The Diamond Bearer's Ring

The Unaltered series: book seven

Lorena Angell

Cover Art: CC Covers

Lorena@lorenaangell.com

or

Fantasy Books Publishing, LLC
3242 NE 3rd Ave. #123
Camas, WA 98607

ISBN: 978-1-969186-93-6

For more titles by Lorena Angell visit:
www.LorenaAngell.com

Books by Lorena Angell

The Unaltered Series

A Diamond in My Pocket, Book 1
A Diamond in My Heart, Book 2
The Diamond of Freedom, Book 3
The Diamond Bearers' Destiny, Book 4
The Diamond Bearer's Secret, Book 5
The Diamond Bearers' Rising, Book 6
The Diamond Bearer's Ring, Book 7
Book 8 coming soon

The Lost Crown Series

Royal Refugee

Non-Fiction

How I Manage Diabetes with C.G.M. Power: My Diabetic Journey and How Continuous Glucose Monitors Changed Everything

License Notes

For more titles by Lorena Angell visit
LorenaAngell.com

DEDICATION

In loving memory of my father,
who taught me life's lessons on the banks of
Sand Creek Reservoir—
coaching me with patience to wait for the right moment,
to hook the taker after the bait was taken,
and how to reel them in to the end.

His quiet wisdom still echoes:
Don't just take anyone's word for it. Think for yourself.
Slow and steady wins the race.

Thank you for every lesson, every laugh, and every moment.

This one's for you.

Contents

Chapter 1 - Vita 1
Chapter 2 - General Appleton 18
Chapter 3 - Terms and Conditions 38
Chapter 4 - Tracking Device 56
Chapter 5 - The Ring 68
Chapter 6 - Irradiated 88
Chapter 7 - Side-Hustle 106
Chapter 8 - Cat's Out of the Bag 120
Chapter 9 - Gift Shop Discoveries 134
Chapter 10 - Vita's Assistant 152
Chapter 11 - Home for Christmas 167
Chapter 12 - Vorherrschaft Unprotected 191
Chapter 13 - The Big Boss? 204
Chapter 14 - Anika's Gift 223
Chapter 15 - Blue Diamond Desires 233
Chapter 16 - Flying Lessons 247
Chapter 17 - Old, New, Borrowed, Blue 268
Chapter 18 - The Coupling 284
Chapter 19 - Crimson's Lack of Vision 299
Chapter 20 - Repercussions 321

Chapter One - Vita

"I'm sorry, Calli. But it had to be this way."

"What do you mean?" I say, yanking violently on the ring stuck to my finger.

"I couldn't stop it from happening, so I kept you from knowing it would."

"Stop what? Knowing what?"

The dream scene in my mind fades to black and my senses become aware of the present. The first thing I see upon opening my eyes is a pale blue wall that appears soft to the touch. I twist my head around and roll to the other side of the bed so I can examine my surroundings completely. It looks like I've been placed in a cell of some kind with padded walls.

I bolt upright, my heart racing against my ribs. Where's Chris? He was in the other car. Is he alive? Is he safe? What time is it? What day is it? I don't know. I run my hand through my hair only to snag a strand with the engagement ring on my finger. I examine the ring and free the strand of hair lodged under one of the prongs. Tugging and twisting on the band, I let out a hiss from the pain while removing the ring. A red enflamed burn wraps around my finger where the piece of jewelry touched my skin.

I focus on my healing power to fix the burn, but no luck. Why hadn't it already healed while I slept? My greater healing power usually heals my injuries in a flash. Is there something wrong with it? Or something specific about this burn?

I slide the precious gift back on my finger, so I don't lose it, and hold out my left hand, tilting my finger up and down slightly to allow the diamond to catch the light. My thoughts drift to Chris and the amazing, romantic scene when he gave me the ring. Then my memories switch to the horrifying moment I realized he was bleeding out, following his diamond insertion, and not healing—technically dead. I remember feeling the ring vibrate on my finger moments before I zapped Chris with power to start his heart. My eyes fill with tears as I recall the fear of losing Chris. My whole world crumbled to the ground during that time on the beach, struggling to bring him back to life, hoping someone would come to help, eventually finding out later that no one was *ever* going to come.

Swiping my tears with the back of my fingers, I stand and walk to the door. How long have I been here? I take a deep cleansing breath and focus on my diamond, reaching out to Chris, waiting for the unmistakable connection, but it doesn't come. I try to connect with other diamonds to no success. I inventory my body, my powers, and my strength levels. Everything seems to be working, except the lingering burn mark still remains under the ring on my finger. I must be in a situation where I'm near obsidian but not affected by it—like at the Denver compound. I recall that while inside the building, I had my powers. However, I couldn't communicate with anyone outside the building.

A sigh escapes my mouth. I can't help but regret the decision to involve the government. If we hadn't come to Washington D.C. we wouldn't have been captured by Max Corvus, at least not like it played out. Who knows how the situation might have transpired if we had been able to approach the government on our own?

What happened to Max, anyway? Did I kill him? He was certainly going to kill me, at least until the woman on the phone told him not to. Whatever happened in the car with Max, my engagement ring became hot and energized, even in the presence of obsidian.

I contemplate my recent decisions. Regret feels like such a simple word against the intense emotions racing through me. Why did I think we would be safe using obsidian when we can't see our futures? The reasons and situations that brought me to the decision to ask the government for help feel so petty and distant now that I'm locked up, so far away from Maetha's island, without knowing what's going on around me. Why did I act so impulsively?

I guess I thought of myself as indestructible.

With a broad spectrum of emotions roiling, I rise up on my tip toes and peer out the narrow glass window on the door. All I can see is a long empty hallway with other windowed doors. I must be at the end of the hall of some sort of jail or psych ward. I pull back from the window and examine the door. A rectangular opening with a metal plate is positioned at waist level. I suppose this is a pass-through for food and the metal plate probably slides open because I don't see any hinges. Small cameras are positioned in two of the upper corners of the room, suggesting I'm being observed. I assume someone will come along soon now that I'm up and moving around.

I leave the door and sit on the uncomfortable bed, tucking my feet under my legs for warmth.

Where is Chris? If he is in this building and I can't connect with him through our diamonds, that means he's disabled by obsidian which could be deadly for him. Or he may not be in the building at all, and that's the reason I can't communicate with him. But that means he might be dead. *Oh God!* I don't even want to think about that.

I try to view the future. Will I be able to get out of this mess? All I see is a soldier attaching cuffs to my hands and the world drifting into the ominous blackness of obsidian.

The jangle of a full ring of keys pulls my attention to the

door. The pass-through slides open, revealing the waistline of the person on the other side wearing military fatigues and a holstered gun. A pair of handcuffs are dangled through the opening by a hairy-knuckled, ragged hand followed by a rough male voice saying, "You have a visitor. They've requested you wear cuffs."

My eyes move up to the narrow window where I see the eyes and nose of a middle-aged man. I try to read his mind but can't, which makes sense because I know he's holding obsidian laced handcuffs. I've already seen my future.

"Where am I?" I ask, staying put on the bed. "How long have I been here? Where's Chris? Is he okay?"

"You have a visitor," he repeats. "They've requested you wear cuffs."

I grunt and move over to the door. I turn around and reach my arms behind me and wait for the snap of the cuffs. As soon as the metal connects with my skin, my powers are canceled, as per my vision moments ago. After securing the cuffs, the man opens the door, and I turn to face him. Behind him stand four more men carrying long rifles with shoulder straps. They aren't pointed at me, but I know they could be at a moment's notice if I decide to be difficult.

The man says, resting his palm on his holstered gun, "I recommend you obey and follow instructions perfectly."

I don't need to read his mind to understand his meaning. I nod and wait for him to invite me into the hallway. He jerks his head to the side and motions with his chin toward the direction he wants me to walk. I obey, albeit cautiously. Behind me I hear the collective footsteps of all the guards. I wish I could read their minds to find out what happened to Chris.

As we walk down the hallway, I glance at the windows on the doors hoping to see Chris peering out, but no. The guard behind me directs me to an interrogation room, complete with a large mirror and cameras in the upper corners. I sit dutifully on the only chair in the room which is positioned at a metal table. He leaves the room, slamming the door behind him. A little overdramatic, in my opinion. I hadn't disobeyed any of his orders. Perhaps he was acting out of fear and wanted to get the door between us as quickly as possible.

Regrouping my thoughts, I assess the current situation as best I can. I'm at personal risk, possibly a life-threatening position, something I'm not supposed to ever let happen. I'd hoped for a better ending by going to the government for help. Not this. I can't even think of a plan because I have no clue where I am, how long I've been here, and how I could possibly escape. The first thing I need is information. My thoughts immediately return to Chris. I hope he is okay.

After a few minutes of being alone with my thoughts, a woman enters the room and walks a full circle around the table. My eyes follow her movements while I take in her appearance: around forty-years-old, thin framed, about my height, long blonde hair, sun kissed skin, and clothing that looks homemade from several decades ago. The woman stops behind my chair. She touches my cuffed hands, making me flinch, then tilts my left hand up a little bit while wiggling my ring back and forth. I yank my hand away, as much as I can while being cuffed.

"I must say," —she speaks in a medium toned voice with an accent I've heard somewhere before— "that is a stunning ring."

I remain silent. I don't know this woman or who she works for, I only know she makes the hair on the back of my neck stand on end. I wish I could read her mind.

"Do you know why you are here?" she asks, walking around the table and stopping in front of me.

"Where is here?"

"Washington, D.C."

I glance around the cold, dank room. "Small area. Always though D.C. was bigger than this."

She frowns, not amused by my sarcasm. "You're here because I need you to deliver a message to the goddess."

I remember where I heard her voice before. She was the woman I overheard Max talking to in the car. She mentioned the goddess and I remember wondering how she knew about Crimson. Presently, I'm concerned I may be dealing with another unknown rogue Diamond Bearer. I decide to play dumb and respond, "Who?"

"The goddess. I know you know who I'm talking about, Ms. Courtnae."

The fact that she refers to Crimson as a goddess tells me she is not a regular in Crimson's circle. I decide to deny and deflect to see if she will volunteer more information. I say, "So, let me get this straight. I was brought here under the assumption I know a goddess and I can deliver a message to her. Why did I have to be kidnapped? Couldn't you have just asked for a civilized meeting?"

"I've found people have more incentive to cooperate if it will gain them their freedom, or if it might save something—or someone—important to them."

I swallow hard as the notion of Chris being used as a bargaining chip enters my mind. My skin prickles. I need to know if he's okay.

"So, with that in mind," the woman continues, "I want you to tell the goddess I'm requesting a meeting with her."

"But I don't know who you're talking about."

The woman waves her hands and arms in a mystical fashion, then produces a piece of paper seemingly out of thin air. She grasps the top with one hand, places the other hand on the tabletop, elbow locked, fingers splayed, and leans across the table, extending her arm toward me so I can see the page—a picture of me and Crimson at the police department when Crimson was invisible. Well, invisible in the room, but not to the camera that captured her image.

Oh boy.

She wiggles the picture in my face. "You *know* who she is and I'm betting you know how to communicate with her. I want an audience with her." The woman pulls back and readjusts her posture before setting the piece of paper down on the table.

I want to ask where she got the image, but I'm still processing how she materialized the paper from nowhere in the first place. What kind of power is *that*? The answer will have to wait till later because she's staring me down, waiting for my reply. Playing coy, I say, "I remember that interview. I arrived alone. The detective and I talked for a short while and I left, alone. I didn't know this person was in the room."

The woman drops her gaze to the floor for a moment, then brings her narrowed eyes up to mine. I note her clenched jaw. I am clearly frustrating her, and I'm not sure if it is a good idea in my current incapacitated state, but it's the only power I feel I have right now.

"I know you think you can fool me, Ms. Courtnae, but you can't. Footage shows she was near you the whole time. We both know she can appear invisible, which is what happened here. Isn't it?"

This woman knows about *appearing* invisible. This changes everything. I choose my words carefully. "Even if I knew this woman, and if I could communicate with her, who should I say wants to meet with her, and why?"

"Tell her you met one of her old acquaintances and they want to talk to her."

"An old acquaintance named . . ."

"Vita."

Vita? My mind races to remember where I have heard

that name before. Then I recall Vita was the name of the Spellcaster who set up the bubble around Maetha's island, and the Hunter's camp. Clara was trying to locate her to ask about the confetti-like pieces we found outside of Max's warehouse in Norway to see if she could help reverse-engineer a key. Ironically, here I sit, having been captured by Max, nearly killed, brought to a location to be questioned by that very woman. I think it is safe to assume she's not going to help Clara figure out how to slip through any bubbles anytime soon. Vita and Max are working together.

Vita watches me closely, probably to see if I recognize her name, or if Crimson has mentioned her to me. I formulate my thoughts and try to respond with the same ambiguity as before. "Well, I can't really look for her while I'm locked up, now can I? You'll have to let me and Chris go, and when we cross paths with the goddess, we'll let her know you were asking for a talk."

Vita makes a sound deep in her throat—a half-laugh, half-determined, almost scoffing sounding. She says, "My assumptions about you were spot-on. I don't know whether to be proud of myself or disappointed in you."

"What?"

"You are predictable, Ms. Courtnae."

I hold my tongue, calming my auto-defensiveness.

She continues. "I figured offering freedom wouldn't be enough for you to admit you know the goddess. Therefore, I acted preemptively. While you were unconscious, I inserted a disabler in your body that only I can remove."

"A what?"

"Think of it like a grenade filled with powdered Yellowstone obsidian. If you try to remove it, the casing will break, and the powder will be released. You won't die, probably, but your powers will be disabled for months or possibly years, until your body processes the obsidian."

I had already performed a body scan earlier in my room and didn't detect anything abnormal. She's bluffing.

Vita continues, "If you want the device removed before it explodes, you need to set up a successful meeting with the goddess for me. If in fact you don't have the connection to her that I believe you do, then . . . oops. Enjoy your powers while you have them."

I still can't believe she could have possibly inserted a bomb into my body. My healing power is such that this wouldn't be possible. I would have detected it earlier, which I didn't. Except . . . my healing power didn't work on the burn and this woman before me *is* the creator of magical bubbles . . . bubbles I've stood right in front of and couldn't detect. I know the power she can create, which is probably why my attempt at rational thinking does nothing to slow the flood of adrenaline in my veins. I must focus on the situation at hand, play it off. Except, I can't rein in my runaway emotions or the increasing panic from consuming my body. I think of Chris. I need to stay strong so I can help him. Focusing on my core, I breathe deeply a couple times, then say as calmly as possible, "So, you're going to let us go to hopefully find this goddess and set up an appointment for you. And then you'll remove the obsidian disabler? Is that correct?"

"That all depends on her and if she'll give me what I want."

"And what is that?" I hear the concession in my own voice and am ashamed of myself for seeming to give in so easily.

She doesn't answer but instead does that magical thing with her hands and arms again, producing two small bundles of medical tape out of thin air. "These are yours. I know you'll probably need these to complete your task concerning the goddess, so I'm giving them back to you. Topaz is so quaint, by the way." A smug smirk slides across her face as she puts the bundles down on the table. "Although, those two are interesting." She points to the pager topazes. "They have Clara's magical fingerprints all over them. It's good to see her expanding her skills beyond beverages."

I inhale slowly to keep my focus and to not allow her to dial up my emotions. I have so many questions, but I already know she won't entertain me. Instead, I ask, "How do I communicate with you, assuming I can get the goddess to agree to meet with you?"

"Max knows how to contact me."

"Max?"

"Yes. I suggest you avoid trying to kill him."

"Kill him? He was the one trying to kill me. Maybe you should be talking with him."

"He's been instructed not to harm you."

"But I heard you tell him he could do what he wants when you get what you want out of me. My information."

She smiles partially. "You have a good memory. Think this through, Calli. Once you've arranged the meeting and the obsidian is removed, Max cannot hurt you unless you allow it."

Hmm. She's using him, like she's using me. I don't like this woman. "I don't have Max's number."

"That can be remedied."

"So . . . that's it? You're going to let us go?" I'm worried because she hasn't acknowledged Chris at all.

"They are going to interrogate you first." She motions toward the door. "Line up the meeting and everything will be fine. But drag your feet and . . . poof!" She wiggles her fingers as she raises both hands above her head. "The obsidian capsule will eventually rupture and then you'll be begging me to help you."

I don't like her threatening words, like she knows she

can control my actions. I respond, "What makes you think I won't figure out how to remove it myself?"

"The same way I know you'll never find this facility again. I've put a protective bubble around it. If you or anyone else tries to remove the capsule . . . well, I recommend you don't." She turns and walks toward the door only to pause and look over her shoulder. "Additionally, know that any traumatic injury, severe bumps, electrocution, or whatnot can also rupture the capsule. So, take care."

"I want to see Chris," I demand as she opens the door to leave. She doesn't reply or even indicate she heard my plea.

The door closes and I'm left alone, sitting on the chair, hands cuffed behind my back. I stare into the mirror, wishing I could see who watches from the other side. Even if I could use my Hunter powers, I still wouldn't be able to do that. I also can't materialize anything the way Vita did with the paper and topaz. I don't know if I've heard of anyone having that power. Maybe Crimson knows.

Crimson.

A wave of nausea washes over me. What was I thinking about leaving the protection of Crimson and the Bearers? Why did I assume everything would go without a hitch for me and Chris to contact the government for help with the Portland blast?

Strangely, I don't feel my life is in danger. I assume this because Vita wants a meet-and-greet with Crimson and I'm the only one she believes has access to "the goddess." However, I don't know about Chris and his future. If he has obsidian cuffs on, his life could be in danger. He said his heart seemed to be rejecting the diamond and he needed to heal his heart often. I hope he's okay. I *need* to know that he's okay.

I take a deep breath and yell, "Hey! Guard! Hey!" If I

could get someone to come in, I could ask questions and possibly get them to remove the cuffs, allowing me to possibly read minds to see where Chris is located. Or maybe I could look to my future and for when I'll see Chris again. That would at least give me some confirmation that he'll be all right. I yell again, "Hey!"

The door unlocks and opens. Max Corvus walks in, or more like limps into the room. A second man follows with a chair. Max directs the man to place the chair as far away from my position as possible, then he sits and stares at me. The man remains in the room by the door.

I speak first, "Where's Chris?"

"Locked up." Max straightens his back and stares me down. "Aren't you going to ask how I'm doing after you electrocuted me?"

Letting out a defeated sigh, I ask, "How are you doing, Max?"

"I'm sore, thanks for asking," he responds, matching my insincerity. "How did you do it? How did you use a power of that magnitude? You were wearing obsidian cuffs. I had a huge piece, too. That should not have happened."

"Like I'm going to just tell you," I mutter. Even if I knew the answer, I wouldn't tell him.

"If you want to see Chris, you will."

"Take my cuffs off first."

"Not a chance."

"I promise I won't kill you, on purpose anyway."

His eyes light up and he slides to the edge of his seat. "So, it *was* an accident. You don't know how you did it."

"Take my cuffs off."

"No."

"Listen, Max. Obsidian obviously doesn't prevent me from using that power. I blasted you while in its presence. Honestly, I don't know why you are risking your life by being in the same room as me." I try to feign concern for his wellbeing.

"I'm not too worried." He points a shaking finger to the surveillance cameras. "If you try anything, they'll see it."

"Mmm hmm. Maybe they are *hoping* I'll use the power on you so they can see it in action."

Ignoring my words, he presses forward. "Was your new power fueled by fear? Anger? Which emotion sparked it?"

"What makes you think it's emotion-based or new?"

"I haven't seen anything in the files that talks about the ability to wield electricity."

"And Invisibility?" I add. "Was that one in the files?"

His gaze drops, and he pauses. "Yeah, no. That wasn't in there either."

"This must drive you crazy, Max."

His eyes shoot back to mine. "Not for long. Soon, I'll know everything about you." Max nods toward the man by the door. "Special Agent Bushman, the best criminal interrogator I know, is going to drill into that head of yours. He gets answers no one else can, at least not legally." Max lets out a delighted chuckle.

Criminal? I hide my concern and ask, "May I use the bathroom first?"

"No." Max stands and nods to the man by the door.

I look over at the guy who entered with Max and brought in the chair. Initially, I ignored his presence, figuring he was only Max's guard. Now, however, I realize he has been observing my behavior, my answers, my body language. More care should have been taken on my part.

Agent Bushman stands probably six feet tall, with a slender build and a dark complexion. He has short well-trimmed facial hair and equally short full head of dark hair. His business suit is clean, pressed to crisp ridges, and is stylish, indicating money and attention to detail.

Agent Bushman steps forward. "I'll have more success if you leave the room, Mr. Corvus."

"I want to stay."

"I insist. And on your way out, tell them to turn off the cameras."

"But . . . her powers!"

"These are my terms, Mr. Corvus. If you do not honor my terms, I won't perform the interrogation."

My heart thuds hard against my ribs fueled by excessive adrenaline. Why does he want the cameras turned off? What does he plan to do to me?

Max storms out of the room in a huff as fast as his injured body will allow. Moments later, the little red lights on the cameras click off.

The man I grossly underestimated eyes me from the other side of the table, angling his head slightly to the left, then the right, his eyes narrowing. He turns without a word and walks over to Max's chair, picks it up, and places it at the table across from me. The strained silence, pierced only by the pounding in my ears, is enough to drive me mad. I've gotten myself into this helpless situation, one where I could be killed or hurt very shortly, all because of what? Because I didn't control my anger. And now a criminal interrogator stares me down with unknown motives.

He abruptly stands, the chair's legs grating loudly against the cement floor. "Ms. Courtnae . . ." He leans forward, placing both palms on the tabletop and leaning in my direction. "Let's get you out of those cuffs." He produces a key and moves behind my back.

I'm completely surprised by this maneuver. Why would he grant my wish of removing the cuffs? Maybe he figures a small concession will get me to talk? I feel him grasp the cuffs and twist the lock, releasing my body from the obsidian. My powers flood into me like a torrential deluge racing through a dry desert riverbed. I immediately search for Chris's diamond, calling out to him with my mind, only to feel nothing. The only voice I hear is Max's outside the room complaining about Agent Bushman's tactics.

I then focus again on the man before me. Agent Bushman's thoughts are easy to hear. He thinks: *Odd that I still can't read her mind, even with the obsidian cuffs off. Max didn't tell me she was run through the machine, too, like Mr. Harding. How does he expect me to do my job if I can't read her mind?*

Bushman is a Reader! What a fortunate find. I dig into his head as he walks around the table to the chair. I'm careful to apply healing powers to prevent him from feeling like he needs to scratch his scalp. He knows quite a lot about the powers of the Sanguine Diamond and the fact I could read his mind if I wanted to. But as his head doesn't itch, he figures I'm not. What I find interesting is he understands if someone goes through the machine their mind cannot be read, like Chris and the many other people who have had their powers removed. But he's unaware that some people like me are born with unaltered DNA, and our minds are unreadable, too.

While sifting through Bushman's memories, I learn he's flown under the cosmic power radar his whole life and naturally became a detective and interrogator. He recalls hearing about the Death Clan's demise and how a young Runner carried the legendary diamond. He even had a chance to see the Readers' diamond amulet before it and all the other amulets were reunited and slammed into Justin's chest. Naturally, he wants to find out what happened to the precious stone, not just what he heard following the recent clan meeting at the Hunters' Forest.

The question zooming through my mind is whether I should alert him to the fact that I know he is a Reader.

Agent Bushman takes his seat. "So, Ms. Courtnae—"

"I want to see Chris Harding first. I need to know he's okay." The words explode out of my mouth like a pressure valve being released.

"He's fine, I promise."

"No offense, but I don't really want to take your word for it. I need to see him."

He pauses and chews on the inside of his cheek. His thoughts consider if he should escort me to Chris's cell or have Chris communicate through a video call.

I press, trying a different route. "If you can't take me to him, maybe you could bring him here instead? I mean, if he's fine, there's no problem with that, right?"

He says nothing, but his mind reveals he doesn't think it's a good idea to bring Chris to the room.

"I won't talk, otherwise." I've decided if he doesn't do as I ask, I'm going to use Mind-Control on him. Every second wasted not knowing Chris's condition is crucial.

"Okay." Agent Bushman moves to the door and issues orders for Max, to which Max lets out a long dramatic rebuttal. Agent Bushman demands Max complies. I can't help but smile and feel a sense of payback, especially hearing Max curse at his loss of control of the situation. I imagine Max felt superior when he captured me and brought me in, but then this Bushman guy orders him around, probably making him feel small and insignificant.

Bushman closes the door and returns to the chair.

While we wait for Chris to arrive, I ask, "How long have you worked with Max?"

"I ask the questions." His shutdown is harsh.

While waiting, I continue to skim Bushman's mind and find he's mentally reviewing everything Max told him about me and my exceptional powers. He's worried that without being able to read my mind, he won't be able to gather the information he was tasked with finding. And catering to my request to have Chris join us may be more trouble than it's worth. We might team up against him with our answers, so he intends to only keep Chris in the room briefly, just long enough so I'll cooperate.

My cooperation will leave when Chris does. I let out a measured exhale to calm my body and mind. I need to think clearly, to stay on top of the situation and shape it to our advantage.

Chapter Two- General Appleton

The door opens, revealing Chris with his hands secured behind his back. A guard holds him at the elbow. His cuffs must contain obsidian stones because I can't use any of my powers on him, although, I don't need powers to tell he's weak and oxygen starved. His pale skin and blueish lips give that away. I want to rush over and embrace him but that would show an extra amount of attachment between the two of us. At this point, I don't know if our engagement is common knowledge, and displaying care and concern might put a bullseye on Chris's back to get me to comply. Instead, I sit patiently while another chair is passed to Agent Bushman, who positions it near mine.

Chris's legs shake as he sits next to me. "Are you okay, Calli?"

I can't help but smile. "Yes, I'm fine. But you don't look so good." I address Agent Bushman, "Does he have to wear these cuffs?"

"Yes," Bushman states. His mind reveals he's concerned Chris might try to overpower him.

"Well, how about you switch his cuffs with regular ones if you're so worried about him overpowering you."

"What makes you think I'm worried about that?" *Did she just read my mind?*

Crap, I think. Then, I say, "Why else would you want to keep him cuffed? Look, you've obviously been told these are special cuffs, but what you don't know is that Chris is affected negatively by them. You can see he's not doing well. Since he went through the power-removing machine—I assume you know about the machine—obsidian has a bad effect on him."

Bushman's suspicions that I have read his mind fade, but not enough for him to decide to comply with my wishes. I add, "I've told you I need to know he's all right. The way he is right now, he's not. For that, you'll have to remove his cuffs or at least switch them with regular ones. Then I'll try to answer your questions."

Bushman huffs then abruptly stands. His thoughts reveal he knows he can't read Chris's mind with or without obsidian because of having been run through the machine. But he figures if exchanging cuffs will get me to talk, he'll give it a try. He moves behind Chris and pulls his own cuffs off his belt and attaches them to Chris's wrists before removing the obsidian set.

I connect with Chris immediately and am relieved to see him inhale sharply, taking in much needed oxygen, while he heals his heart. I lend him extra healing power since he's fairly weak. Meanwhile, Bushman sets the obsidian cuffs on the table and takes his seat.

Calli, Chris says to my mind, *thank you.*

I smile and return my thoughts. *I'm so relieved you have your powers back! Listen, Chris, this guy is a Reader, but he doesn't know you have a diamond. Let's keep it that way.*

Bushman leans forward and says, "All right, now you'll answer my questions, Ms. Courtnae. When did you get the cosmic ability of Running?"

I'm caught off guard with his line of questions, but I suppose he wants to know everything. I respond dutifully, "I was sixteen when my power emerged."

"When did you first meet Maetha the Witch?"

"Um, a couple days after arriving at the Runners' compound."

"Where is she now?"

"I don't know."

Chris asks, "How do you know Maetha?"

Before I can mindspeak to Chris that Bushman won't answer his question, Bushman surprisingly responds, "Here at the Bureau, we all know about her."

Confused by his response, I shake my head and say, "So, you know about Maetha, but you don't know how to find her?"

She seems to have dropped from the face of the earth, his thoughts reveal. "You of all people should understand witches know how to avoid being found."

I resist the urge to grin. Maetha's ability to outwardly change her image has been effective enough to throw off all the top identification techniques currently available. I suggest, "Maybe she's dead and that's why you can't find her?"

Agent Bushman chews on his bottom lip for a moment. "I don't think so."

I ask, "You have another witch, erm, Spellcaster, here in the building named Vita. Why don't you ask her to help you find her?"

"Who?"

Who? Chris asks me.

"The woman who was just in here before you. You know, the woman who ordered you to interrogate me."

Agent Bushman's head flinches back slightly and his eyebrows pinch together. "General Appleton gave the order."

"Is the general a woman?" I press.

"No. I was unaware you had a visitor. Maybe General Appleton sent her. Back to Maetha. When did you last see her, and where was that?"

He clearly wants to move on, but I'm not satisfied with his responses about Vita. This lady claimed she put a bomb in my body, while I was inside this facility, and yet this guy doesn't know who I'm talking about. I ask, "Do you know any other 'witches' besides Maetha?"

"No." His reply is short—and a lie. He knows about Clara Winter, and the more appropriate term 'Spellcaster' but withholds his knowledge out of fear of disclosing his cosmic ability. He focuses on the file of papers presumably about me.

I let his response hang while I consider that Vita is flying under the radar yet obviously has connections that allow her inside the Bureau. Interesting. I'll have to try to get that information out of Max.

Chris speaks to my mind. *I don't know who this woman you talked about is, but we have to focus on why we came here—to ask the government for help with the blast. We need to show them we are on their side. Do you think we could use this guy? He already knows all about cosmic powers.*

We might. I want to test him first. I lean forward and place my folded arms on the table. "To answer your question, I saw Maetha a few days ago."

He redirects his gaze from the papers to me. "You did? Where?"

"I can't tell you where. You wouldn't be able to locate her even if I did."

He doesn't question why, and I can see in his mind he already understands the confusion charm Spellcasters use to hide from the general public.

I continue, "I assume you've been told about the diamond in my heart."

He nods. "Max told me what he witnessed, yes."

Chris jumps in, "I was there, too. I saw it happen."

Moving to the edge of my seat, I ask more pointedly, "Are you afraid of people like us? You know, Runners, Healers, Hunters, Seers, and Mind Readers."

In his mind, he thinks, *I'm afraid of people finding out I'm one of you.* He straightens his spine and responds authoritatively, "I ask the questions here."

Dipping my chin, I say, "I apologize." Then, I speak to his mind. *If you let them run you through their machine, you wouldn't have to worry about people discovering your ability.*

Bushman bolts out of his seat and backs away. His thoughts continue, *Did she speak in my head? That's not possible!* His neck bends forward, then straightens back, while he blinks rapidly. His jaw goes slack and rests in a stunned expression.

I've spooked him. Not good. I'll try to be careful moving forward. *Yes, I can speak in your mind. Please relax. I know your name is Tyrese, I know you are a Reader. You've tried to read my mind and are confused why you can't. I want to help. I will tell you as much as I can, but only if you can give me some indication that I can trust you.*

How is she doing this? He rubs his head.

I continue speaking to his thoughts, *If you put questions to the front of your mind, I'll answer them. But even if the cameras above us are off, they still may be recording us from behind the mirror. You should ask me some other questions out loud, just for show.*

I feel his stomach tighten with anxiety and hear him inhale. His eyes move between Chris and me, then he retakes his seat in the chair he abandoned as if it was on fire. He clears his throat and pulls his words awkwardly. "Eye . . . eyewitnesses said you electrocuted Max. How did you do that? Did you use a taser?"

"Did they find a taser in the back seat?" I respond defiantly to further the image to anyone watching footage or standing on the other side of the two-way mirror.

"No." He then puts a question forward for me. *Are you using a quartz charged with some other power? Is that how you are in my head?*

I continue so there isn't a pause in the spoken questioning. "My arms were cuffed behind my back. How would I use a taser? Plus, I had a bag over my head." *No, no quartz. But I do have topazes. Do you know about them?*

"Yes, I heard about that." His spoken answer addresses both conversations we are having. *I'm unaware of the type of power you're using, and I consider myself an expert in the world of powers.* He speaks again, "Max asked if your ability was emotion-based. You didn't answer him."

"You could try to recreate the situation by threatening to kill me, like he did, then we'd both know." To Agent Bushman's mind, I say, *I don't know much about my new ability, only that I can't control it.*

"I don't think that will be necessary. You clearly don't understand your own strength." He continues with mind-speak. *Before we can form any sort of partnership, I must give General Appleton information from this interrogation. What can you give me to satisfy him concerning Maetha and her whereabouts?*

Chris speaks to my mind so as not to reveal he can also hear Bushman's thoughts. *Calli, press him more on the level of interaction the Bureau has within the government. Does General Appleton have connections high enough that could help us with the Portland blast?*

"Sir, look, we came to Washington D.C. to meet with the government to discuss some important information. We're not going to run. We told this to Max, but he restrained us anyway and treated us like criminals. That unfortunate event wouldn't have happened in the car if he hadn't tried to kill me." I continue, *Maetha keeps to herself. She resurfaces now and then, but if she wants to stay off grid, she has all the resources to do that. I can give her a message next time I see her. I'm willing to do that.*

Okay. I'll pass that along. Bushman flips through the papers in front of him to give the illusion he's formulating his next statement or question.

Would you be willing to wear a tracking device?

No.

Agent Bushman straightens the stack of papers and looks me directly in the eye. "What kind of information did you need to discuss with the government?"

I clear my throat and say, "A cosmic blast is going to hit Portland, Oregon, in about a year and we need help saving as many lives as possible."

"Cosmic rays don't kill people." *You're going to have to tell me more than that.*

"This one will."

"How do you know?"

"Seers." I'm unsure if using the title of Seer will mean anything to those probably watching, but I drop it all the same.

"We have Seers here," Bushman says. "I can ask them about it if you give me more information."

"They probably won't be able to see this event, but you can try."

Bushman tilts his head to the side. "Why wouldn't they?"

"Because they won't know what to search for."

"I don't know. They're fairly good at what they do."

"Do what you've got to do, Agent Bushman. If we don't succeed in evacuating as many people as possible, a lot of them will die. Plus, babies will be born with the new power, which will cause other problems." *Do you know anyone who can help us?*

"What is the new power?"

"The ability to control natural forces like fire, wind, gravity, earth and water."

Agent Bushman doesn't respond verbally or mentally.

Please, Tyrese.

He stands and walks silently to the door. Before leaving, he says, "I'll see what I can do."

I instantly turn to Chris and place my hand on his shoulder. "How's your heart?"

"I hadn't been around obsidian until they put those cuffs on me, so I was all right until then. Thanks for convincing him to switch them."

His words remind me my topazes are on the table. I grab them and separate the pager topazes from the others and strap both sets to my chest. "I'll charge these extra topazes with Healer power, that way you can carry them for emergencies. Or in case they switch you back to the other cuffs."

"Thanks."

"Did Vita visit you, too?"

"No one came to see me until they brought me here. Who's Vita?"

"I'm not sure," I say for the possibility someone is watching or recording us, then I take our conversation internally. *Vita is the Spellcaster that Clara wanted to find about the confetti around Max's building.*

Right. She's here? What did she want?

I don't know if this is true, but she said she put something inside my body while I was unconscious. She said it's filled with powdered obsidian, like a bomb or grenade, and that she is the only one who can remove it. And the only way she'll remove it is if I line up a meeting between her and Crimson.

Huh. Do you know where the bomb is?

No. Frankly I can't detect anything.

Calli, I was so worried about you. The men in the car were scared to death when they saw whatever it was you did to Max. They said it looked like a lightning storm inside the car. How did you do that?

I honestly have no idea what happened, only that Max had an obsidian blade up to my throat and—

Chris's shoulders rise and tighten. *He what? I'll kill him with my bare hands!*

Calm down, Chris. Vita called on the phone and told him to keep me alive. Now I know why—she wants to talk to Crimson. But here's the thing. My ring heated up right before the electrical jolt blasted Max. I don't know what the power is, but I think it's to do with the ring. I lay my left hand on the tabletop and touch the stone with my other hand.

The ring?

We both hear commotion coming from outside the door. I listen and pick up on Agent Bushman's voice.

"I'm in charge of this interrogation, Mr. Corvus."

"You're supposed to be the best! I gave you a list of questions! What's your problem? Now you're suddenly working for her? That's not what I hired you to do!"

"Mr. Corvus, you didn't hire me. Furthermore, the file you gave me was incomplete and lacked significant details concerning her abilities, motivations, and threat assessment. I'm pursuing the logical course of action, given the details I've uncovered."

"Well, you're fired!"

"You're an idiot, Max."

"I'm going to get you fired."

"Take it up with General Appleton. Now, go get them some water and food."

"I don't take orders from you!"

"Fine, The general can order you. He'll be here any moment."

Max grunts exaggeratedly. I imagine he's squeezing his eyes shut with his chin raised toward the ceiling, like he does.

Chris turns to me with a pleased smile warming his face. *I love hearing him not get his way, after everything he's done to you.*

A few moments pass, then Agent Bushman and an older man wearing a military leader uniform enter the room.

"This is General Bernard Appleton." Agent Bushman motions to us and says, "General, this is Calli Courtnae and

Chris Harding."

We exchange cool nods but not handshakes. I note right away the general must be wearing personal obsidian because I cannot use my powers on him. Interesting.

General Appleton speaks with a deep southern drawl. "Mr. Harding, I was sorry to hear about your father. Good man. Tremendous research."

Chris's negative energy emanates, and I pass along healing power to him to help him keep his outward emotions under control.

"Ms. Courtnae, we've been searching for you for a while. Mr. Corvus has quite the dossier on you and your abilities."

"Yeah, he's been busy," I reply dryly.

"Strange behavior caught on camera, abilities we didn't know about—and we know quite a bit about your kind, mind you. Now, thanks to our partnership with Mr. Corvus, we'll learn everything there is to know about the Diamond People. I'm impressed he was able to bring you in so quickly."

"Sir, Max only 'found' me because I asked Chris to bring me here to talk to the government."

The general frowned. "You were coming to us?"

"Yes, maybe not you or this place specifically, but someone high-ranking that can help."

General Appleton sits in the chair across the table and studies me in silence. Then his eyes move to Chris. "How are *you* connected with the Diamond People?"

"I met Calli when she first came to the Runners' Clan. We were on a delivery team together, the one that transported the Sanguine Diamond. We've been associated ever since, in large part due to my father's research."

General Appleton directs his attention back to me. "Special Agent Bushman tells me you have intel on a planned attack."

I answer, "I do."

"Go on, then."

"An event is going to happen in Portland one year from now and a lot of people will die if nothing is done. We're going to need help evacuating."

"Mmm hmm," he pauses, then continues, "Portland, Maine, or Portland, Oregon?"

"Oregon."

"Why would the United States government listen to two young people about an upcoming mass casualty event, that we know nothing about, mind you, and not suspect you as terrorists?"

"Do terrorists normally come in person to announce an impending explosion? We're here to try to get some assistance in saving lives, to reduce the number of casualties."

The general purses his lips and narrows his eyes. "Why aren't you approaching the officials in Portland?"

I say, "We've already tried, but they weren't convinced. We figured we should at least try to get a federal government response to help. This wasn't exactly what we envisioned," —casting my eyes about the room— "but perhaps if you're not able to help, you can direct us to people who can. It's either that, or we follow Max Corvus' example and put up a blog to try to get the word out. Granted, we can expect chaos and everything else that goes with that."

"Well, this division is probably the best suited to hear you out. We investigate the unusual and down-right crazy reports, and this sounds as crazy as it gets."

I exhale sharply, then take a deep breath and say, "We need you to step in and reassure the people they need to temporarily flee from a certain radius around downtown Portland. We believe, then, there could be success with a minimal lasting effect."

"You still haven't told me what the threat is."

The door opens and Max enters, carrying two bottled waters and two bags of potato chips. My powers are sucked out of my body and Chris's shoulders slump forward as well. Max must have a large obsidian piece. He sets the items on the table near the general and moves to the back wall to keep his distance. But it's not far enough. His obsidian is still too near.

I must do something for Chris's sake. "General, I will tell you, but first I need Mr. Corvus to either leave the room or leave his obsidian outside the door."

"What?" Max grunts.

Agent Bushman, who I can only assume is also bothered by Max's obsidian, just not in the same deadly way as Chris, says to Max, "You heard her."

"But—"

General Appleton turns his head to Max with a displeased expression, and that's all it takes. Max quickly strides to the exit and sets his large stone on the floor outside, then closes the door. Our powers return, but I determine Max is still wearing a personal-sized obsidian.

All attention comes back to me to answer the general's question concerning the upcoming power blast. How do I tell him what is coming? Where do I start? Agent Bushman said the general knows about powers, but I didn't get any details of exactly what he knows. If he doesn't know anything about cosmic energy rays, he wouldn't understand the concept of the coming blast. I consider trying to give him a vision, or send him a snippet of what I've seen, but he's using personal obsidian, making it impossible. I need to communicate in his language; in a way he'd comprehend the danger. I say, "A blast will hit Portland capable of killing tens of thousands immediately, and many, many more within the following week or so."

"How do you know about this?"

"I, uh, can see the future." I wait for his scoffing retort, but he remains silent.

"Who is making the weapon? Is it nuclear?" He tilts his head to the side and narrows his eyes to near slits.

"It will be a *naturally* occurring event."

"So, not a bomb."

"More like an invisible bomb. It's a cosmic energy ray. Invisible to the naked eye, like radio waves. The event will happen like a bomb going off, even though no environmental or structural damage will occur, only affecting people."

"Ms. Courtnae, our atmosphere protects us from cosmic energy." He scoots back in his chair and looks at his watch, as if *I'm* wasting his time.

"Not always," I counter. "As someone who investigates powers and abilities, you should know all about DNA alterations caused by cosmic energy that makes its way past our atmosphere to the surface. But, perhaps you don't, and if that's the case, can you direct me to someone who does?"

My words clearly strike a nerve with General Appleton. His posture bristles and he says, "I know what you're talking about. Continue."

"Thank you. Now, let me elaborate. If the upcoming blast is treated like a bomb with a countdown timer, citizens can be evacuated in the preceding days. You could have everything in place with minimal people aware of what's really about to happen. Shelters and housing could be set up prior to the evacuation, secretly, of course. Food and supplies could be prepped, and hospitals emptied in a calm manner without the panicked craziness that would most likely happen otherwise. The public would be both unaware and safe and all the credit could go to you and your team's efficient management."

He doesn't respond right away, but the expression on his face indicates he's in deep contemplation.

A fleeting thought about Vita crosses my mind. Should I ask the general about her at this point? I decide against it.

He clears his throat and straightens his jacket. "I have a few people I can speak to about this. Stay put."

"Where are we going to go?" Chris mutters under his breath as all three men leave the room. The door closes and Chris speaks to my mind. *This is where they lock us up again.*

Sure enough, two guards enter the room. One rattles a pair of cuffs at me, indicating I need to allow him to put them on my wrists. I comply and feel the all too unsettling whoosh of my powers being removed.

After being ushered down the hall to my cell, I turn to Chris, expecting him to be led away to his cell, only to find he is also being placed in my room with me—a surprising twist. The guard closes the door and opens the pass-through slot.

"Put your hands through and I'll remove your cuffs."

I swiftly push my hands through the slot and wait for the cuffs to be taken off. Chris follows and his cuffs are removed, too. I inquire, "Sir, who ordered us to be placed in the same room?"

"Agent Bushman." The metal door shuts.

I turn anxiously toward Chris with the intention of finally wrapping my arms around him, but he steps back. "I'm so relieved you are all right, Calli."

I respond to his cue to hold back on any public displays of affection, which isn't easy, since they are still monitoring us. Instead, I say, "Likewise. How's your heart?"

"It's good. Let's sit down." He walks to the bed, and I follow his lead. He sits cross-legged on the mattress, and I sit on the other end, maintaining our professional distance.

I take our conversation to mindspeak. *We shouldn't talk*

out loud, but it'll seem strange if we are quiet. I have an idea. I say out loud, "You need to rest. Your heart is still weak."

Chris nods and lays on the bed, closing his eyes.

I sit back against the wall and begin to mindspeak again. *At least neither of us is hampered by obsidian, so there's that.*

How are the topazes? he asks.

I check the stones' power levels. They are only beginning to charge, and at this rate they won't be charged till the morning. I let Chris know.

Chris thinks, *Too bad we can't have a setup like this for privacy. We both have our powers, other Bearers can't connect with us, and Crimson can't access your mind. Total privacy.*

Tingles spread throughout my body at the thought of snuggling up next to him in the bed. But reality intrudes. *Except for that camera up there. We are probably on someone's screen right now, and that person is probably Max.*

I don't want Max knowing you and I are close, let alone engaged.

I agree.

Chris takes a deep breath and releases it slowly. *Calli, you didn't ask the general about Vita.*

I know. My gut instinct kicked in and I felt like the time wasn't right, especially since Agent Bushman didn't know what I was talking about. My whole interaction with her was different than what we've had so far with Agent Bushman or General Appleton.

How so?

She makes me nervous. Something's off about her. But she's definitely powerful.

Do you think she's lying to you about the obsidian bomb?

I have no idea, but the thought of it existing makes me feel uneasy. And letting the general know about the bomb made me feel like . . . he might poke around inside me to see if it's true.

Chris opens his eyes briefly and makes a motion as if to reach for my hand but stops mid-movement. I wish more than anything he could.

Agent Bushman comes to talk with us after an hour. "You should know NASA can't see anything like what you're talking about. They are aware of cosmic energy beams and rays but are certain nothing poses a risk to humans because of the atmosphere. That's NASA's take. The Bureau's take is a little different. But, as you said, our Seers cannot see the blast you talk about."

I nod. "Yeah, but it will happen."

"Ms. Courtnae, the Seers have asked for more detailed information that might assist them in viewing the future. I volunteered to talk with you."

I glance to the camera in the corner. "Does that work?"

"Yes. I did not ask them to turn it off." He continues with mental thoughts. *They are watching you closely. By the way, I met the new Seer named Vita.*

"Seers' powers are much weaker than what I possess, and they may not be able to see details." I scoot forward and say, *Vita is not a Seer. She's a Spellcaster.*

What makes you say that? Agent Bushman asks.

Chris speaks to my mind, having also listened to Agent Bushman's thoughts. *Use caution, Calli.*

I think carefully for a moment. I'm still a little unsure about trusting Agent Bushman with vital information concerning Maetha and Crimson. Instead, I respond, *She claimed she put an obsidian bomb in my body while I was unconscious.*

Why?

She wants something from me. Then, I speak to Agent Bushman. "Tell the Seers to look for specific details about the upcoming blast, not destruction, or calamities. The blast itself is not an explosion but more like radiation. They should search for increased sickness in the region, or a time of despair. If we can't prevent mass casualties, there will be a lot of sickness and despair."

"Okay. Anything else?" he asks. *What does Vita want?*

I'm sorry, I can't say. But I'd watch her, and I'd watch your back if I were you. She could reveal your secret to everyone. "Another thing for the Seers to try is to view a specific person's future concerning the blast, like General Appleton's. He'd have to part with his personal obsidian for a little while, but the results may be what he's looking for."

"Good. Thank you for the information." He nods his head and walks to the door and knocks for the guards to open it. *I'll try to keep an eye on Vita. Do you want me to alert the general about what she claimed to put in your body?*

No. Please don't say anything about it.

Okay.

Once he's gone and we are alone, Chris says, "Do you think the Seers will be able to see anything? All the Seers I've ever known couldn't see that kind of detail."

"I don't know, but I hope so." I scoot back on the bed and rest against the wall, closing my eyes and releasing the tension in my shoulders. The scary possibility of a bomb inside my body creeps through my mind. *What is Vita up to, Chris?*

It sounds like she has fooled everyone.

Maybe not Max. She ordered him not to hurt me in the car, not General Appleton.

Is the general aware he has a Spellcaster in his building?

He must. She said there's a bubble around the facility. Everyone here would know about its confusion properties and the need to have a key to enter, that is, if this bubble is like all the other bubbles we know about.

We could ask Bushman. I think we can trust him.

I don't know, Chris.

Bushman is between a rock and a hard place. We know his secret about being a Reader. He's afraid that info will be spilled and he'll lose a good paying job, not to mention his reputation. He's working hard to keep you happy, but also being careful not to suggest you might rat him out. I think we can trust him.

If only there was a way to test him.

Agent Bushman enters the room and closes the door. He points to the camera. "We're not being recorded. The good news is, they're going to release you two, based on Vita's interpretation of the future."

Chris says, "But she's not a Seer."

"Doesn't matter. General Appleton believes her and is moving forward with arrangements."

"This doesn't make sense," I say. "What did she say would happen?"

"I don't know. I wasn't in the room. But when the general joined me, he said the prisoners would be released. Now, the bad news is you'll be monitored and given assignments. General Appleton will give you all the details."

Without a doubt, I want us to be released, and not be held as prisoners, but I feel we need more answers for the new questions that have risen since we arrived.

Chris, having read my mind, says, *I don't think you'll get complete answers about Vita or the obsidian bomb, but we need to find out if Max is still our enemy. Is he involved with the power-removing machines and the Reapers? Is he still trafficking obsidian? What about the bullet he used on you?*

Good point, Chris.

I say, "Tyrese, I'm wondering if you'd like to work directly with me on something."

"That depends. What is it?"

I turn my back to the camera, just in the event it's on and we don't know, then lower my voice to a near whisper. "I want you to investigate Max and see what involvement he has with the manufacturing of obsidian bullets. He shot me with one, so I know they exist. We were on his trail a little while back but he out-maneuvered us. I don't know if he's working alone or if the government is behind it. But, finding out answers is important for all people of powers."

Bushman frowns and responds with the same low tone of voice, "He's not supposed to be doing anything on the side. That's part of his agreement. His immunity is only secure if he cooperates."

"That's good to know," Chris says.

"So, will you do it?" I ask.

"Yes."

"Good. Here's a topaz you can use to contact me." I hand him one of the pager topazes. "I'll keep this one, and you hold the other. Then, when you find details, you can alert me. The signal will let me know you have info and that we'll need to meet."

"Where?"

"How about on the steps of the Lincoln Memorial at noon? However, keep in mind I'll need a minimum of twenty-four hours to travel."

"Right. I understand. So how do I use this?" He twists the stone between his fingers.

I haven't even tried them out, honestly. "While holding it, focus on telling me a message."

"Do I tell the message to the stone?"

"No, simply imagine yourself doing so." I hold the other stone in my hand and wait for something to happen.

He squeezes his eyes closed and clenches his fingers around the little crystal. The topaz in my hand begins to vibrate. His does the same.

"There." I'm amazed it worked, but I don't want him to know that.

"Did you get my message?"

"No. But I got the message you need to talk with me. Yours vibrated also letting you know you activated the power in mine. Once you do this, I'll do my best to be at the rendezvous at noon. Do you have any questions?"

Agent Bushman shakes his head, admiring the little stone, then puts it in his pocket. With his other hand, he gives a pair of cuffs to me. "Put these on Chris. Someone will be by to take him. This way, they won't have any reason to put him in obsidian cuffs."

"I thought you said they were letting us go," Chris says.

"They are. Just, not yet."

"Thank you."

Once alone, Chris speaks to my mind, *Had you experimented with those stones before?*

No.

How did you know how they'd work?

I didn't. I took a guess using the other techniques from other stones and powers. You know, the power of thought and meditation can move mountains, or something like that. It worked and that's all that matters. Let's cuff one of your wrists for now, then cuff the other when the door opens. No reason for you to be cuffed the whole time. We don't know how long it will be.

Later, a guard comes by and takes Chris back to his room. I'm happy he won't be put into obsidian cuffs, thanks to Agent Bushman. However, once the door closes, I'm no longer able to connect with Chris's diamond, and that concerns me.

Chapter Three - Terms and Conditions

I'm awakened in the morning to the loud clunk of my door being unlocked.

A guard and Max Corvus enter my room. "Let's go," Max orders, rattling a pair of cuffs for my wrists.

"Where are we going?"

"Turn around so I can put these on."

He sounds frustrated. If all goes as Agent Bushman said, Chris and I might be released today. That's probably eating at Max.

I allow my wrists to be cuffed, disabled by obsidian once again, and am led out of the room to a larger room than from the day before. Inside, a small group of men and women are seated around a conference table with General Appleton sitting at the far end. Vita is not present. Neither is Agent Bushman. Chris is brought in soon after and I watch his shoulders rise and tighten, then he coughs. My powers are still canceled, but Chris's reaction upon entering the room indicates his cuffs aren't obsidian laced, and he just lost his powers. There must be a large piece in the room that's causing his reaction.

We are directed to two empty chairs at the table.

I ask, "May we please have our cuffs removed?"

General Appleton nods his head and soon our wrists are freed.

My assumptions are correct. My powers didn't return after having the cuffs removed. With a quick action, I reach beneath the neckline of my shirt and pull off the topaz I charged with healing.

"Whoa! What are you doing!" Max rushes over.

A couple of people stand abruptly from their chairs and

move away from the table, clearly afraid.

I hold out my hand to show the crystal. "I'm going to give Chris this topaz because he's not feeling well."

Max shouts at General Appleton, "Don't let her do that!"

"It's either this, or whoever has a large obsidian leaves the room. Chris needs healing power and I can't help him if my powers are gone, so you choose. Let him use this topaz or remove the obsidian."

General Appleton nods to me. "Go ahead."

Max grunts and moves away.

I hand Chris the topaz and he immediately begins drawing from the healing power. His color improves and he takes deep breaths. I ask, "Feeling better?"

"Yes."

General Appleton clears his throat and leans forward in his chair, placing his forearms on the table and interlacing his fingers. "Our Seers can now see signs of the blast you spoke about. Rather than keep you here and operate with your people remotely, I'm willing to release you under certain circumstances."

I'm not exactly happy, but at least they are starting to believe me. "Okay. What circumstances?"

General Appleton says, "We want to take charge of the evacuation of the city. We will spearhead the crisis, control the chaos, and set up evacuation camps. This will be with the purpose of keeping calm and order."

A sigh of relief escapes my mouth. "That's all we wanted. Some help."

"Additionally, I want to be kept up to date on any news or developments concerning the blast."

"Absolutely."

"Like for instance, when exactly will this happen?"

I pause and think about my vision. "I'm not sure."

"Hmm. Well, how long following the bomb before people can return to their homes?"

"I don't know. I'll have to get back to you on that."

General Appleton's head cocks sideways at an angle. "I thought you said you've seen the future?"

I don't want to admit that my visions of the blast are quite limited, so I say, "I haven't looked for that specific information. I've been kind of focused on the save-people's-lives end of things."

General Appleton's eyes narrow. "Why can't you look right now?"

"I'm sorry, it doesn't work like that, sir. However, when I do find out, I'll let you know right away. How will I communicate with you?"

His shoulders relax and he straightens his head. "Mr. Corvus. He will be the go-between."

Chris breaks his silence, protesting, "Seriously? We have to go through him to talk to you?"

"Yes. Part of the calm and order I mentioned will include keeping the existence of supernatural powers largely unknown throughout all of this. If the press catches on, I don't want any hint of Diamond People working with the government, therefore, you will work through Max."

I shake my head. "I can't agree to that condition."

General Appleton's eyebrows rise. "Why not?"

I nod towards Max. "He's already brought more than enough attention to us with his blog."

General Appleton responds, "And that's why we bought his silence."

"Money isn't a guarantee. Someone may offer him more money, or a better deal, to reveal information about us. I swear to you, sir, people with powers are more than willing to stay in the shadows. We don't want any trouble, and we don't want to cause harm. We're all just trying to live our lives, like you."

"Ms. Courtnae, you don't speak for all people of powers. Some are not what you'd like us to believe, so, let's dispense with promises you can't keep."

I sigh again, this time in frustration and say, "Fair enough. I have another concern I'm hoping you can help with. There are others called Reapers who have machines like what General Harding had at his compound. Do you know about them?"

The group of people around the table exchange glances with each other, shrugging shoulders and subtly shaking their heads. Either the group does not know, or they don't want to say. If I could read their minds, that would be nice. I can't wait to get a topaz charged again for moments exactly like this.

I add, "Well, we are actively trying to find and disable their machines. These actions should not be viewed as attacks against peaceful citizens or the government. Our purpose is to protect people with powers."

"And what if your efforts to protect your own kind interferes with our efforts?"

"I believe that with proper communication between us, we can avoid any confrontations. However, I'm concerned about needing to go through Max to talk to you. How can I be sure my messages will get to you?"

Max begins to protest, but the general stops him and says, "I'm positive he will give me everything you give him. You'll see our preparations based on the intel provided."

How do I tell the general that some of the information I'll report directly involves Max? Why would Max pass along damning intel about himself?

Chris crosses his arms but doesn't object. I think he knows we will have to compromise on this point.

Max adds, "I also want to be *directly* involved with Chris

and Calli, go where they go, so they don't try to flee again."

I say, "Where are we going to go, Max? You already have all the state-of-the-art tracking equipment to follow our every move. Besides, we came here for help." I wave my hand in the direction of the group. "There is no reason for us to run away."

"Then there's no reason why I can't accompany you two."

I say, "The last place you want to go right now is anywhere near other Diamond Bearers. You tried to turn the world against us. You put crosshairs on our hearts. You won't be welcomed or protected."

General Appleton intercedes. "I agree that Max needs to remain connected to you. However, that does not necessarily mean physically close. I want you to email Max on a weekly basis. Update him on what you are working on so he can pass the information to us."

Max interjects, "Sir, with all due respect, I captured Calli Courtnae within a week, as I promised I would. I deserve to know everything about their plans and location."

"You deserve? You deserve a jail cell for spilling classified information to the world." General Appleton's veins in his neck protrude.

"Which you bought, because you didn't know everything I knew."

"Young man, the ice on which you stand is cracking. Do you really want to stomp your foot right now? Perhaps you should review the terms of our agreement."

Max goes silent, wringing his hands, then says through a clenched jaw, "Phone. I want Calli to use a phone to check in with me weekly, and I want to always know where she is."

General Appleton rubs his chin for a few moments then says, "Agreed." He turns his head in my direction. "Max will see to the communication arrangements, and that you are taken back to your apartment."

I nod, signifying I agree to the terms as well.

"One last request Ms. Courtnae. I'd like to speak with Maetha. Can you arrange that for me?"

My gaze flickers towards Chris for a moment. "Uh, I'll see if that's possible."

I stand and Chris follows. The group of people take a collective step back from us as if we might attack at any second.

Chris suddenly stops walking and says to the general, "Oh, and by the way, watch out for the Portland mayor and disaster preparedness official. They are quick to disbelieve."

"Mayor Overton and I go way back. I'm not worried."

After being set up with individual phones complete with programed names and numbers, we are ushered by Max and two other guards to a van inside a garage. The guards are Unaltereds, probably from being run through the machine at some point.

"Turn around," Max says as he wiggles plastic zip ties in our faces.

"Why do you need to cuff us?" Chris asks.

"Because you are also going to be blindfolded and I don't want you pulling it off." Max gives the ties to one of the guards.

"That's overkill, isn't it?"

"Turn around," the guard orders.

I speak to Chris's mind as the guard tightens the zip tie on my wrists. *Plastic restraints are better than obsidian-laced cuffs.*

I know. I just don't like Max having any more power over us than necessary.

Though blindfolded, restrained, and stuffed inside the van, we are about to be freed from captivity. There were earlier moments when I worried we would be held in the building long term, studied like lab rats. But the fact that Vita wants a meet-and-greet with Crimson and the only way I can arrange that is from the outside, I knew we would be released. Well, at least I would be. I didn't know if Chris would be, also.

Deep in my gut, I believe Vita is behind convincing the general to let us go, but so many questions remain. Who is in charge of the Bureau operation? Vita? General Appleton?

I do believe Vita isn't bluffing about the obsidian grenade in my body. She must feel like she's in control of my movements enough to let us go. That, or she assumes we will lead her to Crimson and Maetha. I don't know. We will be careful, that's for sure.

The van moves forward, out of the garage and into the obsidian field. The soul-sucking sensation of my powers being yanked from me as the van leaves the premises, and then the rush of them returning once we've driven far enough away, creates nausea like no other. Before I can calm my senses, I'm hit with the thoughts of other Bearers as they link to my diamond. I instantly send out the message: *Don't bi-locate to us.*

Maetha's voice is prominent against the other Bearers' voices in my head.

Where are you? Why are you blindfolded? Are you safe?

Yes. We're in D.C. Is Crimson with you?

No.

Max's voice cuts into my mental conversations. "Well, this is déjà vu—you sitting here with me, blindfolded, restrained, in my control, your life in my hands."

Chris speaks to my mind, *Don't engage with Max, Calli. He wants you to react.*

I hope that's all he wants.

Max continues, "I could kill you both right now." He pauses, clearly waiting for a response from one or both of us.

Maetha cuts in, *Max? You're with Max? How are you safe? You seem to be kidnapped.*

"I *should* kill you and save General Appleton the trouble later. That's what he's going to do with you, you know."

I'm frustrated with the situation and our vulnerability, but also fearful of Max's need to demonstrate he has power over us, at least for a little while longer. The thought of him hurting Chris brings the sting of bile up my throat and I feel my ring begin to buzz and heat up. I must calm myself and control my fear, as it is obvious that emotion triggers the ring somehow. Inhaling a deep breath, I turn my head in Chris's direction and say, "I'm hungry, Chris. What should we have for dinner?

He replies, not missing a beat, "How about Chinese takeout?"

"Yes. I'm craving Chow Mein."

"Sounds good to me."

Max begins laughing maniacally, which makes me think he's losing his grip. "You think I don't know what you're doing?"

I can't resist. I ask, "What are we doing?"

"You're pretending to not be scared."

"Wow. You must have aced your human behavior test. Can you tell what I'm thinking right now, Max?"

"I imagine you're thinking you'd like to zap me with more electricity."

"Nope. I'm wondering how you're dealing with the fact that you didn't get my diamond like you were promised. And how you're probably feeling more out of control than you did when you brought us in."

Max brought you in? Maetha's voice sounds in my head.

"Oh, I'll get your diamond, sooner or later. You'll see. Well, you won't see, 'cause you'll be dead." He laughs again, pleased with himself.

Chris says, "Calli, don't pay attention to Max. He's just talking out of his ass."

"Am I?" his tone reflects his frustration.

I choose my words carefully to both respond to Max and to Maetha. "Max, we all have to play nice, or you'll upset the '*goddess*' Vita talks about. And you know how scared Vita is of the goddess."

"Aren't you?"

"Frankly, I don't know which of the two is scarier. I don't want to upset either right now. I think you feel the same. So, un-bunch your knickers and take a deep breath."

Oh dear, this is worse than I thought, Calli. Tell me where you are, and I'll come get you.

That's not necessary. We're being released.

From whom and from where?

It's a long story. We need to have a Gathering. Would you have Rodger line up a flight back to the island?

Yes, I will. He's in Colorado right now, picking up Brand and Amenembet. I'll make sure he'll be there tomorrow morning. Please do not use obsidian, Calli. I need to be able to connect with you.

I understand.

We sit in silence for several minutes as the vehicle travels along, bumping and bouncing our bodies around.

"Pull over!" Max orders. The van comes to an abrupt halt. Max takes off my blindfold, his fingers grazing my temple as he goes, causing my powers to flee then return instantaneously. The same thing happens when he cuts the plastic ties off my wrists. The door is opened by one of the other men as Chris's blindfold and ties are removed. Max waves his hand as if he's disgusted being around us. "Go on. Get out!" Chris and I exit the van. "You can walk the rest of the way. Don't forget to call and keep me updated." Max slams the door and the van speeds away.

I take in our surroundings. We are in a quiet neighborhood with no one in sight. No one to witness two individuals being dumped alongside the road in the middle of nowhere.

Chris pulls me into his arms and hugs me tight. He says, "I'm so relieved to get out of there and be away from Max."

"I know. Me too. My head is still spinning that they let us go."

"Well, we're sort of let go. We have to check in weekly, and you have that bubble bomb in you, don't forget. Any luck locating it yet?"

"No. Are you able to sense it?"

"No."

"Come on." He takes my hand. "Let's figure out where we are."

We make our way to a high-traffic road a few blocks away. Chris points to the right. "That way." We begin jogging at a regular human pace, not wanting to bring any focus to our abilities.

Soon we arrive at his apartment building. What a welcome sight! I dart my eyes left and right, looking for dark-windowed cars or any trace of Max's van. I don't see anything out of the ordinary. Chris holds the door for me, and then hand-in-hand, we walk to the elevator. I realize we are both wearing the same clothing we had on the night we were forcibly taken. How many nights ago was that? I dig in my pocket, pull out the phone Max gave me, and check the date.

"Chris, it's been four days, well, I mean three nights, and this is the fourth day since we were last here."

He takes my hand and brings the phone up so he can see the date. "Is this right? I don't remember sleeping that many nights."

"Me neither. Maybe the phone is wrong?"

The elevator arrives and we step inside. I become self-conscious of my odor from lack of showering and move slightly away from Chris.

"What's wrong?"

"Sorry, it just became painfully obvious to me that I'm in need of a shower. I don't want to make you suffer."

"What? And I'm *not* in need of a shower?"

"You don't stink."

He kisses my head. "Neither do you. Not to me, anyway."

I smile as the elevator chimes and the doors open on his floor.

"Damn. Hang on," Chris says before we step out of the elevator. "We're locked out. I need to go grab the spare key from my mailbox." He presses the ground floor button, and we wait for the doors to close. "At least my door locks automatically when it's closed, otherwise all my mediocre stuff would be stolen." He wraps his arm around my shoulder and playfully squeezes my other shoulder.

We are soon on our way back to his room, having recovered his extra key. He opens his door and I freeze as I see his bags on the floor exactly where he dropped them when we arrived from Bermuda, as if nothing had happened to us. He walks into his apartment and turns for me. "It's okay, Calli."

My eyes meet the calming warmth in his and I instantly feel better.

"You don't need to be frightened."

"What makes you think I feel that way?"

"Because you look frightened. If I delve into your mind, that's what I'd find. Am I right?"

I appreciate that he's not automatically searching my mind. I say, "I'm not scared. I'm just reliving memories."

"And they are scary memories, to be sure. Come on."

He holds out his hand to me.

I take his offering and clasp his hand firmly. My other hand moves to my neckline. "They didn't give back my lucky necklace."

"Mine is gone as well. I'm sure my uncle can make us new ones." Chris reaches in his pocket and retrieves the phone Max gave him. "We should turn these off. I don't want him listening in on our conversations."

I pull out my phone and turn it off.

After my shower, the aroma of char-broiled beef and deep-fried potatoes tickles my nose. My stomach growls with anticipation, and as I enter the main room, I find Chris emptying the contents of a paper bag.

"All better?" he asks as he divides the food between two plates on the table.

"Oh yeah." I pull out a chair and sit.

"I know, I know," he says, placing a plate in front of me. "You were craving Chow Mein. The wait time was too long, so I ordered this instead."

"It's fine, really. Thank you."

"My turn for the shower."

I point to the food. "Why don't you eat first while it's hot."

"I'll only be a minute. You can go ahead, though."

He's off to the bathroom before I can contest.

Mindlessly, I nibble on a crispy fry while contemplating our next move and evaluating everything that has occurred. My fries are dry, so I fish for some ketchup in the bag. Nothing. I go to Chris's fridge and open the door to survey the contents. There's probably some kind of magazine article or research out there that sheds light on personality types based on what kind of condiments are in one's fridge. I don't know enough about Chris, other than he likes pickled asparagus as he once told me and as is evident by the three different varieties on the top shelf. He seems to be a mustard connoisseur, and a hot sauce aficionado. I smile, thinking about how I have a lifetime to learn more about him.

As for ketchup, there's one squeeze bottle. Perfect. I remove it and close the door.

Taking my seat again, I hear the water in the shower and realize Chris is in there, naked. My entire body flushes with warmth. Did he think about me the same way while I was in the shower? I shift my focus back onto my food and squirt out a puddle of ketchup and drown a fry, then stick the whole thing in my mouth. Mmm. Heavenly. I unwrap my burger and take a bite, desperate to redirect my thoughts.

Chris emerges from the bathroom wearing jogging pants and a tank top. He smells fresh and renewed as he passes by to take his seat adjacent to mine. Once seated, he sets two topazes and a box of adhesive pads on the table. "You left this one on the sink. Can we trade? The other one you gave me is nearly drained."

"Absolutely." I take the drained topaz and affix it to my chest and begin infusing it with Healer power. "This one didn't get you very far."

"I know. Good thing my time around obsidian was limited. I probably need to carry several charged topazes all the time." He attaches the fresh topaz and reaches beyond me for his burger and fries. "Now, this is perfect! You, me, and comfort food."

I follow his lead in changing the subject of impending death in the presence of obsidian and the absence of healing topaz. "I'm a little surprised you didn't order fish and salad, honestly."

"Nah. Since becoming an Unaltered, I've thoroughly enjoyed eating more than a Runner's diet." Chris takes a healthy bite of his burger, exaggerating how much he is enjoying it. He swallows some water and says, "I think we made it through all that at the Bureau without anyone learning I have a diamond in my heart."

"Were you ever x-rayed or scanned?"

"Not that I know of, but we were gone for a while, so who knows what happened to us."

My chewing slows. "How long do you think you were unconscious?"

"I don't know. I remember being injected with something in the car." He takes another large bite of food.

"Agent Bushman's mind didn't reveal anything about a diamond in your heart."

Chris swallows and wipes his mouth. "True. And no one behaved strange around me like they did with you."

"I agree." My mind wanders as he dunks his fries into my ketchup and his arm lightly brushes over mine. We have a whole worry-free night ahead of us. No Max or police or government to interrupt us. Just the two of us . . . and, well, all the other Diamond Bearers who can bi-locate on a whim, and Crimson who can be in my mind undetected. My stomach falls and I take a deep breath. This lack of privacy thing is not something I'm going to get used to. We won't use obsidian, as per Maetha's orders, but also because Chris's heart can't take much of that. I will charge the drained topaz for him, but I don't want to risk him depleting the fresh topaz before the other is ready. I could place the Blue ring of secrecy around us for privacy, but if someone bi-located to the apartment they'd still be able to see us—and they'd see the blue mist and wonder how?

Sheeze! What's wrong with me? Why am I so fixated on this?

I change the subject in my mind and say, "Is it a good idea to go to the island right now knowing Max is following our movements?"

Chris drinks from his water and clears his throat before

speaking. "Well, we need to check out the bubble bomb inside you and tell Crimson about Vita's request. I think we have no other choice."

"Yeah, I guess."

"Besides, he'll know we're flying to Bermuda, but won't know where we go once we get there. I plan on leaving the phones on the mainland."

"Sounds good." I scrunch my eyes tight, as if that will help me figure things out. I relax and look at Chris. "I'm still confused about who runs the Bureau. Max seems to answer to Vita. She is the one who talked to him on the phone when he kidnapped us. But General Appleton bought Max's silence and brought him to the Bureau and Max seems easily subdued by any threat of General Appleton being alerted to his misbehavior. I don't quite understand the power dynamics there."

"I don't either. Vita was acting as a Seer, too, like a subordinate to the general."

"It's all confusing, but maybe we accomplished what we set out to do which was to enlist the government's help with the Portland cosmic blast."

"I *hope* that's what we did." Chris raises his eyebrows and subtly shakes his head.

I help Chris clean up after our meal, and then we sit on the couch. He wraps his arm around me and takes my left hand, admiring the glimmers and shimmers of the diamond ring he gave me.

"After everything we've just been through, Calli, I'd like to get married sooner than later."

My pulse quickens as he speaks, then heaviness consumes me. "Being married wouldn't have prevented us from being kidnapped."

His head hangs low. "I know. It's just, I was reminded

how precarious life is and I don't want to miss out on spending any of it with you."

Like magic, his words lift the consuming weight as if it were a feather, raising a smile on my lips. "How soon is sooner?"

"I don't know, I just wanted to put it out there."

"Truth is, I still haven't fully realized I'm engaged to you. Let's let that sink in first. Tonight, let's enjoy our time together without all the world trying to capture or undermine us."

He squeezes my shoulder and kisses my hair above my ear. In response I snuggle closer to him.

I bring my left hand closer for inspection. "What did you say was this diamond's history? You said it was an heirloom. Correct?"

"Yeah, as the story goes, it was originally from India, used as payment for services given, passed down on my mother's side of the family."

"Won't this break the heirloom tradition by giving it to me?"

"I don't have any sisters, so I inherited it. But if we give it to one of our children or grandchildren someday then that works. Anyway, my mother told me it's more about the history of it being a lucky diamond. Its journey through the ages."

Intrigued, I ask, "What do you mean, 'lucky'?"

"That's merely what it's been referred to over the years."

"Well, I was wearing it when I saved your life, so I guess it is lucky." I smile, but can't help but worry about the devastating effects of random activation like what happened with Max.

He takes my hand and says in a lowered, more serious tone, "Would you show me what happened when I slammed the diamond on my chest. Will you open your memories?"

"You'll be drained of energy. Remember what happened to me when you showed me your past?"

"There's plenty of time to replenish my energy before we arrive at Bermuda, plus, we know how to speed up the healing."

Unable to formulate words, I push aside my worries and welcome the mental replays of our "healing kisses" sessions. I nod, letting him know I'll show him.

He slides his fingertips along my jawline to my lips, sending cool tingles over my skin.

I close my eyes and open my mind and allow him to see what I witnessed when his chest was blown apart by the diamond insertion. The blood and gore are sickening to relive, yet I don't remember there being so much at the time. My eyes tear up in the present as I experience the anguish I felt while healing his heart around the diamond, mending his chest wall, bone and skin, then performing CPR to keep him with me. When the memory of electricity shooting out of my palms flashes for Chris to see, his grasp on my hand tightens to an uncomfortable level. I end the shared memory.

He releases me and wipes his eyes. "Was that everything?" he whispers.

"Pretty much." I dry my cheeks and take a cleansing breath. "Your heart started after that, and I passed out."

"I'm sorry, Calli. If I had known what you'd have to go through, I don't think I would've done it."

I reclaim his hand and send healing vibes to help restore his depleted energy. "Well, it all worked out." I try to sound unaffected by the events and redirect the focus. "This ring somehow gives me the ability to harness electricity. That's how I shocked your heart, and how I electrocuted Max, I think."

"That's a good thing, isn't it?"

"I guess . . . I mean, yes. You're alive. Of course, that's good. We changed the future which wasn't foreseen by Crimson or Maetha. What else have we changed?"

Chris says, "Maybe it's not the ring at all. What if this new power is because of the DNA alteration Maetha orchestrated in you? You know, the super-healing power."

"Maybe. Then why does my finger heat up and become burned when I do the whole electricity thing if it's simply the new power? Besides, none of my family with Maetha's DNA change ever had strange instances of shooting lightning bolts that I'm aware of."

"But they weren't Diamond Bearers either."

"They also didn't have a lucky diamond ring."

We spend the rest of the afternoon and evening talking and learning about each other. I love discovering more about him and his history, his likes and dislikes, his dreams and dreads. I find him enthralling to say the least, and I'm even more excited about being together the rest of our lives.

As the sky darkens and bedtime approaches, Chris says, "I don't want to risk that obsidian bomb going off, or whatever it is, so I think I'll sleep on the couch. You can take my bed."

"I doubt it's that fragile, Chris. The bargaining power goes out the window if it breaks too soon, and Vita wants to meet with Crimson so . . ."

"Still, I'm not going to be the one who causes the thing to take your powers away."

"You could lie beside me, Chris. You don't have to sleep on the couch. I've enjoyed our time together these last few hours; I don't want it to end. And after our four-day ordeal at the Bureau, I don't want to be away from each other.

He brushes away a few strands of hair from my forehead and smiles. "Okay, for a little while."

Chapter Four - Tracking Device

The morning arrives and we take a cab to the airfield where Maetha's plane waits for us. Stepping up inside the plane, we're greeted by Brand.

"Hey, you two! How the heck are ya? I hear you got engaged."

"Yes," I say, holding out my hand for him to see the ring. After he peeks at the ring with a nod of approval I ask, "Did you get your quartz implanted successfully?"

Amenemhet comes over and answers. "Everything went without a hitch. Brand shouldn't have any issues with the stone now, other than it rattling around if he drives on a bumpy road."

"Or turbulence, like on the way here." He smiles and points to his cheekbone. "When it moves it feels like someone is tickling the back of my eyeball."

"That's gross," I say, trying not to imagine what that might feel like.

"Yes, it is. Well, I'm curious why things didn't play out the way Maetha had foreseen with you two."

Chris straightens his spine and angles his head. "What do you mean?"

"You know, you two were supposed to break up." Brand's jovial banter is not received well by Chris or me. In fact, his words indicate that he had knowledge of this information while in Denver.

"Well, we didn't," Chris grumbles.

One side of Brand's mouth lifts with a smile. "Why not?"

"We worked it out." Chris's response now has a clipped growl, which puts me on edge.

"Huh. It's not often Maetha gets the future wrong." Brand wiggles his head side to side dismissively.

I jump in to break the tension. "Brand, have you used your powers now that the quartz thing is inside you?"

"Yep. What's Chris's problem?" Brand asks, as if Chris isn't right there.

"You don't know what we've been through, Brand."

Brand dips his chin. "Oh. Sorry."

The all too familiar spinning sensation fills my head as Brand repeats me back to moments before when I say, "Brand, have you used your powers—"

"Yep."

I shake my head to clear out the nausea. "I mean, have you used your powers, you know, to check on the length of repeating time."

"Have you forgotten who you're talking to? Honestly. The moment Amenemhet finished healing the incision I tested it out. Well, I mean two minutes after he finished. I didn't want to repeat back into surgery."

"Surgery?" I ask.

Amenemhet joins in. "Hardly. He sat on a chair in the washroom while I inserted the quartz. Everything was done in five minutes."

I interject. "Then why didn't this happen sooner, like as soon as Brand decided he wanted the stone inserted in his body?"

"Maetha's orders."

Chris shoots his eyes to the ceiling and lets out a huff. "Of course."

I worry about Chris. I really do. Maetha has been a part of his life for a while now, and usually not in a good way. I don't know if he'll be able to master his anger and frustration toward her. However, I can at least empathize with him now, after experiencing the intense feelings of betrayal by her not coming to help heal Chris's heart after the insertion of the diamond.

Rodger announces, "Folks, take your seats. We've been cleared for takeoff."

We do as we're ordered and sit in four seats facing each other. After buckling in, Amenemhet directs his words to me. "Calli, what happened on the island? Why did you two leave and go dark?"

"Chris proposed on my birthday, and then he, *we* inserted his diamond."

Brand exclaims. "What?"

Chris nods.

"So, we both went through the same thing?" Brand points to his chest, then to Chris.

Still a little irked at Brand's earlier rudeness I say, "Not exactly. Chris died. You got what, a bloody nose?"

"He obviously survived. Have you used your diamond powers since, Chris?"

Chris answers, "A few of them, but mostly healing. We've been around obsidian a lot."

"Huh?"

"My heart acts like it's rejecting my diamond, so I have to heal myself quite often. Obsidian prevents that."

Amenemhet rubs his jaw. "Interesting."

I say, "I'm charging a few Healer topazes for him so he can at least have some relief around obsidian."

One of Brand's eyebrows juts higher than the other one. "Rejecting, as in bad rejecting?"

"Pretty much."

Brand shrugs. "Then take it out."

Amenemhet says, "The diamond cannot be removed without causing extensive damage, fatal damage. The time to remove the diamond was before the heart healed around it."

Brand rubs his eyes. "I should have been there. I could

have told you he wasn't going to heal properly."

"Everything took a lot longer than two minutes, Brand."

"See," Brand waves a hand above his head and presses his body further into his seat, "this is why I'm not eager to be a Bearer. Now Chris has all new problems to worry about. Everyone and their dog has obsidian, thanks to Max and his freakin' blog!" Brand's eyes widen and he points to Chris. "You need a Healer quartz, that's what you need." His waggling finger glides to Amenemhet. "He can put it in your head, too. Then you'll never have to worry about obsidian 'cause the quartz doesn't drain like a topaz."

I look at Chris, hopeful about the prospect of a solution. "Yes."

Chris shakes his head. "Where am I going to get one of those? Didn't we give all the quartz back to the clans?"

"Oh, yeah." My gaze drops.

"And they probably returned the quartz stones to the people who'd been run through the machine."

The plane turns after taxiing to the runway and without delay accelerates for takeoff.

Brand adds casually as we bounce and sway down the runway, "But some of the people are dead, so their quartz is available."

Chris shoots a dangerous glare at Brand. "I will *not* use quartz of a dead person. Those people were killed—murdered."

"Hey, I'm just saying," Brand throws his hands up in frustration.

Amenemhet speaks slowly. "I think you are forgetting that the removed powers stored in quartz is from today's power. Today's Healers cannot use their power on their own body. How would one of their quartzes help Chris if he can't use it to heal himself?"

"That's not entirely true," I say, shaking my head. "Rhonda, the Healer who I gave a quartz to, said she could feel inside her body. Although, she didn't try to heal herself to my knowledge. But I could tell by her reaction to feeling her own body, it was something new to her."

Brand taps his finger to his chin as if he's trying to figure out a work-around. The only word he utters is "Huh."

I ask him, "Did you notice anything different once you held the quartz after it was charged with your powers?"

"No. It felt the same. The only difference with the power since being put into the quartz is that it's immune to obsidian."

Amenemhet changes the subject by asking again, "Why did you two leave the island and go dark?"

I exchange glances with Chris, then say, "We're going to have a Gathering once we get to the island to explain everything, but basically Chris and I decided to go ask the government for help with the coming Portland blast. Unfortunately—or fortunately, it kind of works both ways—we were captured by Max and his goons and were taken to some government-offshoot facility. Max is working with the government."

"Max?" Brand explodes.

Amenemhet calmly asks, "How did you escape?"

"We, um, didn't. They let us go."

Amenemhet's calm quickly devolves. "Are you being tracked? Do we need to turn around?"

My heartbeat pounds in my ears. The possible bubble inside me might be a tracking device, but I doubt it. However, this is a good opportunity to have someone else scan my body. "They gave us cell phones which can be tracked, naturally. Would a tracking device work inside the bubble around Maetha's island?"

"No. Transmitted coms in and out are jammed. No cell

phones, no satellite phones, radios, etc."

"Well, other than that, I don't think we're being tracked."

"Let me take a look." His eyes travel my body from head to toe. I know he's searching for a device of some kind, something that would emit a signal for the government to follow. I wonder if he'll find the obsidian bubble. He brings his eyes back to mine and says, "You're clean."

Hmm. He didn't detect it, which doesn't mean anything, really. There might not be anything inside me at all.

Amenemhet continues, "But if you had a tracking device on you emitting a signal, they would be able to follow it to the edge of the bubble, which would give them enough of a location that a nuclear attack could break the bubble."

I lean forward. "Do you see anything like that in the future?"

He closes his eyes and is motionless for a moment. I dart my eyes to Chris and Brand, then back to Amenemhet, wondering why I didn't think about looking to the future to see if returning to the island was a good thing. Am I keeping a watchful eye on my future? Enough of a watchful eye?

Amenemhet speaks. "The future doesn't show damage to the enchantment around the island. We're good."

"That's a relief. Just so you know, I was planning on turning the phones off and leaving them at the dock in Bermuda."

"Cover the camera for now, at least," Amenemhet says, pointing to the phone.

"Good idea." I remember Jonas telling us about how smartphones can have their cameras turned on remotely. I undo my belt and get up to retrieve the box of adhesive bandages in the nearby cupboard. Finding two of the smallest, I return to my seat, attach my belt, and give one to Chris. Simultaneously, we open and attach them over the lenses on the back of our phones.

"And that one," Amenemhet touches the top of the screen where the reverse camera is located.

I let out a sigh and undo my belt, then collect two more bandages and return to my seat.

While attaching one to his phone, Chris asks, "You said all coms in and out are dead on the island, but what about Jonas' computers? He's online while on the island. How does he do that?"

"Through a fiber optic line that I installed on the ocean floor below the bubble's edge."

Chris adds, "Then our phones could work through the Wi-Fi internet while on the island."

"Technically, yes. But, as Bearers, we communicate through bi-locating as this method is not dependent on server speeds and line integrity."

"Amenemhet," I ask, "How is it we can bi-locate to Maetha's island, but while I was in the Hunters' Forest I couldn't connect with any other Diamond Bearer?"

"They are different bubbles, designed for different uses."

"Oh." I wonder again about the possible obsidian bomb inside me. Vita may have created a specific bubble to guard against any type of detection. "Are you worried at all about the fiber optic cable being a line or trail to the island's location?"

"No outside company even knows it exists. If someone happens to stumble upon it and decides to follow it, the confusion spell would stop them as they neared the island."

I nod my head and shift my questioning. "So, if we used Max's phone on the island through the Wi-Fi, would he be able to pinpoint our location?"

"No. It's the same concept as when Jonas investigated Max's blog. The IP address shows Miami, FL."

"Just to be safe, I still think we'll leave the phones in Bermuda."

Amenemhet holds up one hand in front of his chest. "I want to go back to the other topic. What happened on the island that upset Maetha and caused you two and Jonas to use obsidian? Why did you leave the island?"

Chris's thoughts enter my mind. *I don't know how much he should know.*

I'll be careful, Chris. I respond to Amenemhet, "We learned Maetha thought Chris would die with his diamond insertion and she had no intention of trying to save his life."

Amenemhet replies, "Hmm. Are you sure about her intentions?"

Chris leans forward a little and says, "How about you ask her and let us know the answer?"

I feel another subject change is needed to diffuse the uncomfortable crackle in the air.

I clear my throat and ask Amenemhet, "What do you see for the future concerning the Portland Blast?"

He pauses, as if he wants to pursue the previous topic, before answering. "I can't see much. It's hazy and intermittent whenever I look."

Brand raises an eyebrow. "How come?"

Amenemhet relaxes in his chair. "I believe it means the future is muddled, not set, or is changing from day to day. Your actions, Calli, may be affecting the outcome."

I'm reminded of Jonas' words when he said, "You changed the future."

I turn to Brand. "Did Beth stay at the Denver house while you had your quartz inserted, or did she leave with Clara?"

"She stayed and helped."

Keeping my eyes on his, I lean forward slightly and tilt my head to the side, hoping he'll get my hint to give up more details. He doesn't. I say, "And?"

"And what?"

"Are you two on speaking terms?"

"Yeah." Brand's face lights up a little.

I press Brand. "Well, do you think you two have a future?"

"Boy, that's a big jump to go from 'are we on speaking terms' to 'do we have a future,' Ms. Nosey."

I try not to smile. "I'm just trying to figure out if I need to send you separate invitations, or if you'll be her plus-one."

"You'd send her an invite and not me?" He feigns a let-down expression. "Anyway, we're taking things one day at a time. I guess I'll have to let you know."

"Well, that's a good start."

"I'm happy for you two." Brand points his finger at Chris and me. "It only seems like yesterday we were rescuing you, Chris, from the jail, or whatever it was, right before the other guys died." Brand stops and his expression falls. His chest expands as he fills his lungs and raises his eyes to ours. "We've been on one hell of a journey."

Chris clasps my hand. "We're still on it."

The four of us talk a short while longer, then Chris and I move to the rear of the plane for privacy. Our flight won't arrive in Bermuda for another five hours. I'm not looking forward to returning. We're going to be in trouble, at least I think we will. Maybe not. We did, after all, secure the help of the U.S. government to evacuate Portland before the blast. That's one problem down. I half-expect Crimson to come to me or communicate at least now that we're away from obsidian.

She doesn't.

After we land in Bermuda, and are getting ready to board the boat, I dial Max on my phone.

"Yes," Max answers.

"Checking in. We're in Bermuda. I'll call you next week."

"Why not sooner?"

"I'll be out of service range."

"Yeah, this is what I was afraid of. You guys are bolting."

"I assure you, we're not. Talk to you later." I hang up before he responds.

Chris smiles deviously. "We should toss the phones into the ocean and mess with him."

"Tempting, but probably not a good idea." I approach one of the deck hands for Maetha's boat. "Excuse me, is there a safe place we can store these phones until we return?"

The boat hand directs us to the harbor master building near the parking lot. "There are lockers you can rent up there."

"Perfect. Thanks." I let Amenemhet know where we're going and then we jog up to the building. The lockers are all automated using a credit card to gain access. Chris uses his card to secure the locker in such a quick way that I'm reminded of how Vita waved her hands and produced the paper showing Crimson and me at the police station. Again, I wonder what kind of power she has.

We complete our transaction and head back to the dock. Amenemhet waves at us to hurry up so the boat can leave. Chris takes my hand and leads the way up the ramp.

"I'd like to sit up front. Do you want to join me?"

He looks back at me with a raised eyebrow. "You don't have to ask, you know."

We step off the ramp and onto the deck. Brand is already heading off to the galley for whatever food there is to be had. Amenemhet gives us a nod and follows Brand.

"I ask only because I don't want you thinking I expect you to do everything I do."

We continue walking to the bow and sit on the cushioned bench seat and settle back into the plump-pillowed backrest. The breeze off the ocean whips my hair across my face and I use my free hand to push it back.

Chris wraps his arm behind me, and I lean against his side. He says, "I love that you're independent, Calli."

"Is that code for something?"

"Er, not clingy, perhaps."

"Clingy, I am not, sir."

"Good, 'cause we can't both be." He squeezes my shoulder and pulls me closer.

I lay my head against him, acknowledging my feelings of safety and security, which I know are silly sentiments given that I can provide both myself. I guess I like being with someone who wants to help me be secure. No, I *love* being with him. I gaze out across the endless sea as the boat begins to pull away from the dock and speak to Chris's mind. *I wish we were headed somewhere peaceful and secluded, free from judgment.*

Yeah, I agree. I imagine we're going to be scolded. But I stand by our decision, Calli. We did what we felt was right. He looks me in the eye, then brings his mouth to mine and seals his devotion to our cause, which I happily receive.

We arrive at the island and find Sarangerel waiting for us. I admire how effortlessly beautiful she looks with her mid-length black hair flowing in the wind along with her light and airy clothing choices. I realize my own clothing for the day, jeans and a thick cotton shirt, may not have been the best choice for the climate.

Brand, Chris, and I walk down the ramp toward Sarangerel. As Brand steps past her, her focus remains on Chris and me. She says, "Where have you two been?"

"Uh," I glance at Chris.

Brand says behind her, "Nice to see you, too, Saran."

She places her hands firmly on her hips, ignoring Brand. "Your parents are upset, Calli. Jonas is gone. Maetha is locked in her bedroom. My parents are buried in papers and parts, trying to build the machine with the mechanic."

"You mean my Uncle Don?" Chris's words come out with attitude.

"Oh, you are related to him?"

"Yeah."

I put up one hand. "Wait. You said Jonas is gone?"

"Yes. He left after you two left."

"Where did he go?"

She drops her hands and shrugs her shoulders. "You'd better go to the main house and talk with Maetha. I'm still trying to sort through all of Jonas' files and computers to pick up where he left off."

Brand offers, "I'll help you. That'll give me something to do."

Chris takes my hand and together we walk toward the house. "I'm sure Jonas is okay," Chris says, but I sense the hesitation in his words.

I glance over at him. "What if he's not? I can't sense his diamond. He's either using obsidian or he's—"

"We need to focus on our own butts right now and the best way to tell Maetha and the other Bearers our news."

"You're right."

Chapter Five - The Ring

As we near the main house, a woman walks out the front door and stands near the staircase. I'm surprised to realize this woman is Maetha. I didn't recognize her at first. Her appearance has changed even more in the little time we've been away. Her hair is a rich black color, and her tan skin is now a shade deeper. But her facial bone structure is what makes her image overhaul complete. The shape of her face is longer and oval. Her nose is narrow and more prominent, with thick arching dark eyebrows and deep brown eyes. Her lips are fuller with a natural pink hue. Even though she wears no makeup, her radiant skin, dark lashes, and natural shadowing looks as if she does—all this has been changed to help her disappear off the authority's radar.

Maetha doesn't speak, only waves her hand and motions for us to follow her inside. She guides us up the stairs to the second level and a large bedroom at the end of the hallway furnished with elegantly carved wood dressers, chests, bed frame, and chairs. Even the French doors leading out to the veranda match the style. The doors are open, allowing the warm ocean breeze to flit through the sheer white curtains framing the doorway. My mother would like this room very much.

"Take a seat." Maetha motions toward two chairs against the wall.

We sit while she drags another chair over from across the room. She positions it in front of us.

Chris shifts around in his seat and seems on edge to be around Maetha. I know I am. Since learning she thought Chris would die and didn't plan on helping him live, I've struggled to keep my anger under control. And now, sitting in front of her, on the cusp of revealing the information we gathered from—and revealed to—the government, my heart races and my breathing is shallow and rapid. She is not going to like everything we tell her.

Calli, Maetha speaks to my mind, *use your mind to put up the mist of secrecy around the three of us, but don't get up. Crimson doesn't want other Bearers knowing you have the Blue shard just yet.* She sounds cold and distant as her eyes fall to my ring.

Even though there are no Bearers nearby, I know some can be bi-located in thought only. The mist will block our conversation from them. I do as she asks and install the secrecy mist with my mind. Then I exhale, releasing the tension from my body before I inquire, "Where's Crimson?"

"She left after you healed Chris and I have not heard from her since. Why did you two go to D.C.?"

I answer, "We went with the intention of speaking to government officials about helping with the evacuation efforts."

"With the intention?" She angles her head. "What happened instead?"

Chris leans forward slightly and replies with clipped words, "We were captured by Max Corvus, taken to some secret facility, interrogated by a Reader, aligned with government officials, and were set up with a dangerous extortion by *your* good friend, Vita, before being let go."

Maetha shakes her head as if doing so will somehow make Chris's words make sense. "I, wait, what? Vita? Max? Working with the government?"

"Hey, I'm still reeling from everything." Chris sits back again, a little more relaxed.

I nod. "Me too. Our decision was impulsive, I know, but now that it's done, I think it went well."

"Tell me more details."

Chris and I relay the happenings from our different

points of view. Naturally, there were gaps in the timeline where he and I were unconscious—I'd passed out after shocking Max, and Chris was sedated. As I tell my side of the story, Chris becomes more alert. I realize he isn't aware of all the fine details of what happened to me and the questions I was asked.

Maetha seems extra interested in the details surrounding Vita. "Was Vita interested in your ring?"

"She mentioned she liked it."

"So, she noticed the stone?"

I look deep into Maetha's eyes trying to figure out what she knows about the ring. I've already determined the ring had everything to do with healing Chris and stopping Max. But what does Maetha know? I answer, "Yes. Why does that matter?"

"I didn't have time to tell you and Chris this before you two jetted off the island with those dark anger clouds circling your heads, but," —she holds up her hand to stop Chris from butting in— "the diamond in your ring is the source of your new ability to harness electricity. Additionally, Crimson had a vision of the Elemental blast that showed you wearing it on a chain around your neck, not on your finger. But even so, she never identified it as a powerful stone."

"Wait, she saw I'd wear an engagement ring around my neck? Not on my finger?"

She nods. "Because Chris wasn't going to survive the diamond insertion. You would have found the ring he'd planned on proposing with and you'd have worn it on a chain in remembrance."

I try hard to stay centered on getting answers, even though I really want to hammer out her knowledge of Chris's death. I ask, "How does all of this involve Vita?"

"I think she recognized the stone—a power enhancer. Personally, I could tell right away when I first saw it. Where did you get it, Chris?"

"Family heirloom." His answer is curt.

"Really? Interesting."

I ask, "What does a power enhancer do?"

"Power enhancers give a burst of energy, enhancing whatever powers the wearer possesses. They store power like the Imperial topaz. That's probably why you were able to use it while in the presence of obsidian."

Chris asks, "If these are so powerful, why aren't we using them with our other crystals?"

"They need time to recharge, and they are erratic. There is no saying which stones will work and how often their burst will flow, or, as in your case being a Diamond Bearer with multiple powers, which power will be amplified."

Chris says, "Since they can overpower obsidian's effects, maybe we should all have one, for that reason alone."

"It's not worth the risk."

Chris asks, "So, can't you look to the future and find out what effect the stone will have on the person?"

"For Calli, we can. For anyone who does not have a Diamond Bearer handy to scry the future, it's a gamble. For instance, sometimes the stone can lock a Seer into continual visions, leaving them semi-comatose. Readers' abilities can become amplified to the Thought-Extractor level, debilitatingly so. Those are hunted down and killed."

I say, "Let me guess. Healers shoot lightning bolts."

"Among other things. Apparently, the stone in your ring is latched onto that power for now. Therein lies the danger with your ring: it can become uncontrollable and erratic once it bonds with your body."

I nervously twist the ring, peering down at the burn scar seared on my finger. "Well, that hasn't happened yet."

"Correct, but it will if given enough time." Maetha says to Chris, "You said the stone is a family heirloom."

"Yes." He sends me his thoughts. *I'm sorry, Calli. I had no idea about any of this.*

"Then you have or had a Spellcaster in your family line somewhere, either directly, or in association."

"Why do you think that?"

Enhancer stones are Spellcaster's stones and are passed along through families. Is there a story that goes with this diamond?"

Chris nods his head and runs shaky fingers through his hair. "Yeah. It's supposed to be lucky."

Maetha purses her lips together while looking back and forth at us.

"Well," —Chris's tone flips to sarcastic— "what a *lucky* coincidence I followed tradition and used the *lucky* diamond in Calli's ring."

Maetha reaches forward and places her hand on his. She speaks softly, "Was this your idea? Or was this recommended? Did you feel at all pressured or controlled?"

"My mother gave me the diamond to use in the ring."

"Was your mother wearing the diamond?"

"No. She had it in a jewelry box."

"Did she ever wear it?"

"I don't know."

I ask, "Do you think Vita wants the diamond?"

Maetha pulls her hand back and shakes her head. "She probably has one of her own."

"Maetha," I say, "I've had visions of the blast where I'm wearing the ring on my finger. The diamond turns green. What does that mean?"

"I don't know."

Chris asks, "Can't you see the future, Maetha?"

"Not concerning the fine details like these. The future is unset now that you two have altered it." She turns back to me. "I noticed you had a slight burn the morning after healing Chris. What about now?"

Chris becomes alarmed and speaks before I can answer. "Calli, why didn't you tell me the burn was not healing?"

"I forgot since it doesn't hurt anymore. I don't know why the healing is taking so long."

Maetha glances at my hand then says, "To use the stored power of an enhancer, some power from the user must be sacrificed. This ring will eventually seal itself to your finger—become one with you."

My memories recall the ring being stuck to my finger in one of the visions. I didn't like the panic I felt at not being able to remove the ring.

"How is that possible?" Chris asks.

Maetha responds, "How are you able to have a large piece of carbon inside your heart, Chris, and still be alive? Some answers have yet to be explained by science."

I ask, "What do I do, Maetha? Should I take the ring off? I've seen myself wearing this ring when the blast hits."

"We'll have to consult with Crimson."

I release a slow exhale and say, "Yeah, about Crimson. Vita wants a meeting with her."

"Crimson will never do it."

"Well, she'll *have* to, apparently. Vita says she inserted an obsidian 'grenade' into my body somewhere, protected by a bubble, that will release powdered obsidian if Crimson does not meet with her. And there's an unknown timeframe of when the bubble enchantment will fade, and the powdered obsidian will enter my body. So, I'd appreciate if Crimson would meet with her." My gut churns at the thought of something so foreign inside me.

Chris says, "We're not even sure there's anything inside her. Neither one of us can detect it."

I add, "She also said if I try to remove it, the thing will activate and release the powder."

Maetha looks over my body carefully. I take note of the dramatic change in her expression as her eyes travel, then stop at my belly. "I can't see anything, but I can feel it."

My stomach drops, bringing on an intense wave of nausea. I'd hoped this was all a bluff.

Chris asks Maetha with a trembling voice, "What does it feel like?"

"Confusing. You definitely have a bubble inside, Calli. I'm not sure why your body isn't trying to remove it with the healing power. It should be."

What's wrong with me? I think, anxiety creeping up my spine. *Why aren't my powers working correctly? Is it because of the ring? Is it messing them up?*

"Do you think we can remove it?" Chris presses.

"This will have to be decided by Crimson."

I feel the need to change the subject so Chris will calm down . . . and myself, also. I clear my throat and say, "There's something else, Maetha. The person in charge at the facility knows you. General Bernard Appleton. He wanted to know where you are. I told him maybe you died. He didn't buy it." I watch her face intently for any recognition of his name, but her bland expression gives nothing away.

"I assume I've been caught on camera more often than I originally thought, and with the prevalent facial recognition all around us, we will all have to be more careful from now on."

Chris says, "Or we'll have to change our outer appearance, like you have."

I add, "Perhaps by us inviting the government to help us save lives, they'll work with us instead of against us, and we won't have to take such drastic measures."

"The future is uncertain on that matter, unfortunately." Maetha shakes her head. "Have you heard from Jonas at all?"

I'm taken aback by her question. "No, I haven't. Where did he go?"

"I don't know. He's using obsidian."

I consider asking if he's being punished for divulging all the information concerning him being the backup guy, but I resist. Instead, I say, "I hope he's okay."

Jie Wen appears in his bi-located form nearby, outside the blue mist circle. An immediate scowl crawls over his face as he makes eye contact with me.

Maetha's demeanor changes to something more formal.

I say, "We plan to have a Gathering. Everyone needs to be updated on the government's involvement."

"Yes. I agree. You will take charge of that when you are ready. Our discussion is complete," she says to me, which I understand as a hint to remove the privacy mist, and I comply. Once it dissipates, she stands and moves nearer to Jie Wen's form.

Chris takes my hand. *I can get you a new diamond, Calli. You don't have to wear this one.*

Let's wait for Crimson's opinion. Besides, the two times I've used it, good things happened. I saved your life and saved my own. And for a bonus, I got to give Max the shock of his life.

Chris smiles, which warms my whole body.

Like I said, I've seen myself wearing the ring when the blast hits. I'll try to view the future without the ring to see if that choice will bring better results.

Good idea.

First, I need to announce the Gathering.

With my mind, I focus on the diamonds with owners and send a message, like a group text message, to gather around my diamond in one hour. Chris acknowledges that he received the message.

"Okay, now we wait," I say on an exhale. "I don't want to wait here in the house. I don't really feel like talking to any of the Bearers yet. Let's go find my parents."

"That sounds good."

We leave and walk out on the pathway toward the bungalow where my parents have been staying. Groundskeepers are hard at work, trimming, mowing, and weeding the landscaping. I sometimes forget how large of a job it is for Maetha's island to operate. We come around a corner and see my parents sitting on the deck bench of their bungalow.

"Hi Mom. Hi Dad." I approach and give them each a hug.

"Calli," my dad says, "We heard you'd returned."

Mom says, "Yes, we were about to come find you."

"Sorry, I should have come to see you when I arrived, but I had to take care of a few things first. I have good news. You two can go home now, if you want."

"What changed?"

"The threat to your safety is gone."

My father's shoulders stiffen. "Our safety? What about yours? Did they catch the man who shot you?"

"He turned himself in. He's not a threat anymore." *At least, he shouldn't be.*

My mother places her hand on my arm and I sense her enthusiasm. "We can return? Wonderful. I have a backlog of patients."

"Really? Still?" I ask. "Even after the Shadow Demon threat was eliminated?"

"Yes. Nyctophobia is a very real condition."

My father says, "I am anxious to get back to the office, too. You're in good hands here, Calli. I'm not worried anymore about you."

"Thanks, Dad. Listen, would both of you be able to arrange some time off next August? I'd like to have you help me on a medical project."

"How much time?"

"Two weeks, probably. I don't know for sure yet."

"We'll look into it."

"Thanks. Call me when you get home to let me know you got back okay."

We say our goodbyes and then Chris and I walk back to the main house to prepare for the Gathering. Kookju, Aernoud, Avani, Amalgada, and Ruth are present in person, having arrived the day we left. They sit around the large table in the dining area, talking. Their conversations halt as we join them.

Ruth breaks the silence. "I hear you two are now engaged. When will the coupling take place?"

Chris coughs out, "The *what*?"

"In Diamond Bearer terms your joining is called a coupling, a joining of goals, dreams, and ideas for as long as you both agree."

Chris glances at me and we both smile. He says, "We haven't set a date yet."

"Well, congratulations on taking the first step to cement your lives together."

Avani speaks to Ruth. "I don't think the word cement is appropriate as it implies they will be stuck together."

Amalgada joins in. "We all know what she meant. These two are in love and desire to be stuck with each other."

Chris raises a hand. "I think I prefer cementing over stuck."

Other Bearers begin bi-locating around the table, halting our conversation. The Gathering is about to begin.

After the remaining Bearers arrive, I take charge and say, "As you may know by now, Chris Harding has a diamond in his heart." The lack of reaction from the group tells me they already know. I continue. "After the insertion, we traveled to Washington D.C. and made contacts within the government for help with the Portland blast."

I hear Crimson speak in my head. *Don't mention Vita, Calli.* I take a deep relieving breath upon hearing her communication, finally. She's clearly been eavesdropping to know about Vita's involvement—another reminder of how my mind is an open book. My fleeting relief drowns in my churning stomach.

Jie Wen is first to condemn our actions. "Why would you do such a thing? What were you thinking?"

I decide not to respond to his furious questions. Instead, I continue, "While there, we learned Max Corvus is now silenced by this very department. They have cleared his record in exchange for his cooperation, which includes no longer actively pursuing Diamond Bearers. He is a member of the division that will be helping us."

Jie Wen huffs. "Unbelievable!"

A few Bearers exchange glances.

Duncan asks Maetha directly, "Where's Crimson?"

Maetha doesn't respond.

I increase the volume of my voice a little. "Going to the government resulted in forming allies within, which we'll need to prevent the deaths and disease from the coming blast."

Ruth asks calmly, "What do you mean by disease?"

"I've seen the fallout causing sickness in the days following the blast. Without the government's help, this will be catastrophic."

Jie Wen folds his arms across his chest and juts his chin up. "You don't believe the Bearers can prevent this, do you? You don't think *you* can."

"Correct." Audible gasps seemingly echo through the room. I continue, "I'm not so arrogant to believe I alone can do this. Nor that all the Bearers as a group can do this. We must have help, and that help will come from the non-powered population. Luckily for us, there is a ready-made division with extensive knowledge about cosmic powers and abilities able to comprehend what we need them to do. As they help and observe our intentions to save lives, perhaps the attitudes toward us and people with powers will evolve."

No one responds directly to me, but I hear their discontented telepathic communications between each other. I don't let on to that fact.

I add, "This blast has been seen arriving for thousands of years, by Crimson. It is not preventable. The blast will happen. Life as you have known will change—no matter what. The difference is we can shape the way the world moves on beyond the event. How will the government treat us? How will they treat anyone who becomes affected down the road?"

Chaung speaks up, directing his words more to the group than to me. "I'll be the first to admit I didn't like the idea of Crimson bringing on young Bearers. We've all entered the group in our adult years, with knowledge of life and the workings of the societies we come from." He points to me. "Your young age and lack of wisdom is alarming, yet I see the benefit of this as well. You understand the society you come from. Chris even more so, having had direct involvement with the government. I believe this new development can be positive, without viewing the future. However, I want to make one suggestion. I suggest the disseminating of information concerning the blast, the evacuation, and subsequent fallout be controlled to prevent global panic."

"Thank you, Chuang. I appreciate your support. The government officials want the same control over the spread of the news as you recommend. They don't want the knowledge of powers to become mainstream news, either. That's why they silenced Max Corvus. He's basically under orders to shut up. Our anonymity and that of the general cosmic powers' communities can possibly remain low key even after a major evacuation of such a large city. All the focus will be on the government doing what the government does."

Jie Wen jumps back in. "*If* this goes the way you think it will."

"Yes."

"And if it doesn't?"

"Hopefully we'll be able to sweep up. Once the blast hits, I believe we will all be able to see future forecasts much easier. And before anyone asks, I base that on nothing more than my gut instinct."

Chuang asks, "What about the confusion substance you removed from my body, Calli? Are we any closer to being able to defend ourselves against it?"

Before I can answer, Maetha speaks. "I know more on this topic than Calli." She looks at me and dips her chin slightly. "May I?" she asks.

I nod and say, "Please." I try to hide my relief that she takes over the conversation, because I don't know anything about the recent developments.

Maetha says, "I've been working on this with Dr. Todd. Trying to deconstruct and understand how the substance works and how it was created. This is one of the reasons we are building the machine. We need to reverse-engineer the confusion element. Until we can figure this out, I recommend Bearers always carry a healing topaz on your body."

Mary steps forward. "A topaz won't be enough. We need Healers' quartz, Maetha."

"I understand. However, we don't have that at our disposal right now. Should any of you become affected by the substance in the meantime, Calli can help you."

I volunteer, "Don't forget we have healing blankets.

Even though Chuang wasn't healed while using one, he was able to stay alive until the substance was removed. If needed, we can use those in a pinch."

Several heads nod.

"Does anyone else have questions or concerns?" I pause and wait a few moments.

Avani speaks softly, "I do. Do you know where Jonas is?"

"I don't. Sorry."

Jie Wen steps forward abruptly. "What do you mean, Avani?"

Avani speaks slowly as if she's not sure she's the best person to make the declaration. "Jonas left the island after Calli and Chris and he hasn't returned or contacted Maetha. He must be using obsidian to hide his location."

Jie Wen tosses his hand above his head dismissively. "Another rogue Bearer."

"We'll keep searching for Jonas, rest assured." I pause, then ask, "Any other questions?" After several seconds of silence, I say, "All right. We'll meet later when there's more to discuss."

Bi-located forms disappear almost immediately, and Maetha speaks to my mind. *Calli, take Chris upstairs to my room. I'll be there momentarily.*

The room we met in earlier? I ask.

Yes. Brand is waiting.

I relay the instructions to Chris's mind and together we head to her room.

As promised, Brand sits in a chair near the French doors. He stands once we enter. "How'd it go?"

I tease, "Don't you already know the answer?"

"No. I haven't repeated."

"Oh. It went, you know, good." I rock back and forth on my heels.

Chris wraps his arm around my shoulders and pulls me against his chest. "She was awesome."

I say to Brand, "If you would accept a diamond, you'd be part of these gatherings." I reach up with my hand and clasp Chris's hand on my shoulder, giving it a gentle squeeze.

"Oh, and have it try to rip my heart in half like his? No thanks." Brand motions to Chris.

Maetha enters the room and says with a heavy exhale, "Okay. We're going to have a small meeting."

Crimson, in her invisible form, follows Maetha and stands by the wall. Clearly, she doesn't want everyone in the house to know she's present. This is the first time I'm seeing her since learning she was going to let Chris die, that she knew he would die but didn't tell him. She didn't tell me.

Jie Wen bi-locates to the room and nods to Maetha. As she closes the door, she announces, "I've invited Jie Wen to this private meeting to discuss the bubble in your body, Calli. I've already told him about it."

Before I can respond, Crimson releases her Invisibility, revealing her presence. She forms a blue circle around the room to privatize our meeting. She moves to my side and looks at Chris. He promptly drops his hold on me and walks over to Brand. Taking me by the elbow, Crimson says, "Let me have a look at you." She positions herself directly in front of me and drops my arm, then she scans me with her eyes the way Maetha did.

Brand unexpectedly blurts out, "No! I won't do it."

"Huh?" I ask, looking over my shoulder.

"Jie Wen wants to activate the device to see what happens and have me repeat if it goes wrong. I'm saying no to that."

Jie Wen thrusts his chest out. "I said nothing!"

"You are about to, though," Brand accuses.

Crimson's eyebrows lower along with her tone. "Brand,

I asked Jie Wen here for his strategic wisdom. You are here to repeat for Calli's safety if necessary, nothing more."

Maetha asks Crimson, "Can you locate it?"

Crimson pulls in a breath and lets it out slowly. "No."

Maetha points to my mid-section. "I believe it's in her belly."

Crimson turns me to the left, then the right. She moves her face toward my stomach, then pulls back. She asks Maetha, "Can you detect the general area? Upper, lower, or either side?"

"No."

Jie Wen says, "Exploratory surgery may be needed."

"You won't be able to see the bubble, though," Maetha says. "It's the same concept as the bubble around this island or the Hunters' Forest."

Jie Wen grunts, "For goodness's sake, just activate the device. There's enough time for her body to heal afterward, probably."

Chris exclaims, "Are you nuts? What if it kills her?"

Jie Wen waves his hand as if to shoo a lazy summer fly away, "It's not designed to. It's meant to disable her powers. She could use quartz and topaz until the obsidian is processed through her system."

Chris runs a shaky hand through his hair and says, "I can't believe what I'm hearing."

Jie Wen persists. "Brand can repeat if it doesn't work."

Crimson and Maetha stay silent. Brand has his head down with his index and middle fingers pressed firmly to his forehead. He looks uncomfortable, possibly in pain. Chris's veins in his neck are visible and I worry he might explode in rage at any moment.

Jie Wen adds, "Crimson, if you don't want Vita to have leverage, you need to deal with this issue." He turns in my direction and addresses me personally. "And here you thought everything went well with your jaunt to the mainland. You conveniently left this part out at the Gathering. Now I know why."

"At my request, Jie Wen." Crimson moves away from me. "Vita is right. She is the only one who can remove this. The consequences of activating it are unforeseeable and there's no guarantee Calli will be able to assist in capturing the blast."

"Any one of us can assist, Crimson," Jie Wen says, making me aware of his lack of knowledge on the subject.

Crimson ignores him. "There's no other choice, then. I will need to meet with Vita."

I ask, "Why exactly are you reluctant? Is she dangerous?"

"I believe she wants to disable me. I'll need my own leverage to play her game, which delays when I can meet with her."

"You sound like you've played her game before?"

"Yes."

"Then why did you use her for this island's protection enchantment, or the Hunter Forest?"

"Different times, different situations." Crimson turns to Maetha. "Come." Maetha follows obediently and the two of them leave the room. The privacy circle fades away, leaving me wondering what the next step will be. Will Crimson communicate with me when she's ready to meet with Vita? When will that be?

Jie Wen's bi-located form remains, and I feel him connect with my diamond. I can tell he wants to get something off his chest. If he stays true to what I know about his personality so far, this isn't going to be pleasant.

Chris eyes Jie Wen. "Did you need something?"

Jie Wen straightens his posture even more. "I'm amused by how smart Calli thinks she is, that's all."

I turn and face him. "Tell me what you're really thinking."

He explodes in a tirade that reddens his face. "You think you know everything. Now, arrogantly, you've taken matters into your own hands. No good has ever come from including governments or other officials in Bearer business."

"So far. But you've never had to deal with an Elemental blast. Am I correct?"

He doesn't answer.

"Is this all that bad? The government is working with us to succeed on this mission."

"One government." Jie Wen crosses his arms and pushes out his chest.

Chris defends me. "The government for the country where the Elemental blast will hit. I'd say that's an important one. Plus, they want to keep cosmic powers a secret. That's been a huge concern with all this. I mean, isn't that the whole goal of removing people from the blast radius—to prevent the creation of new people with these dangerous powers? If these new powers aren't out there, the rest of them don't have to become more visible."

Jie Wen moves closer to me. "They want what they've always wanted. Us. Now they have you two. I cannot fathom what Crimson was thinking when she brought in all of you . . . kids."

Mentally, I grunt and think of all the things I'd love to say to him but know better. Instead, I ask him, "Why couldn't you see the future concerning the Portland blast?"

"What does that have to do with anything?"

"You just wondered what Crimson was thinking about bringing us in. I imagine she tried to see if the mission could be accomplished with her existing Bearers, but she couldn't find a combination for success. That would include you, Jie Wen. I don't believe Crimson sees everything with precise clarity, as you seem to think. She's told me she focuses on the long-range future of humanity carrying on after the blast. Without the younger Bearers, it's bleak. So, you do the math. I know she holds you in high regard and would have used you if it meant success. But for whatever reason, it doesn't. Maybe, just maybe, the solution to success will be including the government. The old guard would not ever have done that. Do you agree?"

He remains silent.

I continue. "Unfortunately, I can't see the long-range future the way Crimson does, so I don't know if this will work out. However, we made some extremely important connections, discovered potential allies, learned where the government stands on continuing to keep cosmic powers secret, and now have our nemesis Max Corvus under wraps. His site is down, along with all the information about Diamond Bearers. If nothing else, I'd say our reckless choice had some good results in the end that we can build upon."

Jie Wen points his finger at me and takes a small step forward. "You sided with the enemy. And now you have a ticking timebomb inside you. How do you equate that with good?"

I let out a heavy exhale. "I don't know what else I can say, Jie Wen."

"Admit that you gave up on trying to find a sensible solution. Admit that you acted recklessly and have now endangered us even more."

"The sensible solution *is* to involve the government."

"I disagree."

Exhaustion settles upon me. "You have that right. Are we done here?"

Jie Wen scowls, then turns his back to me, releasing his connection to my diamond, and disappears.

"What an ass!" Brand blurts out as if he's been holding

his breath.

"I agree."

Chris moves to my side. "But you stood your ground, Calli. I'm proud of you."

Brand says, "You'd freak out if you knew all the things I said to him."

Chris asks, "What did you say? I didn't hear anything."

"My words weren't productive to the conversation and kept derailing it. So, I repeated and kept quiet."

Crimson's voice sounds in my mind. *Calli, come speak with me, alone, at your bungalow.*

Another wave of fatigue, but this time it's countered by a rush of adrenaline and anxiety. I glance over at Chris. "Crimson wants to speak privately with me."

"Do you want me with you? Or nearby?"

I smile. "I don't think that's necessary, but I do appreciate your offer."

"Okay. Then, I'm going to go talk to Uncle Don."

"Okay."

Brand clears his throat theatrically. "I guess I'll just go and make myself look busy at Jonas' place."

Chapter Six - Irradiated

I leave the house and walk on the pathway to my bungalow where Chris proposed to me only a couple days ago. I can almost see the events as they played out, along with the diamond insertion and the death of Chris Harding. The beginning of Chris the Diamond Bearer was an entirely different milestone as it marked the beginning of a new chapter, one that had clearly knocked everyone off their game.

Jie Wen obviously isn't completely aware of the significance behind the events that took place only a couple evenings before, and for that I'm grateful. I don't think I could have kept my calm a moment ago if he'd gone off on me concerning Chris's diamond insertion.

The greenery opens to the beautiful view and warm ocean breeze. Crimson sits on the beach with her back to me. I take my place next to her on the hard, wet sand, with so much running through my mind. I want to ask many questions—all the questions.

Before I can open my mouth, she surrounds our bodies with a privacy circle and says, "This is not a time for chastisement or ridicule of instructions tossed to the wind. Nor is it appropriate to debate whether the government's involvement with this task is the right move. I believe your heart was in the right place. You weren't striking out on a rebellious crusade to make a point. I think you reached the end of your rope, in more ways than one, and you acted impulsively, but with good intentions. You still wanted to succeed and save lives."

"That's true."

Crimson says, "Many events did not play out the way I

thought they would, and now you wear a power enhancer that has the potential to throw off the absorption of the Elemental blast. Frankly, I don't know what will happen. The only thing I know for sure is when and where the blast will hit. That, and you'll need to wear the ring to achieve success."

"I know. I've seen a vision that I'm wearing the ring, and it turns green after the blast. It also becomes stuck to my finger."

She turns her head, and our eyes meet. "I never saw that in future visions. Does the diamond you will hold in your hand change colors too?"

"Yes. Also to green. Don't you already know that?"

"No."

"Why are our visions different?"

A pause. "I suspect the reason is you had already thought about going to the government for help and the intention was enough for you to change the future. You began seeing the future as it will play out. That is not the future I saw in the beginning, or I would have intervened and made a change sooner. Now, there is simply not enough time to correct what has happened. I've been struggling to keep the future consistent ever since Maetha and Neema made Henry a Bearer without my consent. I'm not sure this new sequence of events of yours can be massaged into a successful ending."

My cheeks heat and the sides of my throat thicken, making it difficult to swallow. Her rebuke hurts. Maybe Jie Wen was right, and I truly screwed up. "What can we do to change that?"

"Follow your instincts." She pauses. "Now that Vita has inserted herself into the equation, we'll have to evolve."

"What should I pass on about when you'll meet with her?"

"I haven't decided yet. Until then, you should continue forward on the new road you've paved. Try to save as many lives from the coming blast. Keep an eye on your safety and immediate future. Avoid using obsidian if possible so I can keep tabs on you. We are in the home stretch of preparation. Soon, I'll be taking you to Portland to scout locations for our setup."

"What about the ring bonding to my finger? Can that be prevented?"

"I'm not sure. You have to wear it, as per your vision. I've tried to look to the future with your finger bare and I cannot discern what changes, only that it is devastating."

Hearing her words lets me know there's no need for me to explore possible changes to the future. I've seen myself wearing the ring. The vision came after Chris proposed and the ring became part of my life—and Chris almost died and departed it. Like a tidal wave, my emotions crash to the forefront of my mind.

"Crimson," I say, trying and failing to control my quivering chin, "why didn't you tell me Chris was supposed to die?"

"You would have tried to find a way to prevent it, like when you carried the diamond the first time."

"Well, yeah!" The words burst out of my mouth before I can stop them. "I've seen visions of our future together. Why wouldn't I try to protect him?"

She turns her gaze out to the horizon, seemingly unfazed by my outburst. "Being able to see the future is a curse." Her voice is quiet, so much so I'm not sure if she's actually talking to me.

I wipe my eyes and calm my emotions, feeling childish for allowing them to overrule my sensibilities. I notice the gentle lap of waves comes closer to our feet than before. The tide must be turning.

Crimson speaks. "Calli, what was your life like before you could see the future?"

"I don't know. I guess I just rolled with it, wishing I could know what the future holds." I chuckle at the irony.

"Wishful thinking is normal. Being able to see and control the future isn't, and in the wrong hands, humanity could cease to exist." She turns her head to face me. "*In your own hands*, this could happen if you are not careful. Maetha and I have told you to avoid looking to your own future as you may be tempted to try to make a change."

"Crimson, what's the point of being able to see the future if it isn't to make a change? Diamond Bearers do that all the time to avoid death."

"You're right. Initially, *you* needed to view the future and make changes to pass your test. We wanted to see your compassion in practice and your ability to sacrifice for the greater good. You made that choice, even though it meant your life would end. However, since then, your need to see the future isn't vital to the success of the mission at hand."

"I'm confused." I press my palms against my temples.

She turns her whole body in my direction. "Chris isn't a crucial player in capturing the blast. Constantly dwelling on if he lives or dies is complicating the mission."

I default to sarcasm. "So, you'd prefer it if I'd just stop caring altogether. And here I thought I needed to save someone's life to motivate me properly."

"Now that you seem to know the whole story, I guess you don't have to save anyone in particular. You will be saving hundreds of thousands of lives. This moment, right here," —she waves her hand between us— "is why I didn't want you looking to your future. The emotional pain you're feeling isn't helpful to the mission."

I desperately want to tell her exactly what she can do with her mission . . . but, deep down, I know I can't abandon this cause. I've seen the visions. I know the immense powers that are going to hit the Earth and what will result if pregnant women are in the way. My head suddenly feels ten times as heavy and falls forward.

"Calli, we as humans thrive on caring for others. Some care more, but I'm sure you've noticed that. Every Diamond Bearer tries to protect their fellow human beings, to a point, and in conjunction with nature's will. Lifespans are longer these days due to science and medicine, but the human body eventually stops being able to support life without supernatural interventions.

"Your need to care and protect Chris when you first carried the diamond is why you succeeded in ending the Death Clan's reign of terror. But that's where Chris's importance stopped. I never foresaw him becoming a Bearer. He was only to be your love interest, your reason to sacrifice yourself, and later, possibly be your lifetime companion. Yet, as the future played out, he became an Unaltered and I allowed him to be a partial Bearer. I could see that together you two could accomplish great things before the end of his days, as two Diamond Bearers in love. But his days always ended, and they would end when you inserted his diamond. Remember, *you* were instructed to insert it, and to remove it if he wasn't healing fast enough.

"But he would have still died, or at least that's what you thought. Am I right?"

"You are not wrong. However, I wouldn't have been surprised to discover you'd healed his heart after removing the diamond, thus extending his natural life. And yet, saying that out loud doesn't make sense either because in my visions you wore the ring around your neck, not on your finger. What I didn't expect was what you were able to do, that is, heal his heart *with a diamond inside*. But I also didn't know you had the help of an enhancer stone."

I don't say anything.

She continues. "If, before you had the ability to see the future, you had fallen in love with Chris and married him, you might have spent your life with him until death. You would have been content knowing each day was a gift and you would have appreciated the time together. Then, when it was over, you'd mourn, which is normal. But now, you're fixated on whether he lives as long as you."

"I disagree. I'm mad that you didn't trust me with this information."

"And I disagree with you, Calli. Your fixation has changed the future to the extent that I cannot see the details." She thumps her finger against her chest. "*I* cannot see the details. There is a blast coming that will have a drastic impact on the world; that much is still predictable. We can catch it and minimize its fallout zone. That I know. What I don't know is whether Chris will live beyond the event, nor do I need to know."

My anger turns to pity. "How could you turn your back on him after everything you two have been through?"

"I haven't turned my back. I attempted to sway him in the direction of choosing not to insert the diamond. That way he could live a full life. I have grown fond of Chris, and I have compassion for what his father did to him, even if that doesn't seem apparent. I've felt like Chris was my own child in many ways. Restraining myself from helping you save his life was . . . hard."

I am speechless.

"But, that said, he decided to be deceptive and hide his true intentions on your birthday. Maetha saw a different future, one where you and Jonas would be together. That was always a possibility from the outset. With the new knowledge, we put the plans into motion, feeling that you and Chris were about to part ways—until we felt the diamond had no owner." She clears her throat and repositions in the sand.

I take my eyes off Crimson and realize the incoming tide is already beyond our position on the beach. She must be controlling the water because it approaches us, then splits and diverts around us.

Taking a deep breath, she continues. "Sometimes, I think back to when I pulled the Primal Stone out of the skeleton and wonder what that person went through during their possession. Did they reach complete exhaustion, too? Did the Primal Stone end their life unexpectedly? How could someone die with a powerful stone like this inside them? I am nearing mental exhaustion, Calli. I have planned so long for this blast. Maetha has also worked for centuries in preparation, strengthening your DNA to better harness the Healing ability and be able to withstand the blast. Capturing the Elemental power is crucial to be able to deal with the individuals who will emerge in the aftermath. Your recent choices of going to the government have consequences, and I cannot undo what you did."

"Maybe it's not all bad, though." I feel the need to defend myself.

"Vita is involved now. It's bad."

"How do you know Vita?"

Crimson stares out to sea and is silent for a moment. Then she says, "I have known her most of my life. I've collaborated with her on occasion, as you know. But, not as much lately."

"You've known her your whole life?"

"Yes."

"I had no idea Spellcasters could live so long."

"There are several Spellcasters who wander the earth and have done so for thousands of years. Usually, the ones with evil intentions are too impulsive and accidentally take care of themselves and the Bearers don't have to get involved. But we have had to correct more than one over the years. Vita is the only one who has escaped our reform techniques and that's because of her bubbles. She is very good at what she does, and what she does is sow chaos. Vita is chaos."

"If she's so sketchy, why do you feel safe here under her bubble? Isn't she able to enter at will?"

"You're correct, she could enter, but she's not a Diamond Bearer and she cannot protect her life the same as you or I. Vita is mortal and quite fragile. I know she won't come here. She hides out most of the time and is difficult to find. That's part of why she's been able to live so long. Her potions and power enhancer stones will only keep her alive if she's able to continue activating them. If she is away from them for too long, she could die, the same way a Bearer would die if they stopped healing their body." She stands and brushes sand from her slacks. "I need to go, now. I will communicate with you when it's time to go to Portland. Remember what I told you about avoiding obsidian use. I can't speak to you if I can't find you. Until then, do keep an eye on your immediate future to preserve your life, but please avoid the long-term future, especially concerning Chris. I understand that sounds difficult, but your future is more than saving and protecting one person. If you can't see the larger picture, you will create the same death and pain on others you wish to spare with Chris."

I push myself up from my seat and stand next to her. She turns and walks with me up the beach out of the surf zone to dry sand. The water closes in behind us as she releases her hold. I want to be amazed at her ability to control the water, but I need to respond to her request concerning future visions before she leaves. I say, "Sometimes visions just hit me without any effort on my part."

"Those are fine. They tend to happen when the future has changed, yet you can't count on having one of those visions. Clearly, I've been caught off guard with changes to the future. I must go." She pats my shoulder and then begins to float upward into the sky. Then she zips out of sight.

I remain on the beach for a little longer, rehashing her words. She did tell me in Denver there was more to the story but that she couldn't tell me right then. She wasn't lying. But have I heard everything now? Is there still more to be revealed? I don't even want to think about that.

I turn and head back to the main house.

Chris, are you there?

Yes.

Where?

Upstairs with Uncle Don.

On my way.

I enter the room where the power-removing machine is being built, and Uncle Don calls me over to the pile of parts he and Todd are assembling. Chris is with him. I walk over to Chris's side, struggling to keep my mind clear so Chris won't know he was a large part of my conversation with Crimson. I don't want him to feel my dread.

Uncle Don says, "I was told you have a special ring my nephew gave you."

"That's right."

"Well, let me take a look at it." His hand extends impatiently, yet there's a twinkle in his eye. His other hand retrieves a jeweler's loupe from the breast pocket of his shirt.

I wiggle the band off my finger and hand him the ring. I feel safe with Uncle Don and trust that he isn't trying to take the ring, only to inspect it.

His eyes linger on my finger, obviously looking at the burn mark. "You might be allergic to the metal, Calli.

Possibly nickel." He brings both his hands to his face, positioning the loupe at his eye with the ring near the other side. He twists the band forward and back as he examines the stone. "This is platinum. The rash on your finger might be more of contact dermatitis because platinum doesn't contain nickel." He continues to examine the ring, "What kind of stone is this, Chris?"

"What do you mean? It's a diamond." Chris's voice drops.

"I see a faint green tint. Where did you buy it?"

Chris says, "It's my mom's diamond. It's been in her family for generations."

"Here." Don hands the ring back to me, then turns his back and starts rummaging through his toolbox. "I think I brought . . . yes, here it is." He turns around with a long narrow device in his hand. "I can verify the stone with this."

"What is that?" I ask.

Chris steps forward. "What are you doing?"

"This is a diamond tester. It uses electrical conductivity to authenticate mineral types. You see, diamonds versus glass, or moissanite or white sapphire or quartz react distinctively different to heat and electricity and are easily confirmed using this little gadget." He extends his hand for the ring once again, which I hand to him.

Chris bristles. "Why do you feel the need to test the diamond?"

"Because it's green. They are extremely rare in this size." He touches the diamond with the tip of the device and multiple lights illuminate, followed by multiple beeps. Don's eyes widen. "Oh, my!" he exclaims and looks up at us. "Did you know, Chris?"

Chris and I exchange glances. "No."

"Green diamonds developed from being irradiated by uranium millions of years ago deep in the ground."

"Is it radioactive?" I ask.

"No." He chuckles. "Although, there is a process in today's age where green diamonds can be made with radiation treatments. Even so, they aren't radioactive."

I recall how Jonas said my diamond looked green the morning after I received it. My mind slips to Jonas and his whereabouts. I feel he needs friendship and comfort, although I'm not sure why I feel that way. I'm not connected to his diamond at all. Maybe I'm just thinking about what I'd want after fessing up to being part of a huge charade.

Don's voice intrudes my thoughts. "The platinum setting really amplifies the clarity of the solitaire. Beautiful!"

Don hands the ring back to me. "I'd get that appraised and insured if I were you. They will be able to tell if the green diamond is natural or if it's been enhanced. Either way, this is valuable."

Enhanced? I think to myself. *It's an enhancer.* My mind swirls with the memories of my visions where the ring turns intensely green and becomes stuck to my finger. I understand no one will be able to steal it without cutting off my finger, and I have no intention of letting that happen, so having the ring insured against theft or damage seems pointless. As for the value, I don't care how much the ring is worth. This ring came from Chris. It represents his love for me, which in my mind is priceless.

While Chris continues to talk with his uncle, I wander over to Mishell who sits at a desk, working on a computer. Two folded quartz blankets rest on the desk next to her. Mishell has taken quite well to the new life she's been forced to live. Along with Todd and her daughter Sarangerel, Mishell has embraced the necessity for secrecy and respected the confidentiality of the Diamond Bearers—something not everyone can do.

"How are you doing, Mishell?"

"I'm well, thank you for asking."

"How do these blankets work?"

"Quartz was charged with Healer power, then crushed and mixed with the fibers that were woven into cloth."

"Does the quartz separate or fall out of the fabric?"

"Yes, over time it does."

"How much power do the blankets hold?" My thoughts turn to Chris. Would these be a possible solution for his heart?

"Your friend, Chaung, used one for some time yet couldn't heal entirely. In his case, not enough. I've used a blanket when I suffered fever and chills, and I recovered in a couple days."

I wonder if she would have recovered anyway, even without the blanket. Chaung, on the other hand, would have died without the constant healing of the blanket. Perhaps Chris should try the blanket to see if it brings him any relief.

"May I use one of these for an experiment?"

"Certainly. Will you be able to share your results with me?"

"I'm not sure, to be honest. If I can, I will."

"I understand."

Maetha enters the room and joins me and Mishell. "Were you able to get the information I asked for, Mishell?"

"I'm still working on it."

A buzzing sensation hits my upper thigh. I immediately scratch with my hand and feel a lump which at first feels like a huge bumble bee is in my pocket. Then I remember it's the pager topaz. I turn to Chris and find he's already aware the pager is buzzing.

He walks over and says, "I can hear it."

"It's Bushman. He wants a meeting."

Without missing a beat, Maetha says, "Take Brand, Aernoud, Ruth, and Kookju with you. You might need backup."

I muse to myself that of all the names she just listed, Brand is the only one who can truly give me back-up because his Repeater power is immune to obsidian. However, I would like to get to know these Diamond Bearers better, especially Kookju. I think it goes without saying establishing a good relationship built on trust with these Bearers is essential for our future. Plus, I'd like to learn more about when they received their diamonds and what their life was like before.

Chris contests, "I want to go, too."

"Of course. After the meeting, you'll be returning to work." Maetha's answer holds no emotion. She leaves the room.

Chris asks, "What time will you meet him?"

"Noon, the day after tomorrow."

"That's a relief. I thought we might need to head out tonight. We just got here. I'd like to relax a little before diving back in."

"Amen to that."

My parents disembark the island for Bermuda just before the evening meal. They will take a commercial flight home tomorrow. I'm happy for them. Happy they can resume their lives and professions free of being hunted down by Max or any other group bent on controlling me or my actions. At least that's what Maetha said their futures looked like.

In the main house, dinner is served buffet style. As I stare down at the assortment of food items to choose from, my mind wanders. I'm not hungry but I know I need to eat to sustain my physical body. The healing power can only do so much to keep me alive, so I must do my part to nourish and strengthen my immune system. Naturally, the food choices before me consist of nothing processed or preserved and are similar to the Runners' Clan cafeteria food options, minus the Muck soup.

Brand enters the room. "Hey guys, you wanna bring your food to Jonas' place? Sarangerel and Anika are already there. Unless you had other plans."

I glance at Chris. He nods and says, "I'd like that. Would you, Calli?"

"Yes."

We wait for Brand to dish up, then the three of us take our dinner plates to Jonas' bungalow. Even though he has only been gone a couple of days, it appears Sarangerel has already moved in some of her belongings and taken up residency. I'm not sure how I feel about this.

We eat and engage in small talk, laugh a lot, and reminisce, then the topic slides to Jonas. Not that we had avoided it, but I just didn't feel comfortable bringing his name up and apparently neither did anyone else.

I ask, "Sarangerel, are you living here now?"

"Well, I've stayed here the last two nights. I brought some of my things from the main house, so I don't have to run back and forth every day. I just figured someone needs to watch the alerts Jonas has set up, and it's easier to do that here than to try to move the whole system to the main house. But if this makes any of you uncomfortable, I can move—"

I raise my hand slightly. "No, it's fine, I only wondered."

"If Jonas comes back, I'll return to the main house." Sarangerel's words sound strange. I can't imagine Jonas not ever coming back.

Brand fires back, "What do you mean *if Jonas comes back*?"

She bows her head. "Pardon me, Brand. When. When he comes back."

Chris asks, "Sarangerel, what kinds of things are you monitoring?"

"I'm continuing with Jonas' work. He has online alerts set up for any mention of Calli's name. That is tiresome because anytime something even remotely close to your name pops up, I get an alert." She opens a tab on one of the computer screens. "See this list? I will go through these one by one and eliminate most if not all. If anything is related to you, I'll let you know. Also, Jonas is tracking Vorherrschaft with Fabian's and Amenemhet's assistance, except for recently when Amenemhet was with you in Denver. Then there's the power-removing machine hunt and trying to capture Reapers. Oh, and he has this." She reaches under a desk and pulls up a large binder loaded with papers. "This holds all sorts of information about crystals and stones, both fact and fiction."

Brand asks, "Why would he print it out instead of storing it on the computer?"

"He likes to take it down to the beach to read."

I say, "I'm sure he has a digital version stored as well. Sarangerel, can you tell me what he was doing right before he left the island?"

"You're not the first person to ask me that question. He sat here holding a piece of obsidian, twisting and twirling it in his hand for what seemed like hours. He didn't do any work on his computers. He only stared out the window, rolling the obsidian in his hand. I had to leave for a while, but when I returned, he acted like I'd interrupted him and quickly closed down his email and logged out."

"Well, did he say anything before he left on the boat?"

"To me?"

"To you or anyone."

"I heard him tell Maetha she owed him some time off, whatever that means."

I glance over at Chris, who meets my eyes. Chris speaks to my mind. *He said he was going to tell Maetha and Crimson that he told us about their grand plan.*

I can't help but worry about Jonas. Did he leave the island with permission and is he just taking a break? Or is he being punished by Crimson for divulging sensitive information? Is he really missing, or just placed outside our reach?

I'm sure he's fine, Calli.

Chris must have listened to my inner thoughts. I appreciate his attempt to calm my anxiousness, but I don't feel good about Jonas' decision to leave. How would he do that, anyway? He can only fly on Maetha's plane where he can be hidden or disguised because he doesn't have a passport or ID. Jonas Flemming is technically dead. How would he get a flight off Bermuda? Maybe he's in Bermuda taking his break and he'll return when he's cooled off.

Brand breaks the silence. "Anika, how long do you plan on staying here?"

"I'm not sure. I like helping around the island and I have a lot to contribute, but my grandparents have asked that I come live with them around Christmas time, so I might do that. How is Beth doing?"

"She was in Denver with me. She's heading back to the Runners' compound to be with her brother, Nate."

Sarangerel asks, "Nate is a Runner?"

I forget that Sarangerel doesn't know everything about the world of powers or of our lives prior to meeting us.

Brand says, "No, Nate is working at the Runners' compound with Clara Winter. He's not a Runner."

Sarangerel's eyes widen. "Oh, right. The witch."

"Spellcaster." Chris corrects her.

"Oh, do the Spellcasters live at the Runners' compound, too?"

I listen as Chris, Brand, and Anika answer Sarangerel's

questions about the differences between clans and corresponding powers, and how quickly she seems to connect all the dots, remembering names and locations. She is quite intelligent, clearly. A good asset to our team.

Chris and I return our dishes to the main house and help with the evening cleaning in the kitchen, then he walks me to my bungalow. We enter through the door, and I'm pulled into his embrace without warning. I wrap my arms around him to reciprocate.

He rests his cheek on my head and speaks into my hair. "Do you feel like we accomplished what we set out to do by going to the government?"

"Yes. No. Maybe."

He releases his hold a little and pulls back to look me in the eye. "Okay, what do you mean?"

"We talked with the government, sort of, and entered a kind of negotiation. We didn't set out to meet Vita or Max, that's for sure. Whether the government will be a help is yet to be seen."

He brushes a strand of hair away from my eyes. "We found out Agent Bushman is their master interrogator, so we know they don't have other 'secret methods' to extract information out of our heads. That's a plus."

"Yes. But Crimson isn't happy with my choice to involve the government. She worries about the overall outcome of capturing the blast. She's requested I continue to avoid looking for my future, except for impending death, and to avoid using obsidian."

"How do you feel about that?"

"Like a little toddler getting my hand slapped for reaching toward a hot stove, I guess. She's frustrated I have an obsidian bomb inside me she can't detect and that she must now deal with Vita."

"Well, I'm frustrated also over the bomb. I'm afraid to touch you for fear of setting it off. And I really want to touch you," he says with a grin.

"I know. I feel the same. But now that we've found Vita, I'll send Clara a text to let her know she doesn't need to search for her anymore." I snuggle into his arms, content for the moment to forget about the world outside.

Chapter Seven - Side-Hustle

The following day, after docking in Bermuda, Chris and I retrieve our cell phones from the security lockers. No missed calls.

"Should we call Max?" I ask.

"It hasn't been a week yet. I'm not calling him any sooner than I have to."

Our group boards the airplane in the early afternoon, bound for the United States. This back and forth is going to slow down, now that Chris will go back to his job. I glance over at him, noting his healthier complexion. "How is your healing topaz holding up?"

"It's full. I haven't had to use it yet."

"I'm charging two more right now so you can have backups. It's not likely you're going to run into much obsidian while on the job."

After taking my hand, Chris says, "As far as I can see, I don't have obsidian in my near future. You never know, maybe my heart will learn to live with the diamond."

A few hours into the flight, I contemplate the sleeping arrangements for this evening. Having a large group with us will put a damper on any closeness Chris and I may have hoped to have, not that anything would happen anyway. Even if Chris felt comfortable with this potential bomb in my belly, I wouldn't feel relaxed without using obsidian, which we can't use around him or me. I don't know if I'll ever not feel like I'm on stage. I glance down at my finger and at the beautiful ring which symbolizes our love and Chris's desire to live his life with me. How is that ever going to be possible on an intimate level if there's no privacy?

Crimson's voice comes into my head. *Calli, you don't need to worry. I'm sure if you let all the Diamond Bearers know you want privacy, they would leave you alone.*

Sheeze! I can't even think about this without being interrupted. I respond, *I can't deal with the total lack of privacy.*

Intimacy between two people in love is a beautiful thing. Many tribes from long ago would celebrate the merger of families through the knowledge of knowing possible heirs are being conceived. It's normal and natural.

You know, Crimson, when a couple checks into a hotel's Honeymoon Suite, it's pretty obvious what will probably happen. I don't have a problem with people making that assumption about us. My anxiety comes from knowing we are not truly alone and never will be. I feel every Diamond Bearer could be in the same room as us. Sure, I could put up a secrecy mist to mute our conversation but that doesn't stop anyone randomly bi-locating and getting a visual or just connecting without completing the apparition. And then there's your connection, Crimson.

I understand, Calli. There's bound to be a solution that will allow you to feel secure and private.

Yeah. It's obsidian. But I can't use it around Chris.

She adds, *And I don't want you using it at all, if possible.*

I know. I will tell you now, though, I do plan on having Chris use personal obsidian so we can experiment with the quartz blanket once we get to his apartment.

Okay. I'll keep that in mind when his diamond goes dark.

With Brand's repeating, you may not even be aware.

We arrive in Washington D.C. and divide up for the night, with Kookju, Aernoud, and Ruth staying at a nearby hotel after determining my future isn't in immediate danger. Chris, Brand, and I will stay at Chris's apartment to experiment with the quartz blanket. Throughout the flight and car ride to his apartment, I've made sure I was in contact with him in one way or another—holding his hand, or resting my hand on his arm, touching shoulder to shoulder. I crave closeness with him, feel alive when he's nearby, and can't get enough of his touch. For now, that will have to do.

Once we're situated in Chris's apartment, I set the quartz blanket on the table in front of the couch. Then, I dig in my bag while saying, "First up, we'll need some obsidian."

Brand plops down on the couch. "But I thought you weren't supposed to use it."

"I'm not. It's for Chris." Pulling out the metal box containing pieces of what could be responsible for ending Chris's life, I say, "Brand, you'll repeat if at any time you see things turning south in our experiment. I want to see if Chris's heart will heal with the blanket."

"Sweet!" Brand's beaming smile unleashes his dimples. "It will be nice to not be the one she's experimenting on for a change."

Chris asks, "Is this going to hurt?"

"Does it normally hurt when you're around obsidian?" I ask.

"Yes."

"Well, then, I'm sorry, but yes. But we have to do this and find you a solution." I extend my hand forward. "I need your healing topaz, Chris."

"Oh, right." Chris tears off the tape and hands me the stone.

Brand acts as if we're taking up his precious time. "Come on already. Let's get this done so we can chill for the rest of the night."

"Fine." Chris mutters.

I give Chris the box, he removes a small piece and closes the lid. His expression tightens at what I assume is his powers being sucked away. "What now?" he asks with a wince.

"When you feel like you need to put the obsidian away

and use the blanket, then do it."

Brand says, "You'll need about two minutes to reach that point."

"Oh really."

"Uh-huh. What have you got to eat around here?" Brand jumps up and rummages through Chris's kitchen. He comes back with a box of crackers and drops down on the couch. "Okay, you're good. Put it away and use the blanket."

"I thought I was supposed to make that call."

Brand throws a perturbed glance at Chris. "We can do this your way, or we can get this done my way. If you hold that any longer, Calli is going to feel like she needs to help you heal, and for some reason that requires kissing you. So, drop the obsidian and wrap up, dude."

"Uh, excuse me?" I blurt out. "If you're going to repeat, you need to take one of us with you."

Chris drops the obsidian. "Okay, I'm ready for the blanket."

"I could have told you that. Oh wait, I did." Brand shoves a few crackers into his mouth.

I flip open the thin shimmery cloth and drape it over his shoulders, wrapping it around and overlapping it on his chest. "If this isn't working fast enough, tell me and I'll use my healing power on you. Please don't wait too long."

Brand throws his hands in the air. "Why am I even here?" He grabs the television remote control. "What's on tonight?"

After a couple of hours, Chris and I happily conclude he doesn't need the full blanket to mend the heart damage from being around obsidian. I am considering asking if an undershirt could be made from the blanket material for Chris to wear all the time. A thought comes to mind that perhaps I should have one, too, in case something happens to the mysterious bubble inside me. If it ruptures, I'll be powerless. But if I could heal minor ailments during that time, perhaps things wouldn't be so bad. Not that I plan on having the bubble burst.

"Chris, what are our sleeping arrangements for tonight?"

Brand says, "I'm fine on the couch." He waves his hand at us as if to say shoo.

My eyes meet Chris' gaze, and my heart skips some beats.

Calli, I'll sleep out here in the recliner. You can have the bed.

What? Why?

You know why.

I sure hope Crimson meets with Vita soon so you and I can enjoy some time together.

As noon approaches, I take my position near the middle of the steps at the Lincoln Memorial. I sit and face the reflection pool. The day is beautiful, with the sun shining in a clear blue sky and a gentle breeze flowing from the south creating a subtle ripple in the water. Down by the water's edge, Brand and Aernoud stand facing me, while Chris and Ruth are seated together at the base of the stairs facing away. Kookju is inside the memorial with a tourist's pamphlet in his hand, looking up at the seated statue of President Lincoln. Kookju, of all people, is decked out in a flowered button-up shirt, khaki shorts, and a baseball hat. I think about the moment he walked out of the hotel room and how Ruth inhaled sharply and began coughing at the sight. It's the simple moments that keep levity in this chaotic world.

My entourage is here to protect me, even though I already know there's nothing they need to worry about. In fact, everyone here but Brand can view the future. Aernoud brought up a good point that even though this handoff will go well, our views of the future don't include those people in our vicinity who might be here just to watch. I know the Bearers are looking for Max, or other government agents milling around, looking suspicious, anything that would tip us off to Agent Bushman being a spy.

Agent Bushman approaches. I connect my diamond to the diamonds of my team, and ask, *Are any of you able to determine if he's wearing a wire?*

Amenemhet replies, *It's hard to tell from this angle.*

Ruth adds, *I'm not hearing any electronic feedback.*

Chris says, *If he starts asking suspicious questions, that would be a good indicator he's wearing a wire.*

I really wish Brand could communicate with his mind. I don't know if he has repeated or not. He hasn't taken me with him if he did.

Agent Bushman climbs the steps. I'm reminded of my track coach, Mr. Simms, climbing the bleachers to my position after winning the 100m in what seems like an eternity ago, only Agent Bushman is in much better shape. And dressed like a businessman. I half expect that if I look off to the side, I'll find the group of boys who thought I was using drugs. A chuckle escapes my throat at the thought.

"Ms. Courtnae. I'm pleased to see you are here."

"Nice to see you, too." I take note of the briefcase he carries. "What do you have for me?"

"Well, I'm not sure you'll be very happy with this, but it was all I could find on the subject." He sits beside me and unlocks his case, then raises the lid slightly, enough to reach his hand inside and pull out a large orange mailing envelope. He hands it to me while closing the briefcase.

I bend the metal tabs to release the flap. He stops me before I can pull out the papers from inside. "I think it's best if we don't discuss anything out here in the open."

"Should I wait to read them?"

"No, you can go ahead, let's just not talk about it here."

Chris's voice speaks to me. *I guess that confirms he's not wearing a wire.*

Kookju states, *That doesn't mean anything. He could still be wearing a recording device.*

I pull the papers out. There are two pages, both with images and text. I send my thoughts to the other Diamond Bearers and tell them to look through my eyes. As we all read together the information concerning the manufacturing plant where obsidian bullets are being made, I try to maintain the outward appearance of being alone. Agent Bushman has found The Holy Grail and doesn't even know it. Well, maybe he does. He is a Reader, and obsidian bullets would stop his power, too.

I hear Kookjo communicate with my mind. *Do you want him to help find the power-removing machine?*

Chris joins in. *I don't see anyone around. I think we can trust him.*

I say to Agent Bushman, "This is good. Have you heard any information on the location of the power-removing machine I mentioned possibly being in South Carolina?"

"No. I'll keep an ear open, though."

"When you have more information, you can let me know the same way."

He says, "Do I need a different crystal?"

I pull my topaz out of my pocket and examine its power level. "It will work again, at least one more time."

"Good. Just in case, I put my email address on the report, but I'd be careful what you write if you decide to use it."

"I understand."

Agent Bushman stands to leave but stops. "You know, General Appleton is obsessed with finding Maetha. Did you happen to see her?"

Careful, Calli, Chris says to my mind.

I say, "Unfortunately, I don't think Maetha is too keen on meeting with the general. Perhaps she'll change her mind."

"Perhaps. Goodbye for now." He walks away and down the stairs.

We go back to the hotel and sort through the papers. The details state the obsidian bullet manufacturing operation is in Texas, near the Louisiana border.

Chris looks up from the notes. "This has Max's finger-prints all over it."

Ruth leans closer and says, "How can you tell? You can see them?"

Chris says, "Not literally. Max was the one heading up the obsidian processing plant that Brand investigated. We didn't know that till we went to Norway and saw him leaving. Then he posted the video of Calli running behind the truck before he disappeared. Next time we saw him was when Calli and I were captured. We don't know for sure that the bullets contain Yellowstone obsidian, but I'm guessing they do. What I don't know is why this factory is still in operation when Max has been shut down by the government."

Kookju says, "Maybe the government is still trying to disable our powers."

Chris responds, "I wouldn't put it past them. But what I really want to know is if Max is working on this without their knowledge. Calli and I have been placed in Max's care. We're supposed to report to him. This makes me nervous, and I don't like the risks this brings to Calli."

My heart is warmed by Chris's words of concern. I admire his profile and wish I could stretch this moment longer so I could extend my gazing. Instead, I clear my throat and say, "Brand and I will check this place out." I look around the room at the others. "Does one of you want to accompany us?"

Aernoud volunteers.

I notice Chris's shoulders drop forward in a deflated fashion. "I have to go back to work."

I send him mental encouragement to let him know I support his duties.

Ruth and Kookju have other places to be, too.

"Okay, looks like it's Brand, Aernoud, and me. Let's go."

After saying goodbye to Chris and the others, Brand, Aernoud and I board the plane for Texas. Rodger alerts us to a hurricane located off the Texas coast and that he is only able to get us to an airport two hours away from our destination. Another important bit of information is this is a one-way trip. Rodger has another transportation assignment to carry out. Afterward, we'll rent a car and travel that way for a while.

During the next few hours flying, I take the opportunity to take a nap in the hopes of getting some rest, however all I can do is dream about Chris and the upcoming blast. Nothing is different than previous dreams, but that doesn't make the horrific images any easier to deal with.

We arrive at the airport, two hours away from our destination, and rent a car to drive the remaining miles. Ironically, most people are trying to leave the area instead of entering, like us, hence the bumper-to-bumper traffic in the northbound lanes. The southbound lanes are wide open. If only the southbound lanes could be opened to northbound travelers, there wouldn't be such a traffic jam. I saw this type of decision in one of my visions of the evacuation in

Portland.

The wind is already gusting to nearly forty miles per hour, and we have had to drive around several fallen tree branches.

"Is this safe, Calli?" Brand asks as he maneuvers the car to stay clear of a large piece of fencing on the road.

Aernoud answers first. "Our future is secure."

Brand lets out a huff of air. "Whatever that means."

"Seriously, Brand," I say. "You need a diamond or at least a Seer quartz."

"No. I just want to know we're not going to die tonight."

Aernoud says, "That's all I'm searching for. We'll live through the night till tomorrow morning when we wake. That doesn't mean the journey will be smooth, just that nothing is going to kill us."

"Whoa!" Brand's head whips to the right as if he saw something odd on the side of the road. "Did you see that sign? It said seven feet."

"Seven feet what?" I ask.

"The altitude! We're only seven feet above sea level and we have a projected storm surge of fifteen."

Aernoud responds. "That's nothing. In The Netherlands, the lowest elevation is negative seven meters."

"Uh, yeah, but you have dikes and whatever to stop the waves. They don't here."

"Then I suggest we don't dawdle."

Intrigued, I ask, "Aernoud, are you originally from The Netherlands?"

"Yes."

"What time frame?"

"Sixth century."

"Wow. The things you've seen—I'd love to hear about your life sometime."

He nods respectfully.

We arrive at the preplanned destination, two blocks from the listed factory. The area has a couple inches of standing water on the ground due to the lashing rain. This location doesn't have many trees but has plenty of metal and tin roofing materials to threaten our lives if the right amount of wind gets behind it.

Still, Aernoud has seen we will live through the night. So, that's optimistic.

Brand parks the car and says, "Maybe the place will be evacuated. It should be. I mean, honestly, you'd have to be out of your mind to want to go anywhere right now."

The tension inside the car heightens as a large slab of metal roofing flies dangerously close to our vehicle. I know I held my breath as it flew overhead. I'm pretty sure everyone else did, too.

Brand exclaims, "Whose idea was this?"

"We have to surprise them, or they'll pack up and move like they did when you snuck inside the other facility."

"Right, but in a hurricane? That's our cover?"

I say, "I didn't plan this, Brand. Anyway, why are you so scared? You've taken on large groups of fighters and kept yourself safe using your power. Why is this any different? You can repeat us out of bad situations."

"What the hell do you think I've been doing this whole drive? There's a reason I parked here instead of up there where that piece of metal hit the road!"

I notice his eyes seem wider and stress lingers on his words. I hadn't realized how often he must repeat to help us and that we are unaware.

Aernoud raises his voice. "Listen, let's get in there and do what we need to do and get out. I don't like going up against nature any more than you."

We climb out of the car and fight against the wind and

sideways rain as we move in the direction of the obsidian bullet factory. After a few steps, I notice a decrease in the wind speed and less rain blasting our bodies. What's happening?

"Looks like that band of rain has passed," Aernoud says.

Brand says, "Let's hurry before the next one gets here."

Myself, I'm confused. The trees across the street are still bent over from the high wind they're receiving. But we're not. As we move forward, I cast my gaze upward and see Crimson floating above us. Her arms are extended in front of her body, with her hands pulled back at ninety degrees to the ground, fingers straight up.

"What are you looking at?" Brand asks.

He obviously can't see Crimson, and that means Aernoud can't either. I say, "I've never been in a hurricane before." I try my best to sound intrigued and not divulge Crimson's presence, nor her apparent ability to control the weather around us. Mentally, I thank her.

The building is locked and looks deserted, and the power is obviously knocked out. At least we won't have to battle with anyone on this quest. Brand directs us to an unlocked ground-level window that he already located through a series of repeats.

He says, "We have to go through here because the front doors are locked from the inside and I couldn't find a better way in."

"This works," I say as we climb through the window one at a time.

Inside the dark building, I take Brand's hand and lead him while I use my Hunter's night vision to see where I'm going. Aernoud has gone in a different direction to search the office files and possibly take a hard drive or two.

"I can't see a thing," Brand says.

"Don't you wish you had a diamond? Then you could see in the dark, like me." I push open a door and pull Brand inside. Instantly, I freeze in my spot as my powers rush from my body and my vision goes black due to the presence of obsidian.

"What's wrong?"

"Obsidian."

"Oh really? I hadn't noticed. You see, I *don't* have a diamond."

I turn around and playfully punch his shoulder, or at least where I think his shoulder would be at the top of the arm of the hand I hold.

"Honestly, Calli. Don't you have a flashlight?"

"No."

"Hang on a second . . ."

I can feel him wriggle around a moment and then a small bright light begins to shine in the palm of his hand. I begin to hear a subtle heartbeat accompanying the light. "Is that a—"

"Pulse Emitter? Why yes, Calli, it is."

I smile uncontrollably.

"Let's get this done!"

We dig around and sift through papers in file cabinets and through desk drawers, then investigate a large room with assorted machines and an assembly line of some sort. All the while, the storm rages on outside the building with crashing debris and thunder rumbling loud enough to make the hair on the back of my neck stand alert.

"Bingo!" Brand shouts from the other side of the room. "I found casings."

I hurry over to him and see what he's referring to. He shines his light into the box of brass-colored empty casings. Empty bullets.

I say, "Well, I don't know what else we need to do here,

Brand. We came to investigate, and now it's clear this is a facility manufacturing bullets that could harm people of powers and Diamond Bearers."

"How about we damage some of the equipment and slow them up. Maybe the hurricane will get the blame."

"From the sounds of things, I don't think we need to waste the time. This place is going to be flattened."

"Yeah, you're probably right. But sometimes it just feels good to smash some stuff."

Something loud crashes down on the roof. "Later, Brand. We have a hurricane barreling down on us. Let's go find Aernoud."

"Yeah, you're right. Let's get out of here!"

Chapter Eight - Cat's Out of the Bag

With Brand at the wheel, we're soon driving away from the direction of the hurricane's path. Aernoud was able to find invoices for the rounds we found, including addresses and company names that will need to be investigated.

I ask, "Aernoud, will you please share the information with Maetha and then together decide who will investigate those addresses?

"As you wish, Calli."

"Keep me updated. I have other things I need to focus on." Yeah, like the fact Crimson was able to control a hurricane's blasting wind to protect us. I already know she can walk in fire and fly by controlling gravity. What else is included in her ability to control the elements?

I connect with Chris's mind to give him an update. *Hey. Do you have a second to talk?*

Don't bi-locate right now. Max is here, Chris says to my mind. *Are you safe?*

Yes. You?

Yeah. Just dealing with Max. I'll contact you later, okay?

Okay.

I drop my connection with Chris and stare out the window. Maetha directed us to drive to Chicago where we'll stay until Rodger can fly in to pick us up. I'm certain Brand is repeating as he drives to help us avoid speeding tickets and crashes, however, his erratic accelerating and decelerating nauseates me. I use my Healing power to combat the nausea and then notice a police car parked behind a sign waiting for speeding drivers. Brand had slowed at the exact moment to prevent being pulled over.

"You know," I say to Brand, "if you'd just drive the

same speed as everybody else, you wouldn't have to worry about getting a ticket."

"Hey! You wanna drive?"

"I mean, okay, if you don't want to, I can."

Aernoud leans forward from the back seat. "We can all take turns driving, Brand."

I twist my engagement ring as I think about Chris, our time on the island, at the Bureau, back on the island, then in D.C. An overwhelming feeling of doom settles in my stomach as I dwell on the bomb inside of me, somewhere. I can't help but feel violated. While unconscious, and without my consent, my body was tampered with. Not just tampered with, but a full-on surgery of sorts. How else would Vita insert a bomb in my belly? I take a deep breath and let it out slowly and allow my mind to wander into the "what-if" weeds. What if we had not gone to the government? I wouldn't have a bomb inside me now.

My phone beeps in my pocket. I pull it out and see Chris's name on a new text message. I wonder why he's texting when he could simply speak to my mind.

His message says: Calli, Max wants you to check in.

I reply: Okay, I'll call him.

I realize Chris is still with Max and doesn't want Max to know he can communicate with me through the diamond, so he sent me a message instead. To Max's observation, he wouldn't know Chris and I just mind-spoke moments earlier. I locate Max's name in the contacts list and send the call.

Max answers snippily, "Where have you been?"

"You said to call every week." My defensive tone alerts Brand and he directs a concerned look my way.

"No," Max continues. "I told you to call when you have something to report, or when you move."

"I didn't understand the instructions that way, I guess.

Anyway, I'm doing fine, thanks for asking."

"Where are you?"

"I don't know. Somewhere between Texas and Illinois. You're the one with all the fancy gadgets and computers. You tell me where I am." I decide to challenge him to see if in fact he's tracking my movements, or if he's just blowing smoke.

He responds, "Why are you heading to Illinois?"

"Why would you think that?"

"You just said . . . okay, then why were you in Texas?"

I feel at a disadvantage, having all these powers but not able to read his mind over the phone. Did he know I was in Texas, or is he asking simply because I said the name? It doesn't matter. I'm tired of talking to him already and I've got many months ahead of calls yet to come. I say, "We're following leads on the location of the power-removing machine. Look, I'll call when I have something to report or if I relocate my base of operations somewhere else, but don't expect a call every week."

"But that was the agreement."

"Max, I need the Bureau's help with the Portland blast. I'm not going to disappear or run and hide and jeopardize losing trust. I have to go. Bye." I end the call before he can respond.

Brand asks, "So, what did he say?"

"He's itching to know every single move we make."

Aernoud says, "I'll bet he is, especially after we just broke into his obsidian bullet factory."

Brand weaves around two cars. "Your mom is about to call, Calli."

"What?" I ask, then my personal phone rings. I dig in my bag and retrieve it. "Hi Mom," I answer.

"How are you, Calli?"

"I'm good. Are you and Dad okay?"

"Yes, we are. I'm wondering, when do you think you will be able to come home so we can go over some wedding plans?"

Oh right. I'm getting married. I guess I haven't fully processed this in my mind just yet. How can I sit down and discuss colors, styles and venues when I have a ticking time bomb inside my body and a world to save? "Mom, we haven't even set a date yet. What's the rush to plan?"

"These things take time. It's not every day my only daughter gets married."

"I'll carve out some time for a visit, Mom, and I'll let you know soon."

"Thank you, Calli. We love you and are proud of you."

"Thanks, Mom. I love you, too. I'll talk to you later."

I end my call and lay my hands in my lap, cradling the phone. Taking another deep cleansing breath, I try to imagine what my mother must be thinking. She's learned all about the cosmic powers, the diamonds, the quartz and topaz, the machines that can strip someone of their powers, and yet she's consumed with planning a wedding. Honestly, the event is the last thing I want to think about right now. I've never wanted a big wedding. I've never dreamed about what kind of dress I'd wear or where I'd get married, like my friend Suz would. Suz would fawn over celebrities and their weddings and go on and on about what she planned for her own wedding. Her conversations always bored me. I didn't care, and from time to time I wondered if my emotions were disabled or broken. But then I found out I'm an Unaltered. Most if not all those behaviors and reactions, or lack thereof, were because my DNA wasn't affected like everyone else's. I can't decide if I am relieved or if I feel cheated.

Brand cuts into my thoughts. "What did she want?"

"She wants to make wedding plans."

"That's a good thing, right?"

"Sure."

Aernoud leans forward with a small piece of paper in his hand and says, "I've arranged our hotel for the evening. Here's the address."

I take the paper he's holding and type the information into the dashboard GPS, then settle back into my seat and close my eyes.

The next morning, before we leave the hotel, Chris connects with my mind. Thrilling shivers travel throughout my body with the sound of his words, but the sensation is subdued as a twinge of guilt arises for not being very enthused to plan our wedding yesterday.

Calli, Max overheard me on the phone telling my mom about our engagement. I was so careful to not use a recorded line, or the phone Max gave me, but he was nearby when I made the call, and I didn't know. I'm sorry.

Why are you sorry?

Because now I am being transferred back to the Bureau. Max claims our deception is a sign of non-compliance, or something like that.

How is that non-compliance? I called him like I was ordered.

He's afraid of us, well, afraid of you. He just wants some reason to keep control because General Appleton didn't let him be personally involved with us.

Did Max use obsidian on you?

No.

Why didn't you run?

I don't believe he is aware I have a diamond. I'm resisting using any of my powers because I'm not supposed to have any.

How about the Healer topazes I gave you?

They're still full. I haven't needed to use them yet because they haven't used obsidian on me. I wish I had a topaz with Mind-Control—that would be great for emergency situations. They understand how the topazes work so they wouldn't suspect I'm a Diamond

Bearer.

But, Chris, if you are locked up at the Bureau, you and I won't be able to communicate.

Not with powers, but we can use the phones Max gave us.

Oh, how old fashioned.

What did you find in Texas?

Just what we thought. Max is involved in a secret operation manufacturing obsidian bullets.

I'm going to out him!

No. Wait. Let's just get the factory shut down and use his involvement as leverage. He's violating his agreement with the Bureau. You know, this can be our little bit of dirt on him if he tries to raise the stakes. For instance, if they put you in obsidian cuffs, you can get Max to change them out or else you'll divulge his factory.

That's a good idea, Calli. I don't know how much longer we'll have this private connection. When we talk on the phone, we'll be monitored, and we'll have to be careful what we say.

I understand.

Contact Agent Whitman in Denver and tell him about the misappropriation of funds of the Texas obsidian bullet factory. He can get it shut down. That will fry Max's tater tots!

I can't help but laugh. *Okay. I will. If you can, will you thank Agent Bushman for his info about Max?*

Yep. I've got to go, Calli.

I love you.

I love you, t—, Chris's thoughts are cut off before he can complete his word. He must have entered the obsidian field of the Bureau.

Max didn't wait long at all for a reason to insert himself into our lives. I imagine he felt like he struck gold when he overheard Chris tell his mother about his proposal to me. Hopefully, he won't use obsidian on Chris. I regret revealing Chris's weakness to General Appleton and Max. I'm hit with a heavy thought that maybe I caused this rash decision by being too belligerent with Max on the phone. I came across as too defiant by implying I wouldn't call every week. Once Max learned Chris and I are emotionally connected, he jumped on that and took Chris captive to better control my actions.

Looking up Agent Whitman's contact information takes longer than I thought, but at least the in-depth search helps time pass quicker. I link with Merlin's diamond and ask him to communicate with Agent Whitman. I relay the phone number to Merlin and ask that, if possible, he try not to let Max know we were behind the defunding. Let the trail lead back to government investigations. Merlin assures me he can get the job done properly.

We finally arrive at the home of Maetha's friend in Chicago and take turns showering and cleaning up. Fortunately, there are enough beds for all of us to lie down and rest. I use my time to meditate. Brand apparently calls Beth during his relaxation time. I don't mean to eavesdrop but also can't help it due to my Hunter's hearing ability. I'm happy the two of them are on speaking terms again. I like Beth and the strength she brings to our team. I also like Brand when he's focused on Beth. He doesn't try to manipulate every second of the day.

As I'm getting ready to climb into bed, Crimson appears in my room, startling me a bit. "Uh, hi Crimson."

"Calli, now that Chris has been taken back into custody, I want a security detail around you at all times. Brand, for sure, and three other Bearers. We cannot let our guard down and give our complete trust to the government. They've never given us reason to do so. And this situation only solidifies my opinion."

"Okay, I agree. Aernoud is already here. Who else will join up?"

"I'm working on it. I'll arrive soon and will be nearby until the others arrive." She ends her bi-located session.

I assume when Crimson says "nearby" that means she won't make her presence known to everyone else. That's fine. Also, I hope she'll let me know what date she will meet with Vita so I can get this bomb out of my body. And a security detail? Ugh! I'm not looking forward to that. All this because Max can't stand being left out of every detail. I'd better call him and let him know where I am, and hopefully doing so will help keep Chris safe. I select Max's name from the contacts list, press the button, and wait for him to answer.

"Yes," he says on the other end.

"I'm in Illinois. Just wanted to let you know."

"So, you *did* go to Illinois. Why are you there?"

"It's a stopover place while we wait for a new assignment."

"You'll call, right, future Mrs. Harding?"

"Yes. Bye." I end the call, feeling more than a little perturbed. Max has the leverage he's always wanted. Damnit! I only hope Chris is being treated well.

A loud metallic crash from outside my window yanks me upright from the bed. I move to the window and cautiously pull the curtains back. Using my enhanced night vision, I investigate the noise. Relief lessens the constriction in my lungs as I see racoons have tipped over a couple metal trash cans and are feasting on who knows what. Before returning to my bed, I scour the shadows to see if the demons are still following me. Yes. They are pushed back by the streetlights, but I can see them where the light is absent. There seem to be more demons than usual. I guess Aernoud has his own pack that follow him, like Maetha said. Every Bearer who participated in eradicating the demons have eerie followers. At least they are harmless now and people with powers are safe in that respect.

A few days pass with only text messages from Chris. He assures me he's fine, but I wish I could be sure, since technically anyone could be sending them from his phone.

Ruth and Duncan arrive to join my protection squad with Brand and Aernoud, giving me three Bearers and a Repeater to watch my back. Seems like overkill, but Crimson prefers others look for my future's safety whenever possible to prevent me from accidentally seeing too much. Word came in that we will be moving to the Denver house shortly where we can continue with online searches and investigations. We will be stationed in Denver for at least the next month.

Ugh. I don't have enough clothing with me, or patience. And Crimson still hasn't given me a date.

Duncan, Ruth, Aernoud, Brand and I sit around the table eating Ruth's chicken soup. My mind wanders as I slide my spoon through the liquid, dodging carrots and celery, then capturing a chunk of meat. I can't believe how fast the weeks have flown by even though each day also seems to drag on. It's already October and the air in Denver has a brisk chill. I even saw a few lazy snowflakes earlier today out the bathroom window—allowing me to refocus and calm my anxiety after Mary bi-located next to me while taking a shower. I screamed, naturally, and Mary promptly disappeared. Moments later Brand pounded on the door to check on me. I was glad I'd locked the door. Watching those lazy snowflakes helped to slow down my heart rate.

"Calli, are you okay?" Ruth asks.

I look up from my soup to find everyone staring at me.

"I'm fine, it's just . . ."

"Just what?" Brand says with a mouthful of bread.

"I don't like how everyone can bi-locate to me anytime, anywhere."

Brand swallows down some water, then says, "Oh, like in the bathroom earlier."

I nod.

Ruth says, "Maybe you should call a Gathering and ask everyone to announce their arrival prior to appearing, so you are not startled again."

Duncan clears his throat. "I don't recommend she do that."

Ruth turns her focus to Duncan. "Why not? She has the right to her privacy."

"She'll be viewed as weak and prissy, like a hot-house flower.

I ask Duncan, "What does that mean?"

"Hot-house flower? Any flower can appear strong and prolific when all atmospheric conditions are to its liking, but if you apply a little wind or extra heat the flower will tip over or wilt. Some Bearers are waiting for you to tip over, to wilt under the heat. You need to show them you are strong, and your roots and stalk are solid. You can handle the storm. Then they'll respect your privacy but not till."

"I disagree," Ruth rebuts. "Most of the Bearers already regard Calli highly. A gentle nudge for privacy would be respected."

Duncan's gaze shifts my direction. "Do what you want. You know how I feel about it."

Aernoud adds, "I agree with Duncan, although, I don't need you to earn my respect. You have it."

"Thanks." As good as it feels to know I have Aernoud's respect, I can't help but be extremely paranoid someone else is going to barge-locate in on me again.

Brand slurps the soup in his spoon. "I don't understand why Bearers don't respect privacy in the first place. Out here in the real world, entering someone's home uninvited is called breaking and entering. Just saying."

I've called Max on schedule each week. He now knows Chris's father's home is a base of operations, which seems precarious. I guess this is one of the consequences of going to the government, like Crimson had inferred. The Denver house will no longer be a hideout, but more like a rest area on the way to somewhere else.

Chris reports to me through our phone calls that he's being treated well. He's been working with the Bureau team on evacuation logistics for Portland.

We'll soon be leaving for a scheduled trip to Portland for more investigations and planning where we'll meet with General Appleton, his staff, and the Portland team. Maetha's jet will be waiting for us at the airport. Rodger already picked up Chris and Max; Chris was only able to fly with us if Max accompanied him. Nobody wanted Max on Maetha's plane, but it was important for Chris to fly privately to avoid having to go through airport security. We want to keep Chris's diamond a secret for as long as possible. Max, of course, doesn't know that's the reason. My guardians have all looked to the future and found no immediate danger with this plan.

I've been counting down the days till I get to see and touch Chris again.

Brand, Aernoud, Ruth, Duncan, and I wait in the hangar for Maetha's plane. Excited jitters run up and down my body as I think about being with Chris. I've missed him. I don't even care if we have to be accompanied by Max and my security detail.

After the plane comes to a halt, Rodger opens the door and lowers the stairs. Max is the first to exit the plane. Seeing him brings bile up my throat. Second, Maetha descends the stairs. I'm surprised to see her on this trip where we'll be meeting with General Appleton. I wonder if Maetha is coming for that very reason. Finally, Chris fills the doorway. I smile uncontrollably when I see him.

His quick "regular human" strides bring him down the stairs and to me in a flash and I wrap my arms around him, not wanting to let go. His arms encircle my upper body and he pulls me close.

"I've missed you, Calli," he whispers in my ear. *By the way, Maetha is going by the name Janice for this trip. She's trying to stay off the Bureau's radar.*

Got it. "I've missed you, too."

"You know," Max's perturbed voice sounds somewhere nearby, "if I had any idea you two were engaged when I picked you up—"

Chris whips his head in Max's direction. "It's best you don't finish that sentence."

"Are you threatening me, Harding?"

I look at Max and note he's keeping a cautious distance.

"Just matching your tone," Chris replies.

I pull away from Chris and say brightly, "Maybe Max was going to say he'd have brought us a congratulations card, if he'd known."

"Yeah, right." Chris wraps an arm around my shoulders and stands by my side.

Max puckers his mouth as if he's trying not to say words that want to come out, then he walks away and over to the airplane.

I ask, "How has it been being so close to Max all this time?"

"Hard. He's clingy, wants to know everything I do, or everything I think. One thing's for sure, he's nervous to be around you."

"Oh, because of the electrocution incident?"

"Exactly."

"Well, I'll try to mind my manners," I joke. "I'm just happy we get to be together on the way to Portland, versus you being on a different flight."

"Me too." Chris reaches into his pocket, pulls out a topaz and hands it to me.

I accept it and ask, "How's the other one?"

"Still full. There are only a few places at the Bureau where I can't avoid obsidian. I'm so glad I had these."

"No cuffs, though. Right?"

"Right. I'm treated very well. However, Vita visited me and demanded that you hurry with Crimson before your bubble bursts. I tried to get a timeframe out of her, but she wouldn't say, just that the clock is ticking."

"Yeah, Crimson knows. She hasn't given me a date yet."

"Maybe this will convince her to pick up her pace."

I'm sure you're hearing this, Crimson.

No response.

After the maintenance crew completes the refueling and basic upkeep of the plane, we board and are soon up in the air, headed for Portland, Oregon. Once Rodger says we can move around the cabin, I retrieve some medical tape so I can attach Chris's empty topaz to my chest. This time I'll charge it with Mind-Control.

Max watches every move I make, irritatingly so. "What are you doing, Calli?"

"Not your concern, Max."

"Excuse me? Your actions are very much my concern."

"Well, um, this here is topaz," I point to the topaz in my hand and lie, saying, "and I'm going to infuse it with Healing power, if that's all right with you. Next, I'm going to use the bathroom. Do you need to know exactly what I do in there?"

"No. You know what I mean."

I enter the small lavatory and close the door. For a short moment I wonder if giving Chris a topaz charged with Mind-Control is a good idea. What if Max gets ahold of it? It is just a topaz, and the power would deplete after only a couple uses, but if he could figure out how to use it, he would come to know this power—a power he probably isn't aware exists. I really need a Mind-Reader topaz. I'd love to know what's going on inside his mind. Perhaps I should charge this topaz with that instead of the Blue power.

I decide to move forward with the Mind-Control topaz so Chris can have the ability to control his surroundings a bit. Maybe use Invisibility a little. Who knows? I'll pick up another topaz for myself to charge with Reader powers.

Chapter Nine - Gift Shop Discoveries

Our first meeting after landing in Portland is with the airport Transportation Security Administration Director, Janet Welsh. She greets us as we enter her office and shakes hands with everyone. I note she stands nearly six-feet tall with shoulder length brown hair and a fair complexion. My guess is she's close to my mother's age. Her clothing sheds awareness on her expectations for her employees: crisp lines pressed into her business suit, exact fit, perfectly clean. At first impression, I'd say she's tough and possibly former military.

I glance around the room and find General Appleton seated with his guards standing behind him. This is the first time I've seen him since my time at the Bureau. He's wearing a personal-sized obsidian, so no mind reading today. He looks different, older, perhaps more wrinkles. It must be the lighting. Maybe he's tired because he doesn't rise to greet us, which I find amusing. He's been wanting to meet with Maetha, who is standing behind me currently, but because of her identity change, he's unaware. I bet he'd stand if he knew she was present.

Director Welsh speaks, "I apologize for lack of seating. I wasn't aware there would be so many today."

General Appleton raises his hand in a calming gesture. "No need. We won't be long. Ms. Courtnae is our source for the distressing information I shared with you earlier."

She moves her eyes to meet mine. I sweep the thoughts at the forefront of her mind and learn she's familiar with the cosmic powers due to having a friend who was a Healer. That's a head start for us, I deduce. I can skip all the introductory details.

I say, "Director Welsh—"

"Janet. Please call me Janet."

"All right. Janet, will you be able to assist with the evacuation efforts of the greater Portland area? That would also mean rerouting arriving flights."

"Yes, I've been informed, and I've already organized a team to plan ahead for press reports." She motions to the general. "We will strive to keep the media in the dark about the increased arrival of military reinforcements and we'll divert flights that day to the north and south. If necessary, we'll close the airspace and say we have an active bomb threat. That's worked in the past."

"Good. It sounds like you've put a lot of thought and effort into this already. Do you have any questions for me?" I ask.

"Yes. When is this going to happen exactly?"

"Early August."

"You don't have a precise date?"

"No. Not yet."

Janet sits back, twisting a pen between her fingers, lips pressed into a thin line. Her eyes move between me and the general. "Well, do you know approximately how long we will be shut down?"

I say, "At least twelve hours."

"Will we need to evacuate the staff, too, or is there a way to protect us from the blast?"

"I would plan on a full evacuation for the timeframe."

She sets her pen down and stands. Her movements are calm and reassuring. "Once we have a date and timeframe, we'll do exactly that." Janet motions to the door. "Let me walk with you to your vehicles."

I observe how many people are milling about in the airport. I turn to Janet and say, "About how many travelers and workers are in the airport on any given day?"

"Oof, that's a good question. The staffing total would be easy to gather because that's a more static number. We employ around 10,000 people, roughly divided over three shifts per day. The number of passengers passing through the airport, however, is dynamic. Take for instance, when a plane lands and deboards, passengers enter the terminal. Some will board another plane shortly or within a few hours. The others have arrived at their destination. Then there are the departures arriving to the airport from the greater Portland area. My estimation would be several thousand people are in or around the airport during peak hours."

I nod my head. "I know the blast will hit after dark."

"Well, then I'd say the number would be much more favorable. Many businesses close for the night, flights decrease both inbound and outbound, so arrivals and layovers are fewer, along with departures. That will definitely make this effort more manageable."

"Great, I'll keep you updated."

Director Welsh hands me her business card with a handwritten number next to the printed numbers. "My personal phone, if it's urgent." Her gentle, confident nature calms any anxiousness I had going into the meeting. She strikes me as a competent leader with a sensitive side—not what I imagined from the director of the TSA. My past interactions with TSA officers when traveling with my parents had been all business and a little intimidating, but I guess when they're constantly looking for offenders and rule breakers one must assume everyone passing through checkpoints is trying to get away with something. The moment they let their guard down, someone's life may be in danger.

And yet, I imagine Janet to be the type of person who would keep an orderly line moving along while also taking the time to comfort a crying toddler with a lollipop and a loving pat on the head. The framed photos I saw earlier behind her desk give me this impression. She has a gentle heart and a strong conviction to family. Anyone who frames their preschooler's—or possibly grandchild's—artwork and hangs it in their workplace office shows this implicitly.

Our next stop is the Portland Mayor's office. Finding parking for our motorcade on tight streets is not easy, and I'm glad Aernoud is driving and not me. We settle in a parking garage nearby and after my guards look briefly to the future concerning the safety of the next several hours, we make our way to the City Building and Mayor Clyde Overton's office.

The mayor recognizes me and Chris as is evident by his closed expression and narrow eyes.

General Appleton says, "Clyde, let me introduce you to Calli Courtnae. She is our source of information concerning your city."

"We've met." He extends his hand forward to shake mine.

I accept his offer and say, "Mr. Mayor, please don't call security."

"If you're expecting an apology from me for our prior interaction, you'll be disappointed."

"Sir, the only disappointment I'll feel is if you choose not to listen to the general."

General Appleton says, "Mayor Overton and I have had extensive discussions, and he is cooperating fully. We still need exact details like date, time, and radius."

"I only know the blast will hit sometime in August and after dark. As soon as I know the exact date, time, and radius, I'll let you know."

"I hope that is soon."

"Me too."

Max and Mayor Overton react similarly with grunts of disapproval, which I want to respond to but know I wouldn't be able to help them understand why I don't know the precise information yet. So, I say nothing more.

Mayor Overton wrinkles his nose, then swipes the back of his hand back and forth across the bottom of it. He says, "Evacuating the entire city will be next to impossible. Many people will resist leaving, and some business owners won't want to abandon their buildings just so they can be looted and vandalized. This idea of organizing a mass exodus from the city is insane. The roads will end up in gridlock."

An idea enters my mind. "What if we lure people out of the city with different events? For instance, concerts, fairs, vacation incentives. If people left for other reasons one or two days prior to the mass evacuation, there would be less traffic on the roads. We could use busses to minimize the number of vehicles, too."

Mayor Overton replies, "We already plan on using all busses, including the schools', to transport large numbers of people at once. We'll look into what events are already scheduled to take place in early August and see what we can do to relocate them away from the city. But we need to know how far, and when."

"I understand, and I'll get that information to you as soon as I can."

General Appleton adds, "Those that don't choose to travel or attend these events will have to be persuaded by fear to flee. That's where we get into crisis situations."

I suggest, "Reverse 911 calls. Bring in the National Guard. Escort people out. Use all road lanes for leaving the city and block incoming traffic."

"All that sounds well and good, but you don't understand Portlandians like I do. You don't understand the draw to our city for protesting. We are currently going through nightly first amendment rights' displays concerning the latest court rulings."

"Which rulings?"

"Pick one. There are several. My point is if we don't handle this evacuation properly, we could end up drawing crowds rather than evacuating them."

I nod and say, "Well, I trust you'll figure out the best way to walk that delicate line, Mr. Mayor."

After we leave the mayor's office, we travel to the empty shopping center where the government headquarters will be located. Once there, General Appleton singles me out and pulls me aside.

"Have you spoken with Maetha yet?"

I don't know if I should tell the truth or lie, so I send out my thoughts to Maetha. She's evidently using her Hunter hearing to monitor our conversation already. She says to my mind, *Tell him yes, but she doesn't think you'd recognize her now.*

I repeat Maetha's words to the general.

"You told her I wanted to meet with her, right?"

"Yes."

"Tell her I don't care what she looks like now, I still want to talk to her."

"I'll tell her next time I see her."

"Thank you."

We are allowed some "free" time to sightsee. I jump on the opportunity to revisit Multnomah Falls and offer the suggestion to the others, which is met with approval by my guards.

The thirty-mile drive takes nearly two hours due to rush hour traffic, another reminder of how difficult it will be to evacuate the area. Once we arrive and walk the path to the falls, taking in the majesty and power of the falling water, we visit the gift shop. I wander the tight aisles and squeeze between displays checking out the fun and unique "tourist bait," the phrase my father uses to call anything in a gift shop at a tourist destination. In my childhood, if I asked for something from a shop while on vacation, my father would say, "Oh dear, they hooked you." Well, now I'm staring into a revolving glass case loaded with glittering, sparkling jewelry and I'm hooked . . . line and sinker. Before me is a beautiful green stone set in different arrangements from necklaces to rings and bracelets. The color is deep and clear.

Chris approaches me. "What did you find?"

"Some beautiful stones. Are they emeralds?"

A nearby clerk hears my comment. "You're actually looking at Helenite," she says. Her nametag says Erin.

"What's Helenite?" Chris and I ask in unison.

"It's an obsidianite made from the volcanic ash and rock dust from Mt. St. Helens volcano in Washington state."

"Obsidianite? What's that?" Chris asks.

"Well, have you heard of obsidian?"

"Yeah." Chris responds calmly, but I'm holding back a chuckle.

She continues on, as if reciting from a memorized set of facts. "Obsidian is nature's volcanic glass and occurs when magma is cooled very quickly. Obsidianite is man-made using the ingredients from a volcano but processed in a controlled environment with precise heat and pressure. Following the eruption of Mt. St. Helens, heavy machinery buried in the ash needed to be cut apart to be removed. The crews used acetylene torches, which are very hot, to melt through the metal, which in turn melted the nearby ash and caused it to harden into glass, green glass. The particular minerals present in the ash are what make the color. The idea of marketing the ash as a saleable product was of course jumped upon. So, with the right equipment and environment, we now have obsidianite or Helenite."

"Wow, you know a lot about this."

"Well, this is one of the most collected forms of Mt. St. Helens' remains." Erin points to a necklace. "Imagine for a moment that the ash and rock used to create that piece originated miles below the surface of the earth until the eruption ejected the material to the top and by accident was discovered it could be heated into a beautiful emerald-like stone."

"So, lab-created obsidian," I say while casting a glance to Chris.

Calli, Chris speaks to my mind, *I'm looking to the future for our safety tonight and I see danger.*

"That's right." Erin smiles broadly.

I force myself to remain calm. "It's certainly beautiful. Thanks for the information." I take hold of Chris's arm and add, "Have a nice day." We turn away and walk toward the door. I ask Chris, *What kind of danger?*

There will be protests tonight in the Portland downtown area near our hotel that will escalate to a riot. It's going to be a mess, and as it stands right now, we'll be caught in the middle. You'll accidentally use your powers for protection, and, well, we can't have you shooting lightning bolts in a riot. We're going to need to get checked in early to our hotel or relocate all together to avoid this.

Hmm. Lightning bolts, really?

Chris nods.

I'll act as though I just looked for the future and let Max decide where we stay. I locate Max near the obsidian and flint arrowhead collection nearby. I wave my hand and project my voice so he can hear me, "Max, I need to talk with you."

Max is quick to join us and the three of us exit the gift shop and walk over to the car, away from other visitors. Duncan, Aernoud, and Ruth join us.

"What is it?" Max glances at the time on his phone.

"I've seen a vision of some danger tonight." I tell him about the protest and the possibility of being caught up in the riot.

Max eyes me curiously, or maybe it's more of a jealous glint in his eye, and I wonder if he wishes he had the ability to see the future, too. He says, "Then I guess we'll make sure we don't run into them."

"Okay, to do that we need to leave soon and get checked into our rooms. Or, we could relocate to a different place."

Max shakes his head. "All the offices are downtown. We'll go now, then."

We arrive at the hotel and our room arrangements are made. Chris, Max, and Duncan share an adjoining room to mine which I'll share with Ruth. With food on the way, Chris and I sit together on the bed, pillows propped up behind our shoulders for support. Ruth is in the room next door talking to Duncan. Max is slouched into a deep chair by the window. He refuses to be apart from us and it's quite annoying. But even with Max nearby, I'm still happy to be in Chris's arms.

"Max, are you bored now that you don't have a blog to update all the time?" I ask.

"Nope. I have lots to do."

"Does it involve anything other than me or Chris?"

"Yes. I'm helping locate other machine operations like what your father operated, Chris." Max seems overly happy, almost bragging. Then his voice drops. "I will get my hands on one of those prisms."

Chris says, "Well, we all have to have goals, don't we?"

Max shakes his head and stands from the chair to look out the window. "Here comes your riot." He points toward the street below us. "Someday, when I have a prism, I'll be able to see the future like you did today."

Ignoring Max's lust for power, Chris pulls my shoulder a little closer to his and lays his head against mine. "What do you think about June tenth for our coupling?"

"The tenth?"

"It's the second weekend in June. Not too close to the blast date."

Butterflies flit energetically in my stomach as I think about our coupling. "Hmm. I'll check with my parents to see if that date works for them."

Max mutters something unimportant about Chris needing to get permission from the Bureau. I tune him out and relax into Chris's body, cherishing my time with him.

Today, Chris and Max will work with General Appleton while I meet with Maetha and Crimson. Getting Max to agree to me leaving his side wasn't easy, and the only way he agreed was if Chris stayed with him—as collateral.

My bodyguards take me to a downtown waterfront park where I see Crimson and Maetha sitting at a nearby picnic table. I walk over to them while my guards spread out to form a safety perimeter.

I want to ask Maetha about her connection with General Appleton, but I decide to wait. This meeting has some other purpose, which I don't know yet. Perhaps this is when Crimson will give me the okay for her to meet with Vita so I can get this bomb out of my body.

Maetha's gaze is turned in the direction of the buildings across the street that have large sheets of plywood covered with graffiti nailed to the window frames.

I say, "This town sure takes a beating with these riots. I've had my focus on everything to do with the blast and not on the actual happenings in this city. Hopefully, there won't be any riots in August."

Crimson places a large bag on the table and pulls out

three individually cloth-wrapped items large enough to be mistaken for loaves of bread. She sets the mysterious items down on the table one at a time. Each is obviously heavy and thumps the wood slightly even though she tries to be careful.

Maetha turns her head back to me. "You do understand there's a difference between a riot and a peaceful protest, right?"

"I do; it just seems like a protest usually turns into a riot."

Crimson's eyes meet mine and she says, "When authorities allow individuals their freedom to express their opinions, this is what can be expected."

"Riots?" I ask.

"I'm speaking of protests. Many incredible changes over time have come about through peaceful protests."

I shoot a finger in the air. "Like the march on Washington by Martin Luther King, Jr."

"Precisely. And earlier, The Conflict of Orders with the Plebians and Patricians."

"Oh. I guess I haven't heard of that one."

Maetha smiles. "It was a little before your time."

"Did that protest happen in America?"

"No. This was in the Roman Republic around the third century B.C.E."

"Yeah, that was a little before me. What were they protesting?"

"Plebians were commoners, and Patricians were aristocrats born into wealth and power. The commoners couldn't ascend to power or hold positions of power. The protests helped shape new methods and ideas that allowed a qualified commoner to climb the ranks of power, without bloodshed and violence."

I want her to know I understand what she's saying. "Oh,

like here in America anyone can become the president. They don't have to be born into power or money. If they want to run for the position, they can try."

Maetha nods and adds, "Not all countries of the world have the same freedoms. In many places, openly expressing your thoughts can get you arrested, or worse. So, seeing peaceful protests take place over decisions and rulings is a gauge of how much freedom remains. Violent protests or riots should be shut down. Voicing opinions, shouldn't."

Crimson says, "I allow all my Bearers to protest and vocalize their opinions. I listen and if applicable I make changes. Now, let's get down to business."

She opens one of the cloth coverings exposing a giant, mostly clear crystal. One end has a point, although it's a little skewed. The other end is flat.

I ask, "Is that quartz?"

"Yes. It is channeling quartz. These three crystals will direct the ray to you."

"Did you use these when you made the Sanguine Diamond?" These fascinating behemoths catch the light and cast near-blinding prisms all around us.

"No, I used them for the Grecian Blue Diamond."

Maetha asks, "How did you make the Sanguine Diamond, and how was that different than the Grecian Blue?"

I'm caught off guard when Maetha asks this question. Surely, she's asked it before now. How many years has it been?

Crimson replies without missing a beat. "The Sanguine Diamond utilized the electromagnetic energy from the Great Pyramid of Giza. I was able to set up a four-point net of sorts using the four angles of the pyramid. I wasn't trying to only capture one power, I wanted to capture as many as possible and direct them into the stone. When I set the channeler stones at the top of the pyramid, each angle extended to outer space. A vast area where cosmic energy flowed was then funneled down to the diamond atop. The Grecian Blue, however, was a narrow net designed to capture only that power and funnel it into the diamond. That's what we're doing with this one. We're setting up a narrow net with a small radius."

I motion to the channeling quartz and ask, "What are we going to do with these?"

"Nothing, yet. Does seeing these crystals bring any visions of the blast to your mind?"

"No."

Crimson turns her head to Maetha.

Maetha says, "No. I'm not seeing anything either."

"Perhaps we need to give it time."

I ask, "Crimson, when will the blast hit? What date?"

"That will be a detail you pick up from your visions. I don't know the exact date."

My eyes widen uncontrollably. "How is that possible you don't know? You told me you know when and where the blast will hit."

"I did. I know it will hit in August of next year in the area that is now Portland. The exact date and time is unknown to me."

I whip my head to Maetha. "Do you know what date?"

She shakes her head and says, "I've seen visions of the aftermath and of a calendar on the wall. The month and year were visible, but I can't tell what day of the week."

I nervously rub both of my upper arms to try to calm the goosebumps that have erupted all over them. "So that's how you know it will happen in August of next year."

"Yes," Maetha and Crimson say simultaneously.

"Why haven't I seen anything like that?"

Crimson says, "Perhaps because you haven't looked for

it." Her heavy tone sounds like she wants to add the words: *hard enough.*

I feel nauseous and defensive. "You ordered me not to look for my own future, to let the visions come to me. What if I don't ever see that information?"

"You will. I'm sure of it." Maetha smiles at me. Crimson says nothing and begins wrapping the crystal.

"But what if my powers go away, like if the obsidian bomb inside me explodes, and I can't have visions anymore. What then?"

"Try not to worry about it, Calli." Crimson's words are not calming at all.

I clear my throat. Bringing up the subject of the bomb inside me raises my anxiety and I ask, "Have you decided about meeting with Vita?"

"Not yet. I'm still working on it. Let's focus on the quartz crystals, for now, and try to feel the energy, allow the energy to inspire visions."

Only frustration comes to mind.

On the flight home, I wait till I'm alone with Maetha, then I ask, "I thought you knew how the Sanguine Diamond was made?"

"No. And I didn't help with the Grecian Blue, either," Maetha says, having obviously read my mind.

"Uh, I'm having a hard time understanding how you haven't questioned Crimson about them all this time."

"Calli, you live in an intellectual era where people can ask questions, provided you have questions to ask. When Crimson intervened in my life and divided the diamond, I viewed her as a goddess. I was nothing compared to her. Why would I question the gift she gave me or the task she asked me to fulfill?"

I try to imagine what that must have felt like for Maetha to have a goddess entrust her with such a task.

She continues. "During the few hundred years it took for me to find my Bearers, I didn't see much of Crimson. However, once I'd found all my Bearers, she would visit me more often."

"Did you ever feel like she had abandoned you?"

"I never felt that way because I viewed her visits as guidance or course corrections. She had already instructed me on what to do with the pieces of the Sanguine Diamond with the goal of helping humanity progress. However, when the Mind-Control power emerged and the Blue diamond was created, I received a shard and our power dynamic changed. We had quantum entanglement where she could always know what was happening in my mind and surroundings. I was her second set of eyes. You know how it is when she can read everything in your mind, but you can't speak to her. I've lived that for two thousand years."

"Wow." My single word response sputters out of my mouth and my mind blanks out. I've only had the entanglement for a short while compared to Maetha and I already dislike it, but two thousand years?

"Calli, I was okay with giving up my piece of the Blue Diamond and definitely fine with giving it to you and losing the connection with Crimson. Although I must admit, I am jealous of the one-on-one time you get to spend with her. It probably seems normal to you to be around her so much, but it's not. And I'll add, this is probably the biggest reason why other Bearers are struggling to accept you. They feel that the time they've put into this position hasn't been rewarded with being in the presence of Crimson."

I nod. "I guess they probably view her as a goddess, too, and maybe they feel like I don't respect her in the same way."

I rub my temples in the hopes of helping my brain comprehend what she's revealed. "This is nothing like I thought it would be, you know, having the Blue diamond. I have no privacy. None. My parents have always honored my personal space, and I've come to expect it as a rule. But that's all out the window and I guess I've got to get used to it."

Maetha says, "At least with the Blue, you know exactly who has access to your mind, to your private information, private communications. So having Crimson be the only one inside your private life is different than say, the government being able to track your conversations, your whereabouts, your purchases, etc. This is why I'm hesitant to own a phone or use credit cards. I've lived thousands of years with total privacy, except for the time I carried the Blue. Solitude is serene. Now everyone is always trying to follow everyone else's movements. You live in a very monitored world."

"Well, it's all I ever known. Cell phones, satellite phones, and the internet are how we communicate across the globe. I personally find it amazing. Sure, Diamond Bearers can also communicate from across the globe by connecting with others' diamonds, even bi-locate to different positions wherever they may be. But I can use my phone to call somebody on the other side of the world and a video of me will show up in their hands. It's not a whole lot different. And it uses no cosmic energy powers. Oh, and don't forget, phones work in the presence of obsidian. You can use a little self-control about what you say while you're on the phone in case anyone's listening."

Maetha tilts her head to the side and purses her lips. "That doesn't stop the fact that I can be tracked with the thing. Calli, I can see a time in my mind—not a future vision, just the logical progression of what happens when we part with our freedoms and privacy—where people of powers will be tracked and followed using the same technology in phones. The coming cosmic blast will reveal to what extent cosmic powers already exist in the population and fear will be the driver of others feeling like we need to be controlled and monitored. I think this is the greatest problem that will arise from you going to the government."

My body feels heavy and weighted down after hearing Maetha speak her disproval of my actions. I swallow hard and say, "I respect your opinion of my choice." Taking a deep breath to center the emotions that want to become offended, I continue, "I think we're on the edge of a major shift in the history of the world concerning the knowledge of supernatural powers, and this blast will either push us closer to the edge or it will shove us over completely. What it won't do is pull us back from the precipice. Governments already know about us because of Freedom. My choice to include the government with this event felt like the one thing we hadn't tried. In doing so, we discovered more of what they understand about cosmic powers, and we found an ally on the inside. Crimson understands something drastic concerning the blast that I don't fully comprehend yet, or she wouldn't have worried about trying to capture it. She knows there will be trouble with Elementals and that's why we must capture the power . . . so we can have a fighting chance. I believe we need the government's help."

Maetha says, "You are wise, Calli. I hope everything works out." She stands and moves to a seat near the other Bearers.

Chris then takes the seat by me. "Is everything okay?" he whispers.

"As good as it can be, I guess." I try to fill my mind with anything to crowd out Maetha's words of chastisement. I snuggle against his warm body and inhale his cologne. He smells great, but nothing like he used to before he went through the machine—a stark reminder of how much has changed over the last few years since I held his hand on the way to meet with the Death Clan.

Departing the plane in Denver with my bodyguard group, I give Chris a long hug after an intimate kiss. I peek around for Max to make sure he's gone, then I take Chris's hand and lift it toward me. I place a topaz in his palm and bend his fingers around it. His eyes close and he inhales sharply.

Mind-Control, he says, then opens his eyes. *Thank you, Calli.*

Hopefully you'll be able to use it to control obsidian placement around you. That way your Healer topaz will last longer. I reach up and trace his jaw line with my fingertip, lightly gliding over his fresh shave. His head naturally gravitates toward my touch. I say, *Also, I like the tenth of June as our coupling date. Let's plan on that.*

You talked with your parents, then?

No, not yet. They'll just have to clear their schedules for us.

He smiles and brings his lips to mine.

We express our love for one another, and he leaves with Max, heading back to Washington D.C., while I and my group begin our return to Denver.

Chapter Ten - Vita's Assistant

Another month passes by with little to no progress on any front. Crimson has yet to alert me to a time to meet with Vita. Nothing from Agent Bushman, nothing new to report from Portland, just a whole lot of nothing. I've read a lot of books in the down time, learning about world history, geology, military planning, basically whatever books remain in General Harding's home that Chris chose not to throw away. All this learning does little to relieve the constant anxiousness about the obsidian bomb I have residing in my gut. At any moment the thing could disable my powers. I wish I knew what was taking Crimson so long to meet with Vita.

Brand and Aernoud left on a mission a week ago, leaving Ruth, Duncan, and me alone. The future shows no harm to me as long as I remain inside the house, so they felt safe in leaving. At least I don't haves signs of obsidian in my near future, so there's that.

Chris and I talk or text on the weekends. It helps time go by faster to have something to look forward to at the end of the week. Chris reports his weeks are quite slow and uneventful as well. I miss being with him in person, his calming—and stimulating—embraces, his healing kisses, and the overall sense of completion I feel when I'm with him.

Thanksgiving came and went with little notice other than I called my parents and informed them of our June tenth wedding date, and Ruth and I cooked dinner together. I've tried to learn more about Ruth's past, but she doesn't open up much. Her statements are usually one sentence long and pretty dull. Collectively, her single sentence history reveals she gained her diamond around 400 C.E. She had a family, worked as a cook for people with more money than her, an evil clan of Healers were running amok, so she was used to neutralize them, and after her family died off years later, she roamed eastern Europe helping solve land disputes as directed by Maetha.

I wonder if in two thousand years I'll be so non-descript about how I received my diamond, too. I guess my story isn't that different either. An evil clan of Healers raised havoc and needed to be neutralized. Yeah, it seems that's a standard setup. Then again, a different type of beginning story could be centered around capturing the Elemental blast—if I'm physically able to do it. Or maybe my obsidian bomb will explode, and I won't.

As if on cue, Crimson's voice enters my mind. *Calli, you can pass the word along that I'm ready to meet with Vita. She knows the place.*

It's about freakin' time! *Okay. When should I say?*

Tell her I'll be at the place next Saturday. Crimson places emphasis on "the place" suggesting Vita will know based on those words alone.

Okay. I will. I reply, then wait a moment for any other instruction or comment of some kind. Nothing. I wish our mind conversations were more like phone calls with an alert or ring announcing an incoming conversation, and a click, dial tone, or actual words of "goodbye" indicating the end of the conversation. Instead, I'm left feeling like she hung up on me.

Well, I guess a whole lot of nothing just turned into a little something. Picking up my phone, I call Max.

"Yeah, what?" His voice holds frustration.

"Tell Vita that I got the approval for the meeting she wanted. It will be next Saturday at the place Vita knows."

"Where?"

"At the place Vita knows."

"What place is that?"

"Apparently Vita knows and that's all that matters, Max."

"So, what, I just tell Vita the meeting will be Saturday at the place? And she'll know what I'm talking about?"

"Yep. Bye." I end the call and muse that I used the word "bye" to officially end the conversation, unlike Crimson.

The weekend arrives with Brand and Aernoud returning from their task. I, however, am about to call Chris so I excuse myself.

"Hi Chris," I nearly squeal with delight. I've wanted to talk to him all week.

"Hey there. How's everything going?"

"Boring without you, of course."

He chuckles a little, then says, "Well, I had a good talk with Agent Bushman today. He said they found the location of the South Carolina power-removing machine. Unfortunately, the place was cleared out and no crystals were found."

"Then how do they know they found the place if there was nothing left behind?"

"Because they captured a Reaper."

"What?" I exclaim. "When?"

"At the location. The guy was left to guard the building to prevent any squatters from taking over, in case the operation needed to move back and set up again. Agent Bushman said the guy wore a necklace of assorted quartz and that's what tipped them off to his involvement with the Reapers and not simply being a hired guard. He fessed up pretty quickly once Bushman applied pressure of criminal charges and has since been giving intel on the Reapers in exchange for immunity."

"Wow. I mean, wow. That sounds too easy, Chris."

"I agree. I asked Bushman if I could meet the guy. He's working on getting me approval. I'll try to read his mind or view his future to see what I can get, because Bushman can't, you know, because the guy is an Unaltered."

"I don't think the Reapers have anyone working for them who hasn't been run through the machine. Did they confiscate his necklace?"

"Yes. They're studying it."

Crimson bi-locates to my room, startling me, and says, "I met with Vita. She's agreed to remove your capsule."

Overhearing her words, Chris says, "It's about damn time!"

"End your call," she orders. Before I can protest, she angles her head, and adds sternly, "They listen to everything, Calli."

"I'll talk to you later, Chris."

"Yeah, I heard. She's right. Talk to you later."

I end the call, a little frustrated. Crimson barged into my space and then was upset about the phone call? She was the one who blurted out the possibly sensitive information. I take a deep breath, choosing to focus on the good news about the bomb removal. "When will this happen?"

"Soon. Go out to the others so they can hear this update, too."

I get up and walk out to the living room. As happy as I am to hear the bomb will finally be removed, trepidation fills my gut as my mind imagines possible problems or dangers with the procedure. Sometimes my active imagination gets the best of me. I emerge from the hallway to find my guards are seated with Brand. Apparently, Brand has been describing his repeating power. Brand looks up and sees Crimson's bi-located form beside me and stops talking. The others look over.

I clear my throat and say, "Crimson has some news to share."

She doesn't hesitate at all before launching right in. "Calli's capsule will be removed by Vita next weekend in Washington D.C."

"Where in D.C. will this take place?" Duncan asks.

"Yeah, does Vita have like a home or office?" Brand teases. "Perhaps a witchcraft emporium masquerading as a health food store?"

Crimson ignores Brand. "You all will travel to D.C. and wait for the specific location to be announced via Max. I doubt this will take place at the Bureau. Vita instructed us to keep the information of Calli's bomb from General Appleton."

"Well, that doesn't sound sketchy at all," Brand quips.

Crimson responds, "Indeed, Brand. She's up to something large-scale and it makes me nervous."

I ask her, "Will you be nearby?"

"As much as I can. I suspect she'll be using obsidian and probably her bubble technology to protect herself. That's why your protectors will accompany you." She nods to the others.

"Of course," Ruth states.

Crimson nods, then disappears from the room.

Duncan directs his attention to Brand. "So, you were saying, Brand . . ." Clearly, Duncan wants to continue learning about Brand's power. I can't blame him. Ruth and Aernoud also seem more interested in Brand's story, which is fine.

I head back to my room, to my phone, figuring I'll text Chris. Once I'm in my room, Crimson's voice enters my mind.

I know you're worried about this procedure, Calli.

Yes. What if it goes wrong?

The long-range future still looks optimistic. But that doesn't mean the immediate will be smooth. This danger must be removed for Vita to get what she wants from me, and you must be kept whole.

My pulse quickens. *What does Vita want from you?*

She wants to rule the world. I'm getting in her way. Her message to me wasn't any different than a thousand years ago. I didn't like it then, and I don't like it now.

May I ask why you waited before agreeing to meet her?

I wanted to make sure I had, how do you say, all my ducks in a row, first.

To keep yourself safe, you mean.

That, and to be prepared with a concession.

I don't understand.

Calli, she's been trying to capture you ever since she saw us in the picture taken at the police station. By going to the government, you and Chris gave her the opportunity to get her claws into you, to control me.

I'm sorry Crimson.

Save your 'sorry's' for later. For me to retain most of the control, I had to part with a little. I needed time to figure out what I could let go of. As I told you before, you and Chris changed the future with your choices.

I sense she has dropped the connection to my mind, again without a cordial "goodbye." I reach for my phone and text Chris. I apologize for being cut off mid-call. I'm also careful with how I word the conversation between Crimson and me. Chris already heard the main topic, so I only add that I'll be having a "lump" surgically removed, but I don't know when or where yet.

After sending my text to Chris, I call Max.

"Yeah," Max answers the phone.

"I'm coming to Washington D.C."

"I know."

"Oh. Right. Do I need to call when I get there, or will

you be there to greet me?"

"Call me when you arrive, and I'll give you the address to where you're going."

"Okay. Bye." I hang up.

ꝋ ꝋ ꝋ

After arriving in Washington D.C., we rent a vehicle large enough to carry all of us. Then I dial Max and wait.

"Yes," he answers.

"We're here. What's the address?"

"What color and kind of car are you driving?"

"Tan, four-door car."

"Who is with you?"

"My guards."

"She won't want them there."

"Too bad. They're coming. What's the address?"

"Okay," his voice carries a tone of superiority. "Don't listen to me, then." He dictates the address. I write it down and hand it to Duncan who sits in the driver's seat. Max continues, "When you arrive, park near the light post with the letter M. Someone will come to you."

"Okay, bye." I end the phone call.

Brand leans over to see the address. "It's more than two minutes away."

Ruth says, "The future looks good up until the use of obsidian."

Brand turns his upper body to look back at Ruth. "So, where are we going?"

"It's difficult to see. Some sort of a shopping center."

Duncan starts the car and begins driving while Brand enters the address into the vehicle's navigational system. After weaving through traffic for several minutes, following the soft voiced instructions of the computer, Brand laughs.

"What is it?" I ask him.

"Oh, it's too good. I'm not going to tell you. I want to see your expression when you see it." He laughs harder.

Clearly, we are closer than two minutes to arrival and he's already repeated.

A wave of nausea cascades in my belly, causing me to take deep slow breaths to relieve my anxiety. I'm about to see Vita again, probably the one person on the face of the earth who can control Crimson, somewhat. What if Vita refuses to remove the bomb she put inside me? What if we're walking into a trap?

"Your destination is on the right," the GPS states. Duncan slows and signals the impending turn. I see a large signpost near the driveway. On it, several different business-sses are listed: grocery store, pizzeria, Cantonese restaurant, nail salon, tattoo parlor, used bookstore, and others I can't quite make out before we turn and enter the parking lot. We've entered a strip mall, where all the business are linked together, but all have exterior entrances.

Brand is giggling through the hand he's slapped over his mouth. I think he might explode.

Duncan shakes his head and lets out a grunt at Brand's silliness.

Aernoud points toward the other end of the parking lot. "There, I see the M on the post."

As we approach, I read the names of the businesses that we pass by. Most were already listed on the sign by the road, then one comes into view. Mortar and Pestle Emporium: Tonics, Tinctures, Potions and Lotions. That's got to be the place.

Brand laughs hard. "Can you believe it? I was right! I even guessed the emporium word. But look, potions is part of the name of the store. Who puts that word on their building?" He laughs some more. "A witch, that's who!"

Duncan parks the car in front of the post.

"Stop your ridiculousness," Ruth admonishes Brand. "Someone is coming, and we need to be serious here."

Duncan opens his door, climbs out and greets the middle-aged woman. Using my powers, I quickly read her mind and find her name is Dawn and she is only an employee who was instructed to watch for our car. I listen to the conversation.

"The girl and one other may come," Dawn says.

"No. All of us or none of us." Duncan stands his ground.

Dawn exhales and says nothing for a second. Her mind reveals she's incredibly nervous about the owner of Mortar and Pestle being at the store today. "Wait here." She hurries back inside.

Duncan remains outside the car. He leans against it and rests his elbows on the top of the roof.

Brand is still trying to regain control of his laughter. With a slight giggle, he announces, "We're all going inside. Come on." He opens his door and exits the car. I look at Ruth and Aernoud and shrug my shoulders. They do the same and we exit as well. By this time, the woman is returning. She waves her hand and shouts, "All right. Come."

Entering Mortar and Pestle Emporium is an assault on the senses. First up is the smell, some sort of mix of moldy hay, black licorice, and body odor. Second, the music reminds me of what I might hear in the background at a fortune teller's table at the circus. The products for sale are almost as comical as the sounds and smells: love potions, hexing paraphernalia, occult books, tonics for everything imaginable under the sun, and scented candles. Ironically, the candles are the same line of products sold in regular stores.

Dawn leads us toward the back of the store. We pass a

glass viewing case and I'm shocked to find crystals that appear to be topaz and quartz with tags claiming they hold specific cosmic powers. I stop to look closer. The prices are astronomical.

I'm pulled back to the present by the sound of a throat clearing. Dawn is holding a door open, motioning for us to join her. I glance around and find my guards have stopped with me and are also staring at the crystals for sale.

"Do you think they're real?" Ruth asks.

I say, "Probably. Where is she getting the quartz from? I can understand the topaz, but the quartz is only from the power-removing machines."

"To our knowledge, anyway," Ruth whispers.

We follow Dawn through the store and into a hallway that seems to run behind all the stores, like an employee only access area. Across the hall, she opens a door and invites us to wait inside.

I wait for Brand to give directions.

"So far so good," he nods.

We move into the room which is like a small exam room with a bed covered in white paper. I'm happy to be out of the Emporium and away from the strong odor.

Dawn speaks, "I'll let her know you're ready." She closes the door, leaving us alone.

Before we can even take a breath, the door opens, and Vita enters. She wears an emerald-green business suit with high heels, a completely different look than the first time I met her. She doesn't appear like the type of person who owns the shop we just walked through. She looks more like Clara Winter.

"Welcome, Calli. Thank you for doing your part. Now, let's get this done so you can be on your way." Vita motions to the bed. "Lie down there."

"Do I need to undress?" I ask.

"You'll only need to pull your shirt up a little." She slides a tray next to the bed as I lay down.

I throw a cautious glance at Brand. He shrugs his shoulders. I send a quick message to Chris. *Here we go.*

Vita picks up a scalpel and leans forward, bringing it down toward my stomach.

Brand jumps forward. "Seriously? You're not going to wash up or put on gloves or something?"

Vita wags the scalpel in the direction of my head. "She's a Healer. She can fix herself."

"Then why do we need *you* to remove the bubble?" Brand exclaims. "What if it explodes and her powers are canceled for a while? She wouldn't be able to heal herself then."

Her hands freeze mere inches above my belly. "Young man, let me do my job."

Brand's tone changes, leading me to figure he has repeated. "Hold up! You are not going to cut into her without any kind of numbing or painkiller!"

I lift my head to get a better look at the two of them. Brand has my back, that much is clear. Vita, on the other hand, looks as though she's struggling to restrain a smile. *Is she enjoying this?* My skin bristles.

"And what about obsidian?" Brand is on the edge of shouting. He looks at me. "I thought there was going to be obsidian. I mean, your cut will heal faster than she can pull the blade through the skin, and it's very painful."

"You're right, Brand," I confirm. "Vita, What's the plan here?"

Vita lifts her hands slightly, closes her eyes, then raises her eyebrows and exhales. She turns her head toward the door. In an elevated voice, she says, "Joe, come in here."

I don't know who I expect to walk into the room. An assistant, a nurse, an old man, who knows.

Jonas Flemming walks in like this is any other day.

"Whoa!" Brand's hands fly upward.

"Jonas?" I exclaim. My first impression is Jonas is here to help me. Maybe Crimson found him and sent him to be by my side. But, as he moves next to Vita and asks what she needs, my heart sinks. More like it crashes.

The room spins wildly as Brand repeats the two of us back to when Vita instructs me to lie down on the bed. Brand turns to me with a jolt. "Jonas is here?"

Still feeling the utter disbelief of seeing Jonas with Vita, I jump off the table and hurry out of the room in search of Jonas. My guards follow closely.

Vita yells after us. "Where are you going? Do you want that thing out or what?"

Calling Jonas' name, I open doors and peer in empty rooms. Brand is close behind.

I turn around, realizing the distance I've covered is too far for him to have traveled to appear in the room when he did or does. All this repeating still makes my head spin.

Brand says, "Let's go the other direction this time." He repeats me back again to when Vita directs me to the bed. "Come on," Brand takes my hand and pulls me out to the hallway. "He's down here."

Vita's voice trails after us. "Where are you going? Do you want that thing out or what?"

Brand opens the next door, and we see Jonas sitting at a computer, typing. He looks up and composes himself. "Uh, hey, guys."

I stride over and give him a hug. My powers rush out of my body. I release my hug and step back. "Jonas, what are you doing here? Is she holding you captive? Did she put obsidian in your body, too?"

"No. Not at all."

Brand blinks repeatedly while placing his hand on

Jonas' shoulder and giving it a good squeeze. "Then why are you here with her?"

"Her work intrigues me. Plus, her motives are better than you-know-who's." Jonas' gaze moves back and forth from me to Brand, then over my shoulder to Ruth, Duncan, and Aernoud, and then back to me where it lingers.

To say I feel let down can't begin to convey my emotions. I want him to come back to the Bearers. I want him to know all the progress we've made with the preparations for the Portland blast, and how Crimson isn't going to punish him for his decision to leave. But I can't find the words to say, and I can't speak to his mind because of his obsidian. If I could say something that would change his mind about her intentions, maybe that would help. I say, "Jonas, why are you with her? She's dangerous. She put a bomb inside me!"

"I know. I was there."

"What?" It feels like all the oxygen flees my lungs with that one word. My mind blurs with confusion and anger.

"Who do you think healed your incision?"

"You *helped* her?" I can't think straight.

"Yes. I knew the obsidian powder wouldn't kill you if you weren't able to convince Crimson to meet with Vita. Besides, I wanted Crimson and Maetha to sweat some major bullets, after everything they've put you and me through."

"Crimson and Maetha never did anything as extreme as putting a dangerous substance inside me." .

"Are you sure about that, Calli?"

I ignore his question, too incensed to think about that right now. Instead, I blurt out, "You helped Vita use me, use my body, to get to Crimson and Maetha? I've been terrified for months about this thing inside me!"

Before he can respond, Vita swoops into the room. "Let's do this already."

Brand turns and gives Vita the what-for. "You're going to wash your hands, put on gloves and a mask, and give her something for the pain before you touch her!"

"I was going to."

"No, you weren't."

Vita huffs. "No one told me you have Seer ability."

Jonas pulls a small box out of the desk. "And you'll need this," he says as he hands me the box.

I'm hesitant to take it. "What is it?"

He opens the lid, exposing a large obsidian. Again, I experience the whoosh of my powers leaving. He closes the lid as quickly as he opened it, then offers the box again, to which I accept.

"Go lay down and I'll be in there in a minute." Vita points in the direction of the room with the exam bed.

Brand dramatically folds his arms across his chest. "Ah-hem! Gloves? Mask?"

"Fine," Vita mutters. "Joe, get me a syringe of lido-caine."

Duncan stands guard outside the door while Ruth and Aernoud remain by my side. Brand is sitting to my right with beads of sweat dripping down his temples. He's not ordering Vita around so that must mean she's acting professionally or at least up to Brand's standards. Jonas left the room after bringing the numbing syringe.

I remember hearing how bubbles are made using stones of some kind. But, inside the body, too? I crane my neck to try to see what she's doing. I can't see anything, however, I hear the soft click of rock landing on the tray beside the bed. Turning my head, I see the tiny pieces of bloody gravel and then Vita sets a marble-sized gelatinous gray blob down on the tray.

"That's it?" I ask. "That's what this has been all about?"

"Mmm hmm," Vita replies without looking up. She's still working inside my wound.

After Vita finishes what she's doing, she puts the obsidian away so I can heal my wound in a flash. I can't help but notice the glare Vita sends to Brand as if to say, *"See? What did I tell you? She can heal herself."*

I only caught a brief glance of the dangerous object Vita used to manipulate Crimson. What was so important for Vita to say to Crimson that required these extreme lengths? Will I ever find out the details of what the two of them talked about?

"Okay, you're free." Vita orders me and my team to leave immediately.

My first thought is she doesn't want us to try to convince Jonas to return to the island. To be honest, I don't want him to return right now. The thorough sense of betrayal I feel dictates the need to keep Jonas at a distance.

Once we are away from Vita's emporium, Crimson's voice enters my mind.

This is an unfortunate turn of events that Jonas is with Vita. I wondered who she had working with her.

What do you mean?

Vita would have needed a Bearer to heal your incision after inserting the capsule. I had my suspicions that the Bearer was Jonas. I'm sorry to be right.

Chapter Eleven - Home for Christmas

A tense silence fills the car as we leave. I have no words. Between Jonas and surgery, my head has no more room for thoughts. I wish Chris could be here.

"So, where to next?" Brand asks, breaking the quiet, as Duncan pulls out of the parking lot and back onto the main road.

Aernoud places the tips of his fingers to his temple and closes his eyes briefly. "We'll return to Denver until the twenty-third of December, then we'll travel to Calli's parents' home."

I didn't know this. "What? We are? Do my parents know?"

"Yes."

Brand asks, "Could I have time to visit my mom while we're there?"

Aernoud preforms another future scry and then nods his head. "That doesn't look like it would be a problem."

Aernoud catches my eye and speaks to my mind. *I'm sorry about Jonas. His betrayal must be hard for you to fathom.*

I nod in response, not wanting to speak for fear my choked-up throat will give away my emotions. Looking away to clear my mind, I grab my phone and call Max to inform him I'm headed back to Denver. After ending the call, I settle back in my seat and allow the disturbing revelation of Jonas to take residence in my mind. Why? Why would he join up with Vita? She held me hostage. He said he was present when she inserted the potential life-threatening device inside my body. Why would he help her? This leads me to wonder how long I was unconscious, and more importantly, how did Jonas get to the mainland so quickly?

I knew he was upset on Maetha's island after Chris's diamond insertion, but to leave and join Vita seems extreme. The more I ponder on the situation, the more I realize he must have already had contact with Vita before we left, not that he knew where we were going. Or did he? Could he have looked to the future and seen what was about to happen to us? Could he have alerted Vita to our whereabouts?

My head pounds from the holes in the information and from the feelings of disappointment.

I use my phone to send a carefully worded message to Chris. I can't tell him about Jonas. That will have to wait till I know our conversation is fully private. Instead, I let him know my "lump" was successfully removed and I'm doing good.

Chris texts me back. *What a relief! I feel so helpless not being able to be with you for this, but I'm glad to hear the danger is gone.*

Thanks. I'll be going home for Christmas. Do you think you'll be allowed any traveling?

I already asked. I can have three days, chaperoned. I want to take you to meet my mom in January.

Does this mean we're serious now? I type, hoping he'll pick up on my joking manner, but in truth, I'm a little nervous to meet his mother. I type, *What about Max? Will he be tagging along?*

Yeah, like an annoying skin tag, Chris responds. *And yes, we're dang serious.*

I can't wait!

He adds, *I'll let you know what dates we get approved. I love you, Calli.*

I love you, too, Chris. Bye

The last few weeks have flown by so quickly in anticipation of going to see my parents in Ohio. We received word that we would be driving the distance due to Maetha's plane being booked already. A small group of Bearers needed to go to Portland to scout location headquarters for the blast. This seems strange to me that I'm not a part of the process. So, here I am, riding in the back of a minivan, driving across the country, to my parents' home.

It's nearly midnight and my sleepy little hometown streets are quiet, even for being two days before Christmas. The multicolored lights adorning some homes and trees are dusted by a light layer of snow, creating a magical picture like what I might see on a postcard.

A sense of emptiness fills my stomach as I consider I don't really have a set place in this world to call my own. Chris has his own apartment in Washington D.C.—an apartment that stands unoccupied because of him being held at the Bureau—but I haven't had anything to call my own since college. My own homebase. Our wedding, or coupling, is fast approaching, and I imagine we'll find an apartment or home in Portland ahead of the blast due to the fact the aftermath cleanup will take a long time. We will be very busy taking care of anyone affected by the blast—I have yet to learn the date. I'm moderately tempted to look to the future to see, but I choose not to as I understand the ramifications of accidentally changing important details of my life.

Brand tosses a small bag of candy into my lap, startling me back to the present.

"Uh, thanks?" I want to toss it right back at him.

"Hey, look where we are." I follow the direction of his finger and see that we've arrived at his house. A lone evergreen wreath with white lights and a big red bow hangs on the front door. "Keep your phone on you at all times, Calli," he orders.

"I will."

Ruth says, "There isn't anything in the near future to worry about, Brand."

"Not for her, maybe. But for me, we'll see."

I can't tell if he's joking or worried. I suspect he'll visit Suz while he's in town, but I don't want to ask. Duncan helps Brand get his bag from the back of the van.

"You guys don't have to wait around. I'll get myself in the house just fine."

Duncan pats him on the back. "We'll wait to make sure."

"No, man. You don't have to wait. Really."

Aernoud chuckles. "Duncan, let's go."

Duncan remains planted outside the car, determined to make sure Brand can get inside his house.

"Dude," Brand speaks slowly. "I've already repeated. I'm gonna be just fine. Now, go take Calli to her home."

"Fine." Duncan opens the driver's door and climbs behind the wheel.

Brand waves goodbye and Duncan drives away, muttering, "He didn't have to be condescending. I was only trying to watch out for the boy."

We arrive at my parents' home, and I'm pleased to see nothing has changed. The same bushes and trees line the sidewalk and driveway, not any taller or smaller than I remember, with twinkling lights strewn from barren branch to branch covered with the fresh snow. We grab our bags and make our way to the back door. The little frog statue I bought my mom when I was ten years old stands guard near the gate to the back yard where Maetha visited me once-upon-a-time to tell me more about the diamond and its history, among other things—she left out so much during that discussion. It seems like every time I return home I've learned more about my pre-planned life, more about the world of powers, more about Crimson and Maetha, and now the secretive levels in the government. Looking around at the garage doors, the shoveled sidewalk, the dimly lit entryway leading into the kitchen, I feel like this little bit of world has frozen in time while I've been away saving the rest of it. I want to get inside the house, climb into my waiting bed, and enjoy the stillness—to allow time to stop for a moment to take a breath.

"Calli, do we knock?" Duncan asks.

"No need. They aren't home. I'll grab the spare key." I walk over to the frog and reach down and pick up the fake rock beside him to retrieve the key as I've done so many times in my life. Opening the door, I follow Duncan inside and head to the keypad to reset the alarm.

My mother has left a note on the countertop with instructions for sleeping arrangements. I quietly show everyone to their assigned rooms, then head to my own.

Me and my mom are going shopping today for a wedding dress. Over breakfast, she asked Ruth if it would be okay to venture out into the crowds, to which I mentally begged Ruth to answer no. I don't feel like dress shopping is the best use of my time, not when Portland plans need to be made, along with figuring out how to get Jonas to come back to the Bearers. I began to feel a little pressured after everyone agreed with my mom. Their argument was I needed to take a moment for myself. Even though I'm a Bearer, I'm still in my normal lifespan time of living. I should experience and enjoy the traditions and normalcy before the big blast hits because there's no guarantee life will be calm afterward. My mom was happy the others sided with her.

Ruth told me later, away from my mother's ear, the "amount of time spent" is up to me and depends upon how picky I am with a dress.

True.

We arrive at the dress boutique and Ruth comes inside while the men wait outside. She wanders away from me and my mom, eyeing nearby dresses. I think she's giving us some privacy while keeping a lookout for my safety.

"Ooooh, how about this one, Calli?" With large eyes and a beaming smile, my mom holds the hanger and extends the dress in my direction.

Yikes! I can't imagine myself in that dress with all the sequins and pearls covering the bodice. It's too much. "I don't know, Mom. It looks a little warm for Bermuda."

"Oh right. So, you probably don't want long sleeves."

I reach into the mass of white and randomly pull one out. The dress I grab seems a bit closer to what I like: simple construction, low grade embellishments, not too flashy. "Look at this one."

"Oh, honey, we can do better than that."

"What's wrong with it?" I don't quite know what she means.

"It's not that anything is wrong, it's so . . . plain."

"Well, can we find something that's better than this one, but less flashy than the one you found?"

We continue our search. My mind wanders to Chris, naturally. Seeing all these dresses and wondering which one he'd choose makes me recall the day he and I bought the green dress for Anika's parents' funeral. The thought of Chris began as a pleasant memory but became a reminder of how dangerous and deadly things can quickly become as was exemplified with Anika's parents' deaths. The suffering so many people have had to go through in the short time since

I became a Diamond Bearer is sometimes hard to comprehend.

I shake my head and try to focus on the dress in front of me. I can't communicate with Chris while he's in the Bureau, but I will call him later tonight. My mom waves another possibility in my direction to which I shake my head.

My mother and I continue hunting and finally compromise on a gown I really like. The compromise is mine. She thought the dress needed some flash, so I agreed to have some embellishments added. The dress is a one-shoulder, A-line, fitted bodice with a double-bias pleat detail at the neckline. The embellishments will be in the form of a sash around the waist with beaded rhinestone detail.

Standing in front of the three angled mirrors wearing the dress, I feel like a different girl, one with a growing anticipation that I haven't allowed myself to dwell upon. I'm going to marry Chris Harding in a few months! The thought sends heated vibrations throughout my body. I mean, sure, I've thought about where we'll live, what we'll do, but not as a married couple. More vibrations ripple along my skin.

Returning to the house, my mother pulls out a large binder and directs me to sit at the table.

"This is everything I've pulled together for your wedding." She flips through the hole-punched pictures of floral arrangements, desserts, tuxedos, bridal bouquet designs, veils of different lengths, tiaras. The amount of time she's invested in the contents of the binder is impressive, but I feel pressured, again. My stomach rumbles as if it's tumbling rocks. My mom continues flipping pages and says, "If you don't see what you want here, we can order more magazines for more options."

I reach forward and place my palm on the current page to stop her from turning to the next. "Okay, Mom, please listen to me. This is not the kind of wedding I want."

"Like I said, we can order more magazines—"

Waving my hand over the binder, I say, "This is not what *I* want."

My mom clears her throat and closes the binder slowly. "What is it you do want, Calli?"

"Simple. No fuss." I clear my throat. "No frills."

She leans back in her chair and folds her arms. "Aren't you excited to get married?"

"Sure, I am. I just want it done."

Her head tilts to the side, her arms tighten their fold across her chest, and she looks me up and down. I've seen this behavior before. It's what she does when she's evaluating a patient. "*Done?* You could elope, you know."

I sit back in my chair and cross one leg over the other. My dangling foot wiggles automatically as if it's an outlet to dispel my overflowing nervousness. "Mom, I want a small celebration, close family and friends only, with little glamor or frills. My wedding is about joining my life with Chris. There doesn't need to be all the stuff you have in that binder."

"Is this Chris talking or you?"

I'm surprised by her question, "What?" My leg from the knee down starts fidgeting.

"All I'm asking is have you always wanted a small wedding or are you agreeing with Chris to have a small wedding?"

I can't believe she would think I'm parting with my long-held desires to please Chris. "Mom, I have always wanted a small wedding. I've never wanted anything like what you've dreamed about."

She unfolds her arms and leans forward, moving the binder away. "All right. One last question: is Chris okay with a small wedding?

I relax and say, "Absolutely."

"Okay then. I want you to have the wedding of your dreams. *Your* dreams. Not mine. I want you to be happy, Calli."

I reach over and give her a hug. "Thanks, Mom. I love you. If my old friend Suz ever gets married, however, you could be her wedding planner. She'd love your binder."

Christmas day brings mild celebrations, good food, and great conversations. I allow myself some time from the constant thoughts circulating around the upcoming blast. Today I'm just Calli, spending time with family and friends for the holiday. It rejuvenates me. I didn't realize how much I needed a break.

Chris calls around noon, and we talk for a while, discussing several topics including the happenings inside the Bureau. Everything we talk about is safe and hopefully boring for those surveilling the call. Talking with Chris is never boring for *me*, though. He lets me know he'll be able to take me to meet his mother the first week of January. I'm looking forward to it.

Ruth and Duncan are my constant companions, searching my future for any danger, keeping me safe from myself. Aernoud's post is outside. He does the perimeter search on a regular basis and I'm sure he's looking to the future as well. I remember when there were active threats to my life and my parents' lives—not too long ago. Since Max took down his site, there hasn't been much danger to speak of, which is fine by me. But we can't let our guard down even though things feel safer than they have in a long time.

Duncan has talked in depth about his past and the family members that lived since he became a Bearer and up to my mother's birth. He hasn't been a part of their lives in any way, only aware of their existence. Well, until I became a Bearer.

My mother is naturally curious about Duncan's past. He is, after all, her relative. The refreshed realization that she is an Unaltered reminds me she could be a Diamond Bearer. She was approved by Crimson, but not used because the healing alterations weren't strong enough to survive the upcoming blast. That's where I entered the picture. Still, my mother *could* be a Bearer.

She sees me staring at her and asks, "Calli, what does Chris's ring look like?"

"He doesn't wear a ring."

"Not yet, you mean. What does his wedding ring look like?"

"I don't know."

"What do you mean you don't know?"

"Am I supposed to know?"

My father joins the conversation. "The bride usually provides the groom's ring." He's not condescending with his tone, and I appreciate it.

"I, uh, wasn't, um, didn't—" I can feel my cheeks heating as my heart rate increases.

"Not to worry," my father interrupts me. "I'll take you shopping after Christmas."

"Thanks, Dad."

All new panic hits me hard. How am I going to pay for a ring? I've grown up having my needs met by my parents. I've only ever had a few months of actual employment and that didn't bring in much money. Now that I'm a Bearer, all my traveling and living expenses are covered by the mysterious never-ending cash reserve. My financial responsibilities are zero. I suddenly feel like a burden to a lot of people as my life hasn't exactly followed the path of going to college and getting a job.

I'm beginning to understand why Vita has a business in

the human world.

"Calli," my father places a hand on mine, "don't worry about the price. I'll take care of it. Men's rings aren't expensive."

"Could we just *look*? I don't need to buy one till June, so there's time for me to earn some money."

"Absolutely."

The whole conversation has brought my inexperience and dependency under the microscope, and it makes me feel apprehensive and embarrassed. How did I not know I needed to buy a ring for Chris? Where has my head been? I should have paid more attention to Suz all those years ago when she'd go on and on about her wedding dreams.

I make a note to ask my mom what other traditions I may not know about.

That evening, as I sit in my bed, staring at my phone, I decide to search online for men's rings to get an idea of what's available and the price ranges. I doubt Chris would like something flashy or anything that might snag on clothing, so I tailor my searches accordingly. Then, I find an interesting, meaningful band that strikes a chord with me. It is a little pricey due to the rare inlaid stone, but I think this will be perfect for Chris. Now I simply need to get Chris's ring size and figure out how to get some money. I'll talk with my father in the morning and let him know we don't need to go shopping. Maybe he has some ideas on how to sneakily get Chris's ring size.

I close my phone, turn off the lamp, and settle into bed, pulling the thick comforter up to my neck. Subtle glow-in-the-dark constellations on my ceiling still light up, even after all these years.

The day finally arrives to travel with Chris to meet his mother. We head to the airport where Chris and Max will be arriving shortly on Maetha's plane. Brand will be accompanying us with Ruth, Duncan, and Aernoud, too.

I just want to see Chris again.

When the steps of the airplane are pulled down, Max's face is the first one I see. Chris is directly behind him peering over his shoulder. Our eyes meet and my insides melt with joy; however, I realize having Max in between us, quite literally and figuratively, means Chris and I won't get much alone time together on this trip. I can't say I'm not disappointed. I mean, I no longer have an obsidian bomb—or more accurately, a wimpy gelatinous sack—inside me for Chris to worry about harming. Well, that's assuming he and I could get some alone time from my guards, too. Then there's the whole Crimson-inside-my-head-at-all-times thing.

Maybe I need to accept that Chris and I are not going to be able to get too close, maybe ever. That thought is disheartening.

After boarding and having the ground crew care for the plane, we take off for Kansas. We'll have a couple hours in each other's arms, enough time to talk with our minds and catch up on things we can't text or speak into the phone.

Brand moves up to the co-pilot seat to talk with Rodger, and Aernoud engages Max in some kind of boring conversation to get him to stop paying attention to me and Chris. *Thank you, Aernoud.*

Chris raises the armrest between us and scoots closer to me, reaching an arm behind my shoulders to pull me closer. He whispers into my ear, "Now that your obsidian grenade is out, I don't worry about it being damaged and disabling you."

I'm intensely aware of his warm breath on my skin and

of what he's implying when he says he's not worried anymore about damaging anything. My mouth goes dry, and I struggle to swallow. I decide to calm myself by talking about the procedure. "You know, it looked like a little blob of gelatin. That's all. But there were little black stones inside me, too."

"Oh, to form the bubble, maybe?"

"I guess." I cuddle my head against his chest and he rubs my shoulder gently. I take our conversation to mindspeak. *Chris, close your eyes so it looks like we're resting. Maybe Max will leave us alone while we catch up.*

Okay.

I haven't been able to tell you this, but I found Jonas.

What? Where? Chris shifts uneasily under my head.

I take a deep breath. *There is no easy way to tell you this. He's with Vita. He joined her side.*

I can feel the muscles in his chest tighten. *No!*

Yes.

I don't know what to say.

Well, there's more. I take a deep breath. *He helped Vita place the grenade inside me. He healed the wound.*

Chris abruptly moves me off his body and stands. He pushes a hand through his hair with excessive force, then brings his stormy blue eyes to mine. *I need a moment, Calli.*

I watch him stalk to the end of the plane to the bathroom and disappear behind the door.

Ruth looks at me. *What's wrong?*

Chris didn't like hearing about Jonas working for Vita.

None of us are happy about that.

I know. Inside, I didn't know. The other Bearers hadn't talked about it after we left Vita's shop. Well, at least they didn't talk to me about it, other than Aernoud expressing sorrow about Jonas.

Chris comes back with wet hair and a small towel. *Sorry,*

just needed to cool down.

We settle back into our seats again. *Should I have waited until later to tell you?*

No. I needed to know. It's messed up.

I change the subject. *How are things at the Bureau?*

I've got to get out somehow, and soon, before they discover I have a diamond.

Any issues with your heart?

No. I haven't even needed to use the topaz you gave me. The quartz blanket has been good enough.

I hesitate for a moment before returning to the previous topic. *Chris, there's a lot of mystery behind Jonas and his association with Vita. He acted distant, as if he couldn't care less. It wasn't like him. Something is wrong.*

It's all wrong, Calli. Max never said anything to me about having a Diamond Bearer helping Vita. He either doesn't know or they are keeping it secret. I would confront Max, but if he doesn't know, I don't want to give him any extra info he can use. Chris's thoughts pause. *I wonder where Vita is keeping Jonas.*

I don't know.

Well, let me tell you what I found out about General Appleton and Maetha.

I turn in my seat and look at him. He strokes my hair and encourages me to lay my head back down on his chest.

So, get this, Maetha and the general were an item back in the 1980s.

No way!

Yep. They worked together during the Cold War. He lost track of her for a few decades until the video footage surfaced through Max's website of the truck stop robbery when Freedom appeared. Maetha had bi-located to us and was captured on film. General Appleton recognized her right away and he's been hunting for her ever since.

It makes sense now that General Appleton would take notice of Max's work and bring him into the Bureau. He might be able to get some answers about Maetha, like where she's been all this time. Any idea why Maetha doesn't want to talk to him?

No. He wouldn't even recognize her now with her changed appearance.

I wonder how many times she has changed her looks over the centuries.

After landing in Kansas, we try to rent a large vehicle that will hold all of us, but the rental agency is out of stock. We rent two cars instead. I insist that Max and Duncan ride in one car, and the rest of us in the other. Max tries to protest, but Duncan jumps to my defense, understanding Chris and I need some space from Max, even if it's only a car ride. Max concedes reluctantly, then climbs in the car with Duncan.

Chris volunteers to drive and I ask to sit up front in the passenger seat. It's become common practice to ask my guards for permissions such as this that require viewing my future—needless to say, I can't wait to be able to keep tabs on my own future after the blast.

But when exactly will that occur? Chris and I are about to visit his mother and she will no doubt ask when the blast is going to happen. I don't know when. Why don't I know when? Sure, we still have seven months to prepare for an "early August" event, but this lack of detail has me tied up in knots. Besides, it was easier to not be worried when the event would happen "next year," but now it's January and August feels a lot closer.

Chris speaks to my mind. *Are you nervous to meet my mom?*

I turn my head to him and answer. *No, well yes, but that's not what I'm thinking about. I'm stressed about a lot of things.*

Hey, I'm here for you. Let me help. He takes one hand off the wheel and squeezes mine momentarily. Then he looks at me briefly before returning his focus to the road before us.

Thanks, Chris. What are you going to tell your mom about Portland?

I'm not sure. I'll decide based on her anxiety level.

That's a good idea. It's not like you can tell her a whole lot. We don't even know what day it will hit.

Sure, we do. August first.

What? I feel like I've been sucker-punched.

What? He looks over at me again with a quick glance.

What makes you think that? I want to turn all the way to face him, but the seatbelt holds me tight.

I saw it in a vision. Didn't you already know?

"No! I didn't know." The words fly from my mouth as I lose control of my mindspeak. Chris whips his head in my direction, with his eyes wide and jaw clenched.

Brand leans forward from the back seat and asks with a humorous tone, "What didn't you know?"

Chris speaks to my mind. *Be careful what you say, Calli. Our phones are being monitored and I don't want them knowing I can see visions.*

"It's nothing, Brand," I say.

"Okay, I'm not an idiot. Clearly you two are arguing, and that's fine. This time just keep it to yourself, okay?"

Chris begins to react to Brand's words, but the surroundings start spinning viciously as Brand repeats me back. The spinning stops right before I blurt out my words when Chris stated he'd seen the blast date in a vision. My body is twisted toward Chris with the seatbelt restraining me. I feel the exact feelings of utter surprise as I did, but this time I control my response.

I reply to Chris, *No. I didn't know.*

I assumed you knew and were being careful around the authorities, you know, being vague. I just followed your lead.

What did you see in your vision? I ask.

We were driving through deserted streets around seven o'clock in the evening on our way to the capture point. I saw an electronic sign flashing information like the date and temperature. It was humorous because it said 8/1 and then 81F and we laughed at the two numbers being the same.

Did you see the blast?

No.

How do you know that was the blast day then?

Because of the way I felt. I was worried I might not see you again. He turns his head to me. *I'm not looking forward to feeling that way.* He retrains his eyes on the road. *Anyway, the vision ended when we parked the car in the parking garage.*

I relax the death-grip my hands have on the armrest and sit properly, facing forward. *I'm sorry, Chris.*

For what?

I haven't considered how hard this will be on you.

Don't worry about me, Calli. You have too much to deal with already.

I change the subject. *We need to get the word out about the date.*

How about we deal with that after meeting my mom?

Sounds good.

Chris directs my attention and the others to the right side of the road. "There's my elementary school." He swivels his head to the left. "Oh, and there's the pizza shop where me and my friends would hang out after school on our way home. They have the best breadsticks."

He turns the car down a residential street, and I instantly recognize the houses from his memories that I saw long ago when he let me view his past.

I point to the familiar-looking home. "That one was Crimson's, right?"

He nods and slows the car, then turns into the driveway a couple houses down from Crimson's home.

Aernoud leans forward putting his head between our

seats. "What did you say?"

Chris parks the car and engages the parking brake. He turns in his seat and presses his index finger to his lips and holds up his phone. Then he projects his thoughts for us to hear. *She was my neighbor while growing up. I would feed her fish when she was gone on trips.*

Ruth, Aernoud, and Brand's eyes widen with surprise, which lets me know Chris is projecting his thoughts to Brand.

Brand laughs. "She has fish?"

Aernoud shakes his head. *You knew her as a boy?*

I knew her as Jo Jo, my neighbor, not Crimson. She was a regular person. Of course, once my powers emerged and I learned about Mind-Readers I began to suspect she might be one. Chris's thoughts trail off momentarily, then he adds, *And a Healer. I know she used that power on me.*

Ruth says, *So, she was planning on bringing you into the Bearers from an early age, then.*

No, actually, she was watching my father.

Duncan says, rubbing his chin. *I remember those arrangements being put together. Merlin had a big part in finding a home near General Harding's house, but I thought Maetha would be living there, not Crimson.*

Chris speaks, "Uh, would it be okay if only Calli and I go inside?"

Ruth nods. "I've already seen this. It's fine. Just know, however, Max isn't going to be happy. He's quite impatient."

Chris and I both roll our eyes simultaneously, then we get out of the car into the brisk January air. Max is on his way over to us after parking his car.

"Please wait outside, Max." Chris is clear but polite, leaving no room for Max to argue.

Max's pinched expression and narrowed eyes indicate his reluctance to the request.

The front door opens, and Chris's mother stands in the doorway.

"Hi Mom," he greets her with sincerity.

As the two of them embrace and then talk animatedly, I can't help but see the familial similarities, from her blue eyes and blonde hair—now intertwined with grey strands—to her height and posture. She even angles her chin down at times and pulls the same expressions he does on occasion. Knowing about her life of spousal emotional abuse followed by her filing for divorce, she stands before me with an air of confidence of a woman who took charge of her own life and now lives in the moment.

Chris motions to me. "Mom, meet Calli Courtnae."

I shake her hand. "It's so nice to finally meet you, Mrs. Harding." As soon as the name leaves my lips, I regret calling her by her ex-husband's name. She might have changed back to her maiden name. I don't know.

"Please, call me Lynette." She takes my left hand and admires the engagement ring. "Oh, Chris. The diamond looks so beautiful." She tilts my hand side to side with gentle motions as she examines the ring closely. Then she brings her attention up to my eyes. "Are you happy with Chris?"

"Am I happy?" I nearly sputter out. "Of course. Absolutely."

"He treats you well? Respects you?" She looks deep into my eyes while still holding my left hand.

Chris grunts. "I can hear you, Mom."

"I know, I want to hear her answer."

"Yes," I say, lowering my voice in the hopes of conveying my sincerity. "You've raised a respectful, well-mannered, unselfish gentleman whom I love with my whole heart." I bring my other hand up and rest it on hers, giving a gentle squeeze.

Her smile beams brightly and she releases my hand.

"Come in, come in." She steps aside and waves us into the home.

We enter the living room and sit together on a soft couch. Lynette sits nearby on a navy-blue velvet wingback chair. I glance around the room at the many framed photographs of Chris and of his family. I'm amazed Lynette would keep photos of her ex-husband out on display like this, but I guess where Chris is in all of the photos, too, it makes sense not to alter the images.

"I see you've redecorated a bit," Chris says.

Lynette runs her hands back and forth along the armrests of her chair, smiling. "Yes, I've always wanted a chair like this, but your . . . I knew your father wouldn't allow it. He didn't like the style." She looks around the room. "I've found a lot of enjoyment from redesigning my life."

Her words make me wonder if either of my parents feel like they can't express themselves the way they'd prefer. Does one hold the other back? I don't believe so, but I've never really paid attention to that. More importantly, I make a mental note to be mindful of Chris and his opinions and wants, and to be aware of my own desires and wishes to make sure I'm not denying myself the blue wingback chair, if I ever wanted one.

Chris and his mom talk a little about everyday life and catch up on the neighborhood news, then Chris brings the conversation back to us.

He clears his throat and motions to my ring. "Mom, would you tell us about the lucky diamond?"

"Oh, that's just a myth. You know grandma. She was so superstitious."

My mind replays memories of my mother discounting her grandmother's tales of Shadow Demons. It's interesting that both our mothers had predecessors with knowledge of the world of powers in one form or another.

"Still," Chris continues, "we'd like to hear about it."

Lynette smiles. "All right. Let me see what I can remember . . . I know my grandmother claimed that if she wanted something badly enough, all she had to do was clutch the diamond in her hands and wish long enough and her wish would come true. One thing in particular, she claimed she wished for my mother to recover from polio when she was a little girl. My mother had no lasting effects from her sickness, which baffled the doctors. Also, my mother said when she was pregnant with me, she was threatening to miscarry, so she used the lucky diamond to carry me to term."

"Wow," I say, "that's amazing."

"Well, if you believe it," Lynette scoffs. "They were also praying throughout their ordeals. I believe in the power of prayer more than a 'magical diamond.' "

"Did you ever try using it?" Chris asks.

"Heavens no! It's a fairytale. The diamond sat in my jewelry box for years. It's an heirloom, that's all, and I'm pleased to honor the tradition of passing it on to you."

I smile and say, "Well, it's been lucky for us, so we're happy you did."

Lynette beams, then asks, "When is the wedding?"

"June tenth."

"I assume you'll have our minister perform the ceremony. Have you already chosen the church?"

Chris wiggles a little in his seat. "Um, we're going for an outdoor wedding on a private island in Bermuda. I hope your passport is current."

"But, what about tradition?" She points to my ring. "We've always held to traditions. That's why I passed the diamond down to you—tradition."

I'm curious how Chris will handle this with his mother.

"Mom, some things have changed in my life and," —he

takes my hand— "Calli and I want to set some new traditions for ourselves."

"Oh, okay." I note the drop in her excitement. "So, no church? No minister?"

"Just as you've changed some things in your life to improve your happiness, we have too."

Lynette's eyebrows narrow slightly, then relax. "Bermuda, you said? Not many people will be able to attend, like if you had the wedding here."

"We don't want a lot of people, Mom. However, Jo Jo will be there."

"Oh, really?" Her eyebrows shoot up and a pleased smile spreads across her face.

I add, "We'll have a beautiful wedding, and we really want you to be there."

"Of course I'm coming." She looks as if she wants to say more in protest, but she holds back. I choose not to read her mind.

"Great." Chris relaxes back into the couch.

Lynette asks, "I'm curious, though, how did you let Jo Jo know about your wedding? She moved out of her house many months ago. It's a rental now."

Chris squeezes my hand gently and throws a quick glance at me, then says, "Mom, there's something else we want to talk about with you . . . and it involves Jo Jo."

Her eyes perk up and she sits forward slightly.

"In August, there's going to be an event that changes a lot of things."

"I don't understand."

"You know all that stuff Dad studied in Colorado? A lot of those types of things are going to be on the news, and I think it will be a confusing time for you. I just want to help you through all of it."

"Can you be more specific?"

"As more details come in, I'll update you. Right now, it looks like all the supernatural powers Dad researched are going to become public knowledge, and people you know might claim to have some of those powers."

"But they aren't real, powers, I mean."

I speak to Chris's mind. *Should we demonstrate a power?*

No, not yet.

"Well," Chris hesitates, "if you think about normal abilities like sprinters or athletes, there are some pretty fast athletes out there. My speed raised alarms with Dad because it was outside the normal range. That's why he wanted to study me and others like me. There are people who have other abilities besides running that are outside of the normal range. Jo Jo is one of them."

Lynette chuckles a little and clutches her hands together in her lap. "What are you saying, Chris?"

"I'm saying I've had contact with Jo Jo because she's part of our group."

"What power does *she* have?"

I notice her intense hand wringing and can see without using any of my powers that she is extremely uncomfortable. *She's freaking out.*

I know, Calli. I'm backing off for now.

"You know what, Mom, I'm going to let her tell you."

Crimson speaks in my mind. *Calli, tell Lynette I will be performing the ceremony.*

You will?

I always oversee couplings.

I say, "Lynette, I'm told Jo Jo is performing the wedding ceremony."

"She is? She can do that?"

Chris looks at me. *Really?*

Yes. She just told me.

Chris pauses, clears his throat, and turns to his mother.

"Make sure your passport is current. You're going to absolutely love this island resort. I know we do." He brings my hand to his mouth and kisses it.

Chapter Twelve - Vorherrschaft Unprotected

After talking a little while longer about future plans not involving cosmic powers, we say goodbye and leave the house. Chris suggests we should agree to ride with Max to keep him happy. We climb into the back seat of Max's car after getting the go ahead from the guards, Duncan indicating our futures didn't hold any danger. Duncan sits in the front passenger seat. Chris holds my hand and rests his other elbow on the armrest, rubbing his chin while staring out the window. I infuse Healer power into his body out of a deep desire to help him sort through his visit with his mother, even though he has the full Healer power of his own. I understand how easy it is to overlook what we can do for ourselves as Diamond Bearers.

Max looks repeatedly in the rearview mirror at us as he drives through the town. I want to tell him to keep his eyes on the road for safety's sake, but I don't.

"So, what did you guys talk about in there?" Max asks.

"Not your business," Chris answers without pulling his focus away from the view out the window.

"Yeah, but—"

"No buts, Max," I interject. "Personal conversations are just that, personal."

Max tightens his hold on the steering wheel and maneuvers the car through the residential streets of the town in silence. After a couple of minutes, Max asks, "Does your mom know about the diamond, Chris?"

"Again, none of your business." Chris folds his arms and glares at Max's image in the mirror.

"Hmph!"

I send my thoughts to Chris. *Which diamond? The one on my finger, the one in my heart, or the one in your heart, Chris?*

I'm hoping it's the one in your heart and not the other two.

Well, I'm going to charge a mind-reading topaz so I can determine exactly what he knows.

Be very careful, there, Calli. He knows what it feels like to have his mind read.

Good reminder. I will be.

"What the . . ." Chris lurches forward, startling me. "Max, pull over!"

"What?"

"There," Chris points out the right-side windows as Max brings the car to a halt. "Calli, that's the jewelry store where I had your ring designed."

Max vocalizes what I'm looking at. "You mean the shop with all the plywood on the windows?"

Chris gets out of the car and hurries to avoid approaching cars. I climb out and follow him.

"I can't believe it's out of business. I was hoping to get a chance to ask questions about your ring." Chris leans close to the wood and peers through a narrow crack. "Everything is gone. Empty."

The other car parks behind ours and Aernoud joins us in front of the boarded-up window. "What's the matter? Why have we stopped?"

Max steps up to my side and finds a gap to peer through. "I can't see anything in there. It's too dark."

Chris backs away from the window. "This doesn't make sense."

Max cranes his head, still looking through the gap. "How can you tell it's empty in there? It's like looking into a black hole."

"We need to keep moving," Aernoud states with a grimace.

Ignoring Aernoud, Chris says, "Max, look over here through this crack. There's more light that gets through." Chris moves aside and I follow so Max can try again. Chris speaks to my mind, *I used Hunter eyesight. I don't want him to clue in I have better eyesight than him.*

I walk over to a different gap in the boards. "I can't see anything either, Chris. It's too dark. Anyway, we better get going," I say, nodding to Aernoud, hoping Max will sense the need to move along. I walk to the car and get in, not waiting for the guys. Max turns and follows. Chris remains. He looks up at the store sign, then to the left and to the right, as if he's trying to work out a reason why the jewelry store is closed.

Max rolls down the window near Chris. "Let's go, Harding."

Soon, both cars are back on the road. Chris speaks to my mind. *I'll ask my mom if she knows anything about the shop closing.*

Why is this bothering you so much, Chris?

The owner was a friend of my dad. He outright owned the building, in fact, he owned the whole block. Why would he shut down his jewelry business?

Maybe he's relocating.

I don't know. This feels weird.

The rest of the car ride is silent, thank goodness. I just want to enjoy the time I get to be with Chris and look forward to being near him on the flight back.

At the airport, Rodger greets us. "Folks, there's been a change of itinerary. Chris and Max will fly back to Washington, and you four will meet up with other Bearers."

"Why?" Max demands.

Rodger shrugs his shoulders.

A heavy feeling settles into my gut as I realize our time together is cut short. I won't get to cuddle with Chris on the plane like I'd anticipated.

I turn to Chris and wrap my arms around him. "I feel cheated. I wanted to have more time with you."

"Me too. But this trip was really nice, Calli. I love you."

"I love you, too. I love being with you and can't stand being constantly separated." We share an intimate goodbye kiss, to which Max grunts.

After our kiss, Chris pulls me close to his body and embraces me. *I hate being away, too.*

I'm pleased to hear he feels the same and I don't want the moment to end, but reality settles in and I return focus to our tasks. *When should I tell everyone the date of the blast?*

That's up to you.

Max interrupts, "You still have to report to me, remember."

"How could I forget?"

After our group splits and our rental car arrangements are extended, Duncan navigates to an abandoned shopping center parking lot where we can participate in a bi-locating session with Jie Wen and Amenemhet. Jie Wen first sends a mental communication that all phones be turned off. Then they connect with my diamond and appear inside the cramped quarters of the car.

Aernoud says, "Maybe we should get out of the car and talk outside."

"It's not as private," Ruth says, motioning her hand to the windows and roof.

Aernoud presses, "What if someone sees a car full of more people than it can hold, sitting in an abandoned lot. Don't you think that might raise suspicion?"

Brand clears his throat. "Nothing happens in the next two minutes, if that helps?"

Jie Wen nods. "Good. That's more than enough time.

We are confident we've found a Reaper facility with an operational machine, but I don't want to try entering until Brand is here." Jie Wen continues, laying out the plan for us to drive to an address in Texas where we will meet them and formulate a plan of action. The drive will take about five hours.

Lovely. I think I'll meditate and consider the revelation that Crimson will be performing our coupling.

"Okay, Duncan, stop here." Brand orders. "This is as close as we can get before entering an obsidian field.

We've almost reached the guard's gate shack, just a couple of car lengths away. Roughly twenty-five yards beyond the gate is a warehouse that is a suspected power-removing facility.

"The future is unseeable," Ruth says. "Does anyone have a Seer topaz strong enough to visualize the near future to show us how to get inside the building?"

The collective answer is no.

Jie Wen's voice sounds in my mind, and from the way Duncan, Ruth, and Aernoud go quiet, I assume they hear him, too. *Amenemhet and I are behind a nearby building. I recognized one of the Reapers as being from the China facility, and I know he would recognize me. We'll stay out of sight for now. Aernoud, Ruth, and Brand need to get the guard to open the gate. Duncan and Calli will stay in the car until it's safe to enter the building.*

Aernoud takes charge and informs Brand of what is about to happen. Then the three of them exit the car and walk to the guard shack.

I roll my window down halfway. The sun shines brightly overhead, heating the concrete hot enough for heat waves to ripple upward. Distant rumblings of cars and trucks from the highway create an auditory white noise which drowns out the sounds of bugs and birds.

Ruth, Aernoud, and Brand are now at the guard's station at the gate.

I listen as Aernoud asks the guard if they can be admitted to the building. The guard speaks into his handheld radio, asking for permission. After a few moments, the metal door on the side of the building opens and a man wearing a white lab coat stands in the doorway. He communicates with the guard without using the radio, only speaking loudly. I try to listen to his words but can't formulate what he's saying. He's too far away and in the presence of obsidian.

I send a mental question to Amenemhet, Jie Wen, and Duncan. *Can anyone hear what is being said?*

The response is no.

Amenemhet says, *Calli, can your read his lips?*

I'll try. He's pretty far away. The situation is similar to when I read Chris's lips outside the Denver compound, only there we could zoom in on his face with the camera. An idea enters my mind. I pull out my phone and activate the camera, then zoom in on the lab coat-wearing man.

Aernoud replies in a raised voice to the lab coat man with a question. "Who are we with?"

Watching the conversation on my phone screen, I read the response on the man's lips aloud. "Yes, who are you with? What group?"

Aernoud shouts back, "We are. . .with . . .belong to. . ." He's stuttering and pausing, uncharacteristically.

I say to Duncan, knowing Amenemhet and Jie Wen will hear, too, "Brand is repeating. They must be trying many different answers but haven't found the right one yet."

Another white-coated person joins the first standing in the doorway. They talk to each other while facing our direction. I speak the words on his lips, "Are they with the

Oregon group?" The other responds, "I don't know. I thought there'd be more of them."

I put my face to the open window and yell out to Brand, "Tell them you're with the Oregon group." Brand doesn't hear me. Turning to Duncan, I say, "Quick! Go tell Brand to say 'the Oregon group.' "

"But—that's going to look suspicious."

"Brand will repeat you back. Hurry!"

The next second, Aernoud answers, "We're with the Oregon group."

I whip my head to the side and see Duncan with his eyes tightly closed and his mouth twisted as if he's in pain. Duncan grunts, "I don't like Brand's power."

Clearly, Duncan left the car and told Brand and Brand repeated with Duncan.

One of the men shouts, which I relay, "You're early. Where is the rest of your group?"

Brand responds this time, directing his words to the men in white. "On their way. Are we doing this or what?"

I speak what the lab coat man says, "Where are the supplies and equipment?"

Brand lies rather convincingly, "The stuff is in the other vehicle. They'll be here in twenty minutes. So, are you letting us in or not?"

"Just a moment," one man in white says, waving his hand in the air. Then the two men have a discussion with each other.

It's hard to say what they're talking about because they keep turning their heads away from my view.

Jie Wen speaks to my mind. *What are they saying?*

"They're unsure about us. They're thinking of waiting for the whole team to arrive. They were given a different arrival time . . . in one hour. They're going to make us wait. The leader is not with us. They don't want to be punished..."

Duncan asks, trying hard to keep up, "The real team? Er, the one Brand lied about?"

"I don't know." The men are still talking. One is becoming irate, using his hands and arms a lot as he verbally fights with the other. I can't tell what they're saying as I can only pick up one or two words here and there.

What now, Calli? Amenemhet asks.

The irritated man folds his arms across his chest and heaves air in and out, looks toward our direction and says, "Look, it's just us and the kid. I'm not going to risk it."

Before I can even repeat the lab coat's words to my group, Brand runs over to my window. "Really? You're sure there's only three of them?

I nod and see Duncan in my peripheral vision hunched over like he's dealing with nausea.

Brand cocks his head to the side. "Come on, Calli. You know how my power works. Is it true they're alone?"

"Yeah, that's what they said."

"Tell the others we should storm the place right now!" he orders.

Jie Wen and Amenemhet arrive in a whoosh at the side of the car before I can send my thoughts, Brand having repeated without me. I'm glad he didn't take me along, like with Duncan.

Brand says to Jie Wen, "What's more important? Catching the two men or getting what's inside the building?"

"What's inside the building is more important." Jie Wen's response is smug and it ruffles my feathers.

We exit the car and hurry to the others at the gate.

The guard is taken down quickly by Jie Wen, unconscious, as Ruth hits the button to open the gate.

The two white coats disappear inside the building and the door slowly closes.

Brand throws me instructions. "This time, you need to

squeeze through the gate as soon as possible and get to the door before it closes, Calli!" The world spins at an incredible speed as Brand repeats with me back to when he's standing outside my car window, having just confirmed there are only three individuals.

Amenemhet and Jie Wen arrive at the side of the car, Duncan and I exit, and we all run toward the gate. Like a well-oiled machine, Jie Wen incapacitates the guard while Ruth hits the button, and I squeeze through the opening gate, then run to the closing door and catch it at the very last millisecond before it latches. I'm soon joined by the entire group.

Once inside, Jie Wen puts up his hand to halt everyone. He motions for us to be silent, then he and Amenemhet move forward, methodically, like police, to clear each room. But, before they make it to the first room, Brand jumps forward.

"Go the other way, those rooms are clear."

Jie Wen nods and follows Brand's direction.

Brand extends his arm, indicating down the hall. "The third guy is in the breakroom, last door on the left." Then he says to Ruth and Duncan, "Go get the crystals in the lab. Hurry!"

After issuing orders, Brand and I follow the others to the breakroom.

The "kid" the white coats talked about sits at a table with his back to us. His head bobs up and down, earbuds canceling out all noise, as he peels the plastic off his microwave dinner. I imagine the lab coats ran by and shouted at him to flee, but, well, the earbuds.

Amenemhet grabs onto the kid's bicep and pulls him out of his seat. One of the earbuds bounces on the ground. I recognize him from somewhere. College maybe? He's not a "kid" though. No younger than me or Brand.

"What the—" he looks at each of us. "Who are you?"

Amenemhet says, "Break's over, kid. Where are the other two?"

"I don't know, maybe in the lab."

"What's your name?"

"Sven."

I step forward, recognizing him now. "I knew it! You tried to poison me on my birthday long ago at the restaurant. Who does that?"

"What?" he laughs nervously.

"Do you attempt to poison a lot of people, Sven, or should I say, Cody?"

His eyes light up. "You are . . . you're her!" Then confusion takes over. "How? Who?" He looks at Amenemhet. "You caught her? Man, Mr. Schweizer is going to reward you tons!"

Amenemhet pulls out a pair of handcuffs and secures Sven's hands behind his back in one fluid motion.

Sven's reaction time is rather slow. Reality hits him hard and is evident in the high-pitched whining tone as he fights back, cursing, kicking, and flailing.

I'm just happy he dropped a name. Mr. Schweizer.

Brand speaks, "The machine is not operational. The two men have gone. The others are gathering the crystals, hard drives, and files. We need to go help them and get out of here ASAP."

"Is something about to happen in two minutes?" I ask.

"Not yet, but I don't want to be here when the others show up."

We successfully flee the scene and don't run into any trouble. Amenemhet and Jie Wen take Sven with them in their vehicle, and we carry the crystals and gathered information in ours.

Duncan decides to leave the gate guard behind after a quick mind scan revealed the guard was hired from a temp agency to do one thing—run the gate. No surveillance cameras were found. Sven, on the other hand, will be a treasure trove of information once we're able to delve into his mind. There's always a chance he'll cooperate and volunteer what he knows. If not, a Bearer will have to extract his memories, which will drain the extractor's energy, leaving them vulnerable. That's not something anyone wants to risk happening while on the road. I know all too well how exhausting it is to extract memories.

Me and my group check into a hotel for the night after traveling several hours away from the Reapers' building. Ruth and I are sharing a room. I ask for first dibs on a shower and she agrees. Thank you, Ruth.

When I emerge from the bathroom, clean and refreshed, I walk into a conversation between Ruth and Aernoud. A box full of crystals is on the table.

Sitting on the foot of the bed, Aernoud says, "Jie Wen will extract Sven's memories to see what information he holds. We will travel back to Denver and await instructions."

I jump into the conversation. "I thought we were going to the Healer compound."

"They've asked us to wait till the end of February so they can complete their renovations."

"Okay." I look between Aernoud and Ruth. "So, will Sven be taken to Denver?"

Ruth answers, "No. Jie Wen and Amenemhet will deal with him."

"What will happen with Sven when they're done?"

Aernoud stretches his arms above his head. "They'll probably try to recruit him. That's what I'd do."

I can't help but laugh. "How could you ever trust someone like that? Any information he gathers will go right back to the Reapers."

Aernoud lowers his arms and looks at me. "Possibly, but they'll never let him back inside. He will always be viewed as compromised."

My gut stiffens with fear. "Wouldn't you *also* view him as compromised?" I want to yell, *He tried to poison me!*

"Where else will he go? If the Reapers won't have him back, and the Bearers extract all his knowledge—which he would be alarmingly aware of—what options does he have left? Go to the government? Side up with conspiracy bloggers, like Max? Or return to the normal world and try to forget everything he's learned about the world of powers? I think not. Once someone 'sees' the world through the cosmic-powered glasses, so to speak, they can't unsee it. Sven is primed to continue, he just needs a little reprogramming."

"So, we've basically kidnapped him, will scan his brain for knowledge, then try to get him to side with us. Sounds like some kind of weird Stockholm syndrome we're pushing him into." I take a breath and look at both of them. "May I ask a favor?"

They exchange glances then nod.

"Would you inform the Bearers that August first is the date of the Elemental Blast?"

"Of course." Ruth smiles. "Out of curiosity, why have you waited till now to reveal the date?"

"I didn't know until now. Chris saw the date in a vision." I know my tone sounds deflated, but I can't help it. "I will tell Max when I call him, and he will share the information with General Appleton, who should spread it down the line to the authorities in Portland. I believe by knowing the exact date, the Bearers will now be able to see more about the aftermath or at least determine what else needs to be prepared."

Aernoud says, "We will take care of it, Calli. One other question, though . . . you can read lips?"

"What?" I'm confused with the sudden topic change.

Ruth sits forward, head tilted slightly, seemingly eager to hear my answer.

Aernoud replies, "Have you always been able to read lips?

"Um, since middle school. I had a hearing injury and was taught to read lips." I leave Crimson's involvement out of my reply.

They look at each other quizzically.

"We didn't know you could do that," Aernoud states flatly.

"Oh. Amenemhet or Mary never told you all after they saw me do it?"

Ruth sits back and crosses her arms. "No. At least they didn't tell me."

"I never thought about it being important, especially since it's not a power. Should I hold a gathering and let everyone know?" I ask.

"No need," Aernoud says, "Jie Wen has taken care of that." He looks me over. "You need to rest. Your entire countenance feels stressed, which is understandable."

Of course, Jie Wen would be the one to blab to everyone about my skill. He's always hated finding out he hasn't been included in sensitive information. Good thing he doesn't know about my Blue shard.

I pick up my phone. "Thank you. I'll rest after I call Max."

Chapter Thirteen - The Big Boss?

We've been at the Denver house for almost a month now. Word of the exact date of the blast spread quickly to everyone who needed to know. The exact time is still vague—all we know is it will hit after dark. Max was prompt in relaying the information, which was surprising, honestly. I guess I thought he would drop the ball somehow.

Together, we've had time to evaluate all the crystals and information gleaned from the Reaper's facility. Apparently, they were waiting for the prisms to arrive to be able to start using their machine. Boxes of charged quartz and empty quartz were retrieved, and we determined each of the cosmic powers were accounted for. Unfortunately, that indicates that many people have been stripped of their powers. The charged quartz must have come from another facility.

We sorted the different quartzes according to their respective powers. Each will be returned to the clans for redistribution. The empty quartzes will be taken to Maetha's island to be used with the machine there. It does lead to the question of who would be run through the machine to power the empty quartz? Would that make the Bearers any better than the Reapers, harvesting powers? I try not to think too much about it.

A team of Readers stopped by last week and picked up the recovered charged reading quartz crystals. We'll be leaving soon to drive to the Healers' compound in California to deliver their charged crystals. An envoy of Seers will meet us at the Healers' place to collect their clans' quartz crystals. On our way back from the Healers, we'll meet up with Clara Winter to give her the charged running quartzes. That will only leave the Hunters.

Jie Wen bi-located to Duncan yesterday and updated him about the thought-extraction of Sven. Apparently, it hasn't happened yet. Jie Wen and Duncan talked quietly in the other room—as if there is such a thing when you're surrounded by Bearers with Hunter's hearing. Jie Wen expressed frustration with the inability to use his power on Sven, and he's even more annoyed by Sven's grating, defiant personality. Jie Wen made a derogatory statement about attitudes and lack of respect of "kids these days" to which Duncan suggested Jie Wen bring Sven to Denver to "let Brand and Calli interrogate him."

Let us *interrogate him?* I have strong doubts Jie Wen would ever admit he couldn't complete a task and then turn that task over to me.

I've kept busy with the ongoing research and planning for the Portland blast, communicating with General Appleton via Max, and passing along information to Chris to keep him updated, just in case he's not in the loop at the Bureau. I'm not sure when I'll see him next, but with every day passing by, we come closer to our wedding date. I'm struggling to see how we will even be able to get married with the current "captive" situation Chris is enduring. Still, I need to move forward as if everything will work out, meaning I need to get Chris's ring purchased. I asked him for his ring size in one of our texting sessions, rather than trying to be covert about it. After communicating with the ring designer and learning resizing will be expensive, I decided to simply ask.

Sitting in the back of the van, after departing for California, I thumb through the website of the jewelry designer.

Brand leans over. "Whatcha looking at?"

"Rings. A wedding band for Chris."

"Oh! That's exciting. Can I see?"

I pull the screen to my chest, suddenly concerned he

might spill the secret details of the band to Chris.

"Come on, I won't tell him."

I scrutinize Brand to see if I can sense if he's lying.

"I'm not lying!"

"What?"

He drops his chin but retains eye contact with me, causing the whites beneath his irises to become visible. "Seriously? You understand my power better than anyone, but you still forget what I can do."

"Fine." I concede. I show him the screen.

"Ouch! The price. But wow! I want a ring like that."

"I really want to get it for him, but I don't have the money."

"I'll totally lend you some money, Calli."

"You have money? Where did *you* get money? Did you rob a bank?" I jest, but I'm kind of concerned.

"No! I pay attention. I've listened to Jonas and Sarangerel talk about investing in blockchain companies. So, I did."

"Block-what?"

"Calli, you've been really busy with the Portland blast stuff and everything, so, you know, don't feel bad for not being aware of all the new things in the world."

"You've made some money investing then?"

"A bit, yes. If you want to borrow some money, I'm happy to lend you some. I know you'll pay me back someday."

"I'll think about it."

We completed the tour of the Healers' compound and delivered the quartz crystals. I'm impressed with their renovations and increased capacity which will make it possible to care for the many injured and sick following the blast. The only problem I see is the distance from Portland and the fact that their compound is not near a major airport.

The Seers picked up their quartz and went on their way, not wanting to be around the Healers any longer than necessary. I'm a little surprised to see this animosity between them, and I don't understand where it's coming from, but in order for all of us to effectively help the victims of the upcoming blast, they will have to learn to work together.

The Healers are more interested in talking with the older adults than with me, and that's okay. I take the opportunity to wander into an adjacent room that's set up like a trauma unit in an emergency room. Brand follows. The amount of planning and preparation these people have completed is inspiring. I just hope all this is overkill. Hopefully not many people will be affected by the blast.

The walls of the room begin to move, swirling in place, not spinning like they do when Brand repeats. I close my eyes and rub my lids with my palms. When I open them, I see the room is filled with many people. Cries of pain pierce the panicked air. Doctors and nurses move this way and that, issuing orders, administering medications into IV lines, and performing CPR. My heart races as I turn in a circle, taking in the horrifying scene. Then I freeze. My father is one of the doctors working on a man who is writhing in pain. The man lunges at my father and grabs onto his arm, pleading, "Make it stop!"

My father tries to release the man's grip. A nurse and nearby technician come to his rescue, all the while my father saying, "We're doing everything we can. Lay down, please lay down." His eyes soften as his eyebrows rise only on the inside edges above his nose. I've seen the expression on his face before. That's how he looks when he knows he's talking to a terminal patient.

Someone behind me says, "There's too many. We can't handle everyone."

The room then spins and dissolves at the same time, leaving me standing next to Brand in the empty room.

"Calli," Brand says. "What's wrong?"

"Uh, I had a vision. My dad was here . . . or will be here." I turn to Brand, a lump in my throat. "There's still too many people that will be affected."

"I thought you weren't supposed to look at your future."

"I didn't. It just happened. Besides, it wasn't my future."

A loud shriek comes from the other room. Brand and I rush in to see what's happening.

The Healer Rhonda from the Hunters' Forest meeting is standing over a box. "That's mine! Right there." She touches a specific quartz crystal amongst the pile.

Ruth moves beside her. "How can you be sure?"

"It's the missing part of my soul." Rhonda reaches in and lovingly pulls out a crystal. "Now, I feel complete." She presses the quartz against her sternum with both hands.

I say, "Rhonda, how are you doing?"

She turns to me, one hand reaching under her neckline near her collar bone. "Calli! Thank you for bringing my quartz to me. I can't tell you how happy I am to have my power back." She pulls her hand from her shirt, holding a bandage and a quartz crystal. Then she peels the crystal off the bandage and puts it in the box, replacing it with the quartz she identified as her own.

"I'm pleased you could pick out yours amongst all the others. Would you help find the owners of the other quartzes?"

"Absolutely!"

"If you happen to end up with leftovers . . ."

"You mean if someone is dead?"

"I'm sorry. Yes. If a quartz has no owner, please let me know. You can get a message to me through Clara Winter." My thoughts are on Chris. Maybe he would accept a Healer quartz if he felt he would be honoring the individual whose life was sacrificed by the Reapers. Maybe.

Crimson could use a Healer's quartz. I also consider my father. If he could have access to a quartz, he might be able to help with the fallout of the blast more effectively. My mother, too.

Another idea takes shape in my mind. I'm going to contact Clara and ask about the leftover Runners' quartz from General Harding's compound. I'm wondering if Chris's power is amongst the extras. He might like to have the crystal containing that piece of him, like how Rhonda referred to her quartz.

The plans for the next few days have changed. We were headed to Montana to meet with Clara. Instead, we will meet her at a rest area off I-70 in central Utah on our way back to Denver, Colorado. She will be traveling to pick up a new Runner whose power will be emerging soon. I am reminded that the world is still spinning around me even though my mind is preoccupied with the Elemental blast. Clara has confirmed she will bring the extra Runner quartz crystals as I requested.

Two days have passed since we were at the Healers' compound. We've been on the road for long hours at a time, sleeping last night in a roadside motel in Mesquite, Nevada.

We arrive at the rest area Clara directed us to and find her seated at a shaded picnic table, looking more elegant than I remember, her hair perfectly styled up off her neck, and she wears a crisp white pantsuit with stiletto heels. Definitely out of place in the red rock desert landscape.

After our greetings and introductions, we sit and present her with the Runners' quartz crystals retrieved from the Texas facility.

"Thank you," she says, bowing her head. "I'll let the online community know we've recovered some powers."

"Online?" I ask. "Aren't you afraid of imposters or spies infiltrating the group?"

"No. It's an invitation only, token-based group."

"Oh. I'm not sure what that means or how that's secure."

Brand scoots forward. "Token-based? Awesome!"

"I'm sorry?" I look between Brand and Clara.

Brand looks at me. "My investments, Calli. This is the kind of technology I invested in. It's super-secure."

Clara changes the subject. "Why do you want these quartz crystals?"

"One of them might be Chris's. I'd like to give him the opportunity to reclaim his power. I saw how happy Rhonda the Healer was to find hers, so I thought Chris might feel the same way."

She smiles. "I'm sure he'll appreciate the gesture even if his is not here. Go ahead and take these. But, be sure to get them back to me."

"I will." I pull the small box across the table and place it beside me. Resting my forearms on the tabletop, I ask, "Are you coming to Portland to help with the blast?"

"Absolutely. I plan on assisting with the new powers and helping any sick or injured, just so you know."

"Thank you. I'll keep you up to date on the progression and the timing of the blast." I examine my hands, knowing I need to ask her another questions, but not knowing if I'll like the answer. "Clara, did you know Jonas Flemming joined up with Vita?"

Clara's eyes widen and her lips part. "No. When did he do that?"

"Back in August. I didn't find out till recently." My head drops and I study my hands in an attempt to keep the tears behind my eyes.

She reaches for my hand and gently squeezes. "Vita is a good teacher, a little out-there, but still a good teacher. I learned a lot from her."

Clara's physical contact infuses me with energy, not that she's infusing me using a power, only the power of compassion she has for me and my disappointment. However, Clara doesn't know Vita inserted a device in my body. I wonder how she'd view Vita if she knew. I ask, "Are you friends with Vita?"

"I have been, but I've lost contact with her over the years."

"What I know about her isn't comforting. I'm worried about Jonas. I'm worried about a lot of things."

Her face brightens, as if she has an idea. She says, "Nate is working on a recipe for mood stabilization that helps with over-worrying. It may benefit you."

"That's okay. I'm reliant on my excessive worrying. It motivates me to keep trying for solutions. How about you ask him to create something that helps people come to their senses."

We stay in Denver for a couple of long, drawn-out weeks. To pass the time, I focus on other things. I've been in contact with the designer of Chris's ring. He sent pictures of different rings he's made with the inlay of moldavite—the stone I've chosen for Chris—and he's confident he can complete my order by the middle of May. I begrudgingly conclude I will take Brand up on his offer to lend me some money. I feel better about this than having my dad buy it—my dad won't let me pay him back. Brand, on the other hand, won't let me off the hook. I'll reimburse him, somehow.

"There you go, Calli. The transfer is completed. You can use the card now." Brand leans back in his chair and stretches his arms above his head, then brings his elbows back to the tabletop.

"Calli," Ruth says as she enters the kitchen, "did you get the message about the Gathering?"

"No." I set the phone down, after having confirmed Brand's money was received by the ring designer.

Brand pushes his chair back, stands, and places his hand on my shoulder, giving it a gentle squeeze. "I know you're good for it, Calli." His out-of-place words make me think we had a conversation in an alternate future about my stress levels of not knowing when I'll pay him back. He extends his hand, requesting his phone back.

I give it to him. "Thanks for letting me use it."

"No problem."

He leaves the kitchen.

"What about the Gathering, Ruth?"

"Tomorrow at two o'clock Eastern time. Would you let Chris know?"

"I can, but he can't bi-locate from where he's at."

"Maybe he could find a way to leave the compound?"

I shrug then I retrieve my phone from my room and text a message to Chris. My phone immediately begins to ring. It's Chris.

Anticipation of hearing his voice sends exhilarating zings from my head to my toes. "Hello?"

"Hey, Calli, I have a few minutes, what did you need?"

My arms prickle with goosebumps when I hear his

smooth-as-chocolate words. Remembering we might be monitored, I think about a way to be subtle. "Chris, are you able to request some time outside the Bureau where you can meditate? Perhaps meditate on Janice's good heart, like say, at two o'clock tomorrow afternoon?"

"Hmm. I'll have to ask permission. Max will want to come, of course."

"Sure, but it will be boring for him to watch you meditate."

"True. Well, I hope I'm allowed to have a meditation session. I miss you, Calli."

"I miss you, too."

💍 💍 💍

The hours leading up to the scheduled Gathering drag on at a sluggish pace. I'm curious about the news being shared, but more excited to possibly see Chris again, even if only bi-located. General Appleton has been quite generous with Chris, like allowing him to take me to meet his mother. Perhaps meditation time will be granted as well.

After I arrive in my bi-located form, my eyes travel hungrily over the group of Bearers searching for Chris. He's not here. Not yet anyway. I half-expected he'd text or call to let me know if he'd be able to join, but I also understand that sometimes decisions are not finalized until the very last moment.

I nod to Ruth, Duncan, and Aernoud and move my form near Fabian and Mary to exchange greetings.

Amenemhet appears next to me. I greet him and he nods.

I ask, "Have you been able to get any information out of Sven?"

"Not yet. We're on our way to the Denver house for

help with the interrogation. We should arrive today."

"Where's Jie Wen?"

"He's driving right now. We can't both bi-locate with a prisoner. One of us needs to keep an eye on the present circumstances."

"I understand." I think back to when Marketa was my guardian at college. We could both bi-locate if we knew we were locked in our room, secured. Otherwise, she would guard me while I bi-located.

Then Chris appears to my left. My heart leaps out of my chest upon seeing him. I want to hug him and clearly, he wants the same, but we cannot.

He asks, "What is this Gathering all about?"

"I don't know yet. I'm so happy you were allowed to leave the Bureau, Chris."

"Me too."

"Is Max with you?" I ask.

"Yeah."

With a commanding tone, Maetha says, "Let's begin. The power-removing machine is completed, and we will be testing it soon. The first person to voluntarily go through the power-removing process will be the Healer Anika Evanston. She has decided to have her power removed and stored in a quartz. She will give the quartz to Chris Harding to aid with his ongoing heart issues."

"What?" Chris exclaims. "No!"

Anika is not present to hear Chris's response.

Several Bearers talk amongst themselves, discussing the difference of Chris's heart compared to other Unaltered hearts and the acceptance of a diamond.

Maetha continues. "This is her choice, Chris. She feels her power would be better used by you to be able to repair your heart against the strain of the diamond."

I ask, "But what if the machine doesn't work? What if

it hurts her instead?"

"Don has expressed no doubt on the matter, and Anika's future is optimistic. Let's honor Anika for her willingness to help the Bearers attain the next level of defense against the Reapers. The inaugural run of the machine will take place in exactly one week. I recommend Calli and Chris be present for this momentous occasion. Anyone else wishing to be here is welcome. This is a moment of celebration, and we must remember that."

"Wait," my stomach drops in dread, "is this a Surrendering? Like with Yeok Choo?"

"No." Maetha's answer doesn't sound like she's certain.

Chris chokes out a strangled reply, "What?"

"Well, Anika's future is visible, so we know she won't die going through the machine."

"But?"

"No buts, Chris. Anika is choosing this. She has not been coerced in any way." Maetha glances around the circle and adds, "That is all I needed to announce. If there are no questions, the Gathering is over."

Many Bearers' forms disappear instantly. I turn to Chris. "Do you think you'll be able to convince the general to let you travel to Bermuda next week?"

"He's given me many freedoms lately, like this outside meditation time. He might."

"That's good to hear."

"But Calli, I don't want Anika to give up her power just for me."

I wish I could help convince him he needs a quartz to save his life, and that Anika is choosing to support nature by parting with her power, but I can't. He'll have to reach this conclusion on his own.

A few hours after the Gathering, Jie Wen and Amenemhet arrive with Sven.

Jie Wen holds Sven's arm, directing him through the house and into Ruth's bedroom where he sits Sven on the bed. We follow.

Sven has a smirk plastered on his face that reeks of self-satisfaction. Without reading his mind, I can tell he thinks he's pretty resistant against Diamond Bearers' powers, and so far, he's right.

Brand steps forward. "I wanna go first." He rubs his hands together and then sits adjacent to Sven. I'm eager to see Sven crack.

Sven looks at each of us standing before him and then at Brand. "You won't get anything out of me. None of you!"

"Sounds like a challenge to me." Brand inches closer and stares at Sven, who stares right back. They sit there staring at each other for several seconds.

Sven laughs. "What? Are you trying to read my mind or something? No one can read my mind. Didn't they tell you that?" He looks at Jie Wen and Amenemhet.

Brand's eyebrows lower and he clears his throat. Repositioning in his spot, he continues staring at Sven. I know what's happening. Brand is trying question after question, trying to find one Sven will react to or respond with answers. For every second that passes, Brand has asked ten questions—or something like that. He said he loses one-tenth of a second every time he repeats.

Brand bolts up from his seat and storms out of the room in a huff. He must have run out of questions.

I step forward. "My turn." I pull a seat close to the bed and look at Sven.

He moves his mouth like he's cleaning his teeth with his tongue, then smacks his lips as if to say, *"You'll never get me to crack."*

I turn my head and call, "Hey Brand, come back in here."

Brand appears in the doorway.

"I want to try extracting his memories. Would you repeat with me when I ask?"

Brand nods.

Jie Wen throws his hands up, and leaves the room, which is just fine with me. I have the Blue diamond which might give me the edge over Jie Wen's abilities, but I don't want him to know I have it. The other Bearers leave the room, too, leaving only me, Brand, and Sven.

I feel into Sven's mind and detect a strange resistance. I turn to Brand. "Did you feel the block?"

"Yes. I couldn't bring him on a repeat with me. It's a disabler of some kind."

"I think it's the confusion powder we ran into in China."

"Makes sense."

Sven eyes us curiously and opens his mouth to say something, but I interrupt him and say, "Repeat, Brand."

The room whirls around and stops right after the other Bearers leave the room. I decide to try the Mind-Control power from the Blue Diamond. Again, I'm halted by the mysterious blockade.

Sven snarls, "You are pathetic losers!"

Something about his demeanor and tone strikes a bad note in my entire body. I'm frustrated and angry to be called a loser. It's petty, I know, but with Jie Wen in the house, I've already felt these kinds of sentiments being directed my way. And for no good reason. To hear the words hit my ears externally, not originating from my internal thoughts, my heart races and my ring begins to burn on my finger.

Suddenly, his mind opens to mine. I don't ask why but take advantage of the change in the situation. I search for

Sven's memories concerning the Reapers and the power-removing machine. A scene unfolds and I see through Sven's eyes. He's riding in a transport truck with another man, driving by a lake with mountains in the distance. A road sign indicates they are near Salt Lake City, Utah. Sven points ahead and says, "Take this exit to the truck stop."

After the driver maneuvers off the road and parks behind a line of large trucks, Sven and the driver get out and open the back door of the truck. Inside the darkness sit at least ten restrained adults, both men and women.

Sven says, "All right, we're going to let you go. There'll be no trouble if you all keep your mouth shut and don't call the police. I mean, what would you tell them anyway? That your superpowers were taken from you?" Sven and the other man laugh together, then begin releasing the prisoners. In Sven's mind, however, he's relieved the prisoners are all alive and not harmed physically.

I pull out of Sven's mind for a moment to refocus, note his surprised expression at my ability to get inside his memories, then dive back in even deeper. I want to know where the facility is located. Where did these people lose their powers? A scene opens with Sven and the other man waiting in a car at a different truck stop. I can't tell where they are.

"Here they come," the other man says, nodding in the direction of an approaching transport truck.

Sven and the man get out of the car and walk to the transport truck. The driver climbs down and hands the keys to Sven's partner. Sven walks around the front of the truck and climbs inside. His partner speaks with the other guy and then climbs up into the driver's seat.

"Where to?" Sven asks.

"East. SLC."

"SLC? That's a long ride. Will they make it that far?"

"Not our problem."

"Yes, it is. We can't dump bodies."

"What do you suggest?"

"Let's at least get them water."

"You do it."

Sven grabs the door handle and exits the truck. He hurries inside the store and buys a case of water bottles for the "cargo." As he exits the store, he sees a police car parked nearby. The logo on the door says "Reno."

I pull out of Sven's mind. "You picked up cargo in Reno, Nevada, and dropped them off in Salt Lake City, Utah?"

He doesn't answer, but his rapid breathing and scared-to-death expression speaks volumes.

My mind swims with weakness. I turn to Brand. "Go get Ruth. Hurry."

"Do you want me to repeat?"

"No. I want Sven to remember what I saw."

Soon, Ruth enters the room and I grasp desperately for her hand. Once I'm able to draw strength from her, I slow down the exhaustion in my body and prevent myself from passing out.

"Is your finger okay, Calli," Brand asks. The tremble in his voice causes me to look at my finger. My engagement ring is glowing a little. I realize it must have enhanced my Reader ability, which is why I could break through Sven's defenses.

"It'll be fine."

"Okaaay. It's just, well, it kinda had little lightning things." He wiggles his fingers. "You know those glass plasma globes that have lightning inside that connects with your hand when you touch it? That's what that looked like. Sort of."

"Brand, are you going to be okay?" I try to downplay

what he's seen. In truth, I'm happy I didn't electrocute anyone.

Ruth interrupts any answer and asks me, "What did you learn?"

I look at Sven. "Where is the machine located?"

Apparently, me being in his mind has freaked him out. His tough demeanor melts into a puddle. "I don't know. I was instructed to transport. Nothing more. You saw it. The truck came to us. I don't know from where."

The other Bearers return to the room and listen to the exchange. I continue, "Well, Sven, how did you come to work at the Texas facility?"

"I've done a lot of small jobs for Vorherrschaft. Then I got hired on there in Texas."

"Who hired you?"

"Mr. Schweizer. Armin Schweizer. He's like the big boss."

Jie Wen sits beside me. "Let me take over, Calli. Go with Ruth to heal."

I don't argue. I'm weak and I know it. Ruth helps me into the living room and sits with me on the couch.

Ruth touches the ring. "This enhancer works with both Healer and Reader powers. That's unusual."

"It's all unusual. I'm going to take a nap, okay?" It's not so much that I want to take a nap, as it is my eyes are closing and I can't stop them. Restoring my energy will take much longer without Chris's healing kisses, but at least I know I'll be protected while I rest.

I am awakened by the rising sun. How long did I sleep? And how did I get to my bed? Sitting upright, my head swims a little then settles down enough for me to stand. I grab my phone and head to the kitchen for some food.

Jie Wen, Amenemhet, Duncan, and Ruth sit around the

small table talking.

Ruth acknowledges me. "Good morning. Are you back to one hundred percent?"

"Yes. Thank you. What else did you find out?" I ask Jie Wen.

"Sven directed me to a website with an image of Armin Schweizer. I recognized him as one of the men from the compound in China, although I didn't know he was the leader. I never met him personally through my dealings with the group. Sven believes Mr. Schweizer is headquartered here in the U.S. Sven also talked about other machines in the process of being set up in the western states and western Canada ahead of the coming power blast."

Duncan sets his coffee cup down. "How did the Reapers find out about the Elemental blast? This kind of preplanning indicates prior knowledge, perhaps even before we knew about it."

I purse my lips, then say, "Crimson has known for several thousand years this blast was coming. Maetha has known for at least several hundred years. Somewhere along the way, that knowledge leaked, and the wrong people got ahold of it."

Amenemhet shakes his head. "Freedom knew. He found out from Neema, who learned from Maetha."

Aernoud slouches back in his chair. "Meanwhile, I've been off saving scientists who will prevent coming plagues, missing out on all the action."

"Well," Ruth responds, "you're in the thick of it, now."

Aernoud chuckles, "We can hold Bearer Gatherings and share information. Why aren't we utilizing that to keep everyone up to date on all the findings and happenings?"

Jie Wen's countenance darkens. "That's not how Crimson operates. Everything is on a need-to-know basis, and we don't need to know everything." His eyes dart to mine. "Secrets and incomplete knowledge are the name of the game."

"I didn't invent the game, Jie Wen."

"True. You're merely the newest pawn." *—with an exclusive shiny trinket no one else has,* he adds, speaking only to my mind.

You're just jealous I was able to do something you couldn't. Is he talking about my ring or my Blue diamond?

He clears his throat, seemingly aware the tension in the room has centered on the two of us. "But we've all had our turn at being the newest pawn, haven't we." He stands and stretches his back. "Let's get back to work."

Chapter Fourteen - Anika's Gift

Jie Wen, Amenemhet, and Sven stay a couple days, then travel on to some secret location Jie Wen has been busy setting up. Apparently, there are several reformed Reapers residing there. Sven will be given the opportunity to choose for himself if he'd like to switch sides. When I asked where this facility is located, Jie Wen refused to answer. Jie Wen likes to complain about not having transparency with Crimson and Maetha but then goes on to set up his own secret operations.

I wanted to tell Chris all about the events that transpired, but I couldn't risk revealing something by accident. Instead, our conversations have centered on the fact that he will be allowed to travel with me to Bermuda for the inaugural use of the Bearers' machine. Max will not be coming, thank goodness, due to Chris successfully convincing General Appleton to allow the trip. Chris's argument included my diligent phone call 'check-ins' with Max and my willingness to cooperate. Of course, it won't stop Max from tracking Chris as much as possible.

We arrive at the airport hangar in Denver, board Maetha's plane, and find Beth waiting inside. Anika had personally invited her to attend. I'm a bit relieved for Brand to have someone to talk with on the flight so I can rest. She looks good and seems happy and confident with herself, which is wonderful.

Our stop in Washington, D.C. to pick up Chris and refuel is efficiently handled and soon we're up in the air on our way to Bermuda. I use the opportunity to catch Chris up on all the happenings since the last time we could share secrets. He also updates me on information he's learned at The Bureau such as a recent trip to Portland that included Vita and the Seers from the facility. Vita had knowledge of the blast the general hadn't heard before, which felt alarming. I can only assume Jonas is responsible for her visions of the future.

Jonas.

I still feel gut shot whenever I think about him joining Vita.

Once we arrive at the island dock, Chris, Brand, Beth, and I seek out Anika. We find her at the beach, sitting on the hard wet sand, with her arms wrapped around her knees. A gentle breeze ruffles the blonde hair off her shoulders. As we approach, she turns toward us.

"Hey, guys. Come join me." She pats the sand next to her.

We sit. I position myself nearest to Anika as I can feel her trepidation. She's nervous and a little frightened.

Brand launches in with questions. "Why would you want to part with your Healer power, Anika?"

Anika tightens the hold on her knees. "The machine needs to be tested. I want to donate my power to Chris. It's wasted on me." Her words sound rehearsed.

"Wasted. How so?" Brand asks.

"Every time I use the healing power, I feel like I'm taking God's will out of the equation."

I believe I can hear Brand's eyes roll in their sockets.

Chris leans forward and places a hand on her forearm. "But what if it was God's will that you received the power?"

"I don't believe that to be so, Chris. I view this power as an infection, an invader in my body, and I want to be healed from this illness. The machine will clear me of this unwanted thing that I liken to witchcraft."

"Whoa!" Brand seemingly inflates to twice his size. "How dare you compare cosmic powers to witchcraft! You're basically accusing all of us of being evil, which we're not."

"No, Brand, that's not what I'm saying."

"Sounds like you are."

"I don't feel I have the right to decide who lives or dies."

Brand's shoulders hunch forward, no longer defensive, which leads me to believe he's repeating. His irate tone drops a notch, too. "You're just scared to use your power, intimidated by what you can do. I don't think you trust yourself to do good with your ability to heal, so you want it sucked out of your body. And you know how I know this?" His question hangs in the air as he exhales. "Because I felt the same way." His voice softens further, and he dips his chin. "I didn't fight when my power was removed. I wanted it gone. I felt like you feel now."

Anika pulls her knees even closer to her chest and rests her chin on them. "You don't know how I feel, Brand. None of you do." Her words are quiet and heavy. "I choose to go through the machine and donate my power to Chris."

Chris's head drops.

Are you okay? I ask him.

Not really, but I guess by receiving Anika's power, I can protect it in the event she changes her mind and wants her quartz back. Kind of like with Brand and how he's able to have his power.

That's a good way to look at it.

Chris, Brand, and I leave Anika and Beth alone on the beach and walk to the main house to see if we can help with anything. With nearly all the Bearers in attendance, I'm sure there's plenty of work to be done.

We sit outside the room while Anika is run through the machine. The situation feels ominous. I'm worried for Anika because the machine hasn't been used before. Things could go wrong, a misfire, or an overabundance of radiation; even though other Bearers have looked to the future and confirmed she will not be harmed, I'm still concerned.

Anika was supposed to save thousands of lives in the upcoming blast, according to Crimson.

What now?

Tod and Mishell walk toward us, talking to each other. I call Mishell over. "Do you have a moment to talk?"

"Sure, Calli."

"I wanted to let you know how the experiments with the quartz blanket went." I go on to tell her about our tests and conclusions, one being that the healing power isn't magnified by the size of the blanket. Basically, one-fourth of the dimensions is enough to deliver the maximum power. Also, I suggest creating clothing such as an undershirt to deliver the healing properties without needing to wrap in a blanket. This way it can also be worn without having to worry about it falling off the person. She is responsive to my suggestions and thanks me before heading downstairs.

Jie Wen has arrived from the mainland and is talking to Maetha downstairs about something to do with Portland. I can't focus on his words. I'm too busy watching the lights dim and flicker as the process of removing Anika's power progresses and I'm reminded of when Chris's body moved through the machine. Then, the lights regain their full power and I realize Anika is now an Unaltered, like Chris and Brand . . . and Max.

The door opens and Don walks out with Anika. She has an Unaltered's aura.

"Are you sure you're okay?" Uncle Don asks.

"Yes." She beams ear to ear. "I've never felt better in

my whole life!" She glances at us briefly, gives a quick nod, and walks away.

Don says, "Well, so far it looks like the machine works. We will have wait for the crystal to cool before we can test it out."

"Let's get some food," Brand says, rubbing his stomach, as he starts down the stairs.

We follow him to the buffet of prepared food where most of the other Bearers are gathered, talking with Anika. After a short time of questions and answers, we dish up our plates and sit at the table with her.

"So, Anika," Brand asks, "what are you going to do now?" His question feels out of place and too abrupt. He must be repeating, again.

"I don't know. Maybe go stay with my grandparents until I figure out what I want."

I turn to Anika. "You are always welcome to help us with the blast in Portland. We need smart, capable individuals like you to identify and tackle the organizational logistics. Besides, I'd rather have you help than try to find another person with cosmic powers and hope they'll be as dedicated as you."

"Thank you, Calli. I'll think about it." She smiles.

After eating and listening to several reports from the Bearers concerning the Portland blast, Chris and I climb the stairs to the machine room. In the corner, on top of the metal pyramid, sits the charged quartz.

"Do you feel ready to experiment?" I ask.

"Only if that means you and I get to make out." His eyes turn a deep blue as he speaks the words.

"How else would we test the effectiveness if not on your heart? I'd be happy to get your heart racing." I spot a small empty box nearby, pick it up, and scoot the quartz off the pyramid and into the box. "Let's go ask Brand if this thing is dangerous."

"How would he know?" Chris asks.

I blink my eyes repeatedly and let out a puff of air. "He's Brand. He'll know. Come on."

As we enter the room where Brand sits talking to Anika, he pauses and looks up, saying before I even speak, "The quartz is fine. Anyone can hold it."

I glance over at Chris who has a perplexed expression on his face as he chews on his bottom lip.

Anika stands and walks over to us. "May I see it?" I open the box and extend my arm for her to see inside. "Wow. It's hard to understand how all my power could fit inside that quartz.

Not sure what to say, I offer, "Someday, we'll understand how this all works. For now, Chris and I need to go test its power."

"Have fun," Brand chides.

Before leaving the main house, I communicate with Maetha's mind. *Chris and I, well, mainly Chris, will be using obsidian for a little while to see if the quartz will be effective on his heart.*

Thank you for letting me know, she responds.

We take the cooled quartz and head to my bungalow on the beach. My heart races with anticipation to both discover if Chris's life can be protected with the quartz, and to have some alone time with him.

Once inside, Chris opens the metal container holding obsidian and removes a small piece. He winces, squeezing his eyes shut for a moment as his powers flee, then he sits on the couch.

"This isn't enough to threaten my life immediately, well, unless I get a little excited. Then I'll feel pain."

"I can help with that." I sit beside him, setting the box nearby, and wrap my arms around his neck and immediately my powers flee my body. I add, "Not that I want to cause you pain, but I do want to be able to effectively test the quartz."

"I know. I'm willing to feel some pain if it will help us learn new limits. It's for science."

"I'm all about scientific research. Like, if I kiss only your bottom lip, does that hurt?"

"Hurts so good."

"What about if I nibble on your earlobe like this?" I move my mouth to his ear and nuzzle on the soft skin.

Chris whispers, "Okay, where's the quartz?"

I pull my head back. "So soon?"

"You have a hold of my heart, Calli, figuratively and literally."

I reach over and grab the quartz and hand it to him. "Keep hold of the obsidian so your diamond doesn't kick in." Then I stand and move away from him.

He clutches the quartz as if his life depends on it, which it sort of does, then a smile begins to form across his lips. His hold on the quartz loosens a little and his eyes meet mine. "It works, Calli. I can heal my own heart. Anika's Healer power works well. I mean, it's not as quick as the topaz charged with Sanguine Diamond Healer power, but this doesn't drain like the topaz."

"What a relief, Chris."

He looks me up and down as I stand in front of him.

"Is something wrong?" I ask.

"I can sense the diamond . . . in your heart." His eyes rest on my sternum. "You mentioned the Healer Rhonda could sense your diamond with a quartz."

"Yes."

"Now I understand the danger with this. Anyone

holding a Healer quartz could potentially find Bearers." He looks at the obsidian in his hand, then extends his hand to me. "Take this. I want to see if the quartz is affected by obsidian."

I'm hesitant to accept it. "We already know Brand can still use his quartz powers in the presence of obsidian."

"Just take it, Calli. Let's see for sure."

I let him drop the shard of volcanic glass into my hand and again, feel the rush of my powers fleeing away. I don't like this sensation. Chris looks me over, then reaches forward for the obsidian which I am glad to give back. He returns the obsidian to the metal container and I'm able to feel inside his body to evaluate his heart's healthy condition.

He says, "I could sense your diamond the same, with or without the obsidian."

"Okay, that solves that."

"I only hope other, less experienced Reapers won't understand what they're sensing when they're around Diamond Bearers. Still, we all need to be aware they might. I'll take it upon myself to alert each Bearer to this issue, so they can better protect themselves." Chris reaches forward and pulls me onto his lap. I wrap one arm behind his shoulders for stability and to increase our closeness. "Where were we?"

"You want to keep experimenting?"

"Yes." He guides my lips to his and kisses me gently, then says, "I need to see if I can heal my heart as it hurts, while it is in pain." He kisses me again, intensifying his actions, causing my body to react wildly.

Then the fear barges into my mind. Any second someone will appear in our space. Any moment, Crimson will speak to my mind. I remember she can hear, feel, and see everything going on between me and Chris. I push back a little and gather my thoughts.

Chris lays his head back on the couch and exhales long and loud. "I'm sorry, Calli."

"What? Why? I'm the one who ended it."

"I pushed us too far too fast. I wanted to see if I could heal my heart."

"Well, can you?"

"Yes." He lifts his head, his gaze piercing my soul. "Thanks to Anika and her sacrifice, we can be together now without fear of dying. Your bomb has been removed, my heart is not about to rip apart around obsidian, so becoming too excited won't potentially kill either of us."

"But . . . as incredible as this is, there's still the 'no privacy' thing. I'm not supposed to use obsidian for any long lengths of time."

"We just used it."

"I know, and I told Maetha ahead of time."

"Yeah. But she was okay with it."

"To test the effectiveness of the quartz." I pause for a moment. "Chris, I was told by Crimson that the future is dark if I continue to use obsidian for personal reasons. She's tried to encourage me to relax and not be so worried about others knowing we are being intimate. I can't make my brain do that. I really miss my old life and the total privacy and sense of trust I had prior to ever carrying the Sanguine Diamond."

"Help me understand why you feel this way."

"I don't know what you're asking. No privacy, no trust."

"No trust, does that include with me?"

"I trust you."

"You sure about that? I lied to you about being a spy, Calli. I was one of the first people to deceive you. Plus, I basically abandoned you on our delivery run after you brought up the witch."

"I understand why you did. I don't really think that's bothering me now."

"Well, give it some thought. I imagine Maetha and Crimson are high on your list of betrayals, too. Then there's the random bi-locating that takes place, keeping you feeling on edge. Now you can't even use obsidian to block your diamond's locating feature."

"Boy, you're not helping me feel better."

"I'm hoping I'm laying out what I see as the possible reasons you're struggling with us. I'm hoping to help you understand that I know some of what's bothering you and I'm here for you while you work through this. So, again, I'm sorry for pushing too far too fast."

I stare into Chris's mesmerizing eyes for what seems like hours.

He says, "This will take time. Luckily, we'll have our whole lives to take things as slow as we need to."

I smile. For the first time, I feel hopeful that one day we'll be able to truly be together.

Chris takes my hand and kisses the inside of my palm before saying, "For now, let's make the most of *this* time. Why don't we go outside and take in the sunset?"

My smile widens and we leave the bungalow.

Chapter Fifteen - Blue Diamond Desires

Chris and I walk along the beach as the sun drops in the sky. I'm analyzing the strong lack of privacy fears that ended our intimate moment in the bungalow. What I'm realizing is it's been a long time since I worried about Crimson being in my mind. Of course, it's been a long time since Chris and I have had enough time alone to become paranoid about Crimson's presence. That probably has something to do with it. As for the other Bearers bi-locating unannounced, maybe there's a way to block my diamond from the others without the use of obsidian. When I bi-locate to another diamond, I must first feel for the diamond. Maybe I could project a message, an interference of sorts, like an answering machine: *I'm sorry, Calli's diamond is unavailable for connection right now. Please try again later.* I chuckle under my breath. Chris's diamond would also need the message otherwise he could be connected with, too.

Pulling my attention to the present, Chris asks, "What is it about the power-removing machine that makes the healing power stronger in the quartz than that of other Healers of today's power? I mean, it's not as strong as a Diamond Bearer's power, but still."

"I don't know. Maybe it's to do with the quartz prisms that power up the machine. Maybe they enhance the absorption somehow."

"Could they be enhancers, like your ring?"

I shrug, then ask, "Where is the prism you held from your dad's machine?"

"Maetha took it before we inserted my diamond. I guess she didn't want you repeating me back to life."

"Ten seconds of repeating would not have been enough

time to determine if your heart was going to accept your diamond." I squeeze his hand firmly. "I was so scared, Chris. No one came to help. Maybe I should have used the Blue power to force Maetha to come help, but I didn't think about it at the time."

Chris stops and wraps his arms around me. "Hey," he soothes my fears, "I'm alive, you're alive."

"I knew it!" Jie Wen's voice cuts through the air, penetrating my eardrums. "You have the Blue Diamond!"

We turn our heads and see him emerging from the deep brush out onto the beach. As he nears us, Chris moves in front of me as a formidable wall against Jie Wen.

Chris asks, "Were you spying on us?"

Jie Wen taps his ear. "Hunter powers." He walks toward us, his long robe brushing the sand as he moves. "Maybe you forgot about that. Too many powers to keep track of, as you said. How long have you had the stone, Calli?"

I don't answer.

"Is this why you felt so confident when you questioned Sven? I bet Crimson is constantly whispering in your ear, telling you what to say and do. This must be why she brought on kids. They're easier to control than adults."

I lower my voice and speak slowly. "Take your questions and attitude to Crimson, Jie Wen. I don't have any answers for you."

Chris adds, "Yeah, go on." He shoos him away.

Jie Wen whirls in the direction of the main house, his robe and sandals flinging the sand up as he stomps away.

Once he's beyond the bungalow, I speak to Chris's mind. *How could I be so careless?*

I was careless, too.

Yeah, but you never mentioned the Blue Diamond.

This is not going to help you with your privacy issues. You were worried about Bearers bi-locating to you at awkward moments, which

I get; now we can add Bearers physically spying on us, too.

I feel Crimson's presence, or at least she allows me to feel it. I look up and see her entering the bubble, descending in the direction of the main house.

"Crimson's here. Come on." I take Chris by the hand and lead him to the house thinking this is either coincidence or she knew this altercation with Jie Wen was about to happen and figured she'd better be here when it did.

As we near the house, the conversation happening inside becomes audible even without super-hearing powers. I squeeze Chris's hand, and we stop moving to listen.

Jie Wen says, "Why, after everything I've done and accomplished as a Bearer, would the Blue stone go to Calli and not me? Why didn't you tell me, Maetha?"

"You know why I wouldn't tell you that," Maetha answers. "I couldn't. You are my friend, Jie Wen. You are very deserving of the Blue stone as your heart is in the right place, but that wasn't the only requirement or stipulation."

Jie Wen persists. "What did I do to fail you, Crimson?"

Crimson speaks in her classic emotionless, all business tone, "Nothing. The timing wasn't right. I needed Calli to have the stone for upcoming assignments. And now, it is clear she will be the Blue Bearer amongst the Sanguine Bearers. The future depends upon it."

Chris pulls my hand, directing me away from the conversation. We walk to Jonas' old bungalow and knock on the door.

Brand greets us with a sly smile. "How did it go?"

"How did what go?" Chris asks.

"Testing the quartz, duh!"

"Oh, right. It went well."

I nod, swallowing hard as I recall the fear of being watched, and learning soon after Jie Wen was nearby.

We enter and find Sarangerel, Anika, and Beth sitting

around the small table.

Chris adds, "Thank you, Anika. I'll take good care of your quartz."

She beams. "It's my pleasure. And don't worry, I won't be asking for it back."

We talk for a while, learning about what Sarangerel has been up to in her search through the files from both General Harding's compound and the compound in China. I start to update her on Sven's capture and the mention of the big boss, but she cuts me off.

"Jie Wen already told me about them."

"Really? When?"

"Shortly after capturing Sven. I had heard of the man, like Jie Wen, but I didn't know he was the leader of Vorherrschaft, either. Nor did my parents."

"Oh. Maybe there's another person higher up?"

"Whoever set up Vorherrschaft, I would think, is the leader. But we don't know who that is. Yet."

As Chris walks me back to my bungalow for the night along the dimly lit path through the tropical paradise, he says, "I don't want to go back to D.C. tomorrow. Can't we just stay here until the blast? We could pretend we're shipwreck survivors, carving out an existence the best we can."

"Ooh, I like your imaginative mind. We'll be back in June, you know, and that's not far off."

"Just so you know, I've been suggesting to General Appleton that I should be released once we get married. I'm going to push for even earlier. There's no reason anymore for me to be held as collateral. You've complied fully, and

I've been a model prisoner. Besides, we're in the final stages of arranging a full relocation."

"Yeah. I know Maetha is actively searching for housing, as well."

Chris nods and takes both my hands in his and squeezes gently. "You know, with the whole Jie Wen thing that happened today, I have a greater understanding of what you're feeling about privacy, or lack thereof."

"Thanks, that means a lot to me, Chris. Would you like to stay with me tonight . . . you know, platonically?"

"Absolutely!"

💍 💍 💍

After dropping Chris off in D.C. on our return flight, I call Max.

"I'm headed back to Denver," I say when he answers the phone.

"What happened in Bermuda?"

"Family reunion."

"No, really. What happened?"

"Bye Max."

"Wait! Call me when you get to Denver."

"You know, this is stupid. I waste a lot of time keeping you updated on trivial traveling. How about I call when something significant happens."

"That's not the arrangement."

"Well, how long does this arrangement go on for? Because in August the blast hits, and then what?"

"You'll always be on our radar, Calli."

"Bye." I end the call before he can say anything else. *You'll always be on our radar?* I don't like the sound of that.

I sit back in my seat and rest my head. I want to be more involved in the research aspect, combing through the files, like Sarangerel. Instead, I'm headed back to Denver to sit still, taking turns cooking and cleaning while waiting for the next time I get to leave the house.

ܯ ܯ ܯ

After a week has passed, Maetha bi-locates and gives information about a rental opportunity in Portland for me and Chris. This could be a possible "home base" for us, if it suits our needs. She will organize a trip to Oregon so I can go check it out.

I text Chris and give him the update, with promises of photos if the apartment looks good.

Following a bumpy flight into PDX, due to spring rainstorms, we have a quick meeting again with Janet, the TSA Director, for an update on the preparations for August. Her information is succinct and businesslike surrounding the redirecting of inbound flights on that day to relieve the influx of people who will need to be evacuated.

With that meeting wrapped up, we head to the rental car and drive to the address Maetha provided east of Portland in the foothills of the mountainous Cascade Range. The potential landlord's name is Iva Brunelli. Maetha said she's a Healer with a massage therapy practice in Portland. She has a guest house above a stand-alone garage on her property.

I find the location to be perfect—a little over five miles from downtown Portland—in a heavily forested area with ferns and flowering plants everywhere. As I climb out of the car, the tranquility of the forest washes over me. The many different bird species calling out to one another is beautiful to hear, and the smell of ferns, bark, and evergreens ground me in nature's splendor.

Upon meeting Iva, I find her charming and down to earth. She's heard of me and my whole deal with the Death Clan but displays no emotion good or bad to be closely associated with me. I guess that's good. She shows us the apartment above the garage. I love the vibes I feel while walking through the apartment and out on the grounds and can totally see Chris and I living here. There's even enough room for my entourage, too. Not that there's a chance they wouldn't stay with me.

Iva offered her parked camper as temporary housing, too.

We drive to our hotel for the night and Ruth communicates with Maetha who states she will handle the payments to secure the location, then Chris and I can take it from there.

I can't view my future to see how long we'll continue to live in Portland following the blast, so I'm not able to commit to any length of time with Iva. For now, I'm simply happy to have a place lined up.

After breakfast, Crimson speaks to my mind. *Tell your guardians I'm coming to pick you up for a few hours.*

Okay. Can I ask where we're going?

Not far, but dress for the weather.

I inform the others of the impromptu visit and put on my shoes and grab my rain jacket.

When Crimson arrives, she takes me to the elevator, and we ascend to the top floor of the hotel. Crimson leads the way to the staircase for roof access. I follow her up the stairs not knowing what to expect.

We emerge onto the damp rooftop. The rain has ceased for the moment, but more dark clouds are on the way.

"See each of those buttes?" She points to three different hills amongst the buildings and homes, turning in a circle as she does so. "We will position the quartz channeling stones there, there, and there. This spot right here should work well enough to absorb the blast."

"I'm sorry?"

"What?"

I swing my arm in a wide sweeping action. "*This* isn't what my visions show."

She turns and stares intensely at me.

I continue. "In my visions, the Willamette River was between the building and Mount Hood. And the building was taller, with many floors."

"Downtown Portland? How long have you been seeing the blast that way?"

I chew on my lip while I try to remember. "I, uh, don't know. The whole time. Wait, is this place where *you've* always seen the blast hitting?"

"When I started seeing the future blast, this continent didn't even have a name. The indigenous people had villages near the river, so I was able to pinpoint the area and watch as it developed over the last few centuries. The exact location of where the blast will hit isn't as crucial so much as the positioning of the quartz funnel."

"Funnel?"

She motions to the mountains. "I always figured we'd utilize the prominent buttes to set up the channeling funnel, and you'd be in the center with a Sanguine Diamond to capture the ray."

"Do we have to use the buttes?"

"We don't have to. The channeling quartzes need to be positioned higher than you. Naturally occurring high spots are the ideal positioning, but we can improvise. Come," —she extends her hand to me— "let's go find that building."

"Why don't you just view my mind for the vision I saw," I ask as I take her hand.

"I would be weakened."

"I don't understand. You're Crimson. You're always in my mind. Why aren't you able to see what I saw?"

"We don't have time to drive around the city. Come. Let's do this my way." She ignores my question, which frustrates me. She pulls me to her body and I realize she means to fly. My stomach drops. I really don't like flying.

"Activate Invisibility, Calli." She wraps her arms around me, and we lift off, leaving behind the security of solid ground. As we climb higher, I focus on the roads below, watching the traffic snake along, and think about the evacuation routes to occupy my mind. I quickly identify Interstate 84 and where it merges with the I-5 right alongside the Willamette River. Traffic is snarled in all directions at this intersection. Rush hour is fully underway. I hate to admit it, but Crimson was right with her choice to fly versus driving in this mess.

Our bodies float across the river and toward the tallest nearby building. Crimson lowers us to the rooftop. "Keep your Invisibility activated. Now, is this location closer to what you've seen in your visions?"

I can immediately tell it's not. "No, the river is too close. We need to be further west and north." Crimson takes hold of me and again we lift off, flying toward a tall building, closer to the mountains. We touch down and I feel we are close to the location. I walk to the edge of the building and peek over the side. It's so close, but not quite right. I turn to Crimson and say, "Let's move over to that building."

After one more building hop, I glance over the side and see the exact image from my vision. "This is it! This is exactly what I saw." I turn around, feeling satisfied, and find Crimson looking at me with an unreadable gaze. "What's the matter?" I ask.

"Nothing."

"That expression doesn't look like nothing."

"We will have to erect polls or antennas of our own to make this location work."

I survey the area. "Could we use that mountainside over there? Or what about existing antennas on top of buildings?"

"I will look into it. The triangulation formula is precise. It must maintain perfect shape, or we risk a larger fallout zone." Crimson turns full circle looking in all directions, then says, "I believe I can make this work."

I nearly choke on my words. "You believe? Crimson, I've already seen the vision. It works."

"Did your vision reveal where to place the quartzes?"

"No. But I guess it reveals *you'll* figure it out." I smile. I walk to the side of the building and peer down to the roads below, remembering the feelings from the vision after the blast hits. The ring on my finger will turn deep green and I won't be able to take it off. I remember Crimson's words of apology. I don't know what she meant or will mean.

She says, "Let's return to the hotel. Come." She wraps her arms around me and lifts off into the air. We move slowly. I think she is scouting the area with her eyes, and I wonder what must be going through her mind. I know what's going through my mind—*I don't like flying.* We land on the roof of my hotel once again and she says, "Remain invisible until we are inside the stairwell."

I do as she says and follow her through the door. After she drops her Invisibility, I do the same.

"I want to give you a gift, Calli." Crimson pushes her hand inside the pocket of her slacks and pulls out a small brown box.

"What's this for?"

She hands the box to me. I can nearly close my fingers

around the whole thing. It's not heavy, nor is it light. Whatever is inside has substance to it.

"It's an early wedding gift," Crimson says.

I hold the box up and examine it closely. "I guess it's too small to be an electric can opener."

She smiles. Crimson doesn't do that very often. "Open it."

I lift the lid and am greeted by an intense blue glow. The only other time I've seen this shade of blue was when Crimson gave me Maetha's Grecian Blue Diamond. Resting in a satin cradle is what looks like more of the Blue Diamond.

The air has escaped my lungs. "Crimson, what is this?"

"You know what it is."

"But why? More of the diamond won't give me more power."

"The best gift I can give you is privacy. I'm giving you the *full* Grecian Blue Diamond and cutting my connection to your mind, so you don't have to worry about me meddling in your thoughts. Also, so you don't feel the need to use obsidian for privacy. The use of obsidian in your future changes much more than you could imagine. You need to try to avoid it."

I twist the stone between my fingers in admiration. "But what if I need to contact you?"

"Let Maetha know. She'll pass the word along."

"I don't know what to say," I whisper as I gaze deep into the diamond. "How do I insert the stone?"

"You're wondering if you have to swallow it."

"Kinda."

"You don't."

Slight panic erupts in my chest. "Do I have to jam it into my heart?"

"If you want."

"I don't understand."

"Calli, you don't have to do anything with this diamond. You already have the full power in the small piece inside your body. Like you said, more of this stone will not give you more power."

"So, what do I do with it?"

"Whatever you want, but with exception. It is a valuable stone."

"What do you recommend?"

"I recommend you find a safe place, somewhere it can be retrieved easily, yet not easily found by others. I don't need to tell you that in the wrong hands, this power . . . well, you can imagine."

"I understand. Can I tell Chris?"

"If you like. I really want you to not worry about me when making your decisions. And don't worry about Maetha. Do what you feel is beneficial and in the best interests of keeping humanity moving forward. Keep us updated on how we can help with what you decide to do. Oh, and Calli, it's best not to tell Jie Wen."

"May I ask why?"

"The long-range future is dark if Jie Wen has a Blue Diamond; the same is true if you have a prism from General Harding's machine with the Repeater power. Neither of you are evil minded, neither of you disrespect nature's will, but something in your minds click when in the possession of certain stones. The why or how doesn't matter, nor should you waste any energy trying to solve the problem. Just know sometimes some people are not able to resist temptations. We have the luxury of foreseeing a weak spot for you and Jie Wen. Having this knowledge of what to avoid, preventing mishaps along your life's pathway, is a gift."

"Okay. I understand. However, now I'm even more curious."

"A classic human trait, to be sure."

"I'll have to figure out where to hide this."

"For now, put it in your pocket."

💍 💍 💍

As soon as I'm alone, I dial Chris and wait for him to answer.

"Chris, Chris!" I nearly shout.

"What is it, Calli! Are you okay?"

"I'm fine. More than fine." How can I tell him I have the full blue stone without divulging too much information? "I wanted to share something that happened to me today."

"Is it something you could say to everyone at the Bureau?"

I recognize his cautious warning. "I could, but it would be boring to them. I was feeling a little blue earlier today—I'm always missing you, of course—but then I received a gift and it made me feel completely blue."

"That doesn't sound like a good gift. What was it?"

"A trinket. A complete gift from the heart."

"Why did that make you feel blue?"

"It made me think of you and frustrated by the fact I can't be with you right now while I'm in possession of this trinket."

"I'm not sure I understand. What did you get?"

"The gift of privacy."

"Umm, okaaay."

"An old lady gave it to me. She said she didn't need it anymore, and like I said, the moment I held it in my hands I immediately thought of you."

"And you felt *com-plete-ly blue*?" he drags out his words.

Ah! He understands. A giant smile erupts on my face and carries through with my lower-octave words. "That's right. I can't wait to show it to you."

"I can't wait to see it." His tone drops to almost a whisper. "When will that be, though?"

"I don't know."

"Well, coming up in a couple weeks, this whole operation is moving to Portland. Maybe we'll be able to see each other then."

I lay in bed that night, thinking about the fact that I now have the entire Blue Diamond. I need to figure out where to keep it safe because the power contained in the stone is monumental. Someone could control the population and their actions. Control over people is unquestionably against nature—human nature, that is. I marvel at how some people can gain control over others simply by manipulation, brainwashing, and threats, all of which when deployed result in rights lost and power gained.

But then my thoughts switch to Crimson. She is no longer in my head. She doesn't hear my thoughts or words like when we were in quantum entanglement. I'm free. Well, except for the random Diamond Bearer surprise bi-locations and physical spying like Jie Wen. However, if I request that I be "called" first prior to a communication, that should solve the privacy problem. I hope.

The thought of complete privacy with Chris floods my imagination and I drift off to sleep, a smile playing on my lips.

Chapter 16 - Flying Lessons

Crimson asked my guardians to take me to Seaside, Oregon, today. She said she has some training for me. We've been driving for two hours through the coastal mountain range and Brand hasn't stopped talking once. I don't know why he's so inquisitive about everything. At least most of his conversations have been with the other Bearers, not me. I'm happy to stare out the window at the moss-covered trees and think about the errands we ran before leaving Portland for the coast.

Earlier today, we met with the mayor about hospital evacuation plans. He's going to hold off alerting hospital officials just yet. He's concerned it might bring too much attention too soon. I told him I trusted he would make the decision at the right time.

Afterward, we visited a few businesses downtown, including a crystal and rock shop. I asked to stop there to look for a topaz I could charge with Reader powers. I found one. It's currently strapped to my skin, absorbing my power.

The highway we're driving on has many tight curves and it makes me think about how fun it would be to drive my Cooper right now. I've missed my car. Fortunately, my parents are coming to visit soon, and they're bringing my Cooper. They plan to find an apartment or condo to rent for late July and into August. I'm happy to see them again—and super excited to drive my car. Heaviness settles over me as I realize I won't be able to get behind the wheel and zip all over the city until after the first of August.

In fact, I can't do much of anything on my own, except use the bathroom.

Coincidentally, while in the bathroom this morning,

before we left my apartment, I overheard Ruth talking with Duncan about other arrangements being planned for me to be removed from the region two days prior to the blast for safety's sake and then brought back hours before the blast. Apparently, the future shows great unrest in the lead-up and during the mass evacuation of the city. Even though my apartment is outside the blast radius, we are located near one of the main roads out of town, and there will be a lot of traffic during that time. No word yet if Chris will be allowed to stay with me or if he'll still be under government surveillance.

Thoughts of Chris rise to the top and crowd out everything else, bringing flutters to my stomach. I try to hide my smile as I daydream about Chris and the fact that I no longer have quantum entanglement with Crimson.

We arrive at the destination Crimson requested—an obscure local beach access north of Seaside.

She stands on the sand in the distance, staring off at the horizon, her long hair billowing in the gentle ocean breeze. She turns to greet us as we approach. "Good. Let's get started." She puts forth a hand to me and one to Brand. We take them. "You three can wait here or in the car. We'll be about an hour."

Before anyone can agree or protest, she pulls me and Brand close to her sides, then begins to rise off the sand.

Brand squeals with delight. "Yes! We're going to fly!"

My arms wrap around her body for dear life, even though gravity isn't trying to pull me down.

"This is so cool! Isn't this cool, Calli?"

"I don't share your enthusiasm, Brand."

"Are you afraid of heights?"

"That's not the part I don't like."

Crimson says, "Hold on, Brand."

He wraps his arms around her and me, then Crimson launches to the west, out over the ocean. Brand's squeals turn into screams, but they are short lived when Crimson slows our speed as we approach a fishing boat. She lowers us to the bow.

I ask Brand as soon as my feet are on the deck, "So, do you like flying?"

He runs to the railing and vomits over the side. Wiping his mouth, he says, "Hell, yes!"

"Brand, you'll remain on the boat and will repeat whenever the need arises. I will alert you. Here are the books you requested to keep you occupied in the meantime." Then Crimson turns to me. "I'm going to teach you about gravity control, which is found in the Elemental powers."

Brand pulls a book from the box about aeronautics and sits down. "Good luck, Calli."

My stomach flips, but not because of the motion of the ocean.

Crimson pulls my attention back. "Let's talk about Newton's first law. A body remains at rest, or in motion at a constant speed in a straight line, unless acted upon by a force. The force we're dealing with today is gravity."

I nod. "Got it."

"Learn to recognize gravity as a force prevailed upon your body. If you stand in place and jump off the ground, the muscle strength in your legs determines how high you'll be able to lift your feet from the ground before coming back down. If you jump out of an airplane, you fall to earth. You can resist gravity with a parachute, but you will still be pulled to the ground. If you step off the side of this boat, you'll fall into the water. The water provides buoyancy, if utilized by swimming, or treading water. No cosmic ability required. If you stop moving in the water, you'll be pulled to the ocean floor, slower than jumping from an airplane, but all the same.

Gravity never stops.

"Regular people have learned how to defy gravity in the sky with engines, rocket boosters, propellers, and hot air. In the water, by floating devices or water displacement as with boat design. The cosmic ability coming in the Portland blast will give some the ability to control gravity's effect on the body. You will have the power infused into the diamond in your heart. You'll access the power the same way I do—with your mind. But those born with the genetic alteration will have to be taught how to control it. You can't teach them until you know how to control it yourself."

She inhales deeply before continuing. "Begin by re-training your brain to think of falling as actually being pulled down. Your first task is allowing yourself to feel the pull of gravity. She points to the side of the boat. "Go ahead, jump off the edge of the boat."

My heartrate accelerates. "But I don't have the power to resist gravity yet."

"That's right, go ahead and jump. I want you to feel the gravity pull."

"I already know what it feels like to fall into the water, thank you very much."

"Not fall but be pulled."

Brand slaps his book down on the table. "Just jump off the boat already."

"But . . ." I really don't want to jump in the water.

Crimson angles her head in my direction. "You're wasting time. We are in a moment that only happens twice a year. We must take advantage of it today because the next moment won't happen until after the blast."

I don't know what she's talking about—this "moment"—but her serious tone ruffles my feathers. I take off my shoes and look between Brand and Crimson, then run toward the railing and leap up and over, wailing as I fall toward the water. My body slaps the water's surface and I'm submerged. I kick to the surface. My head breaks through and I half expect Brand to repeat me back to the moment before I jumped overboard, but he doesn't. I swim over to the ladder at the back of the boat and pull myself up. Dripping wet, standing before the two of them, I say, "So, I know how to jump in the water. Now what?"

"Do you like being wet?" Crimson asks.

"No."

She gives me a topaz. "This is charged with gravity control."

I take the stone and notice right away the quality of the topaz is low. "Are you serious? You're giving me a topaz to fly with? Do I get a parachute, too, because the topaz will eventually run out and then I'm just out of luck."

"No. That's why we're doing this over water. Softer landing. Don't worry. I'll be with you. Plus, Brand will repeat if needed."

"Yep. That's all I'm good for, it seems." Brand stretches his arms over his head and arches his back.

I puff air through my lips. "Whatever, Brand. If you don't know how important you are to me by now, then I don't—"

He cuts me off. "I do."

"Then what?"

"When people don't want to die, they call me. I mean, you're the Diamond Bearer. View your future or something. See for yourself if you're about to die."

Crimson interjects. "Not a good use of her time when we have you. Let's begin." She extends her hand holding the topaz and produces adhesive tape with the other.

Brand says, "Yeah, no. It's not going to stick if you use that. Stuff it in your bra. That will work better."

"You already know?" I push the topaz in between my

skin and my bra. While my hand is inside my shirt, I remove the topaz I'm charging with the reading power and place the tape bundle on the table near Brand. I don't want to lose it in the ocean.

Brand smacks his lips and lifts his book to eye-level dismissively.

Crimson breaks back into the conversation and says, "This time when you jump off the side of the boat, I want you to push with your knees against the pull of gravity. Think with your mind that you are pushing against the center of the earth. Go ahead." She points to the side.

I exhale and drop my shoulders, still dripping from being in the water. "Fine. Push against gravity." I rush toward the railing and thrust myself up imagining the center of the earth has no hold over me. My body flies upward and out over the water in a large arch, as if in slow motion, and I scream at the unnaturalness of the experience. I just defied gravity! Well, a little. As I fall to the water, I brace for impact. My body slides below the surface completely and I kick to the surface for air. After swimming to the boat—a much further distance this time—I pull myself up the ladder and face Crimson once again, dripping wet but amazed at how light I felt while jumping.

She smiles. "Let's do it again. Try to push harder against the gravitational hold."

I do so. I jump higher than before, go further away from the boat.

When I return, Crimson asks for the topaz back. I give it to her, and she hands me another one. This one is high quality. I can tell by the clear characteristics. "Now, be careful with this one, Calli. When you push against gravity, you want to still feel the hold. What you're aiming for is to levitate, not fly up into the sky. You know how to push against gravity. Well, imagine yourself continuing to push against gravity after your feet have left the surface. Sometimes, it's useful to use your hands, like this." Crimson extends her arms down with her hands perpendicular to the boat deck. Her body rises about three feet off the surface, then she pulls her arms up slowly and lowers to the deck. She makes it seem so easy.

She says, "Pushing against gravity is how you'll propel yourself and also slow your movement. However, if you push too much, you'll release yourself from gravity's hold and then the world will spin below your feet. That's where trouble can happen. That's why we're over water for this training. I don't expect you to master this immediately. I didn't. What I want you to do is establish a meter of sorts in your brain. This meter has a baseline already of what it feels like to use no push against gravity—as in, what it felt like to fall into the water. You also know what it feels like to exert a little resistance against gravity. Now I want you to jump again, only this time, you'll continue to push against the pull. You'll know you're doing it right when you can hover in one place in the air. Go ahead." She waves toward the horizon.

With my heart beating loudly in my ears, and my stomach lurching, I run toward the railing and push up with my knees to clear the top rail. Again, I soar away from the boat in a large arch.

Crimson yells, "Now, push."

I follow her instruction and jam my palms down toward the water below mimicking the push of my knees. The sensation that follows is nothing I've ever felt before, not even when Crimson has taken me flying. My body stops its forward movement, and the water below starts moving rapidly like a river. I look behind to Crimson and Brand, but the boat is not there. Where did they go? I stop pushing with my hands and fall into the water. When my head breaks the surface, I search around at the unending nothingness with a sickening feeling weighing me down. Where is the boat? I don't even know which direction to swim to find them as there are no landmarks and the sun is high in the sky. I'm lost. I scream out, "Brand! Repeat!" I wait for the spin of his repeating, but nothing. Why would there be any response? He can't hear me.

Crimson bi-locates to my position and says, "Push, Calli. Push against the pull to get above the water."

I try but fail. The moment I stop treading water to push against gravity with my hands, my face sinks below the surface and I have to stop the motion and return to treading water to get air. "I can't, Crimson."

The world spins violently as Brand repeats me back to the moment I'm about to jump off the boat. I turn to Crimson. "What happened?"

She looks to Brand. "What happened?"

I think for a moment. Brand can only repeat one person. He repeated with me, not Crimson, so she doesn't know what just occurred.

Brand responds with a tired drawl, as if we are boring him terribly, "You jumped and flew away. Crimson told me to wait to repeat to see if you could instinctively master the gravitational hold. Then she closed her eyes and did the whole out of body thing, then she opened her eyes and told me to repeat."

Crimson says, "Do it again, Calli. Jump again. Brand, this time repeat with me when I tell you to."

I don't want to jump again. The fear of being lost and alone was horrible. However, Crimson is staring me down, and Brand keeps motioning with his chin in the direction I should run and jump. Fine. I start to run but only take one step when Crimson says, "Stop. You released yourself from gravity, Calli. You pushed too hard. Try dialing it down a little."

Understanding Brand just repeated with Crimson and I evidently did the same thing when I jumped from the boat the second time, that I don't remember, which still boggles my mind to try to comprehend, I say, "Explain to me why the ocean ran like a river beneath my feet."

"The water wasn't moving. The earth was rotating beneath your feet. You pushed too hard. This time don't wait to push till you're on your way down. Maintain the initial push from your legs. You may find that you'll jump high, not so much far."

"Okay."

Brand shakes his head. "No, that doesn't work, Crimson. She launches like a rocket and you're not able to bilocate to her."

Crimson and Brand stare wordlessly at each other for a couple seconds. Then she turns to me and says, "I'll need to charge you an atmospheric-control topaz before you can practice further. Let's stay with the super-jumping for now. Would you rather swim back to the boat, or would you prefer Brand to repeat you each time?"

"Repeat, I think."

"Okay, practice until your topaz is depleted."

With Brand's help, I perform the super-jumps, but without the extra effort against gravity. I get to where I can jump a couple hundred yards away from the boat and control my descent down to where I wouldn't break a leg landing if I was on solid ground. If I could land on a hard surface, I think I could do continuous jumps and cover a lot of ground. If I was invisible at the same time, no one would see me. Bonus. The trouble I run into is using the extra push when I jump. Brand only let me experience a little bit of what that feels like to have my body ignite into flames. I imagine when a meteorite crashes into our atmosphere and turns into a flaming ball, it's because of the friction the atmosphere creates. Apparently, that happens to me, too. I've noticed Crimson uses a forcefield to divide the atmosphere in front of her when she flies. That's what I'll have to do.

We practice till my topaz runs out of charge. With Brand's repeating, I was able to utilize the topaz more without it draining as quickly. However, after a few repeats, I asked him to stop due to the nausea. Instead, I chose to swim back to the boat for the remaining power left in the topaz.

After drying off with a towel, I ask Crimson, "How do you propel yourself forward when you fly?

She opens a small cooler and pulls out three bottles of Clara Winter's juice. She passes them to each of us, then says, "When you can identify the feel of gravity, you'll be able to adjust your usage. I move forward by pushing against gravity at an angle. Today, you only pushed vertically. Running and jumping off the side of the boat gave you forward trajectory, then vertical lift with your push. Eventually, you'll be able to focus your push against gravity at an angle which will propel you in the direction you want to go or will bring you to a halt. I recommend you learn more about Newton's laws to better acquaint yourself with motion and also the universal motion."

"Universal?" I take a drink of the replenishing fluid.

"Yes. Our world spins and it is also rotating around the sun. Two motions. However, our galaxy is also spinning and rotating around the center of the universe. You'll eventually learn how to feel the universal motion, which will come in handy for when you *choose* to let go of gravity completely. That's when you fly the fastest. When you can control the direction of your push based on the direction of the spin, you can zip around the world incredibly fast."

"Do you fly that fast regularly?"

"No, only at moments when I know the conditions will

favor what I need. Today was a day where I knew the conditions would favor you if you accidentally let go of gravity. Hundreds of miles of ocean passed beneath your feet before Brand's repeat. If you were near land, a mountain range could have slammed into you at a thousand miles an hour. However, on other days, the universal spin could launch you into outer space if you let go of gravity completely. That, or it could plunge you into the ground."

"I'm confused, Crimson."

"Study up on the laws of physics, and rest assured I'll train you further when you get the Elemental powers. I will bring you a topaz for atmospheric control practice sessions. You can't hurt yourself with that one, and it won't take you long to figure out how it works."

I ask, "What kind of danger is there for someone who can fly? I mean, I would think the fire power, or wind control might be more dangerous to the general public instead of to someone who can fly."

"Depends on the mindset of the individual. If they are a criminal, or evil-minded, it's easy to imagine what being able to fly would allow. Maybe they are destructive. They could disseminate poisons or chemicals over a population. Drop bombs. Bring down aircraft. Or simply drop from the sky into a prison yard and fly out with a convict faster than the guards can respond.

"On the other hand, the control of fire can be fatal, sure, but to a limited number of people. Pyro-power doesn't give its user the ability to ignite a whole neighborhood or town, it's more like igniting a building or area around the user. Basically, pyro-power can be dealt with by regular people. Atmospheric control is somewhat limited. Creating a torrential downpour can only happen if a water source is nearby or if there is adequate humidity in the air. Whirlwinds or tornadoes are probably the easiest to produce, but the size and strength is limited to existing temperature and humidity. I mostly use atmospheric control to reroute bad weather to my needs, like the lashing rainbands of the hurricane in Texas when you were there."

Brand jumps into the conversation. "Wait! You were there? Why didn't you help us? I had to repeat like crazy."

"Between the both of us, Brand, we made the trip possible."

I say, "I saw you there. Do you also reroute fire? Is that how you walked into the fire at Yeok Choo's surrendering?"

"You saw her there?" Brand asks.

"Be quiet." I don't mean to sound so scolding, but I'm finally getting answers to my many questions.

"That was a fire defense or a forcefield. I can start, extinguish, or protect myself from fire. That power is the easiest to master, unfortunately."

"Will you charge me a fire topaz, too?"

"There's no need. That power is instinctual. Once you have the Elemental power, you only have to think the instructions in your mind, like the Invisibility power. 'No one can see me' is enough to appear invisible."

"Oh. Okay. So, gravitational hold is the more worrisome new power coming?"

"That, and anyone who develops multiple powers. Combinations of the powers could be dangerous to a larger number of people. Imagine someone who can fly and shoot fireballs. Okay," she says, extending both her hands to us, "it's time to return to the others."

I pick up the topaz from the table and shove it in my pocket.

Back at my apartment, Brand and I sit in the kitchen,

chatting over our morning coffee. He can't stop talking about what it was like to fly with Crimson. To me, flying isn't fun. I only like the fact that she can go from point A to point B faster than an airplane, and way faster than driving.

The diamond in my heart warms a little, letting me know someone is trying to connect. Crimson's voice enters my mind. *May I come visit you? I have the atmospheric control topaz.*

Yes, absolutely.

I'm trying to recall if Crimson has ever connected to my diamond to speak with me. She's always had the quantum entanglement through the Grecian Blue ever since we went into the Denver compound together.

Brand is still talking nonstop as I stand from my chair and walk to the door. I open it and find Crimson about to knock. "Come in." I motion with my hand.

"Sorry, no time. Here is the topaz with atmospheric control. Use it to shield yourself from the rain or wind, to start with. Form a defense shield of protection like I do when we fly. Once you master that, and if there is any remaining power, try to create whirlwinds."

"What if I can't control the wind and I damage stuff or people?"

"You won't. Topaz doesn't hold enough power to do anything like that. It will drain too quickly. I must go now." She looks beyond me to Brand and acknowledges him, then turns and disappears.

Brand and I walk around the property with the topaz looking for some way to practice the atmospheric control, but there is no wind and no rain, as is common for this time of year in Oregon. I kick at the dry dirt with my foot to loosen it. Then I clench my fingers around the topaz and imagine wind. Nothing happens. I kick the dirt again.

"Well, I can do that, Calli." Brand swings the toe of his

shoe into the loose dirt. As the dust flies up, I swish my hands away from us, willing the dirt to fly away from us. The little dust cloud expands vertically and begins swirling in place. More dust is sucked into the now rotating vortex that is as tall as Brand. "Holy crap on a cracker!" Brand cries out.

I'm as amazed as he is, but I can feel the topaz draining rapidly so I drop my hold on the wind.

"Okay! Now, *that* was cool. Do it again."

I open my hand, showing him the topaz. "I don't want to drain it. I'm supposed to use it to create a forcefield, but we don't have the right conditions other than the little wind I just created."

"Honestly, Calli, do you think I'm going to stand by and make you learn how to use the topaz at regular human speed?"

"What?"

"You're worried that if you drain the topaz, you'll have to wait till Crimson recharges it so you can experiment again—like a regular person." He points his finger back and forth from me to him. "This is like when I first showed you my power and stabbed through my jeans. Remember?"

"Yes."

"You told me to stitch the hole, like a human, but I showed you I could just repeat the hole away. Well, let's repeat with that topaz and master the power already."

"Well, all right then." I mentally slap my palm to my forehead. Why didn't I think of that?

We continue to practice with the topaz over and over again until I can whip up a dust devil with the flick of my fingers. I master creating a forcefield by having Brand splash water on me from a glass. The water doesn't hit my body; instead it is blocked and shoots sideways, up and down, like spraying a window with a garden hose. Now I only need to try it against wind.

The last two weeks have flown by. Chris's ring arrived. It's even more stunning than I imagined. The green moldavite inlay catches the light easily and is enhanced further by the white gold. I put it with the Grecian Blue as I'll be taking both to Maetha's island in June.

Beth, Nate, and Clara arrived in Portland and found an apartment outside the blast zone, as I recommended. I enjoy having them come visit, especially so Brand has someone else to talk to.

My parents came for a brief visit. They hired a mover to bring my Cooper out on a trailer, so now I have my own wheels parked in the garage downstairs. Sometimes I just sit in the driver's seat, recalling my old life of driving the car. Then I remember that my parents bought me the car to cheer me up after my "accident" that sent me home from the "Olympic training camp." I already had a diamond shard in my heart. I was already on my way to being a Bearer. My old life was already over.

Chris's mind connects with mine, which surprises me because he hasn't been able to do this while at the Bureau. *Calli, we're moving now. We've left D.C. and are on our way to Portland. I can't wait to see you again.*

I'm excited to see you, too! Crimson started teaching me how to fly.

Really? But what if you get hurt? Doesn't she want you to avoid life threatening things?

Brand is always around to repeat me back.

Oh, right. Is it as cool as I think it would be to fly?

No. But, I am getting better at it.

Maybe one day you can take me flying.

ఠ ఠ ఠ

Chris's days are spent helping the Bureau haul boxes, office furniture, and computers into the cavernous building south of Portland while construction workers finish partitions and walls and make repairs on the roof. Many of the employees will live in the building in small private dorm-style rooms. Chris is expected to stay there, too.

We're not happy about it.

Beth will accompany me and my guardians when we meet with General Appleton today at the temporary Bureau. I'm thrilled to not have to communicate with Max anymore. He's not, of course. More so, I can't wait to see Chris again in the flesh. Ever since he left the D.C. Bureau, we've been able to have mental conversations. We still send simple text messages and have occasional phone calls to keep up appearances, but otherwise we can mind-chat freely.

"Come in, Ms. Courtnae. Please sit." General Appleton motions toward the chairs against the wall, nodding at myself and the rest behind me.

Beth, Brand, Duncan, and I sit after closing the door. Aernoud and Ruth stand guard outside the office. The thin dividing walls and door barely block the cacophonous whirr of saws and drills outside. I clear my throat and say, "I thought Chris would be able to join us for this meeting."

"He's on his way. Would you introduce me to your friends?"

"Of course. This is Beth Hammond. She is the envoy for the Runners Clan. And this is Brand Safferson, but you've seen him before—"

"Nope," Brand says to me. "This isn't going to work."

"Huh?"

"I'm repeating us as far back as possible. I can't be

here."

The room begins spinning around as Brand repeats. The spinning stops and I find we are just inside the front doors of the government building awaiting security checks.

Brand says, "Beth and I will meet you back at your place, Calli, and I'll explain then."

"Okay."

"Where are they going?" Duncan asks.

"Something's up between Brand and the general. He just repeated with me."

We go through the metal detectors and are ushered to General Appleton's office. Aernoud and Ruth take guard position at the door and Duncan accompanies me to the meeting.

"Come in, Ms. Courtnae. Please sit." General Appleton motions toward the chairs against the wall, nodding at myself and the rest behind me, like before.

I say, "I thought Chris would be able to join us for this meeting."

"He's on his way. Have you spoken to Maetha about my request for a meeting?"

"Yes. She will meet with you, but she doesn't know when yet."

"Good."

"How are your talks with the Portland officials going?"

General Appleton sits forward with his arms outstretched on his desk. He holds a gold pen with both hands and twists it slowly. "We are confident that when we give the official evacuation order, things will run smoothly."

"Where will the city's officials evacuate to?" I ask.

"The city's government, law enforcement, and emergency services leaders will take cover in Kelly Butte Bunker on the east side, along the 205. That will be their base of operations till the area is clear of danger."

I hesitate. "Sir, that's within the blast radius. I'm not sure if it's a safe place for all the heads of government to hide."

"They don't want to leave the city, and the bunker was built to withstand a twenty-kiloton explosion, so it should be adequate. They've been renovating since I informed them of the coming potential disaster. The decision was made to keep the heads of government within the city to minimize the lawlessness that will inevitably follow a mass evacuation."

I try to explain with as much tact as I can. "Cosmic rays are not explosions, sir. The bunker may not withstand the blast. However, I'll talk with the Seers to see if they can foresee any danger with that location."

General Appleton waits a few beats as if certain the bunker can withstand anything, mutters a thanks, then says, "I'm told you have new information to share. What do you have for me?"

I clear my throat. "On the day of the blast, a small number of people, including myself, will be in the downtown area. We are attempting to control the radius of the blast by funneling it into one narrow area."

"Is that even possible? Wait, don't answer that."

"I know it is hard to comprehend, but we're hopeful we can minimize fallout this way."

"What can I do to help with this attempt?"

"Your team should do everything they can to evacuate civilians inside the radius during the day until eight o'clock that evening. Then you should pull your own people out. Don't let anyone back in for at least twelve hours. The blast will hit after dark."

A quick rap at the door, followed by the door opening enough for Max to poke his head in to say, "May I attend this meeting?"

"Come in."

Max enters and makes eye contact with me. I am unable to read his mind which means he is wearing a small obsidian. "Where is Brand and the girl, Calli? I thought they were with you."

"They had to leave unexpectedly." I try to keep my voice level to hide my nervousness.

Chris fills the doorway. "Sorry I'm late." His presence sends ripples of heat through every cell in my being. It's been so long since I last saw him, and I want to jump up and launch myself into his arms.

"Close the door, Chris," General Appleton orders and waits till Chris does so. "Ms. Courtnae was giving me an update." He turns his attention back to me. "Please continue."

"Um, basically, that was all. A group of Diamond Bearers will try to minimize the radius of the blast. I do have a request, though. As you know, Chris and I are to be married June tenth in Bermuda. I have an apartment here in the area. Would you allow him to stay with me and report to you daily in the interim leading up to the blast?"

The general rubs his chin while resting one elbow on the desk.

Max interjects. "Sir, that cannot be allowed. If you let him go, there's no motivation for her to keep updating you on the situation."

I ask Max, "Don't you think saving thousands of lives is motivation enough?" I am tempted to use the Mind-Reader topaz to look into Max's mind but hold back. If he sensed my intrusion, I'd lose all credibility with the general.

General Appleton says, "Chris will remain here till the departure date for the wedding, after which he can move in with you. He will be expected to show up here for work, daily. Any mishaps and we'll have to revisit the agreement."

Chris asks, "Sir, will Calli be able to come visit?"

"As long as our lines of communication remain open and free flowing, I have no problem with that."

After the meeting concludes, Chris and I sit outside on the grass.

"It's so good to see you, Calli." He takes my hand and cups it between his.

My body warms excitedly with his touch. "Well, I'm so happy you're here in Oregon and we can see each other more often, which is more than before but not as much as I'd hoped for."

"I know. At least he's going to allow us to live together after the wedding. I'm sorry I haven't been able to help with the plans and preparations."

I give a weak laugh. "I haven't been able to do much either. Between my mother and Maetha, I think they'll put on a nice celebration for us. Nothing too extreme."

"It's a good thing we're getting married before the blast. Otherwise, I'd probably have to stay with the general till after the fact. Can you imagine that?"

"No. I'm glad you encouraged a June wedding." With a grin, I pull him in for a kiss.

After arriving at my apartment, I ask Brand why he had to leave so abruptly.

"General Appleton called for his guards to seize me."

"Why?"

My guardians join us around the table, all voicing concern over the shocking alternate future that none of them foresaw.

Ruth admits, "I only looked for Calli's future."

Duncan says, "Brand's future is extremely difficult to see."

I nod. "It's because of his repeating. Too many possible futures. So, Brand, why?"

"Max had put it in the general's head that I am government property or at least my quartz is government property. Max referred to me as 'The Invisible Boy.' So, basically, I can't show my face anymore around the government."

Beth asks Brand, "Why now? Haven't you been around Max since he outed you on his blog?"

"Yeah. A couple of times. I don't know why today was the day to try to capture me."

A heavy lump falls to the bottom of my stomach. I say, "I guess I thought since the Bureau bought his silence, he had dropped all those other ideations. He asked me pointedly where you were once we were in the general's office."

Beth reaches over and takes one of Brand's hands. "What happens now? Calli will still need you to help repeat."

He places his other hand on top of hers. "I think I should always have a Runner by my side in case I need one, like I did today."

Chapter Seventeen - Old, New, Borrowed, Blue

I send my thoughts to Chris. *Watch out for Max. He's after Brand's quartz, using General Appleton and his power to get it.*

How do you know?

He attempted today but Brand repeated and ran with Beth.

Shit. That's why he still didn't want me to come live with you. He didn't get what he wanted.

Now that we know this, do you think he'll try to convince the general to not let you live with me once we're married?

I hope not. But you might have to give me another Mind-Control topaz for extra encouragement.

I'll charge one for you as soon as I can.

Calli, when you come to visit, I think we should always stay outside the building, in case you need to run. Make sure your guardians look to your future, too.

They always do.

And I don't think it's a good idea for Brand to be near you. We're so close to the blast date. We can't fail now. Based on what Brand said happened today—or could have happened—you guys probably have shadows, watching your every move. I know how the government works. Alert Brand and have him lead them away from you. He'll do it. He'll also throw them off, like he did that time in the car with Crimson. He needs to be away from you, but that doesn't mean he can't watch over you. He'll figure out how to do that. Please tell him.

Okay, I will.

After discussing everything with the Bearers, Brand, and Beth, it is decided that Brand should leave and see if anyone starts following him. He'll get a hotel for the night. Ruth will communicate with Maetha and give her an update.

Another Bearer will be assigned to take Brand's place as a guardian.

As I lay in bed, Crimson connects with my diamond, asking permission to bi-locate.

I agree.

Her form materializes next to my bed. "Calli, Maetha informed me of the new developments. She recommends you be removed from the area two days prior to the blast. We've already been working on securing a location."

"You mean July thirtieth?"

"Yes. That's when the major mass evacuation will begin to take place. There will be a lot of chaos, a lot of danger, and without Brand to repeat you, your enhancer ring will activate several times."

"I am aware already that I'll be moved out of the area. Do you know where I will go?"

"I'll get back to you on that. Furthermore, I think you should travel to your parents' home soon and then fly with them to Bermuda for the coupling. Let's get you out of this area while we figure out how to deal with Brand's issues."

I remember a time when she said Brand wasn't important in the future of humanity. "Has he grown on you, Crimson?"

"I'm told he'll save my life someday. I'd like to keep him around. But if you aren't able to capture the blast, no one will have a life to save."

Chris and I lay together on a blanket under a thick canopy of old oak trees in the park next to the Bureau's building. I've visited Chris twice now since Brand dropped off the grid. Both times Max asked about Brand's whereabouts. My response to Max was controlled and seemingly non-caring, saying I didn't know. This was the best response because when I read his mind, using the topaz, Max didn't feel like I was hiding something, nor did he feel like he needed to pursue.

Moments ago, I gave Chris another Mind-Control topaz, in the event he needs to persuade the general to let us live together after our coupling. I also handed him my Reader topaz, so he can try to learn more about the government's intentions concerning the Bearers, Brand, and the aftermath of the blast.

"Calli," Chris says, turning his head my direction, "I feel like ever since I saw you sitting on Clara's couch, invisible forces have continually kept us apart."

I look at him. "Definitely! Not always invisible, however. I have this fear you won't be allowed to go to your own wedding."

"Nothing will stop me from going."

"Well, I'll be waiting anxiously until the moment you step off the boat onto the dock. Then I'll allow myself to breathe."

His hand finds mine and he rolls on his side to face me. "One way or the other, I'll make it to the island. I'll be watching for you, too, on the dock." I love how his whispered words are heated with anticipation.

I will be leaving tomorrow for Ohio to stay with my parents prior to traveling to Bermuda. When packing my bags, I take care to remember Chris's ring, the Blue Diamond, and the box of Runners' quartzes.

Crimson stops by my place to take me to the three locations where the channeling crystals will be positioned. After informing my guardians, and getting their thumbs-up on my future, Crimson and I walk into the forest behind my apartment.

"Activate your Invisibility, Calli. We will fly and you will produce the atmospheric shield with the topaz."

"No sweat." I find it curious she assumes I still have power in the topaz. I'm glad I do.

She stands behind me and wraps her arms around my waist, so I'll be able to use my hands to produce the shield. Up we go, above the treetops, then she slows our ascent, and we hover.

"Create the shield."

I do and she launches us toward the west, faster than she's ever taken me before. Yet, I feel great. Being the shield creator makes a huge difference in the flying experience. We arrive on top of a building away from the capture point.

"My topaz is drained, Crimson."

"I know, but you mastered the shield."

Her approval brings a beaming smile to my face.

A metal frame is erected before us. She walks over to it. "This will hold one of the crystals. Each location will have protectors who will guard it all day, every day until the night of the blast when they are moved to safety. Hold on to me. Let's go visit the other two sites."

All three sites are located atop skyscrapers slightly higher than the capture point. She then takes me to the building where I'll be positioned. Drawn in white paint is a triangle shape with an X inside. The three points of the triangle are aimed to each channeling quartz location.

"When the crystals are in place, and you are standing right here, you will see the net. You will see the framework that will channel the power to the diamonds you possess. If something is wrong with the positioning, you will be able to tell because the net will disappear."

"What if that happens?"

"Let's hope it doesn't. There will be a small window to correct any problems. I will be installing the channeling crystals two weeks prior to the blast."

"Will I need to help you with that?"

"I don't know yet. Just be aware that is the time frame."

"So, two weeks out, you'll insert the crystals, and two days out, I'll be taken somewhere away from danger."

"Yes."

"What about immediately after the blast?"

"What do you mean?"

"I'm just curious what you know about the situation immediately following the blast."

"There will be much death and disease, but the long-range future is optimistic for humanity. You are part of the long-range future, Calli."

"That must mean I'll live." I chuckle, then dial back to seriousness. "You said 'optimistic.' You've used that word many times when you've referred to the long-range future. Would you explain what you mean?"

"Certainly. To see an optimistic future is to see one in which most humans still have control over their lives and happiness. They are not suppressed by cosmic-energy-infused, power-hungry tyrants who desire to beat down and control the masses. If the blast is not captured in such a way as what we plan, the Reapers will take over civilization and impose slave-like restrictions, the population will be greatly reduced, all people of powers will be hunted down and stripped of their power, and humanity as you know it will cease to exist."

"Oh. Okay. That explains a lot."

"The future is optimistic on the grand scale, but make no mistake, this blast changes the world. The question is by how much."

Ŏ Ŏ Ŏ

Me and my guardians arrived last night at my parents' home. With Brand out of the lineup, Amenemhet will take his place. I haven't heard from Beth or Clara about Brand's whereabouts or even if he's okay. Hopefully, he'll be able to come to our coupling.

My mother asked if I would water the plants in the backyard. The sprinkler system is broken. Ruth accompanies me, while the other three are somewhere nearby, protecting and guarding the perimeter. I muse about the neighbors and what they must think about the three men stalking about our yard.

Calli, Chris's voice enters my mind as I spray the bushes.

Yes?

I used the Mind-Control topaz to be invisible and I listened in on General Appleton talking to Vita. He was upset that he hasn't met with Maetha yet. Vita told him to follow me to the wedding and that Maetha would be there.

Oh no.

I know. Would you please tell Maetha I don't want our special day ruined because she doesn't want to meet with her ex-boyfriend? I imagine she will want to include some other Bearers for safety's sake when she meets with him. Whatever she decides, she needs to do it before our coupling date. I won't put you at risk, Calli. I won't put humanity's future at risk.

My heart skips a beat and crashes into my gut, or at least it feels like it does. *Yes. I'll tell her. Were you caught on camera when you were invisible?*

No. I know where the cameras are located and was careful not to pull a Brand*. I've got to go. I love you.*

I love you, too.

"What's wrong, Calli?" Ruth asks, placing a hand on my arm.

"I need to bi-locate to Maetha."

"Okay, let's go inside."

After relaying Chris's information to Maetha, she doesn't react. I'm reminded of the time I tried to get her to talk about the strange man named Freedom and how she didn't seem fazed that I knew about him. She'd be a good poker player.

"I'll travel to Bermuda and call Bernard from there," Maetha says. "I wanted to wait till after the blast, but I can't let Chris down again. I'll also increase the protection around the island, and for the yacht, so you don't have to worry about anything."

"Thank you. Maetha, are you worried about this meeting?"

"I'm concerned more about capturing the blast. I'll communicate with your guardians as to when it's safe to travel to the island."

"Okay."

Clara, Beth, and Nate meet us at the airstrip in Ohio to board Maetha's jet on our way to Bermuda. I'm happy they are all coming to celebrate the coupling. With my four guardians and my parents, the plane is full. I sit by Beth and Nate and we talk about the recipes Nate created in Clara's drink factory at the Runners' compound before moving to Portland. I enjoy passing the time listening to him and Beth and seeing them happy and full of life. My mother laughs, pulling my attention to the front of the plane where she sits. My eyes fill with hot tears as it sinks in my parents are with me, traveling to my wedding. Beth and Nate will never have that again.

As if my mother can read my thoughts, she turns her head and looks my way. Her expression softens when she sees my watery eyes. The thoughts at the front of her mind say she thinks I'm having cold feet about the wedding.

I send her my thoughts and speak in her mind. *Not cold feet, I'm just so happy you and Dad are here with me. Tears of joy.*

She nods and wipes her eyes.

Once we arrive on the island, Maetha greets us and directs my parents to the same bungalow they stayed in last time. Beth, Nate, and Clara will be in the main house. I'll stay in my bungalow on the beach. My guardians can leave my side, now that we're on the island. No outside influences will harm me here. I'm relieved to have a little privacy, something I haven't had for quite a while. I imagine they are also thankful to get a break.

I want to ask Maetha about her meeting with General Appleton, but I doubt she'd tell me much. All I know is it happened, and Chris feels comfortable coming to the island.

I head to my bungalow nestled in the line of greenery just beyond the beach. No other bungalow is nearby, not like with the others on the island. I've always loved the location with its prime sunset viewing and secluded setting—perfect for a wedding night party of two.

Once inside, I set my bags down, then retrieve the box of gems. First things first, I need to put the Runners' quartzes somewhere accessible yet hidden from Chris. I choose the cupboard under the bathroom sink. I pile the extra towels on top of the box. Next, I need to put his ring somewhere I won't lose it. I decide I will give it to my father. Last, I pull out the Grecian Blue Diamond.

"Now, where will I put you?" I hold the stone up to eye level and rotate it around.

The walls of my bungalow dissolve away and I find myself in the Healers' compound. I'm sitting at a table with five small Grecian Blue Diamond shards laying in front of me on the tabletop. Chris sits next to me, lending me support. My heart feels heavy with sadness, and I fight to keep my tears behind my eyes. I'm expecting the arrival of some people who I hope will accept the assignment I wish to extend. The scene dissolves as quickly as it formed, and my bungalow comes back into view. I shake my head and think about what I just saw. The Blue will be divided at some point for a purpose, and something will make me incredibly sad.

I'm not going to tell Chris about this. I don't know what I'd say. Why was I sad, or will be sad?

And yet, this is the first time I've seen Chris in a vision *after* the Portland blast. So, there's that.

I look at the stone in my hand and an idea formulates in my mind of where to hide it: the Field of Remembrance. I put the stone in my pocket and leave my bungalow. After making sure the stone is secured, I decide to use my running power to make the trip go faster. Plus, I haven't used that power in a while so this should feel refreshing.

Refreshing, indeed! The humid air blowing my hair straight back as I zip up the trail to the clearing feels warm and sticky, but so nice. I wish Chris were here with me. He will be tomorrow. I arrive at the field and inspect the area to make sure I'm alone. My diamond isn't alerting me to other Bearers and no Bearers are trying to contact me. I stand by Neema's headstone, then kneel down behind it. I push the diamond into the grass against the stone marker, wiggling it back and forth to move the dirt out of the way. Then I remove my hand and press the dirt and grass back into place.

Standing, I glance down to see if I've disturbed the setting too much. Everything looks fine. I feel certain the diamond is safe here, but to be sure, I look to the future for the time when I'll collect the diamond. A scene opens in my mind of me digging up the diamond in a hurried rush, with tears in my eyes and on my cheeks, then launching into the sky and flying out of the bubble. The vision dissipates.

Again, I felt sad in the vision, almost distraught.

What is going to happen?

I know better than to search further into this. I've already seen too much. I risk changing the future if I have more of these visions concerning the Grecian Blue. Time to return to my bungalow, I decide. I need to give the wedding band to my father to hold till the coupling. I return the way I came, running exhilaratingly fast. If nothing else, this jaunt was a great stress reliever. I quickly grab the wedding band and run to my parents' bungalow.

"Come in, Calli," my mother welcomes me with a hug. She waves her hand toward the table and they both join me.

"Is something wrong?" my father asks.

"No, not at all." I show the ring to them.

My mother exclaims, "It's beautiful, Calli."

"Dad, will you keep Chris's ring till the ceremony?"

My father answers, "Absolutely. Do you want me to hold it during the ceremony, too? Or do you have a ring bearer?"

"Will you be my ring bearer, Dad?"

"Of course. Do I get to walk you down the aisle, too? Will there be an aisle?"

"Well, I hope so. I've never been coupled before."

"If there's not one, we'll make one. I want to walk my daughter down the aisle."

I extend my hand toward him and he takes hold. "Thank you."

My mother places her hand over our clasped hands. "Calli, what do you mean when you say 'coupled.' "

I explain to my parents the Diamond Bearers' term for wedding and marriage, to which they both nod their heads in indifference. My dad says, "If it's okay with you, I'd like to continue using the terms I'm used to."

"No problem."

"Me too," my mom chimes in. "Are you excited?"

I smile uncontrollably. "Yes. And a bit nervous."

"That's understandable," my father says.

ὂὂὂ

Maetha lets me know Chris and his mother, Lynette, will be staying in two side-by-side bungalows far away from mine—bummer—although, it's probably for the best that he's with her to help her digest all the new information she's about to witness. After our ceremony, Crimson will stay with Lynette. That seems fitting. They were friends after all.

I walk briskly out to the dock after Maetha informs me the boat carrying Chris and his mother will arrive soon. Chris spoke to my mind about an hour ago, saying they had arrived in Bermuda, but nothing since. I'm incredibly thrilled to see him, to kiss him, to marry him. Another uncontrollable smile erupts on my face.

Wow! I've become like the girls I used to laugh at, giddy and giggly, grinning from ear to ear. I'm fine with it, though. Being head over heels in love is hard to contain.

As soon as I see the boat, I spot Chris standing on the bow, searching for me. Our Hunter vision connects, sending delightful shivers straight to my pinky toes. He looks so good.

No, you *look so good,* he speaks to my mind, having clearly read it.

My cheeks heat as the warm air blows my hair about. *I've missed you, Chris.*

Right back at you. I'd jump off this boat and run right across the water to get to you sooner, but that would probably give my mother a stroke. She just freaked out when the bubble opened up for us to pass.

Have you talked more with her about the powers?

Not yet. But head's up, Jie Wen is onboard and he's not happy that another outsider is allowed on the island.

Maybe tell him to get his own island, then he can decide who gets to visit. Anyway, I don't remember inviting him. Did you invite him? I'm joking with Chris, of course. All Diamond Bearers were invited. The only one not coming is Jonas.

My heart sinks just thinking his name. During the time I carried the diamond for the delivery, I so desperately wanted to heal his cancer. When he was offered the chance to be healed, he declined, valiantly so. Then unselfishly, he allowed Maetha to experiment with his DNA in a sort of donating-his-body-to-science kind of thing, after which she succeeded in making him the first Unaltered of his kind—the only, to my knowledge. He didn't ask to be a Bearer. He was only in the room with Freedom because he had volunteered in my place to be taken to the facility to buy some time and hopefully protect me. I have to wonder if Freedom knew exactly what he was doing when he jammed the diamond into Jonas' chest. Perhaps he saw the future and could see Jonas would join up with Vita . . . eventually.

I shake my head. It's pointless to dwell on this.

The boat comes to a halt at the dock and crew members tie the lines to the moorings. I wait patiently for Chris to help his mother down to stable ground. I had imagined him jumping off the boat and sweeping me up into his arms but watching him take the time to help his mom is endearing to me.

"One second it was all ocean, then this island appeared through a hole!" Lynette exclaims as she grasps my arm for stability. Her hands are shaking, and her face is pale.

"I know. I remember the first time I saw it. Shocking. It's good to see you again," I say.

"Yes. Chris, I just want to lay down for a little while."

I point with my chin toward the bungalows. "Maetha showed me where you two are staying. Let me take you there."

Chris leads his mother's hand into the crook of his arm and says, "Come on."

Her countenance perks up immediately. "Oh! Well, now I feel fine. I guess I just needed to get off that boat."

I catch Chris's eye. He winks at me, having used his healing power on his mother. I find his other hand with mine and clasp it tight as the three of us walk to the bungalows.

Once situated in Lynette's bungalow, she says, "Is it okay to talk about the powers now, Chris?"

Honestly, I don't know where we'll begin to explain the powers to her. Will we demonstrate? I decide to follow Chris's lead.

"Yes," Chris answers. "We can talk about them anywhere on this island and around anybody. Everyone here is aware of cosmic powers."

"That's good. I have so many questions. Ever since Jo Jo visited me and explained everything, I've been aching to talk to you."

I'm taken aback by her statement. *Crimson* did that?

"So, can you fly, like Superman?" Lynette's question is sincere; however, she's comparing our abilities to fictional characters. I guess if it helps her understand, then that's okay.

"Uh, no," Chris responds. "Maybe someday. The powers coming to Portland include flying, so . . ."

"And the government is fine with you having a diamond in your heart, Chris?"

"Actually, they don't know yet. We want to keep that a secret as long as possible."

"Oh." Her eyes widen. Her mind reveals she can't

comprehend how a diamond could be inside a human heart.

Chris says, "As you see more powers in action, this will all get easier to accept."

"I don't know." She squeezes her eyes shut and leans forward resting her head in her hands. "None of this fits into what I've learned all my life, in school, in church . . . and it's not only me, the world doesn't believe in any of this."

"The world will have a hard time adjusting, just like you right now. That's why I wanted to be the one to tell you about everything beforehand, instead of you learning inaccurate information from television."

"I don't know how to comprehend what you're saying, Chris. But I'll try. I'll make an appointment with my therapist when I get back home."

"No, you should only discuss this with others who understand the powers."

I offer, "She could talk to my mom. She's a therapist."

Lynette's face brightens. "She is?"

"I'll introduce you."

Dinner is served inside the main house. The large grassy area out back is being set up for the coupling feast tomorrow night—the same grassy area where Yeok Choo surrendered her diamond, and where I performed mini-surgery on Chuang.

While my parents and Chris's mother talk, Jie Wen pulls me aside. "The rest of us Bearers didn't get to bring our families into the understanding, and certainly not to gatherings like this. I don't envy you when the moment comes for your loved ones to die. They may not understand why you allow it to happen when you can stop it, and you *will* have to let them die."

He leaves my side abruptly before I can respond.

Chris joins me. "Why would he say that to you?"

"I don't know. Jealousy?"

Duncan joins us. "Not jealousy. Pity. He pities you."

"Well, he can keep all his pits." I wrinkle my nose.

"Brand," Beth cries out from across the room as she runs to meet him at the door. "We were worried you wouldn't make it."

Brand's hand rests on the doorframe and he breathes deeply, like he just ran a sprint. "I just landed, sorry, I'm a little out of breath. The crush of the atmosphere was too much for my lungs. I had to keep repeating and telling Crimson to slow down."

Chris and I hurry over to him and Chris takes his hand, infusing him with healing power. I place my hand on Chris's arm to prevent him from draining all his strength.

Brand says, "Great, now we will *all* need a nap."

Beth grabs his other arm. "Let's go up to my room." She looks over her shoulder at us and motions for us to join them. "Come on."

As we climb the stairs, I hear Lynette getting a little loud while confronting Uncle Don about indoctrinating Chris's mind with Stanley's crazy grandiosity. Chris looks torn between going with me or rescuing Uncle Don. I say to Chris, "Go be with your family."

"Thank you." He gives me a quick kiss then turns and hurries downstairs.

I take hold of Brand's arm and listen to the conversation downstairs as Chris suggests they go to Lynette's bungalow and talk about things. The three of them leave.

Once we make it to Beth's room and help Brand onto the bed, I say, "Family arguments at weddings go together like . . . you know what, we should have just eloped."

Beth says, "I never took you as the eloping-type of girl."

"I guess I'm more on board with eloping than dealing with the drama of a big wedding."

"Maybe you'd rather skip to the good part, forget all this noise. So, have you and Chris . . . you know?" She raises her eyebrows suggestively.

I let out an exhale and a grunt. "Come on, Beth." Inside, my heart races at her insinuation. I've never asked her about her intimate life. Why would she think I would readily volunteer extremely personal information? As these thoughts run through my mind, I recognize my frustration concerning the ever-present physical blockades and mental anxieties I've dealt with concerning private time with Chris. It's as if everything in the world wants to keep us apart.

"What? I'm curious, that's all. I mean, you are about to marry 'Bad Boy Chris' from the Runners' Clan."

She makes him sound promiscuous. "I don't know what you've heard about him, but Chris is not like that. I've been all the way to his core with mind reads and watched his memories as if I was a part of them. I haven't seen anything that would label him a 'Bad Boy.' And as for your comment, we've connected on a cellular level through the healing power. I know every millimeter of his body. I've felt inside his bones, muscles, organs, and hell, I've held his beating heart in my hand. I've experienced his sorrows and felt his complete joy in a way that no other couple could possibly do. I don't know how anyone could be closer than that."

"So, that's a no," Beth says with a sly smile. "Sounds like you read the book, but did the book ever make your body feel *alive*? I think you're in for a nice surprise, then."

Chapter Eighteen - The Coupling

I haven't physically seen Chris all day, but I've communicated with him plenty of times. He told me his mother calmed down last night after Crimson, or Jo Jo as she knows her, came and talked with her and Don. Crimson explained the research that Stanley Harding had worked on was dangerously close to revealing the whereabouts of Diamond Bearers and the ways to kill them. Stanley had to be stopped before the Portland cosmic blast occurred or else the whole world would suffer. Chris said his mother accepted the information a little easier, but only because it came from Jo Jo.

I figure if Chris's mom had any idea what lengths Jo Jo would go to in order to secure the future of the human race, like allowing Chris to die at his diamond insertion, she wouldn't be so comforted.

The ceremony will take place on a beach, close to my parents' bungalow, which is perfect for me to get ready with my mother's help.

"Your dress fits you so well, Calli, I'm glad you went with the one shoulder look," she says. "And this sash adds just the right amount of dazzle. Absolutely beautiful! Now, sit here so I can fix your hair." She motions to the chair.

My father enters as my mother pins up my hair. "There's an aisle, now."

"There wasn't one?" I ask.

"Nope. But being the father of the bride, I made it happen."

My mother says, "Will there be any more surprises with this coupling thing?"

"I don't know. I've never attended one. I don't even know if Bearers wear wedding dresses like mine. Then again, I don't know how many years or even centuries ago the last coupling happened. No matter what, nothing can take away from the specialness of the day."

My father looks at his watch. "It's nearly time. Are you about ready?"

"Yes, she is," my mother says, patting my shoulders and giving them a gentle squeeze.

I stand and face my father. "Yes, I'm ready."

He looks me up and down with his gentle, caring expression that I've seen so many times in my life. "I can't believe my little girl has grown into such a beautiful, responsible, young woman. I'm so proud of you."

"We both are," my mother adds.

"Thanks! I love you both."

My father walks me down to the beach where everyone is gathered. Someone had the foresight to place woven mats on the sand to make walking easier in my poorly chosen shoes. Everything is perfect, from the erected arches covered with flowers and greenery, to the tiny lights dangling above. Even the weather is perfect, although I wonder if Crimson has some influence over that. Up near the large arch, Chris stands wearing a tuxedo and looking incredible. He faces me, and I'm lost in his mesmerizing blue eyes.

I barely hear the low music playing the wedding march as my father brings me to the end of the aisle. He kisses my forehead and takes a seat by my mother in the front row.

I take Chris's hand and a huge smile blossoms across my face. This is it. The moment. It's actually happening! We'd been through so much and waited so long. But now we will get to live our lives . . . together.

Crimson, as the officiator, begins. "We are here to

witness and accept the coupling of two Diamond Bearers, Calli and Chris, and the joining of their families, friends, their goals, and their dreams. Would all the Bearers please stand?"

I turn my head to see.

"No Calli, you and Chris must face me during the vote."

Vote? Chris's voice enters my mind.

I didn't know about this. Oh, man! Is this going to be another roadblock coming between us being together? Will we be voted down? Why is there a vote, anyway?

"All Bearers in favor of this coupling, please raise your hand." A pause. It takes every ounce of willpower I have not to peek into the crowd and see how many hands are raised.

Crimson continues. "Your vote is counted, and you may sit. Those who oppose will now have the opportunity to speak their minds, if they desire."

What do you want to bet Jie Wen will be first? Chris asks my mind as I hear my mother ask my father if he knows what's happening.

Jie Wen says, "I speak collectively for the opposition when I say we support the preservation of humanity. We support Diamond Bearers, including these two, but we do not like how this whole operation has evolved into a nepotistic, exclusive club. This island has become a resort, a getaway, not the training ground it once was. Non-powered people coming to the island never happened before Calli became a Bearer. The likelihood of secrets spilling is high."

Crimson waits a moment after he stops speaking. "Jie Wen, I hear your objections. I understand your frustration at not being included in all the details. However, this vote is concerning Calli and Chris and their coupling. You did not raise your hand in support, so do you have anything to say concerning the coupling of these two?"

"Yes. I do not support this coupling because they are emotionally compromised."

Well, duh, Chris thinks.

I know, right?

Jie Wen continues. "Humanity's future hangs in the balance and is determined by these kids and their inability to control their emotional response. They do not have our support at this time for a coupling."

Crimson responds with authority resonating, "You have been heard. You may depart the ceremony if you wish."

"We wish."

I continue facing forward, my back to the crowd, feeling rather offended. Jie Wen doesn't like me because I'm not as cold-hearted as him. I don't ever want to be like him. But I'm also worried about how many others left, how many others feel toward Chris and I the way he does.

Crimson waits for the dissenting Bearers to leave, then she issues calming words to our parents and friends. "My Diamond Bearers' opinions and objections are always heard. Should Calli or Chris ever need to be heard, I will listen and try to resolve the issue. The Bearers who left our ceremony are not against the rest of us, they were speaking freely, as I encourage all to do. I will meet with them later to try to rectify their concerns."

Chris speaks, a touch of heat in his voice. "Why didn't we have the vote earlier instead of now, during what should be a special moment?"

"It's how we've always operated. Regular weddings also hold a vote in a certain sense. Objectors are given the opportunity to speak up or forever hold their peace. Jie Wen spoke up. The question is does his objection change either of your minds to continue with this coupling?"

"No." Chris and I speak in unison as if we'd rehearsed.

"Then let's continue. Coupled Bearers remain together as long as their love continues, and their dreams and passions are compatible. Bearers in love can access the greater Healer power within the Sanguine Diamond which can be utilized by the other Bearers in times of need. Calli and Chris, are you willing to be called upon to help fellow Bearers, no matter who they are?"

Again, we answer yes simultaneously.

"Calli and Chris, Bearers can be immortal if they so choose, and by choosing this you are also committing to adapt to the world around you. Laws and regulations of the land must be followed wherever you live. Are you willing to follow the law of the land?"

"Yes," we both say.

"This coupling ceremony doesn't meet all criteria for legally recognized unions in most parts of the world. It is your responsibility to file the necessary paperwork and have a licensed individual or justice of the peace officially declare you married if you wish to remain in active status as a citizen. Are you willing to do so?"

"Yes," we both say.

"Well, then. With your love for each other and your willingness to help your fellow Bearers and follow the current laws, you are now coupled. Do you two want to exchange rings?"

Chris speaks before I do. "Yes." He reaches inside his tuxedo jacket and pulls out a band that sparkles with different colors. He takes my hand. "Calli, our lives have been, and will be, full of ups and downs, but whether we're up or down we'll be together and that's all that matters. We will be one. Struggles will come and they will go, and we will be one. Children will arrive, grow up and leave our home, and we will be one. With this ring, I promise I'll always love you, no matter what." He slides the ring onto my finger.

I can't make out the details due to the tears in my eyes. I turn to my father for Chris's ring. He pulls out the box from his jacket pocket, removes the ring, and places it in my palm. Then he closes my fingers around the ring and holds on to my hands for a beautiful moment as if to say he's happy for me and gives me his blessing.

I mouth my words, "Thank you, Dad."

He drops his hold and returns to his seat next to my mother who is wiping her eyes with a tissue.

I turn to Chris and extend my hand toward his. I gently slide the ring onto his finger and say, "This ring symbolizes my unending love and devotion to you, just as a circle has no beginning or end, my love knows no bounds and will never end. You are my heart and my soul, and I'm honored to travel this life by your side, supporting you as you support me. I love you."

Crimson leans toward us. "You two can kiss if you want. The rest of you may want to shield your eyes."

Laughter erupts all around as Chris and I close the gap and bring our lips together to seal our love in the presence of our friends and family. My whole body heats up with excitement as his kiss deepens and his intensity matches mine. I become aware of the crowd and their reverent awe for the spectacle we have created. I pull away slightly from Chris and look around. We are glowing bright blue. Chris's mother looks like she's seen a ghost. I'm slightly embarrassed, but the feeling dissipates quickly. In fact, I fling my arms around him and kiss him again, which is met with clapping and cheers.

The party moves to the back lawn of the main house for the dinner. Torches are placed strategically to illuminate the area creating a warm and inviting atmosphere. A large buffet of food and drinks fill a table near the house. This was my request. I didn't want dinner served to us. I just wanted a relaxed party where everyone could help themselves and enjoy each other's company.

Even Jie Wen seems to be enjoying himself. I don't know who else didn't raise their hand in support of our coupling. It doesn't matter. The more I think about his words, the more I realize he's more upset with Crimson than he is with me. I am one of Crimson's choices that he has an issue with. I hope she'll tell him enough information to calm his concerns about my involvement.

As we eat and then mingle with others, accepting their congratulations, I find I'm almost always in contact with Chris whether it's through holding hands, or his hand on my back, or my hand hooked to his elbow. I can't seem to get enough of being near him. During a few brief moments when we're separated, however, my eyes seek him out and when we lock gazes, he has a gleam in his eye that only I know what it means. The look, coupled with our mind connection, makes me wish dinner was over and we could go to the bungalow.

Soon, very soon.

The warm light of the torches lining the pathway cast a romantic glow on Chris's profile as we walk together toward the beach bungalow—our honeymoon suite. Laughter glides along the evening breeze from the wedding party we left behind. I can't ignore the growing anticipation igniting within my body. My feet want to burst into an all-out sprint to the privacy of the bungalow, but I don't think these shoes would cooperate very well.

I stop in my tracks.

"What is it?" Chris turns, his eyebrows raised.

I bend forward and reach down to release the straps of my shoes and slip my feet out. Weaving my finger between the straps with my free hand, I tighten the grip I have on Chris's hand with my other hand and say, "Let's go." I'm a little shocked by the sound of my voice. I sound like a seductress or something.

Chris's pupils grow large, and he squeezes my hand in response.

I grab the front of my dress and hike it up so I can run unencumbered, the shoes clutched in my hand bouncing against my thigh as we launch forward in a dash to the privacy of our room. The journey isn't far, thank goodness. My heart beats wildly against my ribs as we fly along the path through the palm trees and bushes until we arrive at the beach. We turn and run to the bungalow and stop at the door. More torches light the deck, illuminating Chris with golden flickers making him appear more like a Greek god than human. An image forms in my mind: what will he look like in the firelight without all those clothes?

Chris turns the handle and pushes the door open, then he brings his hungry gaze to me. Before I can react, he swoops me up, one arm under my knees, the other around my shoulders. I let out a small squeal, delighting in his romantic actions and wrap one arm around his neck. I toss my shoes off to the side of the door as Chris carries me inside. He kicks the door closed with his heel then sets my feet down. As soon as I find my balance, he cups my jaw tenderly and lowers his lips to mine.

My mind fades to black, or more like my thoughts of everything and everyone fade away. There's only Chris. He is my every thought, my every imagination, my everything. His mouth still claims mine as my hands unbutton his shirt and pull the material out of his waistband. I kiss him back feverishly, as if my life depends on him. Years of waiting and caution and bad timing, keeping us apart, have pent up inside me, ready to burst.

His hands fumble with the zipper on my dress, struggling to get ahold of the tiny metal stick. I'm moving around too much trying to undress him as fast as I can. He wiggles one arm out of the sleeve without breaking kiss contact or dropping the zipper he's finally holding onto with his other hand. I slide my hands over his shoulders and down the front of his sculpted chest, across his belly and down to his waistband. I undo his pants and begin inching them over his hips when he gasps and stops me. He breaks our kiss and rests his forehead against mine.

"Hold up, Mrs. Harding," he nearly growls. "I want us to remember every moment of this."

Mrs. Harding. That's me now. I'm married and his wife. He's my husband. Our bodies belong to each other.

He guides my hands off him and moves them to my sides. Then he returns his attention to my zipper, pulling me closer to his chest so he can get a visual on the annoying closure device keeping my body covered. I take the opportunity to inhale his aroma, his chosen cologne mixed with whatever soap he showered with. He smells so good. I rest my lips against his chest and kiss his skin gently while he curses under his breath over the impossible zipper. I open my lips and let my tongue explore the texture of his body and the taste of him. His body shudders as my tongue glides teasingly.

"All right. I'm going to need your help, Calli. I don't want to tear the dress."

I turn around so he can see what he's doing, then reach back and undo the tiny hook at the top of the zipper allowing the slide to operate with ease. Chris grasps hold and slowly lowers the zipper. I want him to hurry, but he takes his time. Once the zipper slides down to my hips, he places his hand on my shoulders and slowly eases my dress off, helping my arm out of the single shoulder strap, then dropping the gown to the floor in a billowing pile. My back to him, wearing only my underwear, I inhale deeply and turn to face him.

"You're stunning, Calli. I want to kiss every part of

you."

"Yes, please."

Again, he scoops me up and carries me to the bed and gently sets me down.

"You have protection, right?" I ask.

"Yes," he whispers against the skin near my ear, his hands exploring my body as if memorizing by touch. My hands do the same.

One lone fleeting thought enters my head causing me to freeze. My ceasing of motion catches his attention.

"What is it?" he raises his head and looks me in the eye.

"It's nothing."

"No, it's not nothing. Tell me what's wrong."

"No, I mean, it's nothing. There is nothing stopping us right now. Usually something or someone stops us from continuing. But now, there's nothing." I smile and place my hand on his cheek, running my thumb across his lower lip.

"Nothing is a good thing."

He resumes making my body sing in ways I've never experienced. I feel sensations I didn't know could be felt and my mind revels in his attentions to every inch of my skin, and I reciprocate. And as our bodies become one, the room is illuminated in bright blue. What is it about the fever-pitched excitement that causes this reaction, I wonder? The thought flits out of my mind as fast as it enters because my focus is trained on Chris and how wonderful he makes me feel.

Beth was right. I had no idea.

Chris props up on one elbow and rests his head in his hand. His other hand moves in lazy circles over my stomach. "You know, Calli, this moment right now is a first for us.

We aren't running or hiding from anyone. No one is hunting us down. Our lives aren't threatened by any force or thing."

"I know. This is perfect. I wish it could last forever, but let's enjoy the peace while we can."

"Remember when my touch would shift the diamond shard in your heart and nearly kill you?"

"I do. But it was more than just your touch. What about the way you'd look at me?" I laugh. "That gives new meaning to the phrase 'if looks could kill.' "

"Yes, it does."

"Now, your sultry looks and glances send naughty shivers all over my body."

"I get the same sensation when you look at me!"

His roaming hand on my skin slows to a stop on my belly, and he lowers his head onto my shoulder. "I still have nightmares of seeing you on the dining room table in Denver, blood covered, and Crimson trying to heal you, and Marketa dead on the floor. You weren't supposed to be injured. But there you were almost dead. I couldn't keep it together."

I clasp his hand on my stomach. "You kept most of your emotions beneath the surface."

"Probably why I still have nightmares."

"I know what you mean. I've seen you die so many times in alternate realities with Brand. Even though he'd repeat, the memory is seared in my mind. Nothing more so than when you actually died on the beach, though. I can't get that image out of my head. And to think you once lectured me in a steamy bathroom about nature's will."

"Yeah, and I almost kissed the breath out of you."

"That would have been scandalous, sir, no doubt."

"You weren't supposed to be in my life yet. You were too young, but damn, you were you, and you were right in front of me, looking at me with those gorgeous green eyes, having just fought with me over wanting to heal Jonas. I didn't want you to abuse your healing power, because healing was the focal point of my vision. You were a Healer, and you would heal my legs someday. I couldn't let you go down the wrong path. When I saw the acceptance in your eyes, I so badly wanted to kiss you."

"I know." I bring his hand up to my mouth and kiss his palm. "That reminds me, I think I might have a wedding present for you, Chris."

He chuckles, "You think? What does that mean?"

"I can't really explain it, so let me just show you." I move off the bed and throw on my bathrobe. Then I retrieve the box I brought with me and open the case with the individual quartz crystals attached to a removeable flat foam bottom.

"Runners' quartz?" He speaks softly as he moves beside me after putting on jogging pants.

I'm amazed how he instantly identifies the power associated with the quartz. "Yes. I am hoping one of these is yours, that is, if you want to have that power returned to you."

His eyes meet mine with an intensity that dries my mouth and quickens my pulse. "How did you know I'd want my quartz?"

"I saw how happy Rhonda the Healer was when she was reunited with hers, the one we recovered from the Reapers. Her happiness made me think of you."

He points to a particular crystal and whispers, "That's mine."

I don't question his identification. I believe him. I watch as he gazes at the crystal with wide eyes, almost in disbelief of what he's seeing. He reaches forward and ever so softly slides his fingertip across the surface of the quartz. While doing so, his eyes close and his shoulders expand as he fills his lungs with air.

Goosebumps erupt across the back of my neck as I sense his delight. When he opens his eyes and reconnects with mine, he says, "Thank you, Calli. I feel whole, like I've been rejoined with a lost piece of my soul. I don't know any other way to describe it. What a wonderful gift!" He kisses me and pulls me into a hug. Then he says, "I have a gift for you, too." He retrieves a basket full of assorted foods that must have been delivered to my bungalow sometime today because I didn't see it this morning.

"Ah, how did you know I'd be hungry? This is so nice, Chris."

"The snacks are for both of us. This is for you." He digs deep into the basket and pulls out a jewelry box.

"What? Why? You already gave me this gorgeous band." I wiggle my ring finger.

"It's not a ring, Calli. Open it."

I remove the top of the box, slide out the velvet case, then open it. A glimmer of green hits my eyes first as I focus on the necklace attached inside. "Oh! You remembered! It's the Helenite. When did you buy it?"

"Right after we saw it the first time."

"I love it! I love you!" I fling my arms around his neck and kiss him.

Chris places the necklace around my neck and secures it. Then he gently slides his hands inside my robe and pushes it off my shoulders, untying the belt, leaving me sitting naked.

"There. That's the image I pictured when I bought this for you. I wanted to see you wearing only the jewelry I gave you. The green Helenite matches your eyes." He trails his fingertip along my hairline down the side of my face. Then he takes my left hand and brings it up to my chest, placing my palm against my skin to display the ring set on my finger.

"The stones in your band have special meaning. They are all birthstones for August."

"What?" I flip my hand so I can see the ring. The assortment of colored stones glimmer against the candlelight.

"At the jewelers, I asked for your band to have a row of peridot stones because it's your birthstone. Oddly enough, peridot is green, and apparently the diamond is also a green which I didn't know at the time. Anyway, the jeweler asked me which birthstone I was referring to and I just kinda looked at him weird. He went on to show me a chart with all the known birthstones for August from different times and regions of the world. Depending on where you're from or when you lived, you'd have a different birthstone. I asked the jeweler to put one of each in the band because they all have different meanings and powers associated with them."

"It's beautiful, Chris. What are all the stones?"

He points to the channel-set square-cut lineup of stones. "That one is peridot, the birthstone we are most familiar with. The next is sardonyx. It's onyx with orange bands and is recognized in Britain as the birthstone. Then there's ruby from India. Diamond from Tibet. Then traditional birthstones, some spanning back to ancient times: moonstone, carnelian, topaz, sapphire and alexandrite."

"Some of these were on the necklace Uncle Don gave me."

"Exactly. I've become intrigued by all these crystals and stones, like Uncle Don. I used to be so skeptical, like my mom."

"And me. I've never thought of powers being inside a rock or gem. That kind of thinking never made sense to me. But now . . ." I admire the small gems adorning my wedding band.

Chris adds, "I absolutely love the fact that you put a peridot into my band as well. We were both thinking along the same lines."

"Um, well, not exactly. Your stone is moldavite. It's from a meteorite impact site."

"What? Really?"

"Moldavite represents transformation, Chris. You've transformed since the first day I met you and will continue to do so. I wanted something to be a reminder that change is good." Then I look him in the eye. "Take your ring off, Chris."

He grasps his ring and slides it off his finger.

"Look inside the band," I say.

He angles the ring so the dim light will reflect off the inner surface. I watch carefully to see the moment he reads the words. His eyes widen, then soften as he brings his eyes to mine. He speaks the inscription, "I'll love you forever."

He moves quickly and kisses me intensely. Soon, we find ourselves on the bed, again.

There's nowhere else I'd rather be.

Chapter Nineteen - Crimson's Lack of Vision

Chris's basket of food got us a long way, but it's time we finally head to the main house for more, and back to reality. I can see Brand and Beth sitting on the porch together. He nudges her with his elbow and says loudly, "Look who finally came up for air, and just under twenty-four hours. Nice."

Beth looks in our direction and smiles. "Hey, guys. We were beginning to think we'd need to send some more food to you."

"Thanks for thinking about us, and for staying away," Chris says, a gentle ribbing directed to Brand.

It hits me that no one interfered, interrupted, called, or connected in any way for nearly twenty-four hours. We were able to relax, let go of any inhibitions and enjoy each other unencumbered for the first time in all our time together.

"There are leftovers in the kitchen." Beth hooks her thumb over her shoulder. "Go grab some and come chat."

Soon, we are out front with Brand and Beth with our loaded plates of food. We talk about Brand's life of staying off the grid, and Chris's adventures at the Bureau. Then we discuss the coming blast and our roles, mainly mine. The future is not clear to anyone with the ability to view it. Chris struggles, admittedly, to seeing anything beyond driving me to the capture point.

I hesitate a moment, then say, "I've seen a short vision of you and me after the blast."

"You have? When did you see that?" Chris asks, clearly shocked by my declaration that he'll survive the blast.

"The day before the wedding."

"And you didn't tell me?"

Brand looks at Beth. "Uh oh, first fight."

"I honestly didn't think about it. It was really short and lacked detail other than you were alive after the blast."

Beth's eyebrows rise and her voice softens. "I thought you weren't supposed to look for the future."

"I didn't, well, sort of. Sometimes visions just hit me without any effort. Crimson said those are okay." I leave out the part where she said it probably means something in the future has changed. "Anyway, I'm bringing it up now because we're talking about how people are struggling to see anything after the blast. I didn't say anything yesterday because we had other stuff on our minds."

Brand jumps in, "Crimson is taking me back tonight. She had things to do, but she'll return. I hope she flies slower this time."

I suspect he just repeated to interrupt the line of questioning that Chris was probably about to ask—a delay, nothing else.

"We'll be back in a couple days," Chris adds.

Beth says, "I've decided I'm going to stay with Nate at the Runners' compound till after the blast. I feel like I'm under your feet in Portland and Nate wants to work on another drink concoction. He can't do that in Portland. Besides, I'm at risk of being followed because Brand and I are, well, close." Beth and Brand share an intimate glance.

I reach out and touch her arm. "You're not under our feet, but if you feel being with Nate is better, then I support you."

Brand adds, "I'd feel better knowing you're away from danger."

Our landing gear lowers as we approach Portland International Airport causing the plane to shudder a little against the wind resistance. I look out the window at the city below and take in the mighty Columbia River flowing alongside the airport. Small boats dot the water on this beautiful sunny mid-June day. I clasp Chris's hand.

"I wish this time with you didn't have to end."

"It's not ending. We're just beginning."

"Now, that's an optimistic statement. What I meant was—"

"I know what you meant." He brings our clasped hands to his mouth and kisses the back of my hand. "We have a new life now. I get to live with you, Calli. I get to wake up next to you, kiss you goodbye when I leave for work, and then hear about your day when I get home, and then . . . I get to go to bed with you and do it all over again." His voice drops to a sultry level.

"Wow, your day sounds fun. My days will be a bit more all over the board, except for the sleeping part. But on a serious note, we are so close to the blast date and I'm feeling nervous. I liked not thinking about it while on the island."

The plane touches down and we slow rapidly, then taxi to the hangar. A group of people wait for us. Janet Welsh is front and center.

My four guardians, Duncan, Ruth, Aernoud, and Amenemhet speak to each other as they gather their belongings and clean up their seat area while waiting for Rodger to open the door and lower the stairs.

I glance at Chris. "Back to business."

"Yep."

Duncan says, "Calli, stay on the plane until we make sure everything is safe."

I exhale. "If we had Brand with us, he'd already know. I miss his ability."

Ruth adds, "I've looked to the future to see when Brand will be a part of our daily protection of you. I don't see him."

"Is something bad going to happen?" Panic climbs my throat.

"No, I see him, just not as a guardian."

Chris says, "I'll keep my ears open at work for any information about him. If they are still actively claiming he has government property, he's pretty much out of the picture."

After the all-clear, I'm allowed off the plane. A large black vehicle with tinted windows, like the Secret Service uses in motorcades, is parked nearby. Amenemhet ushers me quickly to the vehicle and opens the back door. I climb in and Chris follows. Soon, the other guardians have entered the car.

Amenemhet says, after turning on the vehicle, "No more renting. This is our new transportation."

"What about my Mini?" I ask.

Chris says, "I could use it to get to work, if you're okay with that."

"Of course."

Amenemhet looks at me in the rear-view mirror. "You won't be driving or riding in the Mini until after the blast, when you're able to view your own future. Not with what we've learned about the government recently."

"And what's that?" I assume he's referring to Maetha's recent visit with the general.

"What we've always known. They cannot be trusted."

The past couple of weeks have flown by since our coupling. I sit curled up on the couch with my warm coffee.

Chris left for his day at the Bureau, leaving me deep in thought, recalling the recent past. We had some adjustments at first, like where the guardians would sleep, and when we could have some "us" time. So far, so good. Chris hasn't detected anything unusual or alarming at work, other than Max keeping extra sticky tabs on him, now that I'm not required to check in anymore. Chris does that daily. I've talked on the phone directly to General Appleton. He's never asked about Brand.

I've noticed advertisements for music and beer festivals that are normally held downtown in late July and early August stating the venue will be in Salem, OR. this year. Other concerts around the time of the blast have been canceled outright. Construction companies have set up signs on downtown streets and on one of the main bridges over the Willamette River stating the roads will be closed July thirtieth through August second for maintenance. I'm relieved the city officials are taking this seriously.

We celebrated our first Independence Day yesterday as a married couple. The balcony off the living room gave us a nice view of the valley and all the mini-fireworks displays—a surprising number of illegal fireworks. Chris and I were able to relax and enjoy the show last night.

Crimson connects with my mind. *Calli, I need to visit you.*

Okay.

Without delay, she lowers herself onto the balcony. I jump up and open the sliding door to let her in. She seems distressed.

"One of the channeling crystals is broken. We will need to find a new one, quickly."

"Now?"

"Yes."

"Well, let me get changed." I hurry into the bedroom and change out of my pajamas, while at the same time I connect with Chris's diamond. *Crimson is here. She's taking me with her to go find another crystal. She seems flustered and in a hurry.*

Be safe. Love you.

Love you, too.

I grab my phone and small wallet, shove them inside my jacket pocket, and zip it shut. I've learned when buying clothes to make sure I have the right attire for the right tasks. This is one of those kinds of tasks. We'll be flying and I don't like feeling helpless the way I did in Norway when Crimson and I were separated. I like having my phone, and I like having money for emergencies.

While I change, Crimson informs my guardians of our hunt for a new crystal. Ruth asks how long I'll be gone. Crimson's response is, "We can't be gone longer than ten days."

What? I enter the front room.

"All right. Let's go." She holds her hand out to me.

We step outside and activate Invisibility. I wrap my arms around her, and she takes off into the sky. I squeeze my eyes shut as she pushes the level of g-forces my body can handle again and again, causing me to be in a constant state of healing to prevent throwing up.

We finally slow to a stop, and I open my eyes and peek over my shoulder. We are *way* above the ground. Below our feet, I see a couple airplanes cruising above the clouds. They look like little toys. We must be above 50,000 feet if we're that much higher than the planes. A fresh nausea wave rolls in my stomach, and I tighten my hold on Crimson.

"Why are we stopped, Crimson?"

"Let's talk about your ring," she responds.

"Up here? Can't we land first?"

"You need to get used to being above ground. Plus, up here we don't need to worry about anyone overhearing us."

"I thought we were going to go find another crystal."

"We are. However, your ring just activated when you healed your nausea. We will discuss this first before continuing."

I feel a little ashamed that my ring tattled on me. I can't help it.

"So, your enhancer diamond. It normally activates with fear or anger. Have you experienced both?"

"I don't know about anger, but yes, with fear." Fear of dying at the hands of Max.

"Brand told me he's repeated with you a few times to undo the ring activating."

I'm surprised to hear this. "Yeah, he told me about some moments. Chris also helped me avoid a moment, having looked to the future."

"Until the blast, try to keep yourself in calm settings, absent of anger and fear. There is a chance the band may not fully bond with your finger the way you've seen, but only if you prevent more activations."

"Has the future changed? My visions always show the ring stuck to my finger."

"Not to my knowledge. I recommend that you try to stay as calm as possible."

"Why don't I just take it off until the day of the blast. I know I have to wear it then."

Crimson adjusts her body slightly and cranes her head back to be able to look me in the eye. "Have you tried taking the ring off?"

"Well, no. Not recently."

"You'll find you cannot move it too far from your body before it springs back, like a magnet. The diamond is bonded with you now through the platinum. It protects and helps you. It wants to be a part of you."

I can't even imagine what she's saying. "Is it alive?"

"Not in the sense that you define alive."

"Um, okay. I don't understand what that means."

"You will eventually."

I shake my head. "That doesn't help me now. Can we please land?"

"Not yet."

I let out a heavy sigh. "So, if the ring is already magnetized and drawn to my finger, how would that be any different if I'm able to control my emotions till the blast. What then?"

"The Sanguine Diamond in your heart will absorb the full Elemental powers, one of which is Earth, and you'll have power over platinum because it is mined from the ground. You should be able to prevent the band from permanently bonding with your skin. By preventing the bond, you'll have better control over the enhancer. But if it bonds, your powers will be more difficult to manage."

"So, the enhancer diamond is connected to me forever."

"Yes. Till you die."

"I can't relinquish it to someone, like with the Sanguine?"

"No."

"I wish I would have known this information earlier."

"By the time Maetha identified the diamond on your finger, you had already activated it by healing Chris. It was already too late. She and I have been working tirelessly to find a way for you to be rid of it. Severing your finger has been discussed, so long as the ring remains on the severed finger."

"What?" I exclaim uncontrollably.

"We decided against that, just so you know. Staying calm until you can control the platinum using Earth power is the only other way for you to have better control over the enhancer. Your superior healing ability simply isn't strong enough on its own."

"Keeping me up here in the stratosphere isn't helping me stay calm. Maybe you should send me to some mountain top sanctuary and put me in a coma till the blast."

"Well, that's a little extreme. How about you exercise self-control instead. All right. Speaking of Earth power, we are going to use the Elemental power of Earth to locate a new channeling quartz. One fell while I flew. By the time I realized it, I couldn't repeat back with my prism. Thankfully, no one on the ground was hurt."

"I thought you already positioned the channeling stones. Isn't that why we located the spot on the building that one day?"

"No, we only established where they would be placed. I told you I'd place them two weeks out from the blast. Okay, let's get to the task at hand. The coming blast will contain the Earth power which allows the affected to manipulate anything naturally occurring in the ground. With training, rocks can be identified, along with oil and natural gas pockets, magma chambers, fossils, gems, metals, etc. We're going to use it to locate quartz."

"How is the Earth ability a bad thing?" I ask.

"Well, someone could cause an earthquake by identifying and releasing the blockages on a fault line. They could cause deadly landslides by moving the right boulder."

"They can lift rocks? So, telekinesis?"

"Not exactly. They can shift minor positioning which results in other movement. A fault line will move freely without restrictions, but always at its own pace. An Earther cannot move the continental plates, but by identifying where they are jammed, they can release that spot. Same with a landslide. Find the small rocks holding up the big ones and move them. Then you get an avalanche effect."

My head starts to swim and becomes dizzy. I try to heal

myself but can't find the strength to do so. "Crimson, I don't feel good."

"Our oxygen is low. The atmospheric bubble only holds so much, you know. That's another good lesson about that power." We start moving toward the ground at a rapid pace. "We need to get down to higher oxygen levels. When I fly on my own, I can go much further before I need to descend."

She slows us down and removes the atmospheric control bubble. I inhale sharply, taking in much needed air.

"Hold my hand so you can feel the energy of the Earth power."

I unwrap one arm and take her hand and notice a subtle electrical buzz—then again, my whole body is still buzzing from the lack of oxygen. "What should I be feeling?"

"It's electrical, like a vibration or a buzz."

"Okay, I got that."

"Now, we need to locate another channeling crystal. Reach out with your mind and search for the frequency of large quartz."

"The what? How?"

"You've held charged quartz before. Think back to what it felt like in your hand, the frequency. Feel for the crystal below the surface."

Even though we are closer to the ground than before, we're still incredibly high in the air which makes me sick to my stomach. "This might be easier if we were on the ground, Crimson."

"No, on the ground we are on someone's property or government land. We need permissions and permits and such. But if we can locate where the crystal is from up here, we can determine what action will need to be taken to acquire the quartz."

I shake my head. "I'm confused about why you aren't

able to do this on your own. Why am I here?"

"This is a learning experience. I'm teaching you how to use Earth power, which will be helpful once you receive the Elemental power."

"Can't you charge a topaz with it so I can learn faster? And on the ground."

"There's not enough time for that. We must find a replacement today."

"It's hard to know what I'm sensing while we're in the sky. I'm feeling a lot of things probably not related to the crystal."

"Maybe this isn't going to work," Crimson says. "Try using your Hunter's vision on the ground below us. Look for glints of light or flat edges. Try to see beneath the surface, under the dirt, under the grass, below the trees."

I don't know what she's talking about, nor do I know how to look underground. However, an idea comes to mind. "Where did you find the last crystals?"

"In the Singapore region."

"Why aren't we there, then?"

"Because I know the same types of quartz crystals can be found here."

"Where are we exactly?"

"Arkansas."

"Crimson, have you tried looking to the future to see *where* we'll find a large quartz?"

She turns her head in my direction, inhales deeply, and holds her breath a moment longer than necessary before letting it go. "Some things don't work that way, Calli."

"What?" I'm confused by her response.

"For me, things don't work that way."

Now, I'm totally confused.

Crimson drops her head toward her chest for a moment, then brings her gaze up to mine. "All right, let's land."

Our floating position changes to measured descension. She continues, "It's time I trust you with something that no one else knows, and I don't do this casually, mind you. But, as my preferred future Bearer of the Primal Stone, you need to understand this aspect of the immense power. I focus on the long-range future because my body becomes drained of energy when I look to the short-range. If I try to look for events closer than one-hundred-fifty or so years, I will become ill."

I muse that, to her, one-hundred-fifty years is considered short-range. I can't imagine.

Our feet connect with the ground in an uninhabited area with rocky hills. She continues. "I've been aware of this blast for thousands of years. But as time neared, I started to lose focus on the actual event. I can see the next time this blast will hit the earth in three thousand years, but *this* blast is too near to see without putting myself out of commission for many hours if not days. I cannot afford to be down for that long. Not when every second counts."

My thoughts scramble to understand what she's saying. "But you can heal yourself. Right?"

"I'm limited. Remember, I'm not an Unaltered. I was a Healer in my day, and I could heal my own body before I acquired the Primal Stone. Recall in your mind when the Death Clan died. They were trying to use their power on you while you held the diamond. Their power backfired and killed them. I believe I'm unable to differentiate my natural Healer power from the Primal Stone's Healer power and thus will end up killing myself if I try too hard—like the Death Clan."

"Sounds like you need a Healer quartz."

"Hmm, I will consider that."

I feel emboldened. "May I try looking to the future to see where we'll find the quartz we need?"

"All right, go ahead."

I close my eyes and concentrate on the answers I seek. Nothing comes to mind. I clear my mind and attempt with a different way of thinking.

"How's your vision coming along?" Crimson asks, sounding as though she already knows the answer.

"I'm still working on it. I'll try looking at the quartz as we put it in place for the blast, maybe that will help me find it here."

"No. Doing that can alter the future. If you can't see where we'll find it here, then I've made my point. Near future visions are hard to perform."

"I'm not able to see anything. You must be super-surprised," I add sarcastically.

"You don't know what to look for. This is not any different than when the other Bearers said they couldn't envision the blast hitting Portland. They didn't know what to look for."

"Will I be able to learn how to see the near future at will?"

"After the blast, if you want to learn to scry, there's nothing stopping you. You may find you do what I do and trust the near future to those who can see it with ease, like Maetha."

"So, all this time you haven't been able to see the near future?" I'm truly surprised to learn this about her.

"Why do you think I made the Sanguine Diamond? I needed helpers. I already had my own team of Seers to keep me apprised of the future, but their powers were limited, and they couldn't be trusted all the time. I needed eyes on the immediate future, eyes I could trust, so I created the diamond. This is also why I've maintained an Unaltered line, actually several lines, to have a pool of individuals to choose from for Bearers. With the invention of the power-removing machine, I hoped to expand the pool, but now we know machine-made Unaltereds like Chris are not the same, entirely. They're even more fragile than I am. On the day Chris became an Unaltered, you and I both knew that was going to happen because of your snippet of a vision, yet neither of us could see what would happen soon after."

"You mean, that you would allow him to carry a diamond?"

"Maetha and I knew the two of you were stronger as two Diamond Bearers in love, so we allowed Chris to become a casual Bearer—to carry the diamond on his person. Humanity's long-range future looked optimistic with that choice, so I didn't tell you he'd die or could die if his diamond was inserted. I did, however, insist you do the insertion to ward off any chance he might try to do it without you present. And all those choices were made with the Elemental blast in mind. If we fail in capturing the power, all Diamond Bearers will cease to exist."

"What about Jonas and his diamond?"

"Jonas is a topic for another day, Calli. We must find the quartz."

I sense her disappointment about Jonas, so I don't push. "Crimson, is it okay to tell Chris what you've told me today?"

"If you feel he should know, then you have my permission. Let's get back to the quartz search."

I look to the ground and examine the dirt and rocks, looking for anything that might resemble a crystal. Crimson is peering around also with the same kind of lost look on her face. An idea comes to my mind. "You know, there are several websites devoted to this exact thing. Can't we just look up online sellers of quartz?"

"What are you talking about?"

"Websites. Internet. Crimson, people sell things online.

We should at least try. It might be faster than locating a quartz here and then getting the permission to remove it." I pull out my phone from my inside pocket.

"You can't use your phone here."

No surprise, no service. "Fly us to the nearest town, then, so I can search." I half smile after speaking, hoping she'll comply.

"All right. We'll try your idea. Take hold and activate Invisibility."

I do so and wrap my arms around her body and she lifts us into the air. I have no idea which direction she takes us but assume she knows what she's doing. After a couple minutes, she lowers to the ground in a small town park.

I check my phone for confirmation of service and begin my search. Crimson paces nearby.

Scrolling through images on a popular selling website, I find one and say, "Okay, come check this out." I extend my hand holding the phone toward her.

She walks over and examines my find. "Hmm, that's impressive, but not quite right. The points are off. Can you search for "channeling quartz?"

I continue looking for possible options until I stumble upon a picture of one similar to what she showed me in Portland with Maetha.

"Whoa! That one!" Crimson's finger juts against the phone screen. "Where is that located?"

"Arkansas. Ta-da," I sing, pointing to the screen. "See? Twenty-first century technology wins again. Thank God for advertising algorithms capturing our location and displaying local sellers."

"That one is only about fifty miles away. Let's go!"

After surprising our crystal seller by showing up in person after a brief back-and-forth conversation online, we begin our trip back to Oregon with the new crystal safely strapped to Crimson. No more dropsies. As we soar through the sky, my arms wrapped tightly around Crimson, I think about what she said. She created the Sanguine diamond to form a group of helpers. She's nurtured Unaltered lines throughout history, like Maetha's, and has kept pregnant mothers away from cosmic blasts, like with my mother, to create more Unaltereds. I assume this tradition will carry on with me and my future children, all with the purpose of keeping a line of helper candidates at the ready.

Crimson is creating the Elemental diamond for a similar purpose: to have helpers who can assist in locating and managing affected people. Normally, this wouldn't happen for a few years in the future because the babies that will be infused with the cosmic ray would first have to be born, grow up, and have their powers emerge.

I remember the vision I had about the Portland hotel clerk named James. He will be directly involved with me as we go up against the Elemental power. He will become ill and apparently be healed. In my vision, he wasn't much older than he was when I saw him, meaning the dangerous health effects of the blast will be instantaneous for some people.

But how quickly will the Elemental powers begin to appear in humans?

My question causes a vision to open in my mind: scenes of children moving cars and buses with their minds, adults harnessing fire with their hands and invisible forces causing tornadoes, earthquakes and tsunamis. The scenes are rapid and a bit blurry. The vision ends leaving me breathless.

I tighten my hold on Crimson.

Is everything all right, Calli? She speaks to my mind as we fly, no longer having the quantum entanglement the Blue

Diamond afforded her.

Yes.

I determine we need to double down on plans to remove pregnant women from the city. General Appleton's strategies apparently aren't going to be enough. Additionally, we need to figure out what to do with individuals who develop Elemental powers. Once they're identified, will they be placed in a program to teach them about their power? Will they be dangerous and need to be locked up? I don't know.

We're going to be busy right out of the gates.

July is long and hot, each day dragging on, a slow trudge toward the blast date. More and more people arrive to help with the aftermath. The military has truckloads of makeshift hospital beds and equipment in the parking lot of the new Bureau, waiting to be set up. This will have to wait until evacuations are underway. Otherwise, word could get out that the government is somehow involved with the crisis, that they knew it was coming. Conspiracy theorists would love to shine a bright light on a shadow operation run by the military and supernaturally powered people. We don't want that to happen, not yet anyway.

The reality is that the time of secrecy is coming to an end for people with powers. Between the government knowing our abilities and the Reapers actively hunting us, all that's left is for the general public to be made aware. The "when" is still potentially able to be put off for a while longer, provided we can keep up appearances as long as possible.

Coming up on July twenty-ninth, my parents will come to Portland for an extended stay. I'll be leaving the area the next day to try to avoid fear-related events sparking an accidental igniting of my ring, in the attempt to retain control over my powers after the blast.

Recently, I helped Crimson insert the large channeling crystals into their permanent locations atop three different buildings. Then she flew me to the rooftop from my vision where we further calibrated the three stones to point to the same spot. We did this by having Crimson fly to each of the three crystals and individually point them to me. We could both tell when the alignment was correct because the prism would reflect on my body, similar to having a sun catcher's rainbow dance over me. But once she aimed the last channeler in my direction, I was absolutely blown away by the sudden appearance of the net. It looked like a triangular spider's web made of prismatic-colored silk, or elongated rainbows. Each quartz reflected on me, and each formed a connection with another quartz resulting in a funnel appearance that only I could see. If I stepped out of alignment, I could no longer see the net. We had zeroed in on the exact location where I would need to stand when the blast arrived. Crimson painted an X on the rooftop to mark the spot.

A heavy sense of trepidation settled in my stomach as I stood on the painted X in the center of the ethereal silky rainbow funnel. What seemed like forever away was now just around the corner.

When I questioned Crimson about the stability of the channelers, she assured me the setup was secure and that Maetha had not foreseen any interference that would throw off the alignment. Additionally, six Bearers will be tasked with guarding the three valuable quartzes. They will work in shifts and will basically live on the rooftops till just before the blast, keeping watch over the important crystals.

Each evening when Chris arrives home, I try to focus on us and let go of the world outside the window. We enjoy our time together, cooking, cleaning, even doing yard work for Iva. My guardians and Iva have regular bar-b-ques. They've all become good friends. These last weeks have felt rather normal, and I've made mental notes and pictures of the happiness, contentment, and peace I've felt because deep down, I know this is coming to an end when the blast hits.

Because of this fear, which I'm supposed to be avoiding, I've been meditating whenever I can. I've tried to prevent setting off my ring, and of course, I've tried to remove the ring and block it from jumping back to my finger. It's disturbing, yet kind of fun to watch. But I'm careful not to draw attention to the ring around Chris. He's bothered that he accidentally gave me a lifelong burden. I don't want him feeling like this is his fault. Somehow, I believe he was manipulated into giving me this stone. Too much of a coincidence otherwise.

💍 💍 💍

After saying goodbye to my parents who arrived last night, Crimson lifts me into the air, headed for an unknown location deep in the Cascade Mountain Range. My heart races as I look to my right at Mt. Hood standing ominously high above the other mountains. To my left, I see other volcanoes, but none as tall.

Crimson lowers out of the sky, heading toward a lookout tower. "We'll camp out here."

"Is this a fire tower?" I ask.

"Yes."

"What if there are fires? Who will report them?"

"You and Chris will, of course." She extends her hand, holding a key chain with a few keys. "Let yourself in while I go get Chris."

At least I'll get to be with Chris during the last stretch before the blast, I think to myself as I watch Crimson fly away in a flash.

Ȫ Ȫ Ȫ

Sitting next to Chris and watching the news on the television, frustration and incredulity rise inside me. The evacuation is well underway, and everything is wrong. I feel as if nothing I said to the mayor is being utilized.

"You should turn that off, Calli. I can feel your anger building." Crimson looks at me over the top of her magazine.

Chris massages my shoulders. "She's right."

"But they're screwing this up!" I argue. "They could be opening all lanes of traffic to evacuation, like I suggested, but they're not. More people are at risk of being hit by the radiation because they can't evacuate quickly enough. I don't think their announcement of possible nuclear attack was timed right, either. They moved too early. Now the whole world is talking about this mass evac as being a government cover-up, which is what we didn't want to happen. That will only draw more people toward Portland." I let out a huff. "And then there are the people who believe this is the Rapture and they're not leaving. Anika should have been here to convince them to leave."

The television shuts off. I glare at Crimson who holds the remote.

Chris says, "Let's step outside, Calli." He offers his hand to me, and I take it. We walk to the door and go out onto the deck that encircles the entire tower. The sun hangs low in the west casting an array of orange, yellow and red colors into the sky.

I inhale deeply a few times and exhale my steamed emotions.

"Do you hear that, Calli?"

"What? I don't hear anything."

"Yes, that. Silence. We are surrounded by nature and its natural order. The noise in our lives right now all comes from that box inside. Let's leave it be and focus on us and the task at hand."

"Okay, you're right. It's just, this is it, Chris. Tomorrow is the day Crimson and Maetha have been planning, plotting, and scheming for how many thousands of years?"

"You are nervous."

"Absolutely. Aren't you?"

"Always."

His single word brings me back to my senses; I'm not the only one affected by the events of tomorrow. Chris has had to sacrifice a lot, too.

Crimson steps out on the deck. "My apologies for the order before. You can watch television if you like, Calli. I feel I've explained the consequences well enough of setting off your enhancer. I also feel I've impressed upon you the importance of successfully capturing the blast tomorrow. I'm going to leave you two alone now. I'll be back tomorrow afternoon."

Chris wraps his arm around my shoulders. "I'm sure we'll be just fine. Thank you, Crimson."

She nods and flies away into the sunset.

Chris and I feed ourselves and then enjoy each other while listening to a few movies. Knowing no one except Crimson would interrupt us—and she would announce her return prior to arrival—I allow myself to fully relax in Chris's arms. I haven't felt this detached from the world since being on the island during our honeymoon. I sink into every moment, not knowing when we may have the chance to be this alone, or relaxed, again.

Chapter Twenty - Repercussions

The day begins like any other morning since our coupling in June, opening my eyes to find Chris lying next to me. I hope this never gets old. I wrap my arm across his chest and bring my lips to his temple. "Good morning," I whisper.

He places one of his hands on mine. "Mmm. Morning."

"Do you think they have any coffee here?"

Chris laughs. "Of course, they do. They need to have someone awake all the time to watch for fires."

We pull ourselves from the cozy bed and shuffle to the kitchen area and find the makings for coffee, then we wrap up in blankets while waiting for the brew. The sun is already up in the east.

I say, looking up to the ceiling, "Somewhere up there in the sky, a beam of energy is hurtling toward us, ready to change our lives. Are you ready?"

"Nope. You?"

"Nope. But I am ready for this to be done."

Crimson returns when she said she would. She looks frazzled.

"All right, you two. I'll take Calli first, then come back for you, Chris."

"Is everything okay?" I ask her.

"Things will be better when you can fly yourself, my dear."

"Or maybe things would be better if you could carry both of us at the same time?"

"That, too. But Chris it much larger than Brand, so he'll have to wait. Let's go."

I give Chris a hug and a kiss and go with Crimson.

We fly quickly to the city. As we approach, I see columns of smoke at different places from fires. Sirens blare from every direction and traffic snakes along the main roads heading out of town. However, all lanes are being used to exit the city, now, which is a relief.

I note the difference in my mind between viewing the destruction and pandemonium in person compared to watching it unfold on the television. At the fire lookout hideaway, I felt angry the leaders weren't using my suggestions. I was caught up in my own head, thinking the orchestration of evacuation was handled poorly. But now, seeing, hearing, and smelling the panic the residents are experiencing causes me to become sick to my stomach, yearning for their safety, wishing I'd done more to help the people escape the coming blast.

"Crimson, did you have something to do with this change of using all lanes to evacuate? They weren't doing this yesterday."

"You raised a lot of good points last night. I did the best I could to help out. Unfortunately, the rioters and looters don't seem concerned about their safety, and some of the homeless camps downtown are unwilling to give up their spots. There have also been several homeowners and store owners who refuse to leave their premises. However, most of those cars down there will make it past the five-mile radius point."

"Most?"

"Unfortunately. At least by using all lanes on the major highways to evacuate, no new vehicles are coming into the city."

She lowers me to the ground near the mayor's office. It looks like a war zone. A noxious haze lingers in the air from the riots last night. Alarms blare. Windows up and down the street are smashed out, including the door to City Hall. "Go inside. Amenemhet and Duncan are waiting for you. I'll be back with Chris."

I do as she says and quickly get off the street.

Mayor Overton stands in the reception area. "Any last changes to the plan?" he asks when I enter.

"No."

"How long will the radiation last?"

"At least till noon tomorrow. It looks like things have been rough here."

"Well, considering nothing like this has ever happened in our city, I think it went as well as could be expected."

General Appleton enters with Max and some other military personnel. The general says, "Mayor, it's time to go." He turns to me. "Calli, good to see you're still alive."

"I'm sorry?"

"Max couldn't reach you on your phone. Or Chris."

"We weren't able to take calls in the mountains."

Max snarls and puffs out his chest. "Well, you just kind of disappeared at the moment everything went crazy here."

"Calm down, Max," I say, admittedly a little heavy on the condescending side.

Max lunges toward me. Startled, I take a step back. Amenemhet moves faster and blocks him. Max shouts, "Don't tell me to calm down! What are you hiding from us? What's with all the secrecy? Why are the Diamond People all over the city? Where is Brand?"

I can feel my anger building and my ring warming. This guy is not going to cause me to lose control over my emotions. I inhale deeply, close my eyes, and send my thoughts to Chris.

Hey there.

Yes, what is it?

Tell me something you look forward to after the blast.

Uh, I can't wait for you to take me flying instead of Crimson. She definitely goes too fast.

I smile. *Thanks.*

"What's so funny?" Max yells as I open my eyes.

I don't answer. Instead, I turn my back to him and say to the mayor, "There is still quite the traffic jam out there, sir. You should probably evacuate now, so you have enough time to get to the bunker. Unless you have a helicopter or some other means of transport."

General Appleton joins our conversation and says, "We've barricaded a bridge and several roads to secure an open path to Kelly Butte Bunker for the city officials."

"What about you, General?" I ask.

"We have air transport back to the Bureau hub where we'll finish the field hospital set-up. Hopefully, we won't need to use it."

We discuss logistics for several more minutes, then Chris enters the building and glares at Max as he passes him. "You guys better get going," Chris admonishes.

I say, "I already told them that."

He turns to me. "We'd better get going, too. Two-hour traffic jams are common in this city under normal conditions. This is anything but."

Amenemhet ushers me out to his large vehicle. Chris and I get into the backseat with Duncan. Amenemhet drives us along the deserted streets and past the sign on the corner flashing the numbers 8/1 and 81F. I look over at Chris and together we chuckle. Then his smile falls.

"Calli, I was driving in my vision. We were in your Mini."

I smile, nervously, while trying to ignore the eerie feeling deep inside. "Something's changed. I hope it's for the better."

Amenemhet enters the parking garage and parks near the elevators. The four of us ascend to the top floor, then take the roof access stairs for the last leg. Out on the roof is Crimson, holding a bundle of off-white fabric.

Crimson says, "Calli you will need to wear this for when the blast hits."

"What is it?" I ask, taking the bundle from her. My stomach is in knots and my hands shake as I fumble with the clothing.

"It's a cotton robe."

I unravel the robe that looks more like a nightgown my grandma might wear and hold it out at arm's-length. I don't see any metal clasps or plastic buttons, only two ties at the neckline to draw it together. I ask, "What's significant about this?"

Crimson waves her hand dismissively. "Nothing. It's that, or you don't wear anything at all."

"I don't remember wearing this in my visions."

Chris's eyebrows scrunch together. "You don't? What were you wearing?"

I think for a moment but can't recall anything. "I don't know. It wasn't a focus point. I mean, I never really looked myself over, only noticed the ring turned green and became stuck to my finger. I always felt like I was wearing normal clothes, I guess. I certainly wasn't naked." I take my wedding band off and hand it to Chris. "However, this band wasn't part of my vision. You'll protect this for me, won't you?"

"Of course." He takes the ring and slides it onto his little finger. Chris takes both my hands with his and pulls me close, his eyes connect with mine. "This is it."

"Yes," I say, "This is the moment they planned my life for. I sure hope there's more after this blast hits, and that it's in *my* control."

"Me too. I have a lot of plans that include you."

His words bring hope to my overloaded brain. So much has happened in the last couple of hours, so much realization, revelation, and despair has inundated my senses that I find I'm struggling to keep my focus. But his words and closeness bring me comfort. I feel revitalized. Then it hits me. He just infused me with healing power, strengthening my resolve to face down my task.

Thanks, Chris.

Just repaying for all the many times you've extended healing to me.

Crimson says, "Okay. Chris it's time for you to go. Calli, you need to change."

I give Chris a desperate hug and kiss him, pouring all of my hopes and fears into this one gesture of togetherness. "I love you."

"I love you too, Calli. We've got to stop having so many dramatic moments in our lives." He winks at me

"But they're so fun." I try to joke.

Crimson says, "You two are Diamond Bearers and have defied all the odds, especially you Chris. Should everything play out the way it needs to today, you *will* have more drama in your life, you can count on that."

"What do you mean should everything play out right?" Chris asks.

I look at Chris and say, "She always talks like that. Just go. It'll be fine."

Crimson tells Amenemhet and Duncan, "Take Chris and go pick up the other crystal protectors who should be on their way down to the street. Then go to Calli's apartment."

Chris leaves and I change out of my clothing and into the robe. I set my clothing down in a pile by the door.

Crimson says. "Okay, Calli. We're down to the final stretch. You need to take your place on the X inside the triangle with the diamond. Once you're inside the net, you will be all alone. You won't be able to communicate with other Bearers or with me. No one will be able to bi-locate to you nor you to them." She reaches inside her pocket and pulls out a Sanguine Diamond. "You'll hold this in your left hand. And something else—" She walks over to a pile of boxes and pallets and grabs a metal handcart. She inserts it under a frame built of metal rods and wheels it toward me. She positions it over the triangle. "Stand here, and I'll strap you in."

"I'll be tied down?"

"You must be, Calli. The blast will weaken you and you will fall otherwise. You need to remain positioned correctly for the diamond to absorb the blast properly. So, come on. Let's get you situated."

I move to where she directs me, and she wraps long strips of the same cloth as my robe around my waist and feet. Then she extends my arm forward and creates a sling hanging from the bar above to rest my wrist. Finally, she wraps my chest to the frame. I'm completely bound.

I don't like this very much.

"There. Now, look around. Do you see the net?"

"Yes. The triangle spider's web."

"Perfect. I must go and clear a path for Chris and the others to get to safety. I won't be back till after the blast, but I know you're ready and I know you can more than handle this."

"How will I know it's done?"

"The funnel will disintegrate on its own, and then you'll heal any remaining harm to your body. I will return as quickly as I can. Until I do, just stay put."

She flies away leaving me feeling strange. I don't recall any of this in my vision. I wasn't bound. The sun hasn't even set. The blast hits in the night, doesn't it? One thing's for sure; I can't communicate with anyone. This is like being surrounded by obsidian, except I can still feel all my powers.

I can see the last rays of sun illuminating Mt. Hood's peak. The distant sounds of business and car alarms echo across the valley. An airplane climbs into the sky heading east. Hopefully, it is the last flight out. I'm not able to see the main highways from where I'm standing to see if the traffic is moving any better. I sure hope all this planning and preparation works. Now, all that's left is to wait for dark to settle in.

I stand in the triangle with the diamond in my hand waiting for the elemental blast to reach the earth. Everything I've learned in school about the universe, the stars, and the planets helps me understand how even though a few thousand years seems like a long time for a cosmic beam to reach us, it's nothing compared to the size of the universe and how fast light can travel.

Across the rooftop, the door to the staircase unexpectedly opens.

Vita emerges.

Shock, followed by animosity, hits me. What is she doing here? "Vita?" I ask, immediately aware that I can do nothing while bound.

She grins and walks a circle around me, reminiscent of the time she entered the room at the Bureau, stopping when she completes the circle. She faces me, her eyes a little too bright, and says, "Calli, I wouldn't miss this for the world." Her exuberance is alarming.

"With all this chaos going on, you decide to come and watch? Didn't you listen to Crimson, or the warnings? It's not safe."

"I listened. I also found her solutions and preparation wanting. I've decided to intervene and help this work out better." She waves and wiggles her hands side to side, back and forth, and mysteriously produces a small leather pouch. *What is that power?* I don't have the time to dwell on that right now as she reaches in and removes a black rock, then bends forward and places it on the ground nearby. I can tell it's not obsidian as I still feel my powers.

The immenseness of the situation comes back to mind. The blast is coming soon. As much as I dislike Vita, I don't want her to die from the radiation fallout. "Listen. You need to get out of here while you still can."

"Always thinking of others. How touching. Don't worry, I'll be protected. But your refugees might not be." She begins to walk around again, depositing more black stones in a circle around me as she goes.

My mind reels, replaying Crimson's instructions and detailed descriptions of where the three points of triangulation should be located. I quickly glance around and see the rainbow net is intact. Then, I stop cold as Vita's words sink in. "What do you mean about the refugees?"

She continues her movements and says, "I've made some adjustments to the calibrations to expand the fallout radius."

Ice creeps up my spine. *Expand* the radius? "How could you even know about that?" I twist my head to the right as far as I can to try to see what she's doing.

"My dear child, Crimson is following *my* collection method and calibrations from when we channeled the Mind-Control power into the Blue Diamond. She did not know how to do it, so she came and asked for my help. I was more than happy to help the goddess." Vita has nearly completed the circle with the black stones. "I monitored the triangulation points and watched from afar as she held the diamond in her own hands while it was blasted with the cosmic ray. Not that I can see the rays, but the diamond glowed a brilliant blue once it was empowered. The fallout from that blast was controlled due to my precise triangulation. Today, I'm once again in control of the triangulation, unbeknownst to Crimson. I know this because she hasn't fixed my recalculations of the stations. Or maybe she knows and is choosing not to fix them. Hmmm." She taps her finger on her chin while looking upward with her eyes.

Becoming enraged, blood rushes through my veins. "Why would you want to mess this up and hurt people?"

"You and I are different, Calli. You want to keep everyone safe. I, however, want as many people to be affected by the blast as possible."

"But, why?" My voice cracks.

She removes one more stone from the pouch and tucks the pouch inside her pocket. She does not put the stone on the ground. Holding the stone at arm's length in front of her eyes, she examines it. Her focus shifts from the close object in her hand to my eyes. She lowers her arm and says, "The world used to be ruled by the gods and goddesses. Those with special abilities were revered—whether received naturally from the stars, or learned, like in my case. We were the Healers, the Prophets, and the correctors of the ordinary humans. We were respected. Then, thanks to Crimson and the Diamond Bearers, the world view changed, and we had to go into hiding to avoid ridicule and incarceration, even death. I say enough is enough. We must take back the rule of the planet. We must rise above the regular humans and make them bow to us once again."

I really wish I could communicate with someone, to warn them. I try to connect with Chris's diamond. I know it's futile, but I try anyway. *Chris, can you hear me? You have to move further away. The blast is going to reach beyond what we estimated. If you can hear me, please go!*

I wait for a response but hear nothing.

She continues, "I, for one, am quite thrilled there will be many individuals to run through the machines. We've already amassed a large quantity of quartz stones that are waiting to be charged, and soon we'll have new Elemental powers to extract as well." She bends forward to set the last stone down.

"Wait, what? You are involved with the machines?"

She pauses and tightens her grip on the stone, not setting it down. She stands again. "Yes. I've worked on this for centuries, young one. I recruited Henry the Diamond Bearer to help me pull together more resources and tools to further the goal. He helped set up the Bureau, and he got General Harding up and running. Henry was my right-hand man." She thrusts her stone-clenched fist toward my face, with her first finger pointing accusingly as if she's picking me out of a police lineup. "He was supposed to be here beside me to welcome in the Age of Supremacy!" She lowers her arm and takes a deep breath. "I suppose he is here in some form. You have his diamond in your heart and his essence is present."

My head spins ridiculously. "You worked with Freedom, er Henry? Who are you really? I mean, I know you worked with Maetha on her island, and evidently you worked with Crimson. You are with Max and the government now, too. What else do I need to know about you?"

"Why should I tell you anything more about me?" she hisses, then softens her demeanor and tone. "Unless you want to join me, like Jonas."

"You probably have him under some kind of spell."

"I didn't do anything. I didn't need to. Jonas found me, which is not an easy thing to do. He asked to work with me, and who was I to turn him away?"

"How did he find you?"

"Through my company. Vorherrschaft."

"*You* are Vorherrschaft?" I actually want my ring to activate so I can . . . do what? Kill her? Detain her? My emotions are all over the board, yet my ring is calm.

She seems to be energized by my exclamation. "I can't tell you how happy I am that Jonas found me. I learned from him that all Bearers have Shadow Demons following them. I wondered what had happened to my friends. You see, the Grecian Blue cosmic ray hit during the day, not at night when the Demons are out. I'm curious to find out if they can be affected by the incoming power, now that you've discovered how to turn them into blank canvases."

"There's too much light for the demons." I nod in the direction of the lights on the top of the building.

"We'll see, right?" As she says this, I struggle against my bonds. I have to be able to communicate to someone about Vita's plan. But before I can wiggle enough, she adds, "But more than anything, I am interested to see what happens with your ring."

I feel like I've been punched in the gut. "What?"

"Yes. I'm sure you've been told about its significance."

I don't answer. I'm shocked she's even bringing it up.

"I want to know which powers will be absorbed by the enhancer diamond, and if the powers from your Sanguine Diamond will also be transferred. Chris was essential to the quest, you know."

I am speechless and breathless.

"Yes. He was going to select white gold for the band, so I 'encouraged' him to upgrade to platinum. It's the only way to form a proper conduit from your heart to the ring. I'll be sure to thank him for access to his impressionable, feeble mind."

The level of anger heating my body is so high I feel I might explode. I want to break free from my bonds to attack this woman and to alert my loved ones to flee further away.

She continues. "Then again, you've always been the sacrificial lamb, Calli, so, thank *you* for that."

"You sound like you think I'm about to die."

A tinkly laugh escapes her mouth. "Of course you will. Don't worry, though. The ring will be taken care of with great respect, believe me. Your essence will be a part of the new Supremacy era, just as Henry is part of this moment today." She takes the black rock in her hand and vigorously rubs it against her other palm, then bends forward and taps it against the nearest similar piece before placing the last stone on the ground to complete the circle. I hear a crackle and sizzle similar to the sound of a match igniting. The sound encircles me, one black rock at a time, seemingly igniting one after another. She stands, then turns and walks away.

"Wait, what are these rocks for? What are they?" I shout in her direction.

She waves over her shoulder and enters the door to the staircase. My mind is flooded with new information. I don't remember anything about the black stone circle in my visions. Where is Crimson? I know I'm not about to die. I've already seen beyond the blast in my vision. But that vision didn't show me bound or these stones near me. My heart rate increases, and I feel rushing in my ears. Is this why I wasn't allowed to view my future? Too many changes would have shown me I'm going to die?

The power grid for the entire city begins to turn off in an ominous patterned succession, leaving me in darkness, allowing my Shadow Demons to become visible. They've been around me the whole time. I want to make them go away, wish I could order them to leave, but I know that I can't. Without adequate light, that's not possible.

I try for Chris again. Nothing. The crackle in the air around me intensifies and I sense the blast is near. I look up to the sky expecting to see something but can't. The stars are visible now that everything is dark around me. I use my Hunter's vision to search the night sky as far as I can. Then I see it. A white pinpoint directly above me growing larger in diameter as it approaches. The diamond in my hand begins to warm. My heart pounds faster. I identify that the racing is coming from the diamond within my anxious heart. My ears plug as my blood pressure does strange things. My head is filled with a vibration and deafening roar as if I've placed my ear on a train track and a large freight is barreling down upon me. The fear that I feel is more like being tied to the train track, unable to free myself.

The pieces of black rocks on the ground rise from the rooftop and float in the air at the same level as the diamond in my hand. My body feels as though it is rising as well, even though I can still feel the cement under my feet. This sensation causes my heart to erupt in panic, bringing pain as it heats the diamond in my heart to white-hot. I remember how my chest burned when I was on the stone altar with the diamond on top of me. It was excruciating then and is no less now. The agony radiates through my left arm to the diamond in my hand. I squeeze the stone as hard as I can and focus on healing but find it harder and harder to do so. The pain intensifies and covers more of my body; my other arm, and my legs.

I close my eyes and focus on the diamond in my hand and the ring on my left finger as they heat up. The soles of my feet feel like they are ablaze and are going to burn right off of my legs. My skin feels like thin crisp paper. The roar in my head continues its brutal attack. I don't know if I can do this. I don't know if I'll survive. A scream escapes my throat, having lost the ability to fight against the torture.

No less intense, isolation threatens to tear me apart. Nothing can be worse than dying a painful death alone. No, wait. Knowing Chris or my parents died alone and in pain would be worse. Their faces swirl in my mind's eye. Chris's imagined form tells me, "You've got this, Calli." Vita's words follow with her revelation that she's intentionally trying to harm everyone I love. Adrenaline rushes through my burned and broken body as I recall her gleeful prospect of expanding the blast radius. I must heal myself! I must go help them!

The ring on my finger buzzes violently. I open my eyes to check the ring and color of the diamond in my palm, but I can't see anything. My vision is gone! The electrical activity of my ring is enough to distract me from my lost vision. I can feel the lightning bolts shooting out, hear their deafening crack and boom. Clearly, my hearing is intact.

Pain stops increasing the more my ring responds. The enhancer stone is boosting my diamond's Healing power, slowly, but noticeably, fighting against the onslaught of the blast. I wish the healing process was faster so I could go to Chris and my parents.

The roar in my head finally begins to lessen, and I no longer feel the blast attacking me. Unable to see, a void of nothingness surrounds me, yet in this darkness I can sense the Shadow Demons nearby. I can feel them as if I am the same. Have I died? No. I still feel pain and burning. Even though my diamond and the enhancer stone are actively repairing my damaged body from the inside, I think about external forces that could help lessen the heat. Cool water. I'm so close to the river. If only I could jump in and quench my burning pain.

Without warning, and being unable to see what's happening, my body is engulfed with water, not unlike the time I ran into the river during a vision when we transported the diamond, except this time I can still breathe. Instinctually, I tighten my grasp on the diamond to protect it, and in doing so, I realize I'm no longer bound to the metal frame. I lower my left arm, the diamond still firmly held, and wrap my arms around my body in an effort to comfort the agony raging within me. My brain wants to know where the water came from, but the excruciating pain throughout my being prevents that. I try to focus on the healing power.

The roar in my head is nearly gone and my vision slowly begins to heal, but the cool wetness is fast becoming hot. I blink vigorously to try to make out my surroundings. The darkness is now due to the lack of light, not lack of sight. My vision is returning. Using my Hunter vision, I can see I'm surrounded by water. I'm still on the roof, but a bubble of water encapsulates me, defying gravity, holding a form that is not found in nature. What's more, the water is *boiling*.

I stop thinking about water and the cooling effect I thought it would have and instantly the bubble drops flat to the surface of the roof and with it, the metal frame falls into a pile of rubble. I look around and see steam wisping up from the wet surface. The once floating black rocks have fallen and the Shadow Demons have transformed again to nearly translucent non-shapes.

The simple cloth robe has burned off my body and the heat within continues. I need relief. If there was a breeze, it could blow on my wet skin and cool me. As if my thoughts alone were enough to make it happen, a gust of wind comes from nowhere and knocks me to my knees. I steady myself and allow it to blow all around my position. The moisture on the roof begins to rise as a mist and floats in the air, encircling me. I've nearly returned to normal temperature. The pain is lessening with every breath. The wind slows and the water drops once again. I stand with the diamond still clutched in my hand, and my breath hitches in my throat as my mind swirls with new sensations and obvious Elemental abilities.

Power is restored to the downtown area in the same manner as it shut off, grid by grid. My ring has changed to the deep green from the vision. I drop the clenched, now green Sanguine Diamond to the ground, and I close my eyes, inhale deeply, and focus on completing the mending of my organs which have been decayed and virtually destroyed in the process of being hit by this blast. I scan for any remaining injury or abnormality and come across a tiny mass in my stomach area. It's confusing, to say the least. I focus harder and feel my ring heat up again. I'm drawing Healer power from the enhancer stone to help investigate the mysterious mass. The edges of the mass start to chip off like hard-boiled eggshell pieces, leaving a soft center below my belly button. My mind traces all my internal organs, scanning for imperfections or scarring, and healing them as quickly as possible. Then, I stop with an almost audible screech. The shell was protecting my body, surrounding my uterus . . . and the tiny lifeform attached to the side.

I'm pregnant?

Oh no! How could this have happened? We were safe! But even more confusing is why didn't I detect a pregnancy as I prepared for this mission? Why didn't Chris pick up on it? Or Crimson? What's happening?

Crimson approaches in the sky. All I hear in my mind is her previous words from my visions, "I couldn't stop it from happening, so I kept you from knowing it would." A pregnancy must have been what she was talking about. My ears pound from the rushing blood coursing through my veins as I try to comprehend everything I've just experienced.

I storm over to my pile of clothing, sit down, grab my pants and put them on not even caring about underwear.

Crimson slowly lowers her body to the rooftop as if she's reluctant to speak with me.

I don't wait for her to speak. I throw my words at her like daggers as I awkwardly shove my arms into the arm holes of my shirt. "I already know what you're going to say," I explode. "Just tell me why I had a bubble in me, hiding the fact I am pregnant?"

"Calli, take a breath." She pats the air with her hands in a calming gesture. "First recognize what you accomplished. You captured the blast in more ways than one: in the diamond in your heart, and in your hand, and in your child who will be the only full power-wielding Elemental. You did this and you survived!"

"Don't try to redirect this, Crimson. You prevented me from knowing I was pregnant, didn't you."

"Yes, and I'm sorry to deceive you, but it had to be this way."

"What do you mean?" I say, yanking violently on the ring stuck to my finger.

"Once you changed the future by going to the government, I wasn't sure if this could be massaged into a success. Remember when I told you to save your "sorry's" for later? Creating an Elemental baby was the only recourse. I couldn't stop it from happening, so I kept you from knowing it would, for fear you'd want to change it. I tried everything I could to help your choices have favorable results."

"So, you went to great lengths to have me become pregnant. You gave me the Blue so I'd feel comfortable. That is sooo . . . eww. I wouldn't be surprised to learn you and Vita orchestrated the whole baby-making process. I can't even—"

"Calli, you're right. I gave you the Blue so you'd feel private and secluded, and yes, the timing was right for you to conceive. You and Chris's love created a life that will go on to become a formidable force in the war against the

Reapers. You are the ultimate powerful force now, Calli."

I don't take the time to put on my shoes. Instead, I hurry over to where I dropped the green diamond and pick it up. I need to get to Chris and the others as soon as possible.

Crimson points to the diamond. "You'll select individuals to receive a shard of the new Elemental Diamond, and they will be powerful helpers. Your child with full Elemental abilities will be more powerful than anyone who receives part of that charged diamond, that is, once he or she learns how to control the power. With this group of Elemental fighters, you'll lead the war against the Reapers."

"So, you had Vita hide my uterus so I wouldn't be aware of the baby. When did she do that?"

"When she removed the obsidian bomb. She created a new bubble at the same time, at my request, to protect your womb."

I'm absolutely disgusted. Crimson allowed Vita to coerce my insides even more. "What did you give her for her services? What was the tradeoff?"

"We have more pressing things to worry about right now than Vita."

"I think it's very important—enough for her to come visit me and place these black stones."

A confused expression crosses Crimson's face. "Excuse me? She was here?"

"Yes, and she told me more about her relationship with you than you did, like how she set up the triangulation for capturing the Grecian Blue Diamond's power, and that this whole system you and I set up was her design. Oh, and how happy she was that you hadn't realized she moved the channeling stones to include a larger radius of radiation. And do you know why? Because she is Vorherrschaft! She is the Reapers' leader. She is who we are fighting, and you had her place a bubble in my body thinking you were one step ahead of her, using her for your gain. Or maybe you two are working together, using me and everything else. I don't know anymore! All I know is you and I are *done,* Crimson. I can never trust you again. I'm leaving." I turn away from her.

She takes a step towards me and reaches forward with one hand. "Wait, we don't know the effects on the enhancer stone."

"Stay away from me," I reply angrily. "I mean it."

Bending my knees, I take hold of one of Vita's black rocks on the ground with one hand, the Elemental Green Diamond in the other, then crouch as if I'm in the starting blocks for a race. The air freezes in place as my eyes connect with Crimson's.

"Calli, please, wait!"

I push off with all my force, into the sky, surround myself with an atmospheric shield, and accelerate with increasing speed across the city far below. I know where Chris should be. I just don't know what I'm about to encounter now that I know Vita expanded the fallout zone of the Elemental blast.

Hang on Chris, I'm coming!

Thank You!

Thanks for reading my books! I'd really appreciate it if you'd take the time to leave a review wherever you purchased the book. Reviews (also "liking" other helpful reviews) help new readers decide what to read and you could be a big part of that. Additionally, by leaving a review you are helping my book-writing process and hopefully new readers will find the series and share your enthusiasm. The best way you can help me as an author is to talk about my books with your friends and other readers.

ABOUT THE AUTHOR

Lorena Angell is the internationally bestselling author of the YA fantasy series, *The Unaltered.* Inspired by an interview from J.K. Rowling, Lorena began to write and published her first book in 2011. Since then, she's earned over 4,200 reviews (average of 4.5 stars), has been a #1 bestseller in over 11 countries and wants nothing more than to write more books for her readers.

Connect with Lorena Angell at:

www.LorenaAngell.com/contact-me

Facebook: The Unaltered Diamond Series

Instagram: the.unaltered.series

YouTube: LorenaAngell

TikTok: @LorenaAngellAuthor

www.ingramcontent.com/pod-product-compliance
Lightning Source LLC
Chambersburg PA
CBHW030340310726
48979CB00001B/118
9781969186936